# DEAD
# LINE

**Books by Marc Cameron**

*The Arliss Cutter series*
OPEN CARRY
STONE CROSS
BONE RATTLE
COLD SNAP
BREAKNECK
BAD RIVER
DEAD LINE

*The Jericho Quinn series*
NATIONAL SECURITY
ACT OF TERROR
STATE OF EMERGENCY
TIME OF ATTACK
DAY ZERO
BRUTE FORCE
FIELD OF FIRE
ACTIVE MEASURES
DEAD DROP
THE TRIPLE FRONTIER

*The Jack Ryan series*
TOM CLANCY: POWER AND EMPIRE
TOM CLANCY: OATH OF OFFICE
TOM CLANCY: CODE OF HONOR
TOM CLANCY: SHADOW OF THE DRAGON
TOM CLANCY: CHAIN OF COMMAND
TOM CLANCY: RED WINTER
TOM CLANCY: COMMAND AND CONTROL

# DEAD LINE

# MARC CAMERON

**KENSINGTON**
PUBLISHING CORP.

kensingtonbooks.com

KENSINGTON BOOKS are published by

Kensington Publishing Corp.
900 Third Avenue
New York, NY 10022

All Kensington titles, imprints, and distributed lines are available at special quantity discounts for bulk purchases for sales promotion, premiums, fundraising, educational, or institutional use. Special book excerpts or customized printings can also be created to fit specific needs. For details, write or phone the office of the Kensington Special Sales Manager: Attn. Special Sales Department, Kensington Publishing Corp., 900 Third Avenue, New York, NY 10022. Phone: 1-800-221-2647.

Library of Congress Card Catalogue Number: 2025934260

KENSINGTON and the K with book logo Reg. US Pat. & TM Off.

ISBN: 978-1-4967-5270-3
First Kensington Hardcover Edition: August 2025

ISBN: 978-1-4967-5272-7 (e-book)

10 9 8 7 6 5 4 3 2 1

Printed in the United States of America

The authorized representative in the EU for product safety and compliance is eucomply OU, Parnu mnt 139b-14, Apt 123 Tallinn, Berlin 11317, hello@eucompliancepartner.com

For John V. Palmer
World War II British Army Officer, fiercely proud Canadian,
quiet example of service, and the best father-in-law this Texas
boy could ever dream of.

*A man said to the universe:*
*"Sir, I exist!"*
*"However," replied the universe,*
*"The fact has not created in me*
*A sense of obligation."*

—Stephen Crane

# CAST OF CHARACTERS

**Arliss Cutter**—Supervisory deputy US marshal, Fugitive Task Force

**Lola Teariki**—Deputy US marshal. Alaska Fugitive Task Force

**Mim Cutter**—Arliss's widowed sister-in-law, registered nurse

**Michael Cutter**—Mim's nine-year-old son (twin)

**Matthew Cutter**—Mim's nine-year-old son (twin)

**Constance Cutter**—Mim's sixteen-year-old daughter

**Ethan Cutter**—Arliss's older brother (deceased)

**Grumpy Cutter**—Grandfather who raised the Cutter brothers

**Ursula Rogers**—Arliss's mother

**Geoff Rogers**—Ursula's husband

**Jill Phillips**—Chief deputy US marshal, District of Alaska

**Nancy Alvarez**—Anchorage PD patrol officer assigned to Task Force

**Sean Blodgett**—Deputy US marshal, Fugitive Task Force

**Paige Hart**—Deputy US marshal, Prisoner Operations

**Micki Frank**—Deputy US marshal, pilot

**Paul Gutierrez**—Fairbanks suboffice deputy US marshal

**Ryan Madsen**—Fairbanks suboffice deputy US marshal

**Joe Bill Brackett**—patrol officer, Anchorage Police Department

**Holly Burns**—helicopter pilot, Alaska State Trooper

**Nick Haslet**—helicopter pilot, Alaska State Trooper

**Special Agent Finnan**—FBI New York Field Office

**Special Agent Ramos**—FBI New York Field Office

**Sam Lujan/Luke Trejo**—Government witness

**Josie Lujan**—Sam Lujan's mother/professor Arizona State

**Royce Decker**—Former SWAT/LEO wanted for murder

**Suzi Massey**—Decker's girlfriend. Former teacher

**Butch Pritchard**—Royce Decker's associate

**Tina Massey**—Pritchard's girlfriend, Suzi's sister

**Merlin Tops**—AKA Butterbean—Pritchard's associate

**Lazor Kot**—Organized crime boss, New York City

**Valeria Kot**—Kot's daughter

**Bobby Gant**—Kot organization
**Dusty Baldwin**—Kot organization
**Nils "Peewee" Halverson**—Kot organization
**John Blackwell**—Kot organization
**Mads Nash**—Kot organization (Australian freelancer)
**Browny Nash**—Kot organization (Australian freelancer)

**Note: Temperatures are in Fahrenheit unless otherwise noted**

# PROLOGUE

*Florida*
*1987*

FEW PEOPLE ON EARTH CAN HOPE LIKE A TEN-YEAR-OLD BOY.

Arliss Cutter glanced up from his miserable attempt at building a campfire and nudged a lock of sweaty blond hair out of his eyes with a bandaged knuckle. The tightly wound growl of an approaching outboard grew louder by the moment. He squinted hard into the sunset, past his grandfather's patrol boat that bobbed in the shallows a few feet offshore, beyond the spider-legged mangroves that guarded the protected bay where the old man had brought Arliss and his older brother for a weekend camping trip. The boy willed the driver not to turn before coming just a little farther into the bay. Even at ten, Arliss knew he probably had an exaggerated view of life-or-death scenarios—but this situation sure felt like one. He just *had* to have a better look at the woman in the passenger seat.

Four and a half feet of scarred knees and grubby elbows, Arliss wore a faded pair of cutoff jeans and a hand-me-down marlin fishing T-shirt his older brother had outgrown before it went into the rag bin.

The outboard motor growled louder. On the Gasparilla Sound, a low sun dazzled the rooster tail of spray behind the fiberglass runabout. It was the second time in ten minutes the boat had come by.

The woman in the passenger seat was blond and wore a green swimsuit. Green. That couldn't be a coincidence. It was hard to get a good look at her face, silhouetted against the sunset like it was. Arliss came up on tiptoe and craned his neck, praying the extra few inches of reach might give him a better view. The runabout cut a wide arc, roaring in close. Peals of high-pitched laughter rolled in with the surf, fizzling against the sand.

The boy's heart sank. Mama's laugh was low and husky. It wasn't her.

Deflated, Arliss went back to his attempt at a fire, hoping against hope that nobody had seen his foolishness.

His grandfather, a small giant of a man everyone called Grumpy, sat on a battered Igloo ice chest just above the tideline and whittled on a piece of sea-grape wood while he stared out to sea past his anchored Boston Whaler. The old man stopped whittling for a second and touched the Colt Python on his hip with the hand that held his Barlow pocketknife. He did that every now and then, like he wanted to make sure the gun was where he'd left it. Khaki slacks and a loose cotton shirt took the place of his usual slate-gray uniform, but the gold badge clipped to his belt identified him as a Florida Marine Patrol officer even when he was off duty.

Twelve-year-old Ethan stood in the mottled shadows of a strangler fig a few feet up the beach, munching on Fritos and bean dip.

If either of them had noticed Arliss, they didn't let on. They seemed more interested in seeing if he could get a fire going without resorting to matches.

Arliss unscrewed the top of a small tin Grumpy had given him and cursed under his breath. He hadn't said one of the really bad words, but he checked to see if Grumpy had heard just the same. He hadn't. Probably. Arliss peeked in the tin, careful not to let any of the precious contents blow away with the breeze. There were only two pieces of charred cloth left. This better work soon. The last thing the boy wanted to do was ask his brother for any of his. That was admitting defeat.

Careful not to destroy the fragile cloth, Arliss lifted out a square about the size of four postage stamps and placed it gingerly in a nest of punk he'd grabbed from the crown of a palmetto—Grumpy called it a cabbage palm. Tongue out and parked between his teeth to help him concentrate, he struck furiously against the flint with his steel striker. (It was a point of contention between the brothers whether you should hit steel with flint or flint with steel. If Grumpy had an opinion on the matter, he didn't' share it.) A shower of sparks landed on the charcloth. Two of the sparks caught immediately as Arliss had known they would. Burning up the charcloth wasn't the problem. Glowing orange lines pulsed in time with the boy's coaxing breaths, working outward from the initial sparks as they consumed the fragile tinder. The whole thing winked out in a matter of seconds with no effect on the nest of cabbage palm. It was gone in an instant, along with the boy's hope.

Arliss pushed his hair out of his eyes again and chewed his bottom lip in frustration. He wanted to kick the whole mess of sticks into the ocean—and would have had Grumpy not been there.

A stiff breeze blew in off the sound, past a dark line of mangroves to rustle the big Walmart dome tent Grumpy had helped the boys set up on the beach. The wind cooled things off, so that was good. Trouble was, that same breeze came in on the tail of a heavy squall that had drenched every bit of bark and twig suitable for a fire.

Ethan leaned in, whispering but not nearly quiet enough. "That wasn't her, ya know. If she was gonna come back, she woulda done it by now."

Arliss clouded up like a thunderhead, voice quivering through clenched teeth.

"I know that."

Grumpy whittled away like he was oblivious.

Ethan sighed, the way grownups did when they thought they just weren't getting through to you. "I know you've been trying to find her, little brother." He folded the top of the Fritos bag tight, as if that was the end of his snack and this conversation. "You need to stop it."

Arliss's throat tightened, angry at Ethan for pointing out his weakness, angrier at himself because he knew his brother was right.

Ethan plowed ahead. "She ain't worth it—"

Grumpy cleared his throat at that, weighing in.

"*Not* worth it," he corrected. "Right grammar, but wrong sentiment. Who's to say what thing's important to another man?" Grumpy lowered the pocketknife to his lap and swiveled around on the ice chest to look directly at Arliss. "Son, if you want to know where your mama is, I can surely find her. Hunting down folks who don't want to be found is a big part of my job." The old man peered over the top of his glasses, looking Arliss up and down. "But I will say this, I'd be much happier if you didn't sneak around with such things."

Tears welled in the boy's eyes. It gutted him when he disappointed his grandfather.

"I just . . . I just wonder what she's doing sometimes. That's all." He turned to Ethan. "Don't you ever wonder?"

"No," Ethan whispered, his eyes now glossy, too. "I don't care if we ever see her face again . . ."

Grumpy usually didn't stand for lies, but he let Ethan's slide and went back to carving on his sea-grape wood. "It's completely up to you boys," he said. "Just say the word and I'll hunt her down for you."

Arliss's face flushed. His chin began to quiver.

"I guess . . ." He closed his eyes and took a breath, trying to get his throat to relax enough to make words. "I guess she just stopped lovin' us?"

Grumpy cocked his head, gazing out at the ocean past his boat. Sometimes the old man's advice was found in his silence, when he just whittled or looked at the water and let you work through stuff on your own.

Arliss was five years old when his father passed. They'd said it was *idiopathic.* An awful big word for dying. Grumpy explained that idiopathic just meant the doctors didn't know what to call it. Mama had run off a few months before. Arliss was too little back then to know for sure, but Ethan figured her leaving probably had a lot to do with Daddy's idiopathic stuff. Aunt Rita said she thought poor Daddy just plain gave up on life after she left. There'd been no choice but to come and live with Grumpy. To Arliss, the old man was ancient as the big live oak tree in his yard off Alligator Creek. In reality, he'd not yet reached fifty when the boys came to live with him.

Grumpy took up his whittling again. "You know I'm not one to say a harsh word about your mama," he finally said. "But I will offer this opinion. A person who stays gone more than five years has her reasons."

Ethan crossed his arms, frowning, crunching the bag of Fritos in his fist. "I wish we'd stop talking about her."

"Suit yourself," Grumpy said. "You don't have to talk about her at all, but if Arliss wants to, we need to listen." He gave the boys a wink. "A campfire's as good a place as any to talk a little philosophy. Cowboy TV."

"If Arliss would ever get one lit," Ethan groused.

"He's doing just fine." Grumpy gave Ethan a side eye. "Is the boat unloaded?"

"Yes, sir."

"Very well," Grumpy said. "Then eat your corn chips and mind your business."

The runabout roared by again, staying out beyond the mangroves this time. Arliss didn't bother to look up.

Most of his charcloth had turned to ash, but he hit his flint and steel together over and over anyway, cursing under his breath at his own stupidity while he showered the damp tinder with sparks. He was an idiot for holding out hope like that. Mama wasn't coming to get him. Not now, not ever—

One of the sparks finally caught a remaining thumbnail of charcloth next to what was probably the only dry piece of cabbage palm on the beach.

Openly sobbing, Arliss picked up the nest in cupped hands like he'd been taught and blew and cursed and blew some more, coaxing a coal and then a growing flame out of the tinder. Grumpy and Ethan looked on in silence, loving the boy enough to let him blame his tears on the smoke.

# FRIDAY

# CHAPTER 1

*Anchorage, Alaska*
*Present day*
*9°*

SUPERVISORY DEPUTY US MARSHAL ARLISS CUTTER STOMPED HARD
on the gas, drifting his government-issue Ford Escape through a
tight right turn off Baxter Road and onto the icy side street. He
hadn't heard his partner on the radio for two full minutes. That
much dead air was a long time during a pursuit—an eternity for
someone as talkative as Lola Teariki. His window down despite
the bitter wind, Cutter scanned the surrounding yards and houses
as he straightened the wheel and poured on the gas, searching in
vain for any sign of his partner's whereabouts.

It wasn't like Lola to go dark. She was smarter than that, especially when they were chasing a hired killer. Butch Pritchard had
murdered a twenty-five-year-old woman in her sleep in Missouri.
His victim was four months pregnant at the time of her death.
This guy wouldn't think twice about killing a deputy US marshal.

Cutter was a big man, six three and a shade under two hundred
and thirty pounds, barely able to fold himself behind the wheel of
the little SUV.

He hammered the wheel with his fist. His grandfather taught
him to take care of his partner at all costs—and now Lola was
NORDO—no radio—alone and on foot after a murderous bas-

tard who from all accounts would be happy to pick his teeth with her bones.

Cutter tapped the brake, slowing a hair, listening, scanning motley patches of snow for fresh tracks as he sped through the neighborhood. A biting wind burned his face and brought tears to his eyes. He didn't care.

Cheney Lake lay ahead, hidden from view by a stand of frosted spruce and bone-white birch. The twenty-two-acre gravel-pit-turned-lake was now a sheet of ice tucked in among the evergreens at the dead end of Colgate Street. Locals cleaned off a good portion of it for hockey when the ice got thick enough. Christmas was only a few weeks away and the cedar-sided houses, built during the pipeline boom of the 1970s, looked like so much gingerbread with twinkling lights and candy cane lawn ornaments.

A warm Chinook wind had barreled in shortly after Thanksgiving, making the ice iffy. Most of the snow was gone, leaving only a few grimy drifts, mainly where city plows had thrown up berms. Lawns were left patchy and blighted. Now a high-pressure system had camped out over southcentral Alaska, gripping Anchorage in bone-numbing cold with no snow to insulate the ground. Inflatable reindeer sagged in the cold, doing little to chase away the brooding darkness of midwinter. A white Christmas wasn't in the cards.

Cutter snatched up the radio as he sped toward Lola's government Tahoe parked in the wood line at the end of the long block.

There was no sign of her—or Butch Pritchard.

He keyed the mic. "Hello, Lola!"

Nothing.

He tried again, this time reaching out to task force Deputy Sean Blodgett. According to Lola's last transmission, Blodgett was in the middle of arresting someone who'd come out of the target residence with Butch Pritchard.

"Sean, Sean, Cutter," he said, using the "hey you, you, it's me" format to communicate.

Dead air.

He pounded his fist against the steering wheel again, pouring on as much speed as he dared on the slippery street.

The thermometer on his dash read nine above—seven degrees

colder than it had been when he came to work that morning. The forecast said temps were going to drop hard over the next few days. White crystals drifted through the flat light, as if materializing out of the winter air. The little Ford's defrost roared like an oncoming storm.

Cutter scanned more frantically. "Come on, Butch," he growled out loud. "Where did you go . . . ?"

Pritchard wasn't even their top priority. That line on the dance card went to Royce Decker, a former St. Louis Metro PD SWAT sniper who'd hired Pritchard.

Decker had contracted his wife's murder with the full knowledge that she was fifteen weeks' pregnant with their first child. Pritchard shot her to death as she lay sleeping on the couch. Authorities in Missouri had the idiot coming and going on the doorbell camera. The day after the murder, twelve thousand dollars had shown up in his bank account. Had Pritchard known that eight million in seized cash had disappeared from a vehicle in police storage shortly before Decker dropped off the radar, he might have charged a lot more than twelve grand to do the killing.

A murder-for-hire case involving a dirty cop threw the media into a frenzy. Worse yet, it gave the district attorney's political rival ammunition in his election campaign. The DA pulled out all stops to get Royce Decker behind bars—which included calling in the United States Marshals Service Eastern District of Missouri Metropolitan Fugitive Task Force. The deputy leading the MFTF was an old classmate of Cutter's. A court-authorized phone dump of Decker's cell records revealed twenty-nine calls to IP addresses and cell numbers that appeared to be coming from inside Russia. Analysts at US Marshals Headquarters Enforcement Division linked at least two of these cell numbers to a man named Fyodor Pugo, a Russian businessman with a fleet of offshore fishing vessels based in Vladivostok and Petropavlovsk. Decker's new girlfriend appeared to have ties to Alaska, and it was feared he would use some of his newfound wealth to flee to Russia where he would be out of their reach. For all Cutter knew, he was already there.

The Missouri task force sent a collateral lead to Alaska via Capture, the Marshals Service internal fugitive and prisoner tracking database. Cutter and the Alaska Fugitive Task Force (AFTF) hit the ground running.

A known cell number for Decker's girlfriend, a former middle-school teacher named Suzi Massey, had pinged near Ester, Alaska, a small community south of Fairbanks. Shortly after, that number had gone dark. The Air Guard warrant analyst assigned to the task force had identified five addresses in the Fairbanks area with a possible connection to Massey or her known associates. All of the locations were rural.

Royce Decker was a trained police sniper facing the death penalty with eight million bucks in his war chest—not an easy man to approach. Rather than have Fairbanks sub-office deputies stir up neighbors and alert Decker by checking the individual addresses, Cutter planned to take the entire task force to Fairbanks for a more methodical approach.

Then a day before they were scheduled to fly north, Suzi Massey's cell phone went active again just long enough to call a cell that came back to the target house near Cheney Lake. Lola spoke to her contact at the post office and learned that a man who looked like Butch Pritchard had been seen at the residence earlier in the week.

USMS HQ insisted that though Pritchard had been the one to pull the trigger on a sleeping Heather Decker, her husband, Royce, was the focus of any manhunt. Both men needed arresting, and both appeared to be in Alaska—but politics dictated priorities. Fortunately for Cutter and the rest of the fugitive task force, the chief deputy for the District of Alaska believed that good sense trumped politics. Pritchard crossed their sights, so they focused on him.

There was a possibility Decker was also there, but even if he wasn't, nabbing Pritchard would get them a step closer.

Cutter put the Fairbanks trip on hold for the time being and set up on the Cheney Lake residence, rotating surveillance for three solid days.

No joy.

Deputies Teariki and Blodgett were on the house this morning. Cutter liked to lead from the front, sitting surveillance and kicking doors alongside his people, watching over them, ensuring that they were safe. Supervisory duties had pulled him away, forcing him to schmooze with Alaska State Trooper brass on Tudor Road. He'd ordered the deputies on Cheney Lake to sit tight if they saw any movement and wait for other members of the task force to back them up.

That was the plan anyway, until Lola got eyes on Pritchard and her ass magnet took over. At least she'd had the good sense to send a text.

Cutter quit his meeting before he'd finished reading her message and contacted Task Force Officer Nancy Alvarez, a TFO on loan from the Anchorage Police Department. Alvarez left the federal building with Paige Hart, a court ops deputy the chief had temporarily assigned to the task force. Alvarez and Hart were still five minutes away by the time Cutter turned off Baxter Road.

According to Lola, Butch Pritchard had come out of the target house with a second white male. She couldn't identify the other man except to say he was too big to be Royce Decker.

Butch Pritchard was six one and tipped the scales at around two-sixty—no small fry—but Lola described the mystery associate as over six five and pushing four hundred pounds. Cutter's grandfather would have called such a man a butterbean. From the sound of the radio traffic, Sean Blodgett was dealing with Butterbean while Lola chased after Pritchard.

Alone.

Cutter slid the little Ford to a stop at the end of the street and keyed the mic again.

"Talk to me, Lola!"

He resisted the urge to hurl the handheld through his windshield. She had to quit running off on her own like that.

A moment of garbled squelch poured from the radio before Teariki came through. Her voice crackled, wobbly from the chase. ". . . still on foot . . . trail . . . running toward lake . . . west." Her Kiwi accent—always stronger when she was under stress, transformed *west* into *wist.*

Cutter bailed out of the G car, squinting against the cold. He snugged a black wool hat over shaggy blond hair, then keyed his handheld with one hand while he tapped the Colt Python in the holster over his right hip. He trotted toward the trees as he spoke.

"Nancy, Nancy, Cutter," he said.

"Go for Nancy." It was Paige Hart. Alvarez surely had her hands full careening over the slick streets.

"Y'all come in via Baxter," Cutter said. "That'll put you on the west side of the lake in case our guy makes it across the ice before Lola grabs him."

"Copy that," Hart said.

Cutter clambered over a frozen hillock at the end of the street. Fresh tracks on the frosted trail disappeared into the trees. He recognized the long oval "football" in the tread pattern of Lola's Lowa Renegade boots.

A feral growl like the snarl of a cornered animal, came from the shadowed bushes ahead. Cutter clenched his teeth to keep from freezing his lungs as he broke into a run. He left the Colt Python holstered but his jacket unzipped, giving him quick access to reach the weapon if he needed it.

Deputy Blodgett's muffled commands sifted through the spruce forest.

Seconds later, a giant of a man crashed out of the brush. Roaring, he barreled straight for Cutter, jowly face a bright crimson, puffing great clouds of vapor in the cold air.

Butterbean.

# CHAPTER 2

"**S**TOP HIM!" BLODGETT BARKED FROM THE TREES.

St. Louis Metro PD had Butch Pritchard on video murdering a pregnant Heather Decker. He was a killer and there was a better than average chance his associates were killers too.

"US Marshals!" Cutter snarled. "Get on the ground, now!"

Butterbean kept coming.

Tasers were problematic in the deep freeze of Alaska where even the longer probes weren't likely to penetrate thick layers of clothing.

This guy had a good three inches and well over a hundred pounds on Cutter. Getting run over by him would hurt. Beyond that, Cutter didn't have time to mess around. Lola was out there by herself, possibly tangling with Pritchard.

Butterbean croaked something unintelligible as he attempted to chug past.

Cutter stepped off the trail like a matador. He crouched low, and then pushing off with his legs, drove his shoulder low into the big man's thigh.

With any normal human the knee would have been toast. Take out the underpins and even a brick house will collapse. Butterbean was no normal human. Some injuries were immediately incapacitating, ending the fight on the spot. Others required time to take effect. From the looks of Butterbean, this one was apparently neither. The force of Cutter's blow knocked the big man off balance, but it took its toll on Cutter as well. His ribs and arm had taken a severe beating while bringing his brother's killer to justice a scant two months earlier. Everything worked, just slower and with varying effect. He'd learned years before that if you weren't prepared to fight hurt then you might as well be out of the fighting business. Unfortunately, Butterbean was on to the same concept.

The big man rolled with a ferocious growl, quickly pushing himself up on all fours. Cutter winced through his pain to deliver what should have been a devastating knee to the man's ribs. He may as well have driven a knee into a side of beef.

Butterbean shook off the attack and continued to his feet. Cutter knew he should have stepped away to gain distance, but his predator drive pulled him forward, a deadly but much smaller lion clamping down on the nose of an angry Cape buffalo bull.

"On the ground," Cutter barked again. "Police!"

Butterbean shook off all two hundred and forty pounds of deputy marshal, hand on one knee to push his massive bulk to his feet. Beyond pain now, Cutter plowed into the giant again, driving forward while he was still trying to rise and knocking him face down on the frozen mud. The ground shook. Frost rained from overhead branches.

Blodgett ran down the trail, panting like he'd just finished a marathon. His parka was open, the tail of his wool shirt untucked. Blood poured from his nose where Butterbean must have clocked him. Without slowing, Blodgett jumped on a prone Butterbean's back. The outlaw's parka had ridden up during the scuffle with Cutter. Blodgett exploited the opening and drove the prongs of his Taser into the unprotected flesh above the man's belt.

Butterbean howled as fifty thousand volts surged through his body. The barbed probes weren't far enough apart to incapacitate a large muscle group, but five seconds of molten electricity coursing up and down his spine got his attention. He gave a half-hearted growl and attempted to scramble onto his hands and knees again. Blodgett pulled the trigger a second time, delivering another river of fire immediately on the heels of the first.

Cutter backed away a step and held the howling outlaw at gunpoint. His mind was still on Lola. He waited a beat while Blodgett daisy-chained two pair of handcuffs together making them long enough to cuff Butterbean behind his yard-wide back.

Lola broke squelch again on the radio. ". . . Pritchard . . . crossing the lake . . . northwest . . . Behind him . . ."

"Go!" Blodgett said to Cutter, wiping blood off his face with his forearm, patting Butterbean down for weapons. "I got this guy."

Deputy Hart broke in, her voice buzzing with tension. "Lola! Nancy says stay off the ice! She's not sure it's solid enough."

Lola came over the air with a sardonic chuckle, now crystal clear. When she wasn't arresting fugitives, she virtually lived in the USMS gym. It would take much more than a little footrace to wind her. "Too late for that," she said. "The ice is holding Pritchard's fat ass. I . . . I should be—"

A hollow shout came over the air, not quite a scream—and then silence.

"I got him," Blodgett said to Cutter. "Go."

Cutter paused as Butterbean launched into a tirade of curses.

"Seriously," Blodgett said. "I'm good here. Go!"

Cutter broke out of the trees at a dead run. Frigid air seared his lungs. Flat light made it nearly impossible to make out much detail. Butch Pritchard wasn't fat, but a heavy parka and clodhopper winter boots made it look as though he was waddling over the ice. By some miracle, he'd made it more than halfway across the frozen lake without being rugby tackled.

A sputtering cough jerked Cutter's attention a hundred feet to his right. Only then did he discover the reason Pritchard had been able to outrun a gym rat like Teariki.

Two outstretched arms waved above the ice, almost invisible against the monotone gray of winter.

She'd fallen through!

Lola gestured frantically toward an escaping Butch Pritchard. "I'm good!" she screamed. "Get the bastard!"

Cutter ignored her, moving quickly but carefully, testing the strength of the ice with each step. He wouldn't do her any good if he fell through himself. The crust crunched beneath his feet but there was no telltale sound of cracking.

Paige Hart came over the radio again. She and Alvarez were stuck in traffic a half mile out. It didn't matter. Pritchard was as good as gone.

Lola gave an exasperated growl. Her hair, usually in a high bun, had fallen into a thick black tangle. The Lamilite insulation in her parka didn't absorb water, but trapped air to push the entire coat up around her neck and shoulders, framing her Polynesian face.

"I . . . said I'm fine!" she stammered, fighting the bulky parka as she alternately treaded water and pounded the jagged lip of ice in exasperation. "This is . . . a good three inches th . . . thick. It'll hold me."

Cutter gasped as she sank out of sight, only to break the surface again, spitting and cursing, now out of the bulky parka. Black water churned as she kicked and thrashed, bracing her elbows on the edge to pull herself up. Behind her, a shelf of ice roughly the size of a refrigerator door teetered precariously on the far edge. She'd apparently hit it at a dead run, her weight causing the slab to surf half out of the hole while dumping her in the water. Held in place by friction alone, the commotion in the water threatened to bring the slab of ice back down on top of her, plugging the hole with her under it.

Cutter clocked the gravity of the situation at once.

"Lola, stop!" he barked. "Grab my hands."

"But . . . Pritchard's getting away—"

A scant five feet behind her, the ice slab groaned as it began to slide from the shelf, canted like a giant blade directly at her neck.

Cutter dropped to the seat of his pants, legs stretched out straight in front of him. Elbows on the ice at his sides, his butt in the water, Cutter braced the small of his back against the edge of the hole and caught the oncoming ice against the soles of his boots. The shock of a sudden dunking took his breath away but sent a shot of much needed adrenaline. Certain his ribs would detach from his spine at any moment, he strained, leg-pressing the oncoming ice, slowing but not completely stopping the advance. Even the thick parka gave him little padding between his back and the toothy edge.

He groaned, pressing with everything he had. "Now would be a good time to get out."

Lola launched herself prone in the water. Kicking powerful but half frozen legs, she wallowed her chest and elbows on the edge, and then managed to put one foot and then another against the oncoming slab. The advance pushed her forward, sliding her out and onto the ice.

At the same time, Cutter straightened his back and legs, letting the closing trap door shove him out of the water.

Soaking wet, the pair wrenched their freezing clothes away from the ice and turned to watch the four-by-six-foot slab shriek back into place, plugging the hole where Lola had been only seconds before.

Cutter arched his back, trying and failing to catch his breath from the strain he'd just put on his injured ribs.

"You have got to stop running off on your own like that."

"No shit . . ."

He frowned, shaking his head. "I mean it, Lola. Don't do that again or—"

"Or what?" Lola snapped. "How about you let me thank you for saving my life. Then you can chew my ass for poor tactics—which, by the way, I learned from y . . . you."

Her parka lost beneath the ice until spring, Lola's teeth began to chatter. The color had bled from her normally bronze face. Cutter shrugged off his, which was still reasonably dry and draped it over her shoulders.

"We'll talk about this later," Cutter said.

Lola stared transfixed at her former prison. "Holy . . . h . . . hell, Cutter. That thing gobbled up my coat. If you hadn't . . . That could have been me."

"Well, it wasn't," he said.

"What d . . . do you reckon that slab weighs?"

"Three or four hundred pounds, give or take." Cold seeped through his wet clothing. "Looks like someone cut it." He nodded at the series of eight-inch holes someone had made side by side with an ice-fishing auger, each drilled close enough together to form a rectangular "trap door" of free-floating ice in the middle of the lake. Half frozen slush left the cut lines nearly invisible. Pritchard's tracks showed he'd led Lola to the trap where he'd jumped across, leaving Lola to step directly on top, dumping her into the frigid water. Fortunately, her weight and the angle of her step had caused the floating block to wedge up on the far surface for a time instead of instantly sliding shut on top of her.

"That asshat tried to kill me," she whispered.

Cutter nudged her toward the vehicles, holding her tight around the shoulders.

"We'll get him," he said. "Sean has Butterbean in custody."

"Who?" Lola sputtered. She reached up to wring out her sopping wet hair.

"The guy who was with Pritchard," he said. "He'll know where we should look."

"His name's Butterbean?"

"It is for now," Cutter said.

Lola finally started to walk without him pushing her.

"That was almost the end of me."

"It was," Cutter said. No reason to sugarcoat it.

Lola stumbled. Cutter caught her.

"I'm calling an ambulance," he said.

"Holy hell, boss, I just tripped." She brushed a damp lock of hair out of her eyes. "Ice baths are supposed to be invigorating."

"That wasn't just the dunking," Cutter said. "Your wet clothes are essentially like wearing a refrigerator."

Lola shrugged off his arm. "Seriously, Cutter, I am fine. Please tell me this Butterbean has felony warrants."

"Seems the type," Cutter said. "Warrants or not, we have him on resisting. He smacked Sean in the face and fought me when I identified myself."

"Good," Lola said.

Cutter hit the auto start on his Ford as soon as it came into view through the trees.

"We'll take my car," he said.

"Mine's parked right beside it."

"We'll have Paige bring yours back to the courthouse."

"You think I'm not able to drive? Shit, Cutter, I was in the water for all of five minutes. Joe Rogan takes ice baths longer than that."

"I'm not arguing with you," Cutter said. "We're taking my car."

Lola stopped in her tracks. "Look," she said. "I get that you want to yell at me some more, but can we at least check the house? Decker could be inside."

"Alvarez will have APD to back her up and do a knock and talk."

"We can't screw around with this guy," she said. "I feel like we're only going to have one chance at him."

"That is no reason to go off half-cocked by yourself like you did."

A pained expression crossed her face, like she might throw up.

"Arliss, I coulda died . . ."

"And whose fault is that?"

Cutter knew exactly whose fault it was, which explained why he was so angry. It was his.

# CHAPTER 3

*L*OLA WAS QUIET ALL THE WAY TO THE FEDERAL BUILDING, SURELY
some kind of record for her.

They'd swapped wet coats for dry wool blankets from the back
of Cutter's G-car. The heat blew full force and their wet clothes
had gone from freezing to clammy. Lola pulled her blanket over
her head like a hooded robe. Cutter draped his over his shoulders.

He used his proximity card on the Seventh Avenue side. It was
closer to USMS office space and kept him from having to deal
with the contract security guys at the Eighth Avenue entrance.

Lola finally broke her silence while they waited for the rolling
metal door to rumble open.

"You said we'll talk about *this* later," she said. "What does that
mean?"

"Forget I said anything."

"Cutter! Talk about what?"

"Your accident," he said. "An after-action review."

"It wasn't an accident," she said. "That asshole tried to kill me,
but he failed. Would it be an accident if he'd shot at me and
missed?"

"It's not the same thing," he said.

"I reckon it is."

"Not for you to decide."

Lola's voice shot up an octave, and for a moment, he thought she might come across the console. "Cutter, I . . ." She closed her eyes and took a deep breath. "I guess it would be inappropriate to refer you to the whole pot-and-kettle thing."

Cutter parked directly across from the USMS sally port entrance and threw open his door. "It would indeed. Seriously, we're both still processing. We'll discuss it later."

Lola bailed out without another word, her angry footfalls echoing off concrete pillars. Melting ice and even some scant snow from vehicles belonging to people who came in from the Hillside ran along the concrete floor in tiny rivulets to strategically placed drains. Like most underground garages it was humid and dusty and smelled of vulcanized tires and antifreeze.

Cutter pushed the button to activate the electronic Hirsch ScramblePad, but the door buzzed open with a loud click before he had time to enter his four-digit code. Cutter waved his thanks at the pan-tilt-zoom camera mounted above the door. The court security officers in the control room had seen them approach.

Another click of static and Bill Ferguson, a retired Air Force Security police officer turned CSO, spoke over the speaker.

"Might want to hustle. Sean's having some trouble in the cellblock with that big guy he and Paige just now brought in. We're sending the elevator down for you."

Cutter pulled open the heavy steel door.

"Thank you, Bill." He turned to Lola.

She held up her hand. "Please don't," she said. "I'm right-as. I promise."

The door from the parking garage took them into a small ten-by-ten "mantrap" with a door to their left leading out to a vehicle sally port. The elevator opened dead ahead. It was a small car with a prisoner screen divider that left room for no more than five or six people.

A short ride up deposited the deputies in the secure hallway of reinforced concrete blocks and a steel mesh ceiling. A series of doors to the right would take them out to Marshals Service operational office space. To the left was the heavy steel door to the booking area with a computer, camera, fingerprint machine, and shower for particularly filthy arrests. Angry shouts and growls came from another set of doors beyond the booking area—the cell-block proper, literally three large steel cages complete with steel benches and combination toilet/sink/drinking fountains. Directly in front of Cutter as he stepped off the elevator was the USMS control room—cameras, duress alarm systems, and doors. It was staffed by two court security officers, including Bill Ferguson, who stood at the window.

The CSO pushed a steel banker's drawer out toward the deputies, allowing them to secure their sidearms and blades before going into the cellblock. Ferguson, an old-school military lawman had put two boxing Everlast mouth guards in the drawer as well.

Cutter snatched up the rubberized mouth guards and passed one to Lola. Ferguson buzzed them through to the booking room as soon as he'd shut the gun drawer.

Slipping the mouth guard between his teeth as he moved, Cutter flung back the steel door and kept going. He crossed the booking room in less than a second and grabbed the handle for the cellblock, ready for it to buzz as soon as the outer door shut behind him. Lola stayed hot on his heels, Taser at the ready. They'd trained for this. She, too, had put in her mouth guard. Kinetic arrests on the street were one thing. They didn't get paid enough to get their teeth kicked in. Government dental insurance was a joke.

The door buzzed and Cutter was greeted by Butterbean going whirling dervish in the center cell. His coveralls were torn from chest to crotch, leaving a wheel barrow load of pink belly flailing around the cellblock. Sean and Paige were both on top of the spinning giant, each holding to opposite sides of his muscular neck with both hands, like counterweights on a spinning top. Blood poured from Blodgett's nose. Paige Hart had lost a shoe. Both their Tasers had been fired at least once and lay on the concrete floor amid a tangle of gossamer wires and confetti-like chaff the Taser deployed each time it was fired.

"Merlin Tops!" Cutter roared around the mouth guard, using Butterbean's real name. It had no impact.

"Ready with your Taser?" he said over his shoulder to Lola.

"I got no target!"

"I'll hit him low when he comes around," Cutter said. "You pop him with the Taser when the others are clear."

Cutter was vaguely aware of the cellblock door clicking again, bringing in reinforcements. It hardly mattered. Too many hands could make it more difficult.

"Sean!" Cutter barked. "Paige!"

He charged as soon as the words left his mouth. Hart saw him coming and spun out of his way. It took Blodgett a half second longer. Hart staggered backward, smashing against the mesh cell wall. Blodgett slid across the tile floor, coming to a halt when he hit the stainless-steel bench. Both scrambled to their feet immediately. Ready to rejoin the fight.

Cutter timed his rush so that all two hundred and forty pounds drove through rather than into the side of Merlin Tops's left knee. It's what he'd wanted to do by the lake. This time, the leg folded, sending Butterbean listing like a sinking ship, yowling in pain.

Cutter kept going, ignoring the searing pain in his ribs. Behind him, he heard a chorus of, "Tase! Tase! Tase!" By the time he turned, Butterbean lay face down on his ponderous belly, back arched, chest and face off the floor. His howl had turned into a low groan through tightly clenched teeth. Both Chief Jill Phillips and Lola stood at the cell door with Tasers deployed. Paige Hart had recovered her Taser and stood to the side ready to add her darts and voltage to the mix if Butterbean started to fight again.

The five-second Taser ride over, the big man's body went from perfectly rigid to slack with a long, low moan.

Phillips, a half a head taller and twelve or so years older than Lola, took immediate command. "Don't move!" she ordered in a smooth but forceful Kentucky drawl. "Mr. Tops, I swear to you, you hurt my deputies and I will mess you up! Do you hear me?"

The whisper-thin electric wires ran between each Taser and the two sets of darts embedded in Merlin Tops's back and buttocks.

"Holy shit!" the man said, a line of bloody drool trailing from split lips to the tile floor when he lifted his head.

"Do you hear me?" Phillips said again.

"I said I hear you!"

"You said holy shit," Phillips said. "Two different things." She winked at Cutter. Stone cold.

Blodgett and Hart moved in quickly, snapping leg irons on Tops's ankles and a pair of "big boy" cuffs—which were essentially another pair of leg irons with a chain shortened to handcuff length—behind his back. Only then did Lola don nitrile gloves and come forward to yank out the barbed metal Taser darts.

"Y'all good?" Phillips asked, glancing from deputy to deputy like a mother hen checking on her chicks. "I want a CA-1 from each of you on my desk before you leave today." A CA-1 was a federal government employee injury report, memorializing any physical issues that might come up later. Phillips turned to go, then stopped. "That means you, too, Teariki."

"But I didn't go in the cell—"

"For earlier," Phillips said.

"Ah," Lola said. "Righto."

Phillips gave Cutter another wink. "Good thinking leaving those mouth guards in the control room, Big Iron."

Blodgett helped get the outlaw rolled into a seated position, then handed him off to Cutter, Lola, and Hart while he got a tissue for his bloody nose. "We're leaving him handcuffed during his initial appearance. Right?"

"Without a doubt," Cutter said. "But hospital first."

"Hart and I can handle that," Blodgett said.

"We'll tag along," Cutter said.

Tops maneuvered himself onto the metal bench, a gasping, wheezing pink blob. His injured knee stretched straight out in front of him. "Why'd you go and arrest me anyway? I know I don't have any warrants."

"Assault, for starters," Blodgett said, holding a paper towel to his nose. "I just wanted to talk, and you broke my nose. Twice."

"Yeah, well, I wasn't interested in talking. Then or now."

"Suit yourself," Cutter said. "Truth is, absent you trying to kick our ass—and doing a good job of it, by the way—we have no interest in jamming you up."

It wasn't lost on Cutter that video of the present situation would show a restrained and bloody prisoner surrounded by four deputy US marshals bent on interrogating him. Not the best image to portray if it ever went to court. Beyond that, this guy would just clam up if he felt backed into a corner. He sent Hart for the biggest wheelchair she could find. Blodgett's nose was bent at enough of an angle to leave no doubt that it was broken, putting him out of the game. Cutter sent him ahead to see a doctor.

Once only he and Lola were left in the cellblock, Cutter leaned against the steel mesh wall. "I'm serious, Mr. Tops. We don't necessarily have to charge you. We just need to know about some of your associates—"

"And I'm serious," Tops said. "You can kiss my ass." His nostrils flared. Cutter thought he might fight again, but his good knee began to bounce. This meat loaf of a man who had zero issues going gladiator against four deputy US marshals was suddenly scared.

Lola shot a glance at Cutter, who gave her a nod.

"You're on state probation for theft," she said. "And now you're looking at two new assault charges, both federal."

"Running my mouth is a good way to fall out of a window." He looked Cutter directly in the eye. "Lawyer."

"Suit yourself," Cutter said. "First we'll get your knee checked out."

Tops winced, reminded of his injury.

Cutter pushed the cell door shut, waited for the electronic whir, then gave the door a tug to be certain it was secure after the CSOs in the control room had activated the lock.

Two cells down, Lola grabbed the handle of the block door, the signal to the CSOs to unlock it as soon as the cage itself was secure.

Head down, Tops spoke as Cutter was walking away.

"Those people," he said. "They'll kill me, then they will kill you . . . and they will kill my family, they'll kill your family . . ."

Lola scoffed. "Butch Pritchard can't kill anybody if he's in jail."

"Hang on!" Tops wallowed to his feet, no easy task with his hands cuffed behind his back and one bum leg. Breathing hard, he leaned against the door, pink belly waffled against the steel mesh. "You're after Butch?"

"That's right," Cutter said. Whoever Tops was scared of it wasn't Butch Pritchard. "You've already asked for an attorney. We can't have a conversation."

"Well, I'm taking it back!" Tops said. "I can do that, can't I? I mean, I have the right to remain silent. I don't *have* to."

"Nope, you don't," Cutter said. "That's up to you."

"Pritchard," Tops said. "That's it."

"And Royce Decker," Lola said.

"Decker?" Tops said. "Whatever. I don't know anything about him. But don't drop the assault charges."

Cutter bit his tongue. This guy really did need a lawyer.

"Just lower them. Make 'em misdemeanors or something so I can get out but still have to pay a fine or something. It'll look like I'm talking if you let me off completely. They'd kill me for sure."

"Who are you so scared of?" Lola asked. "I told you. Pritchard can't get to you if he's in jail in Missouri."

Tops looked at her from his steel cage. He started to say something else but stopped like he'd thought better of it.

"Everything alright?" Lola asked.

Butterbean shook his head as if coming out of a trance. "You want to write this down or what?"

"What was that all about?" Lola mused when they were outside the cellblock and on their way to change into dry clothes that didn't smell like Cheney Lake. "Butterbean rolled on Pritchard like a jelly donut, but he's scared shitless of somebody out there."

"Yep," Cutter said. "Whoever it is, he thinks they're more dangerous than a contract killer."

"Butterbean genuinely doesn't seem to know much about Decker," she said. "So, that's not it."

"One thing at a time," Cutter said.

"When have we ever gotten to handle one thing at a time." Lola scoffed at that. "Anyway, something out there's scaring him, and it's kinda creeping me out."

# CHAPTER 4

*Four years earlier*
*Las Vegas, Nevada*

TWENTY-TWO-YEAR-OLD SAM LUJAN WATCHED THE GUY IN A GRAY hoodie and torn skinny jeans hanging out on the balloon side of the fake Arc de Triomphe across the half-moon portico off Paris Drive. Tall, sparse gray beard, skinny but with the catfish gut common to heavy drinkers and light eaters. He checked out every limo as it arrived, like he was waiting for someone special. You could never be sure, of course, but as a rule, guys with catfish-gut bellies and skinny jeans didn't run in the same circles with people who arrived in limousines. Sam could spot a loser from a mile away. His mother had dated a string of them on and off the Rez. That hadn't really been her fault, though. Josie Lujan always saw the good in people, even when there was little of it to see.

Sam shook off the memories. That was a long time ago, before his mom got her PhD and started teaching Apache history at the University of Arizona. Sam had flown the coop shortly after high school, headed for Vegas to earn a little cash for college. Judging from how his tips were trickling in tonight, school would have to wait.

As if to prove his point, a kid driving what had to be his daddy's tanzanite-blue 7 Series Beemer rolled up and tossed Sam two crisp ones with the key fob. Two lousy bucks from a guy driving a car worth a hundred grand. Yeah, college wasn't in the cards any-time soon.

Sam eyed the loser in the gray hoodie—still lurking—and hopped in the BMW and headed for the garage.

A talent scout from Chippendales had approached him earlier in the week about a stripping job. "A strapping six-foot-three In-dian kid with arms like tree-trunks would be a showstopper for sure," the guy said. "Soccer moms on vacay would go crazy." The scout was one creepy dude, but Sam kept his card anyway. He needed money.

Sam parked the Beemer and sprinted back under the portico to the valet station. The loser in the gray hoodie was still there, leaning against the base of the Arc. What was up with this guy? Sam had heard it said that there were only three kinds of people on the Strip—cops, tourists, and those that preyed on tourists. He supposed valets fell into the latter.

Martin, the other valet working that night, had just gotten the keys to a new Stingray. Lucky bastard. Vette owners were usually older and liked to impress their girlfriends by peeling a hell of a lot more than dollar bills off their cash rolls.

Sam drew a rented Chevy Tahoe next. A couple from Nebraska in their early forties with the doe eyes and stoppy-starty demeanor of first timers to Vegas. The way the husband clutched his key fob said it was his first time letting a valet park his car as well. He took a wallet from the pocket of his sport coat.

"Do I tip now or when I pick it up?"

Yep. A first-timer.

*I have to park your car a block away, sprint back here, and then I have to sprint to retrieve it when you're done stuffing your face or feeding the slots.*

Sam kept his thoughts to himself and forced a smile, handing the man his claim ticket.

"That's entirely up to you, sir."

His attention was already on the brunette stepping out of the rear driver's-side door of a black Escalade limo that had just pulled up.

She was on the shorter side, a shade over five feet with a pile of hair in a sexy updo. Dark brows and piercing green eyes accented a handsome if not classically beautiful face. Sam's attention was immediately drawn to her tiny black dress and muscular legs. He saw dozens of such dresses every night, but none of those girls wore it quite like this one. Matching black heels, not so tall as to make her wobbly, were high enough to turn tan calves into baby-smooth baseballs. The bellmen were all busy, so one of her guys—a balding dude who looked like Jason Statham on a diet of too much McDonalds—had opened the door and led her around the Cadillac. The passenger door swung open by itself, drawing an exasperated groan from fat Jason Statham. He bowed his head to trot around the car to do his job and get the door for the man who was obviously his boss.

The loser in the gray hoodie crossed the ellipse from the Arc to the hotel side about the time the boss's shoes hit the pavement. Fat Jason was still in the process of lumbering around the Escalade. He was heavy, but it was easy to see that a good deal of that heft was muscle.

Sam watched Gray Hoodie work his way around the rented Tahoe and then turn to stand with a small group of curious pedestrians lining the street. There were probably more limousines per capita in Vegas than anywhere else on the planet. Sometimes, when the door opened, Donny Osmond or Beyoncé spilled out. Sometimes, it was a bunch of drunk chicks with smeared eyeliner. Either way, looky-loos were common.

Gray Hoodie took a step into the street. That was weird. At first glance, Sam thought he must have believed the handsome brunette in the little black dress was someone famous. But she wasn't his target.

Sam caught the glint of steel an instant before Gray Hoodie shoved the Tahoe driver to the pavement and lunged forward with a knife.

"Lazor Kot!" the loser said, his voice tight, like he was being strangled.

Fat Jason was five steps away.

Sam was there in two.

Still holding the keys to the rented Tahoe, he sent a powerful right cross directly into the would-be attacker's jaw, dropping him like a stone. The knife skittered across the pavement.

Fat Jason shoved Sam out of the way and stooped to see if the attacker was armed with anything beyond the knife. Finding nothing, he urged the boss to return to the Escalade.

The boss, a muscular old man, waved off the notion. Apparently, an assassination attempt wasn't enough to throw him off a dinner. The brunette stepped up and whispered something to him. Moments later, he beckoned Sam over with a flick of a beefy wrist.

"I'm Lazor Kot of New York City." He nodded to the brunette. "My daughter, Valeria. We have reservations at Gordon Ramsey Steak, and she'd like you to join us."

Fat Jason's head snapped up, glaring daggers.

Sam gave a polite grin. "That's very kind." He held up the key fob for the Tahoe. "But I'm in the middle of my shift."

He hadn't knocked out the knife-wielding attacker to get a tip, but he wouldn't refuse one either.

"It's the least we can do," Mr. Kot said. "You saved our evening." He looked Sam up and down for a long moment, like Sam's uncles perused a horse before they bought it. "The thing is, Mr. . . ." He raised a brow.

"Sam. Sam Lujan."

Kot put a hand on his shoulder, a surprisingly powerful hand. "The thing is, Mr. Lujan. I learned a very long time ago, it's best not to cross my daughter. Valeria can be—"

The brunette shrugged. "It's alright, Papa," she said. "If Sam Lujan doesn't want to come to dinner with me . . . with us . . . we can't force him."

Kot gave what looked very much like a sure-we-can scoff. He stared hard at Sam, like he was looking through him, at the back of his skull. "How much do you make parking cars for this casino?"

Fat Jason must have known where this was going because he darkened like a rain cloud.

Sam grimaced. "Mr. Kot—"

"How much?"

Lazor Kot of New York City seemed like a man you needed to answer when he asked a question.

"Eighteen an hour plus tips."

"Let me run a background check at the very least," Fat Jason said. "We know nothing about him."

"We know everything we need to know," Kot said. "We know Sam Lujan risked his life to save mine when he didn't have to. And we know Valeria approves. What other vetting shall we do, Olek?" Kot spun on Sam, bushy gray eyebrows arching skyward. "Do you have any unpaid traffic tickets?"

Sam stifled a smile and shook his head.

"No, sir. I—"

"Boss . . ." Olek all but pleaded.

Kot continued his interrogation, much to the amusement of his daughter.

"Are you wanted by the police?"

"No."

"Have you ever been caught in bed with a dead woman?"

"No."

"Did you torture small animals as a child?"

"Sir?"

Sam stole a glance at Valeria, who was shaking her head.

"Papa . . ."

"I did not," Sam said.

"Outstanding." Kot clapped his hands. "We'll start you at five K a week, plus expenses. How does that sound?"

"It sounds terrific, sir. What will I be doing?"

"Other than stopping people with knives from killing me?" Kot gave him a narrow grin. "You'll earn your money. I promise you that. Until then, you'll have your hands full keeping my daughter happy . . ." He raised a playful brow at Fat Jason—who didn't look like he wanted to play. "And staying out of Olek's way."

Valeria Kot snaked her arm around Sam's waist. Snaked. That was a good word for it. Something about the way she moved at once thrilled Sam and terrified him. "Come on, Sam Lujan. Have you ever been to Gordon Ramsey Steak?"

"I have not."

"Good," she said, her voice a little huskier than it had been a moment before. "You're sitting beside me."

Working for Lazor Kot probably wasn't much removed from stripping at Chippendales. The guy was probably a mob boss, but he seemed like a nice mob boss who paid well and had a handsome daughter.

# CHAPTER 5

*New York City*

$S$AM COULDN'T GET THE BLOOD OFF HIS HANDS. HE TRIED TO DIG IT out from beneath his fingernails with the tip of his pocketknife and scrubbed with water hot enough he thought it might blister his skin, but there was always more. Images of Henry Vargas's skull haunted the boy's memory. Stains to remind him what an idiot he was for getting tied up with Lazor Kot in the first place. His mother had warned him—

"Relax, Sam Lujan," Valeria called into the bathroom from her side of the bed. "You have to put this sort of thing behind you. Now, come to me. I'll fix everything."

He'd been working for Valeria's father over two months, and she still called him Sam Lujan even during their most intimate moments—as if she knew a whole bunch of Sams and needed to keep them all straight in her head.

Sam sat on the edge of the bed, facing away from her, elbows on his knees, face in his hands. He closed his eyes, slowing his breathing so he didn't vomit right then and there all over Valeria's expensive Persian carpet.

"Your father said go to Brooklyn and *talk to Mr. Vargas*," he said. "The next thing I know that psychopath Olek puts a bullet through the back of the guy's skull." Sam rocked back and forth, teetering on the verge of tears. "Vargas was just a tired old man.

I . . . I never saw anybody get shot in the head before." He turned to face Valeria, looking for some sign that she found this whole thing as repugnant as he did. "It was . . . it was horrible. That Olek . . . he's got dead eyes. I'm positive he wants to put a bullet in my head, too."

She gave a dismissive flick of her hand. "Why would you say that?"

"Because he said the words, 'one of these days I'll put a bullet in your head, *mlody.*'"

Valeria laughed, deep in her belly. "He's calling you a young-ster."

"That he wants to shoot in the head!"

"He's joking around." Valeria pulled the sheet up under her chin.

"Like he joked with Henry Vargas?"

"Olek does serve a purpose." Her chest rose up and down with her deep sighs. She was flirting, like she always did when he tried to have a serious conversation. It usually worked. Just not today.

"Who keeps a psychopath on hand to serve a purpose like that?"

Valeria pursed her lips, trying not to laugh again. "If you think Olek is bad . . ." She changed her approach. "I'm really sorry you got dragged into this sort of business so soon."

Sam recoiled like she'd slapped him. "What does that even mean? *So soon?* Your father told us to *talk* to Vargas, not splatter his brains all over his kitchen."

"Sometimes talk means talk," Valeria said. "Sometimes talk means . . ." She shrugged. "Well, sometimes it means what you saw."

"You're telling me Lazor wanted us to kill that old man?"

Valeria rubbed a hand over her face, as if she were tired of ex-plaining such a simple thing. "Vargas was in the pocket of the FBI. He planned to testify in federal court. My father has to think about his business. He has to think about me."

Sam dry heaved. "You knew this was going to happen?"

"Not exactly," she said. "But I trust my father's decisions and so should you."

"I didn't sign on to murder people."

Valeria let the sheet fall, revealing honey-tan skin all the way to her belly button. "Then I guess you'll just have to walk away."

"Yeah, right," Sam said, at once mesmerized by what he saw and disgusted at the memory of what he'd seen. "I know too much. Your father would send Olek to 'talk' to me."

Valeria leaned her head back and pounded it softly against the headboard. "You've been here two months and still you don't realize how much my father listens to me. I'm serious. If this is all too much, if you feel you need to leave, I'd be terribly sad, but I wouldn't let anything happen to you. I promise you that. Our secrets are your secrets. I trust you wouldn't do anything to hurt us." She affected a resonate stereotypical Native American voice and quoted *The Outlaw Josey Wales.* " 'There is iron in your words—' "

He hated it when she did that. She might as well have said, *How, Ke-mo sah-bee,* but right now, racial sensitivity was the least of his problems.

"This is serious," he said.

"I wish you'd stop worrying." Valeria reached for his hand. "I knew I could trust you from that first night in Vegas. More importantly, my father trusts you. You're no rat, Sam Lujan." She patted the silk sheet beside her thigh—which had somehow slipped out into the open. "Maybe you should sleep on it . . . here beside me."

Sam woke with a ripper of a headache half an hour before his alarm. In truth he'd spent most of the night wondering how he'd gotten tangled up with Lazor Kot. His mother's disappointed face plagued his dreams—not the sort of image you wanted in your brain when you're lying next to a naked woman.

Valeria stirred when he sat up.

"Stay," she whispered, her voice husky with sleep.

He slipped on his pants, speaking over his shoulder as he buckled his intricately tooled leather belt—a gift from his mother. "I have to meet Olek and the others in Chinatown at nine."

"You keep forgetting that Olek works for me," Valeria whispered. "Come back to bed. I'll tell him you called in sick."

"And give him another reason to blow my brains out?" Sam said. "I don't think so. Anyway, my stomach is killing me. I need to stop and grab some toast or something before the meeting. You can come with me if you want. A breakfast date."

"Go then," Valeria said, bottom lip in a full-blown pout. "Come back to me after you're finished with today's murders."

Sam turned to stare at her, mouth agape.

She held the sheet in her teeth, stifling a giggle. "I'm sorry," she said. "I shouldn't joke. I know this was traumatic for you."

"It doesn't bother you?"

"Of course it bothers me," Valeria said. "But this business we're in, it's a war. You should remember that. If my father were to show weakness, he'd be the dead one. I'll talk to him. You don't have to be involved with any more killings."

Sam closed his eyes. "You're awfully damned cold about it."

"Listen to me, Sam Lujan," she said. "When you grow up with Lazor Kot as your father, you see things. It's a shame you had to see them so early in our relationship. I hope it didn't change your feelings for me."

"Not at all," he said, almost believing it.

# CHAPTER 6

$V$ALERIA'S APARTMENT WAS ON EIGHTY-SIXTH ON THE UPPER EAST Side, a place befitting Lazor Kot's daughter. Sam's salary of twenty grand a month left him enough for an efficiency over sixty blocks to the south. It did get him a sweet car though. Nothing too fancy, just an older black Audi TT with a six-speed manual transmission. He was tall and broad enough that he appeared to be wearing the car instead of driving in it, but he didn't mind. It had just the right amount of flash to zip around in Manhattan traffic. Not too bad for a boy from the Rez.

New York was one of those places where it was almost impossible to find a good place to double-park. Sam got lucky and found an empty loading zone a half a block from his favorite diner across from Grand Central Station. Working for Lazor Kot had taught him that NO PARKING signs were for others. The little Polish flag hanging from his rearview mirror told folks who might call for a tow truck to mind their own business or they might . . . Sam had never thought about what might happen, that is until he saw Olek kill Henry Vargas.

Sam sat in a booth by the window where he could keep an eye on his Audi. Depressed to the point of tears at his own stupidity, he ordered dry toast and three scrambled eggs. What he got was a man and woman who flopped down in the seat across the table from him.

"What the hell, man—"

"Special Agent Karen Finnan, FBI." The female of the duo held up a black wallet with a smallish gold badge. She was tall with frosted, pixie-cut hair and what Sam would have taken for a genuine smile had she been anyone other than a cop. The Feeble Eyes didn't exactly have a great reputation on the Rez. The male agent, also smiling, flashed his credential case like he wanted the guys in the next booth to see it. "Ramos," he said.

"You've got me confused with someone else," Sam said.

Special Agent Finnan—Tinkerbell with a badge—thumbed through some notes on her cell. "Lemme see, lemme see . . . Oh my gosh, I must have gotten my wires crossed. I'm looking for Samuel Redhorse Lujan on the rolls of the San Carlos Apache tribe?" She glanced up. "That's not you?"

Sam didn't move.

Special Agent Tinkerbell charged ahead.

"So, I guess you're not the son of Dr. Josie Lujan, professor of Native American Studies at Arizona State University? The same Sam Lujan who is presently sleeping with a mob boss's daughter . . ."

The agents wore khaki slacks and dark three-button polo shirts—like they didn't care if everyone in the diner knew they were feds. It took Sam all of two seconds to realize that was exactly what they hoped.

He closed his eyes and listened while the agents laid out the evidence against him.

The waitress brought Sam's eggs and poured the agents some coffee. Surprisingly, Finnan ordered eggs, too, like she planned to stay awhile. Finished with her pitch, she leaned back in the booth and gave a soft smile, sad, like she felt sorry for Sam—or at least wanted him to think she did. Ramos licked his lips, no doubt salivating at what this case could do for his career.

Sam put both hands flat on the table. "Not a chance," he said. "No. No way. You've got me figured wrong."

Special Agent Ramos had a ridiculously long neck that crawled out of his polo like a turtle every time he leaned across the table—which he did each time he wanted to make a point. "Look, kid. We can place you at the murder." His voice had a deep Southern twang.

Sam felt the blood drain from his face. "Then you also know I had nothing to do with it!"

"That's not quite right," Ramos said. "You drove Olek and the crew to Henry Vargas's house. Held their horses, so to speak."

Sam clutched at the table in a vain attempt to stop the room from spinning. "Why didn't you stop it if you were there?"

"I wish we could have," Finnan said. "We didn't know what was going down until after the fact. The thing is, Vargas's wife was hiding in the adjoining room. She filmed the entire thing."

Ramos took out his phone. "Want to see the footage?"

Sam wanted to scream. "Are you on crack?" he snapped, then lowered his voice, wagging his head at the insane suggestion. "No, I don't want to see the footage!"

What he wanted to do was run, to go back to his old job parking cars for losers in Vegas.

Ramos craned his long neck out again. "Ya know, if this was Texas, all y'all assholes would be facing capital murder charges."

"Lucky me," Sam said, his voice hollow. "Look, this whole deal makes me sick to my stomach."

"Henry Vargas isn't feeling too good about it either." Ramos smirked like he'd just made the world's best joke. Finnan rolled her eyes, almost as sick of this guy as Sam was.

"Think whatever you want," Sam said. "I'm not a killer."

"No," Special Agent Finnan said. "You're not. You're a drowning man who's in over your head—and you think Valeria Kot is your life raft. You believe we're the bad guys in this little shitshow. I promise you, we're not."

Sam lowered his voice and pushed his eggs aside. "Not the bad guys, huh? Then why are you trying so hard to get me killed?"

Ramos scoffed. "We're trying to keep you alive, bud."

Sam glared at him. "I'm not your bud."

He felt Finnan nudge her partner under the table, warning him to reel it in.

"What do you know about Lazor Kot?" she said. "I mean, really know?"

"Nice try," Sam said. "I'm not telling you shit."

"Off the record," Finnan said. "Hypothetically. Where do you think his money comes from?"

"Hypothetically?" Sam was only twenty-two years old, but he wasn't stupid.

"Alrighty." Finnan sighed. "Let's try it this way. I imagine you believe Kot's a bookie, runs illegal gambling, maybe a little harmless protection racket with guys like you as his muscle. Goons who are big and scary enough no one ever actually gets hurt . . . until yesterday. Am I close?"

Sam gave an almost imperceptible nod. "Hypothetically."

"Well, that is not the half of it, my friend," Finnan said. "Are you willing to go to prison for a man who makes most of his dough from human trafficking?"

Sam sat up straight. "Human trafficking? You mean, like kids?"

Finnan gave another sad nod. "Mostly young women out of Eastern Europe. Poland, Bosnia, Romania. Hundreds each year, some of them as young as twelve years old."

"I didn't . . . I mean I would never do that kind of . . ."

"I know you wouldn't, Sam," Finnan said. "Like I said, you're in over your head—"

"What do you want from me?"

"Testify to what you know of Kot's organization. We have him on human trafficking and racketeering. We have Olek and the others on Henry Vargas's murder. We need you to help tie that to Kot. Did he order it?"

"I don't know if Kot ordered Vargas killed," Sam said. "But I was there when he told Olek to talk to the guy."

"Did he often order Olek to *talk* to people?" Ramos used air quotes when he said "talk."

"All the time," Sam said. "But he seemed pretty pissed about this guy."

"Testify to that," Finnan said. "Just tell the truth."

A sudden realization seized Sam's already tortured gut. "Vargas was going to testify!"

"Now you're tracking," Ramos said.

"We're not going to let anything happen to you, Sam," Finnan said, looking like she almost believed it.

Sam slumped in his seat. "What am I supposed to do now? You want me to go back in and keep a book on him or something? Because that would be suicide."

"Oh, yeah," Ramos said. "They'd kill you before you jumped back in the sack with Valeria."

"Shut it, Art," Finnan said. Then to Sam, "Just walk away."

"It's that simple?"

She clarified. "Walk away with us. We get up from this table and we walk out together. We put you someplace safe and then testify in court when the time comes."

"You're from the government and you're here to help," Sam scoffed. "No Indian ever heard that before."

Finnan fell back against the booth like she was about to give up. "Sam—"

"Will I have to do time?"

"Oh, yeah." Ramos gave an emphatic nod. "You did stand by and watch Olek Vrobel blow a man's head off."

Finnan reached across the table and touched Sam's wrist. "It's possible you will have to do some time in prison, but maybe not. I'll personally recommend probation to the US Attorney. You would have to tell the whole truth, even if it implicates Valeria."

Sam pulled away, hands up in front. "Then, no deal. She's not a part of her father's trafficking shit. I know her. Valeria could never . . ."

Finnan gave Ramos a nod, like they'd rehearsed it, turning him loose to do what he'd obviously wanted to do all along. He slid an eight-by-ten photograph across the table. There in living color was Valeria with half a dozen other young women about her age, all of them dolled up like they were about to go clubbing. A sign on what appeared to be a bakery behind them was written in Cyrillic.

Ramos jammed his index finger at the image of the girl standing nearest to Valeria. "This pretty young lady is dead," he said. "Murdered by her pimp in Barcelona."

Finnan affected a gentle, motherly tone. "Valeria's not what you think she is, Sam." She slid the photograph closer, tapping another girl, taller than the others. "This one got out. She provided us these photographs, described how Valeria lured her and seven of her friends, all from the same school in Mostar, Bosnia, with promises of modeling jobs in Berlin, Barcelona, and right here in Manhattan. Valeria is the bait, Sam. The pretty girl to lure other pretty girls into the scheme."

"The Judas girl," Ramos said.

This was impossible. How could Valeria be involved in something this evil?

"No jail time and then I get protection. Olek would just love a reason to shoot me in the head."

"We'll see about the jail time thing," Ramos said. "The Marshals will stash you someplace safe. New name, new job, the works."

"The Marshals? You guys just use me and pass me off?"

"That's the way it works." Finnan chased the last bit of scrambled egg around her plate with a piece of wheat toast. No reason to let a shitty turn of events in Sam's life spoil her breakfast. "The Marshals are the experts. They haven't lost a single witness during the entire span of their program." She captured the eggs and popped them in her mouth, talking around them. "But you have to follow their rules."

"What if I break a rule?" Sam asked. "You know, accidentally."

"You won't," Finnan said. "These aren't those kind of rules."

"But say I did?"

"Don't," Ramos said. "Or Olek's bullet will find you before you can apologize." The agent gave a long-necked nod toward the window. "Speaking of Olek, he just drove by the diner for the second time in five minutes."

"Are you shitting me?" Sam blanched. "You think he saw us talking?"

Ramos chuckled. "I'm sure of it."

"You knew he would look for me here!"

Finnan pointed at him with the corner of her wheat toast. "We followed *you*, Sam," she said. "You chose this place."

"I didn't choose to have you two Feeble Eyes sit down beside me in broad daylight. Now I look guilty."

Ramos scoffed at that. "You are guilty, whether you help us or not."

Sam let that one slide. He was too sick to argue.

"Time to walk away," Finnan said.

"What about my stuff?" he asked, deflated.

"Forget it," Ramos said. "No stuff's worth dying for."

Finnan stood and threw a wad of cash on the table.

"Life as you knew it is over," she said. "All your meals, including this breakfast, will be on Uncle Sam for the near future."

Sam sneered. "Thanks?" He glanced out the window, scanning the street for Olek's Lincoln Town Car. He fully expected to die in a hail of gunfire the moment he stepped out the door. Hell, Valeria might even be the one to pull the trigger.

He'd just climbed in the back of Special Agent Finnan's black Chevy Suburban when another cold reality washed over him. He leaned forward, pounding the back of the passenger seat enough to draw a sheep-killing-dog look from Special Agent Ramos.

"What?"

"My mother!" Sam said. "They know where my mother lives. Valeria and I are . . . were planning to visit her in Arizona for Christmas this year."

"Already taken care of," Finnan said. "This isn't our first rodeo, Sam. We had agents watching her before we contacted you. Your mom's fine. Everything is fine. You're going to be fine."

That was a hell of a lot of *fines*. It sounded an awful lot like she was trying to convince herself.

Sam groaned. "Lucky me."

# SATURDAY

# CHAPTER 7

*Present day*
*Anchorage, Alaska*
*2° below*

*P*ERFECTION WAS A STRAIGHT RAZOR, ALL WELL AND GOOD UNTIL YOU moved the wrong way.

And everybody moved.

Arliss Cutter stood in front of the stove, completely still, eyes closed. He'd imagined many different outcomes to his life, most of them grim. But here he was, in the kitchen making pie with his dead brother's widow—the woman he'd loved since they were sixteen years old. His teenage niece was in her room—as usual—and his nine-year-old twin nephews played outside, sledding down the ice-covered hill behind the house. He didn't deserve it. This homey stuff was just too perfect. Excruciatingly wonderful—and so very easy to lose.

And then there was his mother. She'd run off when he was five and Ethan was seven. Cutter had only seen her a handful of times after that, always from a distance when she came looking for money from their grandfather. No phone calls, no letters, no birthday cards. She'd not even come to Ethan's funeral. Not a single word until she'd appeared at Mim's over six weeks ago. Thanksgiving had come and gone. Christmas was just a few weeks away and Cutter still had no idea why the woman had suddenly decided to darken his door—forty years after she'd tossed him aside like yesterday's garbage.

She'd bought a used Nissan Pathfinder in Anchorage and disappeared for a good portion of each day, returning in the evening to sit on the sofa and scroll through her phone. What attention she did give went to her grandchildren, chatting in her amiable Southern way as if she'd not been estranged from the family for four decades. The kids took it in stride. Apart from pleasantries—which Cutter found far from pleasant—she'd barely spoken ten words to him. He knew the look on her face though. He'd seen it a thousand times on people he was chasing.

She was on the run from something or somebody. Whatever or whoever it was, she was keeping it to herself.

"You okay there, mister?" A pie pan in each hand, Mim blew a lock of straw-colored hair out of her eyes. Cutter's quiet philosophizing was holding up her process. The kitchen was small enough to require a sort of dance to get things done without colliding with one another. Lately, periodic brushes of shoulder or hip had become more and more frequent as that dance went from a waltz to a tango.

Cutter had transferred from Florida to Alaska almost three years earlier, as soon after his brother's death as he could find an open position with the US Marshals office. Since his arrival, he'd been Mim's confidant and protector, a surrogate father-figure for her children. He'd even helped with the bills when Ethan's engineering firm held up the insurance payout. He was everything but the one thing he'd wanted to be since the moment they'd first met all those years ago.

Their relationship evolved in Alaska but at a glacial place and always on Mim's terms. Then, two months ago on a trip to South Dakota to look for Ethan's killer, everything had changed—like a bursting dam. Cutter still wasn't sure exactly where things stood, but they were different than they had been, and different was good.

Mim spoke again, firmer this time, drawing him out of his stupor. "Arliss, I said, are you okay?" She nodded at the oven door directly behind him and gave his thigh a little bump with her knee.

Sweet as she was, Mim considered baking pie crusts serious business.

Cutter lifted his head, outwardly calm, but severely wobbled on the inside. This woman did things to him. She always had.

"Maybe I was praying," he said.

"Well, I'm glad to hear it." Her voice curled in a beautiful Southern drawl. "That being the case, I'm sure the good Lord suggested you let me go on and pop these crusts into the oven."

"You know what." Cutter mustered a grin. "The Big Guy did mention you make an awfully mean chocolate pie. Reminded me not to fudge it up."

"Sounds like something He'd say."

Cutter opened the oven door, cup towel thrown cavalierly over one shoulder, the sleeves of his white shirt rolled halfway up on powerful forearms. His ribs and wrist still ached from the horrific sixteen-penny-nail wounds he'd gotten bringing his brother's killers to justice. He ignored the pain as best he could, but Mim caught the tension in his jaw. Her fingers trailed down his shoulder.

"Arliss—"

"I'm fine," he said. "Just worried about Lola."

Mim checked the temperature on the oven, then stepped back to lean against the counter. She bounced slightly on her hips, as if to the beat of some song in her head. "Falling through the ice like that . . ." She grimaced, then moved closer, pressing her shoulder against his.

He winced at the sudden pain from the old wounds.

She popped up straight. "Sorry about that."

"Totally worth it," he said. "I'm good. Really."

"Of course, you are," she said. "I'm a nurse, Arliss. We're trained to notice when people are in pain."

"Better every day." Cutter opened and closed his hand, curling his index finger like he was pulling the trigger before tapping her on the lips. "Everything works like it's supposed to."

"I'm sure . . ." She grinned, eyes holding a glint of mischief but left it at that.

Cutter stifled a groan.

Along with closure, solving his brother's murder had brought an emptiness that he hadn't anticipated. Mim felt it too and told him so. Change was hard, even when it was for the better.

He and Ethan had been inseparable growing up, the best of friends learning how to be good men under Grumpy's guidance. Then when Arliss was sixteen, he'd met Mim at the bait shop where she worked on Manasota Key. She had been, and still was, the most beautiful, mysterious, and perfect girl Cutter had ever seen. Though a tough and supremely confident man now, at sixteen Arliss had been all nerves and elbows. He'd just worked up the nerve to ask Mim out when his big brother swooped in with his barbershop haircut and football star charm to cast his spell. There'd been no contest. Ethan swept Mim off her feet and left Arliss standing dumbfounded by the minnow buckets.

Somehow, he survived the singular misery of watching the girl he loved each and every day joined at the hip with his older brother.

Ethan proposed.

Mim accepted.

Arliss joined the Army.

He met another girl in North Carolina just after he finished basic training. She had the same peaches and cream complexion and straw blond hair that had drawn him to Mim. They were married before he made E-3. That first wife might have looked like Mim, but she had the heart of a water moccasin. They divorced within a year.

Grumpy wrote letters with family news nearly every week, mostly in pencil. Arliss successfully passed the grueling Ranger Indoctrination Program in the red Georgia clay and months of Ranger School, joining the ranks of the 75th Ranger Regiment. Ethan graduated college and then went to work raising his family.

Arliss went to war.

Gobsmacked that he'd survived deployments to Afghanistan and Iraq, he interviewed for a deputy position with the United States Marshals Service a few months before his second enlistment was over. After a year and a half turning a wrench at an old Army buddy's motorcycle shop in Fort Myers, he at long last got a report date to the US Marshals Academy at the Federal Law Enforcement Training Centers in Glynco, Georgia—FLETC, or, as he and his friends often called it, FLEA-TEC. He was on his second wife by then. She ended up handing him divorce papers as he climbed into his truck to make the drive up to Glynco. A rare smile had escaped his lips as he signed the documents and shoved them back without a word. The fact that she wanted a divorce wasn't a surprise. Her timing was just laughable. She'd chucked rocks at his pickup as he backed out of the driveway, accusing him of mocking her. He supposed he was. This one also happened to look like Mim. And she sure as hell knew how to chuck rocks. What she did not know how to do was plan ahead. If she'd held out in the marriage for just a few more months and served Cutter the papers after he became a bona fide federal employee, she would have been entitled to half his pension when he died or retired.

Or, maybe she knew all that, but hated him so much she just wanted to be shed of him as quickly as possible. Cutter couldn't blame her.

The Marshals academy had been a breeze compared to Ranger Selection. He made good friends, shot gobs of ammo, and mixed it up in the mat room as often as anyone wanted to spar. Good times under the Georgia pines.

Cutter had never mentioned it to anyone—he wasn't much of a mentioner—but from the time he'd joined the Army at eighteen, he'd always assumed he wouldn't live long enough to get old.

Federal law enforcement wasn't generally as dangerous as his time with the Ranger Regiment, though this US Marshals gig had sure seen some moments. Still, he felt lucky to have a job that was tailor-made for him—a man with a resting mean mug and the skills imparted by his late grandfather.

As a POD—a plain old deputy—in Miami, he'd done his share of hooking and hauling prisoners, spent mind-numbing hours in federal court with everything from money launderers to child traffickers. Each new deputy was assigned a handful of fugitive warrants, most of them for low-level criminals or cold cases in folders so old they fell apart in your hands when you took them out of the filing cabinet. Cutter worked weekends and evenings, doggedly clearing every warrant that landed on his desk. Three years in, the chief temporarily assigned him to the enforcement side of the office. A welcome change from letting his brain go moldy sitting in court all day.

Deputy Cutter soon established himself as one of the preeminent manhunters in the Southern District of Florida. His tenacity locating and arresting two homicide suspects that USMS HQ had designated "major cases" saw him assigned a permanent desk in warrants. The fulltime assignment to Enforcement had cost him his third wife—an assistant clerk with the US district court.

The fact was, all of Cutter's ex-wives probably wanted to kill him worse than any Taliban insurgent ever had—maybe with good reason. Three failed marriages left only one person to blame. Like Grumpy always said, if everyone else in the world seemed like an asshole . . . the asshole was likely the man staring at you in the mirror when you shaved.

By the time Arliss and the assistant clerk of court split the sheets, Ethan had Mim, three beautiful kids, and his dream engineering job.

Then the big heart that had shepherded two abandoned grandsons into adulthood just exploded while Grumpy stood on the deck of his Florida Marine Patrol boat. Arliss was sure that was exactly where the old man would have wanted to go out. Not one to cry, Arliss had wept his heart dry during his grandfather's funeral, a bitter, ugly cry that cursed the heavens and made his head throb for days. He'd thought his mother might have the common decency to attend the funeral of the man who had raised her boys.

She hadn't.

Three hundred others came—family, longtime friends, honor guards from a host of law enforcement agencies including the Florida Marine Patrol, the Marshals Service, and the Parker County, Texas sheriff's office where Grumpy had started his career as a lawman. Surprisingly, some of the folks he'd arrested over his thirty-year career came to pay their respects. Even they wept. Four of his old Army buddies showed up in uniform, complete with green berets of Special Forces operators—a part of Grumpy's life he rarely mentioned, even to curious young grandsons.

Southern funerals are basically reunions with prayers and hymns. The Cutter brothers and Mim spent the evening around the firepit in Grumpy's backyard where the boys had grown up on the muddy gut called Alligator Creek. They traded Grumpy stories and talked more than they had in years.

Later, after Mim had gone inside with the kids, Ethan took a long pull of his beer and glanced up the hill toward the little stucco house as if to make sure they were alone at the fire.

"Listen, brother," he said. "I've got a line on a position with an engineering firm up in Alaska—if I can convince Mim."

Arliss had scoffed at the notion. "Seems to me she's a Florida girl to the bone."

"True enough," Ethan said. "But she'll come around." His brown eyes sparkled in the firelight, the way they had when the boys were young, and they'd stood in this exact spot to plan their adventures. "Alaska is . . . well, it's just magical, ya know. Wild and hairy with a hell of a lot of things that can stomp the puddin' out of you." He gestured to Arliss with the neck of his beer. "Right up your alley, brother." He took another drink. "Anyhow, life's short. You should come visit. We'll fish, hunt some caribou, do all the stuff we used to do with Grumpy—except there'll be grizzly bears and snow . . ."

Cutter had returned to Miami the next morning and thrown himself at his work. He'd met the woman who would become his fourth wife a short time later during a judicial protection detail in Fort Lauderdale. Barbara was a third-grade teacher, working a summer job at the Marriott Courtyard where the detail deputies were staying. That marriage might actually have worked out, but both Barbara and Ethan died within six months of each other, her from breast cancer, him, murdered on an oil rig on the North Slope.

And now, three years down the line, Arliss was here in Alaska, in Mim's kitchen making pie. Heart-wrenchingly perfect.

Except for Ursula.

# CHAPTER 8

*Arizona*
*Present day*

S WEAT RINGED THE NECK OF BOBBY GANT'S BLUE OXFORD BUTTON-up, blossoming from his armpits and dripping like a leaky faucet down his spine. Bobby G to those who knew him, Gant sat behind the wheel of the dusty white Ford panel van and tried to work out what he'd done to piss off Valeria Kot. Wavy hair hung to his shoulders, damp with just enough product to make it look as if he'd just stepped out of the shower. His dark beard was going gray in two perfect vertical lines on either side of his chin. A hooker in Queens once said it made him look like he was wearing a skunk's ass on his face, but he thought it gave him character. A Golden Gloves boxer as a teen, he was six three and a trim buck-ninety-five, even staring fifty in the face.

He'd missed New York at first, the action, the tempo. Hell, he'd even missed the noise. He figured Valeria held it against him because he'd been at the dentist with a broken tooth the morning Olek popped Henry Vargas. Gant had committed the unpardonable sin of not getting arrested with everyone else, so she'd banished him to the desert to keep an eye on Josie Lujan until she led them to Sam.

Four years had felt like banishment in the beginning, but he didn't mind it at all now. Hell, Arizona felt like home after four years—and Josie felt like someone he might like to know, maybe invite out for dinner and a date milkshake—except that he'd eventually have to kill her.

Everything had been going smoothly until Valeria recalled his normal partner to New York and sent this brainless gym bro, Dusty Baldwin, who now parked his ass in the passenger seat of the white panel van. The kid delighted in passing gas made all the more noxious from his steady diet of protein shakes. If Gant had been ten years younger, he would have stabbed the muscle-bound smartass in the throat.

Instead, he cranked up the air conditioning, partially to keep up with the oppressive heat, but mainly to chase away the stench of Dusty's latest protein gut bomb. They'd parked beside a cinder block wall a block and a half from the target pay phone.

On most evenings about this time when the desert sky turned that purple-blue color that made you imagine old Western movies and coyotes yipping, Gant would have been watching Josie through her windows while she made dinner or sat in her Eames chair and read a book. Not tonight. Tonight, Josie was on the move, probably going to one of the pay phones she'd been visiting for the past two weeks.

There was only one reason a woman like her would drive all over town just to make a call.

She had to be contacting her son.

Outside the van, a streetlight cast long shadows through a scraggly velvet mesquite tree over a waist-high green plastic box. Wires ran from the box through a crack in the van's window where Gant could sit and listen in the relative comfort.

Waiting.

He'd been following Professor Josie long enough to establish the patterns of life that defined her. He knew where she liked to stop for coffee on the way to her office at the University of Arizona Tempe campus. She had a fondness for Charmin toilet paper as long as it was on sale and preferred Snuggle fabric softener over Downy no matter the cost. She hit the gym near her house four times a week, two of those times for a spin class that Gant would have joined if he'd not had a partner looking over his shoulder all the time. Wednesdays were reserved for book club or painting classes. She went hiking nearly every weekend—locally if it was cool enough or up toward Sedona or Flagstaff if the desert was angry—which, as far as Gant could tell, was most of the time. Twice a month, she visited the San Carlos Apache reservation, likely to visit family. Gant wasn't sure. A New York mobster with a beard that looked like a skunk's ass barely blended in in Phoenix. He steered clear of the Rez and left Josie to her own devices. He wondered if she ever felt a difference when she wasn't being followed. She traveled some, which mixed up the routine every now and again—once even going to Machu Picchu with some of her Native American Studies students. When she was home in Arizona, her life had a rhythm—comforting and predictable.

At least it had been.

The first whiff of a change had come two weeks earlier. Gant's heart skipped a beat when she left her office and turned her cream-colored Subaru Crosstrek south when she should have gone north. Tonight was book club—a sacrosanct appointment not to be broken. Instead, she jumped on the Maricopa Freeway and drove in the other direction to the REI outdoor equipment store in Chandler. The REI in Phoenix would have been closer to her house. All of this was outside the norm, but not enough to report to New York.

She'd gone south again the following day, staying off the highway, sticking with surface streets, doubling back a couple of times like she didn't want to be followed. Gant stuck with her, but just barely. She ended up at a pay phone outside a trailer park on the outskirts of Gilbert.

A pay phone.

Dammit. What was she thinking? This would be the end of her and the end of Gant's time in Arizona—the end of their time together.

Pay phones were going the way of the dodo. Josie bounded all over the city, hitting three of them at least twice over the past nine days. He'd let it ride for the short time when he was between partners, telling himself he needed more information. Then Dusty arrived and he was forced to report up the chain.

Now Gant sat behind the wheel with a pair of headphones, praying Josie wasn't going to do what he knew she would.

"Finally," the kid said. "We got something to work with besides tilapia and toilet paper." At least he'd read the reports.

The kid had obviously been in more than one fight. His left ear was a pink cauliflower of tissue. A jagged smile cut unevenly across his face, just one of many scars.

"Patience," Gant whispered through clenched teeth, though he was fast running out of that himself.

Dusty lifted a coffee tumbler to his lips. Massive triceps looked like they might split the bunched sleeve of his muscle mapping T-shirt. Lifting the coffee tumbler was just an excuse to flex.

"How's that patience thing working out for you so far, Bobby G?" The kid sneered. "You've been trying to locate Sam Lujan for four years and what do you got to show for it? I say we pull out some of the old lady's fingernails, turn the tables and use some of her Apache methods to get what we need."

Gant shifted in his seat, trying to decide if this guy was as dumb as he looked.

Bald as an egg, the kid's massive arms were covered in tattoos from wrist to shoulder. His upper arm was encircled with the stylized word "Regulator," a nod to his self-appointed nickname, Dusty the Regulator. What a jackass. You didn't get to pick your own nickname. The rest of the guys called him a lot of things, but Dusty the Regulator wasn't one of them.

Conventional wisdom suggested a bald head, dark goatee, and full sleeve tats might not be the best idea for someone who needed to work in the shadows, but that didn't matter so much nowadays. There had to be ten thousand warriors and former warriors on YouTube running the exact same style. Whatever his faults—and he had a million of 'em—Dusty the Regulator melded with the crowd. And anyway, Valeria hadn't hired him for his brain. Ironic since bringing aboard a handsome rat is what got her father killed in prison and nearly brought down the entire operation.

Dusty took a long swig of coffee and whey protein—a sickening combination—and leaned forward in his seat to glare through the grimy portion of windshield outside the reach of the wipers.

"What do you say, Bobby G? I slide open the door, snatch her ass off the sidewalk and you drive away."

"Sit tight and listen. She'll make another call."

"Screw that," Dusty said. "We're two blocks away from the phone booth. You could be tied into the tamale stand up the block, for all you know."

Gant made a futile attempt to explain how he'd used a device called a Hound to send a tone from the target pay phone down the street. Then, using a wand called a Fox, he'd scanned the nest of wires in the green box outside his door until he got a straight tone, giving him the paired lines associated with the target pay phone. At first, he'd thought Dusty might want to learn. Fat chance.

If he was right, this would all be over soon. If Josie Lujan was anything she was a creature of habit. She'd use the target pay phone again and when she did, Bobby Gant and Dusty the Regulator would be sitting in a van around the corner listening to every word.

Bobby Gant heaved a melancholy sigh.

Such a waste.

# CHAPTER 9

*Anchorage*
*5° below*

CUTTER GOT A CARTON OF HEAVY CREAM FROM THE FRIDGE AND passed it to Mim.

"How is Lola anyway?" she asked.

Cutter shrugged. "I chewed her out pretty good for screwing up."

"Sounds like it."

"She knows I'm only trying to protect her."

"Hmmm." Mim glanced up. "Don't y'all jump through a hole in the ice every Christmas to raise money for Special Olympics?"

"She could have been killed," Cutter said.

Mim gave him a sad-eyed smile. "You were there too, buddy. Are you trying to scare me to death?"

"I want her to think before she runs off half-cocked."

"Says the man who took a canoe upriver to arrest his brother's killer all by himself. Now you know how I feel."

"She's my responsibility," he said.

"And you're mad because she chased this Pritchard guy on her own, before you got there?"

"Onto the ice." Cutter rarely found himself on the defensive, but Mim was a different story.

"You told me Pritchard murdered a woman and her unborn

child," she said. "Looks like you would have wanted Lola to go after him."

"I absolutely did," Cutter said. "But with backup."

Mim stood still and looked at him for a long moment, like she was trying to make sense of what he'd said.

"And now Lola thinks you're mad at her?"

"I am mad at her."

Mim began to crack the eggs into a mixing bowl. "Does she know?"

"Oh, yeah," Cutter said. Mim glanced up, eyeing him the way she did her boys when they told her they'd washed up for dinner, but their hands were still bone dry. He looked away, sheepish. "Lola knows what I mean. She's . . ." He heaved a heavy sigh. "She's like family to me."

"You ever consider telling her that?"

"She knows."

A wave of chilly air rescued Cutter, rolling into the kitchen ahead of chattering voices and the stomp of heavy snow boots on the hardwood floor.

Cutter readied himself for the stampede of twin boys coming his way.

"Boots off!" Mim reminded them from her spot by the stove.

Matthew rushed in first, cheeks rosy from cold, eyes welling with tears. His parka was unzipped, his wool hat cockeyed, revealing a shock of sweaty blond hair. A yellow scarf twice his size that said CRIME SCENE DO NOT CROSS draped over one shoulder and trailed along behind him. The youngest by twelve minutes, he was by far the more emotional of Mim's nine-year-old twins. Of the two, he looked the most like his Uncle Arliss. Michael, the older twin, blew in tight on his heels. This one was darker like his father. Both boys were panting hard from whatever game they'd been playing outside.

In the middle of separating eggs, Mim turned sideways like a matador to protect her nascent pie filling from the teeming horde.

Cutter gave the boys a nodding salute. "Hello, men," he said. "Why don't you take off your coats and stay awhile."

The boys both started talking at the same time, growing louder and more intense with each word. Matthew, on the verge of tears, threw up his hands and glared at his older brother. Michael closed his eyes and said, "Okay, you tell it then."

Mim dried her hands on a cup towel and cocked her head, checking her youngest son for wounds. "What's the matter? You hurt?"

Matthew shook his head, sniffing back a sob.

"We were sledding down the hill on the ice and—"

"And you broke something?"

"No-ah!" Matthew said, exasperated, as if *no* was a two-syllable word. "I'm fine. We were sledding and I told Gordon Brown that I was going to be a marshal someday like Uncle Arliss."

Mim shot Cutter a look he couldn't quite discern. He shrugged and bowed his head. He'd not encouraged the boys, but he'd not discouraged them either.

Matthew kept going. "Gordon said you were only a marshal because you wanted to hurt bad guys. I told him it was because you wanted to help good guys. But Gordon said his dad told him that you were just a bully who liked to push people around. I said you were not. He wouldn't take it back. I shoulda punched him."

"Nah," Cutter said. "Guys like that aren't worth it. I probably arrested someone Gordon's dad knows."

"Maybe Gordon's dad," Mim said under her breath. Then, "You boys need baths."

"We were going back out," Michael said.

"Thirty more minutes," Mim said.

Calming as quickly as he'd gotten his blood up, Matthew peeled off his wool hat and got himself a glass of water from the fridge door, gulping it down. "Did you?" he said to Cutter.

"Did I what?"

"Become a marshal so you could hurt bad people?"

Cutter felt Mim's eyes lock in on him.

"Nope," he said. "Sometimes the bad guys do get hurt. That's for sure, but I never plan to hurt anyone. The choice is always theirs if they want to come in peacefully when I arrest them."

"Even the really bad ones?" Michael asked.

"Even the really bad ones," Cutter said.

"So, I was right," Matthew said. "You did do it to help people."

Cutter mussed the boy's hair. "You weren't wrong," he said. "But truth be told, I do hate a bully."

The boys blinked up at him, taking in the information.

"Anyway," Cutter said, "you don't need to be in law enforcement to help people. Your dad helped out folks all the time. Never told anyone about it."

Michael seemed to chew on that for a moment then changed the subject completely. "Can you take us to see the dead whale?"

The carcass of a forty-seven-foot fin whale had washed up on the tidal flats near Anchorage, drawing hundreds of locals to look at its frozen remains.

"We'll talk about it," Mim said. "Might be interesting."

"Cool," Michael said.

Matthew put his glass on the counter and wheeled toward the door. "I'm going to go tell Gordon I was right!"

"No punching," Cutter said.

"Okaaaay," Matthew said.

"Thank you," Mim said after the door had slammed shut behind the boys.

"I'll be more careful about encouraging him," Cutter said.

"That's not what I mean." She put a hand to her chest, stifling a sob. "I'm saying thank you for being a man the boys can look up to." She sniffed. "And anyway, I know the real reason you went into law enforcement. Ethan told me."

"My Tarzan complex—the need to swing in and save the day?"

"There is that," Mim said. "Ethan said it was because of Grumpy's friends."

Cutter couldn't help but smile. "Ethan was right. I have to admit I always did crave that brotherhood Grumpy had with his buddies."

"Trauma-bonding will do that," Mim said, her eyes glassy with tears.

Cutter took her hand. "You okay?"

She nodded, the kind of quick, tight-lipped nod that said she was anything but. "This is . . . this is just a lot. That's all. Seems like something is always getting in the way." She sniffed back a tear. "Have you tried to sit down and talk to your mother?"

"Kind of," Cutter said.

Mim lowered her voice to a whisper. "Well I have," she said.

"And?"

"And nada," Mim said. "She has gobs of advice for the way I should parent and clean my house . . . but still nothing about her or why she's here."

Cutter glanced at the empty doorway. "I can't figure out what it is," he said. "But that woman is hiding something."

Ursula floated in on cue, clinking the ice in her glass as if to announce her presence.

Mim pulled away and went back to making her pie filling. Cutter opened the fridge door, treating it as a shield between him and his mother. He frowned as she walked by, or at least, didn't smile.

In her early sixties now, she was still blond as ever, though Cutter suspected that came from a bottle. She loomed so much larger in his memory—a beautiful blond goddess with tan shoulders and a green sundress. High cheekbones accentuated a slightly puckered mouth, as if she'd just taken a bite of something a little bit too sweet. A green sweatshirt nearly swallowed her up. She wore a ring on nearly every finger, butterflies and flowers— and a tiger's-eye Cutter remembered her having on when she ran off. Bracelets of all shapes and materials—from metal to braided cotton to something that Cutter thought might be elephant hair— decorated deeply tanned wrists. The powdery scent of Mary Kay cosmetics wafted over as she walked by, putting a lump in Cutter's throat. He frowned, unwilling to admit that this woman still had a hold on his emotions and swallowed the feeling. She planted herself in a seat at the end of the bar as if she owned the place.

"The boys want me to take them to see a frozen whale," she said. "What's the point of that?"

"It's a whale," Cutter said. "That is the point."

Mim shot Cutter a behave-yourself look before smiling at his mother.

"Hey, Ursula." Mim moved a bowl with the egg yolks next to a small saucepan on the stove. "You should take them. It would be nice to spend some time together."

"Looking at a dead animal," she said, unconvinced.

"Come jump right in here," Mim said. "Cooking's therapy in this house. I'm interested to learn some of your favorite recipes."

Ursula scrunched up her nose like she was about to sneeze.

"You know that thing that's the opposite of a green thumb for gardening," she said. A strong Southern accent turned *thing* into *thang*. It would have sounded nostalgic had Cutter not been so bitter.

Mim laughed. "I don't know. Numb thumb?"

"Yeah, well, hon, I have that same thang when it comes to cookin'." Ursula settled into her bar stool, elbows on the counter, chin in her hands. "Sounds like Constance plans on driving to the mall with her friends. Don't you worry about her on these roads?"

Mim exchanged a glance with Cutter. Ursula may as well have been a stranger breezing in off the street to give parenting advice. Cutter started to stay something, but Mim beat him to it, calm and sweet. Defusing.

"Of course I do," Mim said. "I worry all the time. But I'd worry a lot more if she just camped out in her room all the time. Your granddaughter can be kind of a loner. We're just glad she's made some friends she wants to spend time with."

Ursula gave a little nod, like she understood the words, but didn't quite agree with them. She made the sneeze face again. "I've been biting my tongue, but it seems awfully cold and dark for the boys to be playing outside."

Cutter scoffed. "That your new job, ratting out the kids?"

"I only—"

"It's fine," Mim said. "Cold and dark is what we get this time of year. I don't care as long as they're bundled."

Ursula appeared to let Cutter's jibe slide off her back. If she cared what he thought, maybe she wouldn't have run off and left him.

She glanced up at Mim, chin still smushed against her fists.

"Matthew told me the teachers make them go outside for recess until it's colder than ten below zero. That can't be right."

"Oh, he's telling you the truth," Mim said.

"That's criminal," Ursula mumbled. "At least it's not snowing."

Cutter put the carton of cream back in the fridge. "We need more snow," he said.

The weather was as good a reason as any to argue.

Mim jumped ahead, again, working to defuse. She was good at that. "The snow keeps the underground pipes from freezing when temps drop." She stood at the stove, stirring the contents of her saucepan, glancing up as she spoke. "Anyhow, it's good the boys are going out while it's still relatively warm."

"You mean it's fixin' to get worse than this?"

"Oh yeah," Mim said. "Supposed to drop to fifteen or sixteen below zero tonight. We'll leave all the cabinets open and the faucets dripping."

"This godforsaken place . . ." Ursula changed the subject, gesturing with her chin toward the stove. "You're makin' Chester Mae's chocolate pie."

Mim raised a brow.

Cutter's frown bordered on a glare. The name sounded vaguely familiar. "It's the recipe for Aunt Rita's chocolate pie."

"Do you even know your great-grandfather's name?"

"Which one?"

Ursula chuckled. "The one named Chester, smartass. You don't have to be ugly about it. Anyway, your great-grandpa's firstborn happened to be a girl, so they named her Chester Mae." Ursula's accent made it sound like *Chesta-Mae*. "She didn't start going by Rita until high school. Most of the family was still calling her Chester Mae when I came into the picture."

"Good to know," Mim said as she stirred the pie filling.

Cutter rolled his eyes. "Scintillating."

They were quiet for a time, then Ursula spoke out of the blue. "You two seem to be getting along awfully well." She turned to study Cutter. "The boys told me you've been married four times?"

"I have indeed," Cutter said.

She chuckled under her breath. "My son, the serial monogamist."

"Guess I missed out on your guiding influence."

Ursula turned, her chin still in her hands, and stared out the window. "You know, I thought about coming to get you a dozen times over the years."

Cutter braced himself. She'd finally decided to talk.

"I made it all the way to Wayne's screen door once. He had you boys sitting on the couch darning socks while you watched Westerns on that little TV of his. You know, the one you had to use pliers to change the channels..." She shook her head. "Like he couldn't afford new socks."

Cutter slammed the fridge hard enough to rattle the condiments in the door.

"It wasn't about the socks," he said.

"Don't you think I know that?" Ursula pushed away from the counter and stood with a low groan that sounded a lot like Cutter felt. "You know, when a young mother realizes she can't provide her baby the life it needs she gets praised as a selfless hero for giving it up for adoption. Me on the other hand . . . I'm a demon bitch for doin' essentially the very same thing."

"Imagine that," Cutter said.

Mim touched his arm. "Arliss—"

Ursula didn't slow down.

"I wish you'd stop and think for just one minute," she said. "Wayne was the only person I knew who could give you boys what you needed."

"We needed a mother," Cutter whispered.

Ursula laughed, low in her belly. "Oh, that's rich. It's easy to say now, sitting here when I'm old as dirt with the rough ridden off me. You have no idea what I was like when you were little—"

"You're right about that—"

"Your grandfather knew," she said. "He saw the crowd I was running with, how young and ignorant I was. To tell you the truth, he seemed relieved when I left your daddy. Then even more relieved when I broached the subject of having him raise you boys when your daddy died."

Arliss fought the urge to open the refrigerator door just so he could slam it again. "What do you think killed him?"

"Oh," Ursula said. "I killed him. No doubt about that. Truth is, your daddy was dying well before I ever met him. I think my leaving just put him out of his misery." She leaned against the wall, bracelets clicking when she folded her arms across her chest. "I would have ruined you, son. But look at you now. Wayne gave you—"

Cutter suppressed the urge to scream. "I wish you'd call him Grumpy like everyone else."

"He was just D Wayne Cutter until you came along and started calling him Grumpy. It fit him well enough, but as far as I can tell, you're the grumpiest person I've ever met."

"Whatever you say—"

"I'll make you a deal, Arliss," she said. "I'll call D Wayne 'Grumpy' if you'll call me Mama like you used to."

"Call him whatever you want."

Ursula turned to Mim, her voice softer. "I know it sounds like I was being selfish . . ." She trailed off. "Because I was, but believe me when I tell you Wayne was exactly what those boys needed. Both of them, but for different reasons."

"I got to know Grumpy pretty well," Mim said. "He was an incredible father figure."

Ursula looked Cutter dead in the eye and gave a somber shake of her head. "You remind me of him, you know."

"Sure, I do."

"I'm trying here, son," Ursula said. "I really am."

"Good for you," Cutter said.

Mim took his hand in hers, holding it tight.

Ursula threw up her arms. "You want the truth, Arliss? Well, here it is. It's uglier than you'll want to hear. Your big brother would have been fine if I'd dragged you boys around with me. Ethan came out of my belly already a half-grown man, knowing how to handle things. But you and me, we were too much alike. I mean, look at yourself, four marriages for pity's sake. If I'd have stuck around, you and me woulda been a couple of drunks living in some travel trailer on cinder blocks, waitin' on our welfare checks every month."

"I would have had a mother," Cutter whispered, trying desperately not to sound like an abandoned five-year-old. "Anyway, you seem to be doing fine."

"That's because I didn't have two kids to worry about while I was still a kid myself. Don't you get it, hon? Grumpy not only raised you boys. He gave me a chance to get myself raised. Arliss, sweetie, I'm not looking for forgiveness—"

"Outstanding." Cutter paused, cocking his head to one side. "And just what exactly are you looking for?"

"To be honest, I do not know." She stared at her feet. "At least as far as my leaving you is concerned. A chance to explain, maybe."

"Okay, then," Cutter said. "Beyond that. Other than absolution for running away when I was a little boy. You had to have some reason for coming here after all this time."

Ursula gave an exasperated sigh. "You don't make this easy."

Mim gave a long sigh. "He's got a point, Ursula," she said. "You've been here over a month, and we still don't know—"

"Six weeks," Cutter said.

"Six weeks," Mim said. "And we still don't know why."

Ursula met Cutter's gaze head-on. Her lips trembled. "You're absolutely right, of course." She closed her eyes, pressing tears through her lashes, looking even more drawn and hollow than she had only a few moments before. "Arliss, hon . . . I need you to help me find my daughter."

Cutter felt as if someone had stabbed him in the heart. "Hang on . . . You're telling me I have a sister?"

Ursula nodded, lips pressed into a tight line like she might break down at any moment.

Mim stood and stared directly at the mother-in-law she'd known now for mere days. Her face flushed red. Her entire body began to shake with rage. "Let me make sure I understand. You want the son whose heart you broke to help you track down a daughter you want to be with."

"It makes me sound like such an awful person when you say it that way," Ursula said. "But life's messy—"

"You can say that again," Mim fumed.

Cutter's phone rang before he could speak. He considered ignoring the call, but saw it was Lola. With any luck it would be a callout and he could get some distance from this freakshow.

"Cutter," he said, sounding far gruffer than he intended.

"You still talking to me, boss?" Lola asked.

He couldn't tell if she was being flippant or really wanted to know. Likely a bit of both.

"Tell me what you've got," he said. He turned to face away from Ursula.

"Okay," she said. "Here's the deal. Joe Bill's working swing shift tonight. I thought I'd ride along, do some follow-up on that information Butterbean gave us."

"I thought we decided to wait until Monday," Cutter said. "It's been a hell of a few days. You need to go home and get some rest."

"Are you ordering me?" Lola's voice hummed with emotion.

Cutter took a beat to think. "No," he said. "It's advice you should listen to."

"So," Lola said. "I'm your kid now?"

"If you were my kid I'd send you home," he said. "I'm leaving it up to you."

"Testing me," Lola scoffed. "To see if I make the right decision?"

"I've already told you what I think."

Lola softened, trying a different tack.

"This *is* resting, boss," she said. "If I wasn't on the street, I'd be in the gym doing heavy squats. Anyhow, what are the odds I'll come to grief twice in the same week."

*Astronomically high*, Cutter thought. *You work with me.*

# CHAPTER 10

*Anchorage*
*7° below*

"**H**E HATES ME," LOLA TEARIKI SAID. "I THOUGHT IT YESTERDAY. Now, I'm positive."

She wedged herself in the passenger seat of Joe Bill Brackett's patrol car and tucked her parka around her thighs so she could shut the door. Still relatively junior with Anchorage PD, her boyfriend drove one of the Chevy Impalas instead of the more spacious Ford Explorers or Expeditions. The mobile data terminal, or MDT, took up heaps of room on the passenger side, forcing Lola to swing her legs toward the door. An air freshener scented like Hoppe's No. 9 gun solvent hung from the rearview mirror mingling with the pungent odor of Lysol that drifted through the holes in the plexiglass screen from the rear seat. Swallowed up by wool scarves and her personal down parka—her issued Wiggy's was under the ice on Cheney Lake—Lola Teariki looked like a pile of laundry with a head stacked on top. Black hair spilled from beneath a wool beanie.

"Cutter doesn't hate you," he said.

"You didn't hear him," Lola said. "I'm telling you, I'll be back in ops hookin' and haulin' prisoners next week. They're already grooming Paige Hart."

"She'd be good," Brackett said.

Lola reached across the console and slugged him in the arm. "I know," she said. "That's the problem. The chief already wants to shake up the task force."

"She told you that?"

"The chief doesn't tell me shit," Lola said. "But I hear things. Do you know what she calls us? The 'task force of misfit toys.'"

"I'm sure she's joking."

"Maybe," Lola said. "But that doesn't mean I'm not back in ops next week."

"I think you might be overreacting," Brackett said.

"Wow, that's exactly what a girl wants to hear," she said. "Just drive, would you. I want to think about anything but my stone-faced boss right now."

"That's pretty much how I feel all the time," Joe Bill said.

Lola turned to look out the window. There wasn't much to see. The pitifully weak winter sun had set hours before, leaving nothing but frosty streets and twinkling Christmas lights the city would leave up all winter. They were supposed to help people cope with the interminable hours of darkness and cold.

Joe Bill drove west through downtown, humming some annoying ditty in time with the beat of road gravel popping under his tires. They passed the iconic log cabin visitor center and park that would have been filled with tourists under a midnight-sun summer. For now, bitter temperatures had chased even local Alaskans inside, leaving the streets eerily deserted for eight p.m.

"You okay?" Joe Bill asked, his face ghostly green in the light of the dashboard.

"Right as." She gave him a glaring side eye. "What the hell are you humming?"

Joe Bill gave an embarrassed chuckle. "I didn't realize I was humming." He flicked his hand toward the windshield and the frozen world outside. "We're driving down Fourth, so . . . It's the . . . you know, the Fur Rendezvous song—."

Lola rolled her eyes. "Brilliant." She softened immediately. "Sorry. I don't mean to be pissy."

"Fugitaboutit," Brackett said.

She couldn't help but smile at the childlike innocence. He reminded her of that Raymond Chandler quote—*Down the mean streets a man must go who is not himself mean . . .*

"You are an unusual human being, Officer Brackett," she said.

"Thank you?"

"I'm pretty keen on unusual," Lola said, snuggling deeper into her nest of parka and scarves. "I wish you could have seen Butterbean's face."

Brackett glanced sideways as he drove. "Who?"

"That's what Cutter calls Tops," Lola said. "That guy is terrified of someone."

"Could be he owes some people money."

"Yeah-nah," Lola said. "This was weird. His eyes got all flighty-like and he said, *they'll kill me, they'll kill you, they'll kill my family, they'll kill your family.*"

"Sheesh . . . that's dark."

"No shit." Lola shrugged. "I'll never forget the look on his face. I'm gonna dig into it more after we get Royce Decker. Bugs me to think somebody that bad is out there."

"Oh, hon," Brackett said. "You and I both been on the job long enough to know there are a hell of a lot of somebodies that bad out there."

"Job security, I guess," Lola said. "Until then, Butch Pritchard will be a worthy consolation prize. I got a bone to pick with that asshole."

Merlin Tops/Butterbean had vomited information, providing cell numbers for Pritchard and a dancer named Tina Massey, his girlfriend of the moment. A search warrant for phone logs revealed Pritchard had called Massey shortly after he'd slipped away from Lola. Both phones pinged off the same tower a few minutes later near Russian Jack Park where Massey had presumably picked him up. Then both phones had gone dark. Lola stayed up on both numbers, monitoring just to be sure. If either phone was activated, or in the unlikely event someone made a call, she'd get a notification on her cell. Good in theory, but Pritchard was too smart for that.

Active cell phones weren't the only way to track down an outlaw. Logs built patterns of life if you knew how to look at them.

The night before she'd picked up Pritchard at Cheney Lake,
Tina Massey's phone had pinged downtown near the PD. Previous records showed outgoing calls to a number registered to one
Regina Orr. A quick check on APSIN, Alaska's secure law enforcement database, revealed both Massey and Orr had several arrests for prostitution. Orr had two for misconduct involving a
controlled substance. In her case, prescription oxy.

It made sense. According to Butterbean, Regina Orr worked at
the Pioneer Bar. Pio (PIE-OH) to locals, the Pioneer as well as the
bar next door called the Gaslight spilled into the same parking
area in an alley between Fourth and Third Avenue. APD units
working area 1 had plenty to do during bar break.

Brackett stopped singing long enough to nod at the Gaslight's
front door, painted bright red against the snowy walkway out
front. "Pio's entrance is around back," he said. "Which is good. I
don't particularly want the noses at the PD to see me going into a
bar with my hot deputy marshal girlfriend."

"Am I getting you in trouble with this ride along?"

"Sergeant Hopper gave his blessing," Brackett said. "The lieutenant's got heartburn for feds in general. And the fact that
you're my girlfriend doesn't help. Past bad actors have forced the
implementation of a strict, 'no booty on duty' rule."

Lola smacked the laptop and MDT stand. "I need more space
than this for my booty to express itself!"

Brackett shifted uncomfortably in his seat then shot her a grin.
"Let's talk about something else."

"So, your LT doesn't like that we work together for these investigations?"

"We've always gotten results," he said. "The chief likes results.
As long as we don't get in a shooting—"

"Or engage in the booby-on-duty, thing—"

"*Booty*," Brackett corrected. "You're killin' me . . ."

He turned down the alley off H Street.

Lola zipped up her parka and pounded the door with a fist.
"Let me off here. I reckon everybody will clam up the second you

walk through the door in that sexy blue uniform." She gave him a wink. "Or the badge bunnies will start hitting on you and I'll have to knock some heads. I'll text you if I see Regina Orr. Then you can come in."

Had it been summer there might have been a dozen patrons hanging out in the parking lot shooting the breeze, trying to hook up, or score some dope. Every one of them would surely have been giving a stink eye to the white Impala that was backed into a parking spot near Third Avenue for quick egress—as cops were known to do. Eight below zero turned the lot into a deserted wasteland. Lola's cover remained intact as Brackett rolled up to meet her, tires crunching gravel five minutes later when she popped out of the Pioneer Bar and into the nose-pinching cold. She gave Brackett a thumbs-up, then made her way to the driver's side and banged a fist against the window.

Frost chattered against the rubber seal as Brackett rolled it down, streaking the glass. He squinted at the sudden rush of Arctic air.

"Hey there, pretty lady," he said, breathless from the cold. "Need a lift?"

Lola's words came haltingly on a series of gasps against the frigid air.

"Bartender in the Pio was a Chatty Cathy. Said she hasn't seen Regina Orr or Tina Massey in two days."

"That tracks." Joe Bill shifted in his seat, eager to roll up his window.

"I guess Orr likes to hang out next door at the Gaslight." Lola coughed, whispering as the cold air gripped her throat. "Chatty Cathy said the bartender over there will help me out. I'm gonna go talk to her." She patted the door with her mitten. "They still got a mechanical bull in this joint?"

"As of three days ago."

"Good," Lola said. "Maybe I'll go for a ride. You stay toasty out here."

"Hang on a sec," Brackett said. "The bartender at the Gaslight. What's the name?"

"Hannah something or another," Lola said. "Goes by Hank."

"Hank Fielder." Brackett shot her a tight-lipped grimace. "You're right. Better if I stay outside."

Lola's eyebrow jumped up, disappearing into her wool hat. "Something you want to tell me?"

"Not at the moment," he said. "Hank's good people. She'll help you out—as long as I'm not there. We sorta parted on bad terms . . ."

Brackett drove back to his original parking spot near Third and backed in, giving him a clear view of both bars' entrances. Lola had been too cold to quiz him about Hannah "Hank" Fielder before going in. She'd just thrown back her head and looked cross-eyed down her nose in her terrifying Polynesian warrior princess face. He was certain they would talk about it later.

He'd barely had time to throw the Impala in park when two men came out of the Pio Bar. It was impossible to tell much about them in heavy winter coats and wool hats pulled down over their ears. The tallest one, wearing a green stocking cap, hooked a thumb over his shoulder toward the Gaslight. The smaller of the two—not really small at around six feet—had a bushy red beard that filled the V left by his partially unzipped parka. The men scanned the parking lot for a few seconds, both hunched up against the cold in their not nearly warm enough parkas.

Brackett had positioned himself behind a large dually pickup, hopefully giving him some cover in the darkness. If the men noticed him at all, they didn't act like it.

Brackett decided Green Hat was probably the younger of the two. Red Beard's facial hair made him appear older. The men continued to scan the lot, leaning forward like they were looking for someone. Since Lola was the last one to leave the Pio, Brackett suspected that someone was her. A cloud of vapor blossomed in front of Green Hat's face as he spoke. Red Beard gave a curt nod and then grabbed his parka by the waist as if to hitch up his pants underneath. Someone with less experience might not have noticed, but Red Beard grabbed slightly farther back at the four o'clock position. Odd for a man just hitching up his pants. He'd just checked to make sure his gun was where he left it on his waist-band. Like most Alaska-grown kids, Brackett had been raised around firearms. He was a gun guy through and through. But guns and bars were a deadly combination, especially bars where his girlfriend happened to be looking for a hired killer.

This was sure to piss Lola off, but Brackett didn't care. He threw the Impala into gear and stomped the gas at the same moment the two men ducked out of the cold into the Gaslight.

Brackett crunched to a stop adjacent to the curb, just a few feet from the Gaslight's door. He locked the Impala but left it running against the cold. Anyone with enough balls to break a window and try to steal it wouldn't get very far without disabling the hidden kill-switch.

Brackett waited until he reached the entrance before keying the mic on his handheld radio.

"1A-2."

The dispatcher came across his earpiece immediately. "1A-2."

"1A-2. I'm out at the Gaslight bar, alley entrance." He gave the descriptions of the suspicious males and advised dispatch there was a plainclothes female deputy marshal on the scene.

"10-4, 1A-2," Dispatch said. "Any unit near the Gaslight bar . . ." She paused.

"Xray 23, go ahead and attach me to that."

Brackett groaned as he opened the barroom door. He'd just as soon not have Sergeant Hopper respond as backup when he was trying to save his girlfriend on a hunch. Lola Teariki was not really the sort of woman who liked to be saved.

Throbbing music carried out to meet him on a bubble of humid air, warm and heavy with the odor of alcohol and good times. He stopped just inside, taking a moment to let his eyes adjust to the darkness. Green Hat and Red Beard were impossible to miss. They'd already found Lola and were moving toward where she'd parked herself, back against one of the long high-tops that encircled a pit of foam pads—the bull ring. Behind her, a twenty-something kid wearing a shit-eating smirk and a sleeveless T-shirt settled onto the mechanical bull, psyching himself up to ride.

The battered straw hat, pulled down low enough to make his ears stick out, looked like he'd slept in it.

A couple of girls at the table nearest the door must have felt the rush of cold air from Brackett opening the door. They peeled their eyes off the urban cowboy long enough to check him out. They giggled and grinned when they realized he was a cop. He ignored them and pushed his way through the crowd.

All eyes except for Lola and her two gentlemen friends were on the mechanical bull. Lola's face darkened when she saw Brackett. She gave an almost imperceptible shake of her head before turning to face Red Beard. Her message was clear.

Back off. She had this.

Red Beard raised his hands as if to concede some point—then suddenly bladed, reaching behind his back.

# CHAPTER 11

*Two minutes earlier*

AS WAS HER HABIT, LOLA STEPPED TO THE SIDE AS SHE ENTERED, putting her back to the wall while she scanned her surroundings. Flashing red and green lights illuminated a milling crowd. The Gaslight's reputation notwithstanding, no one jumped out and tried to murder her right off the bat.

She chuckled to herself, remembering her time in the Marshals Service Academy just a few years earlier where virtually every scenario involving a bar ended up in a sim-round shootout. There was a reason, of course. Deputy US marshals died in the line of duty every year. Academy instructors felt the enormous responsibility of training newbies for the worst-case scenario. It took Lola a couple of years to realize that though she needed to stay aware, sometimes a bar was just a bar.

It wasn't yet nine p.m., but plummeting temps had a way of chasing the good times that usually happened in the parking lot, indoors. Patrons milled in small knots here and there. A few people at high-tops nearest the door glanced up from hushed conversations when Lola breezed in, attempting to stomp the cold out of her feet. Even then they were more interested in the chilly air that followed her than who she was. A squad of girls in tight leggings and University of Alaska Seawolves jerseys egged a young guy into the bullring.

But no sign of Regina Orr.

The tall, tan drink of water behind the bar had to be Hannah "Hank" Fielder. She zeroed in on Lola from the moment she saw her. The chatty bartender from the Pioneer had surely called ahead. Hank threw her bar mop over her shoulder and leaned forward, resting on both elbows, smiling a friendly smile. Muscular bronze arms and a skintight white tank top said she could have been working in a Hawaii dive bar rather than a roadhouse in the frozen north. Lola nodded slowly, muttering to herself. "Well, well, Joe Bill Brackett. You, sir, have a type."

Lola glanced behind her as she began working her way through the crowd. She clocked two bozos from the Pio immediately after they came in. Big guys. Red Viking beard and a guy in a green wool hat. She'd noticed them before. That could have been a coincidence, but even in the strobing lights of the bar it was easy to see by the whites of their eyes that they were focused on her. Her hand gripped the phone in her pocket. She thought about calling Joe Bill or getting the bartender to do it.

"No!' she whispered to herself, loud enough that two girls next to her looked in her direction. The day she couldn't handle a couple of idiots in a bar was the day she needed to turn in her badge.

The guy with the red beard approached first, his taller buddy hanging back a half step. Both men swayed in place—drunk or stoned . . . or both.

"You're a cop," Red Beard said, head canted. He leaned in slightly as if telling her a secret, but shouted like she was all the way across the room instead of eight feet away.

Lola gave him a curt nod, stone-faced.

"US Marshals," she said.

Red Beard took a step forward.

Instead of raising her hand to ward him off, Lola dropped her right foot back a hair, shifting her weight. She put on her serious face and barked, "Step back."

Both men stopped in their tracks, blinking at this sudden ferocity.

Joe Bill walked in at the same time as Red Beard raised both hands.

"We don't want no trouble," he said. Then, inexplicably, his right hand dropped to his waistband.

Her back against the railing of the bullring, Lola had no way to retreat. Instead, she lunged forward, closing the distance between herself and Red Beard in the blink of an eye. Her left hand came down like a hammer, impacting the man's forearm as she rocked back slightly at the waist. Her Glock was out in a flash, held tight against her side.

"Wait-wait-wait!" Red Beard whimpered. "Just getting my phone."

The Gaslight was spacious as bars went, but somehow Joe Bill covered the thirty feet from the door to Lola in an instant. He grabbed Green Beanie by the arm and shoulder, push-pulling him into a 180-degree spin.

"Your phone?" Lola said, still aimed in. She glanced down at Red Beard's cell on the floor.

To his credit, Joe Bill stepped away. Across the bar, Hank Fielder stared daggers at him. Lola would have felt sorry for him if she'd had time.

"Gentlemen," she said, "how about you keep your hands visible and tell me what I can do for you." She holstered her pistol but kept her hand on the butt.

Red Beard turned to see Joe Bill standing in uniform by his partner, and then bowed his head. He took another step forward. "Hey, listen. We should really go outside and talk."

"That's not happening," Lola said. "I told you to step back."

Red Beard complied.

"Sorry," he said, a half whisper, leaning in so far he almost fell over. "It's just that . . . I . . . we don't want to broadcast to everybody in here that we're . . . you know, helping the cops."

Lola nodded at Joe Bill. "A little too late for that," she said, as much for Joe Bill as Red Beard. "You have something to say, go ahead and say it."

"We heard you guys give reward money for information," the guy in the green beanie said. "That true?"

"Depends," Lola said, relaxing a notch. "On the case and the information provided."

Red Beard's eyes shifted back and forth beneath bushy brows, obviously worried about being overheard. "We couldn't help but hear you say you're looking for Regina Orr." He gave a little nod, puppy-like. "I got some pics of her on my phone." He gave a lascivious grin. "Some of are even of her face."

"I know what she looks like," Lola said. "I need to know where she is."

"That's easy," Red Beard said. "We know where she works."

Sometimes a bar was a bar. Sometimes a bar was a jackpot.

Lola tucked her parka around her hips and slammed the patrol car's door against the icy air. "I'm about to freeze my butt off," she said through chattering teeth. "It's gotta be colder than it was ten minutes ago."

Joe Bill had waited in the warm vehicle, letting dispatch and his responding sergeant know he was no longer in need of backup while she stomped her feet in the parking lot, working out details for a Crime Stoppers payment with her two new informants—if their information panned out.

"Sorry about moving in on you like your knight in shining armor back there. I know that pisses you off. I just—"

Lola bounced her head softly against her headrest. "Joey, Joey, Joey . . . I'm happy for the backup—" She shot him a side-eye. "I just don't want you to think of me as a damsel who needs saving all the time."

"I know you're plenty capable," he said. "But you've gotta admit you've been through it in the last day or two. When I saw that guy go for his—"

"His phone," Lola said. "But it could have been a gun." She waved away the apology—and the excuse. "You did what partners do. Anyway, what do you know about the Nordic Spa?"

"Down at Alyeska? That's where Orr works?"

"Yep," Lola said, the beginnings of a plan already forming in her mind. "Have you been?"

"Once," Joe Bill said. "Saunas, cold plunges, hot tubs, all tucked back in the woods. Pretty swank."

"According to these bozos, Regina Orr's a masseuse there working afternoons."

Joe Bill looked sideways, eyes glinting with mischief. "I'm happy to go undercover and get a massage—"

Lola smacked him in the thigh with her mitten. "Alyeska is in Anchorage patrol zone, right?"

"Technically," Joe Bill said. "But they pay Whittier PD to respond because we're so far away."

"But you'd still be in your jurisdiction if you came out there with me tomorrow and had a look around?"

A big grin spread across Joe Bill's boyish face.

"Oh, hell yeah."

"Outstanding," Lola said. "It's a long shot. We don't even know for sure that she works tomorrow. Makes sense to surveille the place for a bit."

Joe Bill checked his watch. "I get off in a couple of hours. We should drive down tonight . . ."

Lola looked up from her phone.

"Alyeska Resort has a room." Her thumb hovered over the screen.

"Book it, baby!" Joe Bill said. "We stay the night, then we can be at the spa waiting for Regina if she comes in to work."

They rode in silence until Joe Bill reached the federal building eight blocks away. She passed him her proximity card, which he scanned to activate the roll-up garage door.

Joe Bill passed the card back to her as soon as the door began to rattle upward.

"You think Orr will eventually lead you to Decker?"

"Worth a try," Lola said.

"Still think he's in Fairbanks?"

"That's the general buzz," Lola said. "Our suboffice deputies have been watching a few likely spots. Heaps of places to hide out. Hard to do much when we don't have an actual location. Big frozen country and not many people."

"Twenty-three below at the Fairbanks airport last I checked," he said.

"And falling." Her head lolled sideways again, looking him in the eye. "Hey, you should come if the hunt moves up there. Help keep me warm."

"Fat chance of that," Joe Bill said. "The LT's pretty sure you're gonna infect me with your fed gunk as it is."

"We'll just have to get you a spot on the task force."

"Talk about fat chances . . ." Joe Bill pushed the laptop around so Lola could see the screen. "Looks like the warrant gods have smiled on you, Madame Marshal. No new warrants for sex offenses, but Regina Orr's wanted for failure to appear on a shoplifting charge from Home Depot last year. That gives us a little something to hold over her head."

"An hour drive down to Alyeska—in the dark," Lola said. "You up for that?"

"I feel like I need to make it up to you for . . . you know, trying to save you."

"I'll swing by the store and grab some road snacks before you're done with your shift." Lola pounded the armrest with her fist. "Well, dammit! I never had a chance to meet your bartending ex-girlfriend."

"Let's consider that a blessing," Joe Bill muttered.

"Why did you guys break up?"

"It's a long story," Joe Bill said.

"I have time."

"Lola—"

"Is it something bad? I mean, she does work in a bar with a stripper pole."

"Nothing bad."

"Because I'm happy to go back and kick the shit out of her. I'm kind of in a mood, in case you haven't noticed."

"It's not that," Joe Bill said. "We were always fighting. Didn't end well."

"What did you fight about?"

Joe Bill gave her a sheepish grin. "She . . . she thought I was always trying to fix things . . . you know, charging in to save the day."

Lola chuckled softly.

"Imagine that."

# CHAPTER 12

*Arizona*

Bobby Gant pressed the phone tight to his left ear and plugged his right with his index finger in a hopeless attempt to understand his boss. Folks in his line of work didn't much worry about ear protection, except maybe if they were shooting at beer cans on the Kots' farm across the river in New Jersey. Even then ear-pro consisted of an unspent .38 round hanging from each ear. Decades of exposure to gunfire made hearing Valeria Kot's mercurial tones a crapshoot. Telephone conversations were especially problematic. Gant wasn't entirely sure the woman didn't walk around with a mouthful of marbles. Her men's inability to understand her graveled mumbles was their fault and had nothing to do with the fact that she'd ruined her voice screaming orders and insults after Sam Lujan ran off.

Gant had watched Valeria grow from a giggling child to a pretty, if not classically beautiful, young woman. Four years ago he'd sat in the gallery of the federal courtroom for the Southern District of New York and watched Sam—one of their own—turn rat. The betrayal had ripped Valeria's heart out.

Then Mr. Kot got himself murdered in prison.

His daughter ran the show now—numbers, extortion, drugs—everything her father had built. She had a soul for the business—or the lack of one. Valeria ordered more people whacked during that first year her father was in the joint than he'd ordered killed over the entire previous decade. Under Lazor, murder was a means to an end. Each hit was carefully discussed among his trusted advisors, planned to the smallest detail. Murder was reasoned, surgical. If someone was late on a payment, they'd get a visit from Gant or one of his associates. A few broken ribs, or, if they were flagrantly delinquent, a baseball bat to a knee—but only one knee. A guy needed to be able to hobble around to make money.

Valeria's business model was less nuanced. Warning visits and grace periods were a thing of the past. The late notice was a bullet in the face. Everyone who owed her money witnessed what happened if you didn't pay on time. Message received, loud and clear. Valeria Kot lacked the elegance of her father—but Gant had to admit her brutality was effective. Murders went up but beatings went down—and the money rolled in on time.

Valeria gave the order for the cellmate who stabbed her father to be gutted in the showers, but most everything else was just business. The lion's share of her anger, she reserved for Sam Lujan. After all, absent his betrayal, her father would never have been in that cell to be murdered in the first place.

After the trial, they'd thought to kill Lujan's mother, Josie. She was easy to find. According to Valeria, the kid talked to his mommy all the time. Killing her would smoke Sam out, but his government protection would be problematic. Contrary to her natural disposition, Valeria decided to play the long game. She'd assigned men to go to Arizona and follow Josie, screen her mail, comb through her social media. Eventually, mother or son would grow impatient. And when they did . . .

Gant's money had been on Sam coming home to Arizona. He'd been wrong.

Following Josie, as he liked to call her, became a sort of vacation. Winter months were the best, when the weather around Scottsdale was far preferable to the bitter winds of New York, not to mention the foul temperament of the boss.

On the phone, Valeria's voice grew louder. It was still slurred from her evening whiskeys, but more understandable than it had been.

"So she bought camping gear? Why is this important? Has she never been camping in the last four years?"

"Camping gear for cold weather," Bobby G said.

"Hmm," Valeria said. "Imagine that. Cold weather gear in the winter."

"You wanted us to call you if we believed there was movement."

"Movement toward Sam Lujan," Valeria said. Her voice grew distant again. She must have set the phone down and walked to another part of the room. "This isn't news."

Water began to run, loud. Gant pictured her drawing a bath. The sound of breaking glass, then a husky curse. She'd knocked over her whiskey.

He waited for her to finish her rant.

"I think this is different," he said. "She's bought wool underwear, snowshoes, and a mountaineering parka at the REI in Chandler. She's making calls from pay phones now instead of her cell, and shopping on the opposite end of town from where she lives. I didn't bother you with it before, but wanted to let you know what's going on before it gets too late on your end. She's planning a trip. I'm sure of it."

Valeria picked up the phone again. Her voice suddenly clearer, her interest piqued.

"This pay phone business is interesting," she said. "But she's been on dozens of trips since the trial. Didn't she go to the Andes last year?"

"She did," Gant said, pleased Valeria remembered at least some of what he'd reported. "A trek to Machu Picchu."

"What makes this one any different?"

"That's the thing," he said. "Josie Lujan is San Carlos Apache. She has a loyal following on social media, especially among the members of the tribe and her Native studies classes. When she goes on a trip, she posts maps, video logs of her getting her gear together, planning her route, basically taking her friends and students along with her virtually."

"Okay," Valeria said. "Use her posts to find out where she's going—"

In the passenger seat, Dusty farted.

Gant shook his fist in the air and mouthed a silent curse. "That's the thing, boss," he said. "Every other time there are lots of posts. This time, it's crickets. Nada. She's prepping for a trip somewhere cold, someplace wild enough she'll need snowshoes—but she's not made a single post about it."

"She's going to see Sam," Valeria whispered, barely audible.

"That's my guess," Gant said.

"Bobby," Valeria said. "You find out where and then call me. You hear what I'm saying? I don't care what time it is."

Dusty spoke up now, trying to stay relevant.

"You want us to slip into her house when she's not there? Maybe see if we can find airline tickets, maps, that kind of thing?"

Gant breathed a sigh of relief when Valeria said no. Too big a chance she'd figure out someone had been there and call off the trip. They'd waited four years. It wouldn't hurt to be patient a while longer.

"Don't you lose her, Bobby," Valeria said. "You hear me?"

"Loud and clear, boss," Gant said. "I've got a box on one of the pay phones now. We'll have a lot more info when she makes another call."

"Good," Valeria said. "You guys buy yourselves parkas. I want you to stay tight on her ass. Now go. I need to call in Mads."

"Mads?" Gant heard himself say. He closed his eyes and gave a silent moan, regretting the slip immediately. Valeria Kot did not like to be questioned.

Fortunately, she appeared to be too focused on revenge to notice. "Yes, Mads," she said. "Things are about to get bloody."

You can say that again, Gant thought.

The box in Gant's lap gave an audible chirp.

He swallowed hard. This was it.

"Sorry, boss," he said. "I'll call you right back. Someone is making a call on the pay phone now . . ." He listened. "A 907 number . . . Alaska."

"Explains the parka," Valeria said. "Call me when you know more."

Gant ended the call and adjusted his headset.

"Who's Mads?" Dusty asked.

Gant shook his head, tapping at the headphones, though the line was still ringing. Mads . . . The last person he wanted to think about was that psychopath.

# CHAPTER 13

*Fairbanks, Alaska*
*23° below*

*H*IDDEN SOMEWHERE ON THE KITCHEN COUNTER UNDER A PILE OF gloves, wool hats, and paper grocery store sacks, the telephone rang once then fell silent. Sam Lujan—now Luke Trejo—was alone, as usual, sitting on his couch playing *Rainbow Six*. He froze, game controller in midair. No one called his landline except telemarketers and—

It rang again. Only once. Ten seconds later it began to ring a third time, carrying even more urgency, if such a thing were possible.

The signal had been his mother's idea. *One ping only . . .* She watched way too many spy movies.

The boxy apartment off College Avenue was Alaska Pipeline chic with dark wood paneling and baby-crap-yellow countertops of the 1970s. Thankfully, the landlord had replaced the shag carpet with Berber everywhere but the bottom of the closets.

Luke Trejo was only four years old, less than that if you took out the time it took for the government to get his identity built and backstopped. He'd better get used to it, they said. Sam Lujan was gone.

He snatched up the handset, belching a nasty pizza burp as he answered. This cloistered life was making him soft.

He held the phone to his ear without speaking, like they practiced.

"It's me, Piñon," his mother said. She used the third of three rotating code words they'd established when he'd first gone away.

The sound of her voice melted away his new identity and he became Sam Lujan again.

"Good to hear your voice, Mama," he said.

He could hear the tears welling. "Oh, my son."

"Don't be upset, Mama," he said.

"One day you will learn. A mother is never happier than her saddest child. I worry for you."

"It's been four years," Sam said. "If they were going to kill me, they would have—"

"Please don't talk about killing—"

"I'm saying there's nothing to worry about if you're being careful. You are, right?"

"Of course," Josie said. "I carry around a can of Lysol now to disinfect these nasty pay phones. Anyway, as your great-grandfather used to say, I'm brushing out my back trail."

Sam gave an inward groan. Once his mother started telling stories about her grandfather, there would be no stopping her.

"Did you hear about Valeria's father?"

"I did," she whispered, as if she'd had the wind knocked out of her. "Killed in prison last month."

"Kind of sad for him to go out that way," he said.

"Pffft! The man was a murderer, Sam. He's the reason my only son has to hide out like an animal."

"You're right." Sam always felt a little sheepish around his mother. "It's just that, Mr. Kot was such an easy guy to like—"

"That kind of thinking is what got you into this mess in the first place." His mother went quiet, as she often did after telling him something she deemed important, letting her lesson *sink into his bones.*

"Anyway," Sam said. "Could be I'm not in as much danger as we think. Valeria and I were . . . we were very close."

"Ahhh, you poor, naive child," Josie said. "That just tells me how little you understand women. Look at it from your enemy's point of view. What do you think I would do to someone who betrayed my father, especially someone to whom I had given my body?"

Sam shivered. He'd seen his mother on the verge of real anger twice in his life and it had terrified him both times.

"That wouldn't be good."

"No," she said. "It would not."

"Mama, if you're trying to freak me out," Sam said, "you're doing a good job of it."

"A woman betrayed would just as soon gut you as look at you," Josie said. "And likely look at you while she's gutting you. You keep that in mind when you think of Valeria."

"Anywaaaay," Sam said. "The aurora forecast is off the charts. We could see them from my apartment balcony. We don't have to go all the way to the cabin. Supposed to get really cold."

"I know it'll be a bit of a hike to get to—"

Sam laughed out loud. "A bit of a hike? Mama, you don't hike at thirty below zero. You ski or waddle on snowshoes. Slowly, so your lungs don't freeze solid. The truth is my car is in the shop. We should just—"

"I'll rent a car," she said. "A waddle on snowshoes will do you good. I can tell by your voice that you're getting soft. And anyway, you need to get back to your roots. Our people knew cold. Maybe not that extreme, but I can guarantee you that we'll be safer at a remote cabin surrounded by wolves than you ever were with these murderers you called your friends. And who knows, you might even learn a thing or two about the land from your old Apache mama."

Two blocks away under the swaying shadows of a velvet mesquite, Gant retrieved his hardware from the phone box. Never in his life had being right left him so depressed. Inside the van, Dusty Baldwin bounced his fist on the armrest. "We got your ass now, Sammy Lujan. You and your 'Apache mama!'" He looked sideways at Gant. "What are you waiting for? We need to go pack."

Gant threw the van in gear and pulled away from the curb. "Nah," he said. "We'll fall in behind her and follow for a bit longer."

"We know where she's going," Dusty said. "Hell, she gave him all the flight information on the phone. We got shit to do to get ready ourselves. Why would we waste time following her?"

*Because it might be the last time*, Gant thought, but kept it to himself.

# CHAPTER 14

*Anchorage*
*11° below*

Mim rolled her Toyota Sienna to a stop in the hinterlands of the Carrs grocery store parking lot, far away from other vehicles. A walk in the cold would help clear her head. She threw the minivan in park and grabbed the steering wheel with both hands, rocking forward and back, screaming until her chest hurt. Her nose ran and tears coursed down her cheeks. She didn't care. She would have kept screaming had a Jeep Gladiator not crunched to a stop on the ice in the parking spot across from her. It was one thing to cry your eyes out in the grocery store parking lot. Having some judgy teenager witness the ugly mess was out of the question.

Mim wiped her face with her parka sleeve and tried to paint on a smile as the kid got out of his Jeep. Ears plugged with a wool hat and headphones, he ignored her completely.

Done with her cry for the time being, she reached to kill the engine but stopped, mesmerized as a story about wolves played over Alaska Public Radio.

Constance had come home from school talking about wolves venturing into the city and snatching family pets.

Mim gripped the wheel again. *That's all I need, something else to worry about,* this time with teeth and claws.

According to the guy on the radio, snow was to blame, or lack of it. Like any other animal, wolves needed a great deal of food in the subzero weather. A warm wind had melted much of the early season snow. What little was left turned into ice as temperatures fell. Wolves were fast but without deep snow, moose held the advantage. Packs were driven to desperation in their search for food. Skittish creatures that normally kept to the mountains came to the city for the next best thing.

Family pets.

Eight dogs had already been snatched, five in Eagle River, three on the Hillside above Anchorage, not far from Mim. A poor little King Charles spaniel had been yanked from the doggy door when it stuck its head out to investigate a noise on the back deck. The wolves had apparently learned that tasty treats popped out of these little doors multiple times a day.

Mim made a mental note to barricade their unused doggy door so she didn't end up like Red Riding Hood's grandma.

The news story kept going, but Mim killed the engine. Bears, earthquakes, mudslides, and bitter cold weren't enough. Now she had wolves to worry about.

She checked her face one last time in the rearview mirror, and after another swipe with her parka sleeve deemed herself presentable enough to shop late on a Saturday night. Hand on the door handle, she leaned forward and scanned the deserted parking lot for wolves. Then, laughing at her own paranoia, she stepped out to meet the cold.

She'd lived in Alaska for almost five years now and had only ever seen two. Her Alaska friends at the hospital and church assured her that wolves steered clear of people. There'd been only one recorded predatory attack on a human by healthy wolves, in decades. Russian wolves apparently weren't so skittish. According to the internet, entire Siberian villages were sometimes terrorized by packs of hungry wolves that picked off the drunk or elderly when they stumbled home in the Arctic twilight. Apparently, "Peter and the Wolf" was more of a documentary . . .

It was hard to tell the difference between true and fantastical, but now, crunching across the ice in the lonesome grocery parking lot, it was easy to imagine good old American wolves might find their inner Russian predator. They were, after all, suddenly going after family pets. It wasn't much of a leap for them to work their way to the other end of the leash.

The weather app on her phone showed the temperature had dropped more than ten degrees in the last hour, stalling at fifteen below. Ethan had made sure they always had blankets and hand-warmers in the vehicles, along with road flares and other emergency supplies. In his view, anything less than half a tank of gas might as well have been sitting flat on empty—especially in winter. Mim wore a better than average Canada Goose down parka, Smartwool long johns, and a down wraparound skirt that added an extra layer to loose flannel-lined jeans. Steger moosehide mukluks kept her feet toasty warm, even in this nonsense. Down mittens hung on tethers from the sleeves of her bright red parka. Frostbite came knocking quickly if you lost a glove in this weather. Arliss had brought her a neck cowl called a smoke ring from the Arctic village of Deering on his last trip. Hand knitted from gossamer musk-ox wool or *qiviut*, it was light as a feather. Pound for pound it was the warmest thing she wore.

It was not even nine p.m., but the biting cold kept all but the most intrepid shoppers home beside their fireplaces and wood-stoves. Mim should have been used to it by now—but how do you get used to something that freezes your eyelids shut every time you walk outside. Ursula was right about one thing. The boys whined because Anchorage schools made the kids play outside for recess until it dropped below minus ten. What she didn't know was they didn't whine because they had to go out. They whined because they had to stay inside when it got colder. But even they huddled up when it dropped to minus twenty-five. That was just miserable.

The cold, wolves, Ursula . . . Mim had plenty to worry about—and that wasn't the worst of it.

She grabbed an abandoned cart from the parking lot and leaned into it, determined to return it to the store. It was the kind of thing Arliss always did—a living example of Grumpy's man-rules she was glad he was teaching her boys. Far from flat, the

Carrs grocery parking lot was a confused minefield of gravel and frozen sludge built up by constant traffic during periods of freeze and thaw. Any sign of pavement had disappeared by mid-November and wouldn't poke through until March—if they were lucky.

The cart rattled along like a snare drum on crack cocaine, giving Mim an excuse not to think—about anything.

Mim unzipped her parka the moment she stepped through the doors. Absent the ice and gravel, the wheels rolled along the shiny waxed tile with little more than a mild squeak as if the cart, too, was happy to be out of the biting weather. She leaned forward, arching her back as she looked around for familiar faces. It seemed she always ran into someone she knew on Saturday nights. No one. Good. She wanted to get in and out unseen.

Face flushed from the sudden warmth of the store, Mim turned up the shampoo aisle. A muffled cry behind her made her crouch like a rabbit at the screech of a hawk. She spun, using the cart as a shield, grateful for the qiviut smoke-ring that hid the terrified look on her face when she saw Lola Teariki.

"Sorry for scaring you," Lola said. She was hunched over like she'd just walked in from the cold, shoulders rounded, hands clasped at her waist, chin tucked into the neck of the sweater beneath her parka. "I was just listening to a story on APRN about wolves!"

Mim gave an emphatic nod toward the door. "Me too."

Lola peeled off her wool hat and mittens, throwing them in her own shopping basket.

"Shopping late," she said.

"Yeah," Mim said. "I kind of needed to get out of the house for a minute."

"Cutter's mum?"

Mim smiled at Lola's Kiwi accent. It was endearing. She liked the way it turned Mim into "Meem" and Cutter into "Cuttah."

"I'm afraid so," Mim said.

Lola leaned over her shopping cart, rolling it back and forth in place. "I've been wanting to ask you something."

"Sure."

"Do you think Cutter . . . I mean, does he ever say . . ."

"For heaven's sake, Lola," Mim said. "Arliss isn't angry with you. If anything, he's angry with himself for not being able to be everywhere at the same time."

"Does he ever talk about moving me off the task force?"

"That's work," Mim said. "I'm not divulging any—"

"Sorry. I shouldn't put you in that kind of spot."

"Forget it," Mim said. "Just know Arliss loves you."

Lola groaned. "That clinches it. I'm off the task force."

"No," Mim said. "I mean, I have no idea. Arliss doesn't talk to me about that kind of stuff. He knows you and I are friends."

"Alright. I guess I can live with that."

"Shopping late yourself," Mim said, changing the subject.

Lola gave her a wink. "Picking up a few things for an overnight trip to Alyeska with Joe Bill."

Mim raised her eyebrows up and down. "Now that sounds exciting."

"We're gonna get a room and then do the Nordic Spa thing in the morning—saunas, couples' massages, the works." She brightened. "You should totally get the boss to take you!"

Mim looked down at the basket of the cart. "We're still . . ."

"Yikes." Lola grinned. "Don't tell Cutter I was so cheeky."

"Pretty sure he knows."

Lola gave a contemplative nod. "Anyway, sorry to hear you're having mother-in-law problems."

"Strangest thing," Mim said. "I don't mind having her around so much, but it's hell on Arliss. And it got a lot harder tonight."

"How's that?"

"Ursula finally spilled the beans about why she's here."

Lola frowned.

"Turns out," Mim said, "Ms. Ursula wants Arliss to get her teenage daughter back from an estranged husband."

"A teenage daughter." Lola whistled under her breath. "How old?"

"Fifteen."

"How old's Ursula?"

"Sixty-three," Mim said. She knew where this was going. She'd done the math herself.

"So, she had the boss's baby sister when she was . . . forty-eight."

Lola gave another low whistle. "Hang on a minute. This woman wants the son she abandoned to help her find a daughter she wants to keep. That's stuffed up."

"That's exactly what I said! Still, I think Arliss needs to cut her a little slack—for his own mental health."

"I'd ask how he's doing," Lola said, "but I don't want you to violate any confidences."

"He's getting by," Mim said. "In the garage cleaning gear at the moment, I imagine. Anyway, you'd better not keep Joe Bill waiting. Good to see you."

She started to push her cart away but stopped. "When is the task force heading up to Fairbanks?"

"Any day now," Lola said. "We've got leads on Kodiak as well. Depends on what Joe Bill and I find out."

"Well, crap," Mim said. "That means I'll be entertaining my mother-in-law without him."

"Maybe it won't be so bad," Lola said. "You might learn something about Arliss by spending a little time with the woman who gave birth to him."

Mim leaned on her shopping cart and stared out the store windows at the frozen parking lot.

"Yeah," she said. "I think I'd rather be out there with the wolves."

# SUNDAY

# CHAPTER 15

*Alyeska Resort*
*42 miles south of Anchorage*
*18° below*

JUDGING FROM THE TANGLED SHEETS—AND THE SEVERE LACK OF JOE Bill, Lola Teariki must have slept like a crocodile doing death rolls. Images of black water and giant slabs of ice plagued her dreams. She opened one eye to find her boyfriend sitting in a chair beside the bed. He had a towel around his waist and was sipping coffee while doomscrolling on his phone.

Lola routinely woke before five a.m. so she could hit the gym before work, but she liked to take her time, essentially stretching her way out of bed, coaxing back to life whichever body part she'd decided to hammer with her workouts the day before.

He glanced up from his phone and blew her a kiss, the well-rested jerk. It was hard not to be mad at him for having such a good night's rest. Joe Bill was like a little puppy. When he woke up, he was up for good, far too chipper for the way she felt at the moment. He stood and flung open the drapes, peering out the window toward the mountain.

"Man, oh, man," he said. "Eighteen below zero and two more hours until daylight. They gotta be diehards to hit the slopes this morning."

Lola pulled a pillow over her face.

"Come back to bed."

"I could," Joe Bill said. "But I know you. You're aching to go to the gym, and the Nordic Spa opens at ten. I did some checking and it sounds like Orr's shift starts this afternoon at two. We should get there when it opens, have a soak, get the lay of the land." He shot her one of his boyish grins. "I could book a couples massage if you'd like. Before Orr gets there, of course."

Lola frowned. "I don't feel like getting naked in front of a stranger."

"You're not actually naked."

She scoffed. "Have you ever had a massage?"

"I guess not . . . Do you really have to get naked?"

"Just shut up and come back to bed. I don't want to go to the gym."

Joe Bill's mouth fell open.

"Who are you and what have you done with my girlfriend?" His voice softened, genuinely concerned. "Seriously, are you okay?"

"I'm fine," Lola said. "I just . . ."

"It scares me when you don't want to work out."

"It scares me when you don't want to come back to bed." She forced a smile, batting dark lashes. "Besides, who says I don't want to work out?"

Two hours later, after a considerable amount of exercise and a visit to the buffet breakfast in the hotel, Lola and Joe Bill braved the short trudge across the icy parking lot in the shadow of Mt. Alyeska. Stepping inside the Nordic Spa was like a warm hug from a favorite aunt who was fond of eucalyptus.

Inside the locker room, Lola slipped into her swimsuit, plastic slippers, and one of the heavy hooded robes provided by the spa. An electronic proximity bracelet allowed her to lock her belongings, including her sidearm and handcuffs, in a private locker. Joe Bill was waiting in the hallway by the towel desk.

A wall of intense cold bit her nose and shoved her breath back down her throat the moment Joe Bill pushed open the glass doors to the ice planet outside. Plastic slippers protected their feet from the cold, slapping on the concrete as they hustled toward their objective. She picked up her pace, pulling the robe tighter around her legs to reduce the airflow.

"Breezy!" she gasped.

Rising steam flocked surrounding trees and signage with crystalline hoarfrost. Couples and small groups lounged here and there in the numerous concrete soaking pools. Some read books but most chatted among themselves, mouths agape at the fairyland scenery around them. A man about Lola's age had fashioned his shoulder-length black hair into a mohawk, where it froze solid in the subzero air above the steaming water. An older couple who probably ran marathons stood facing each other, waist-deep in one of the cold pools, shoulders hunched, faces taut, battered by a frigid waterfall.

"Those two are out of their minds," Lola muttered as she padded by.

Hustling past the firepits and two Swedish saunas, Lola and Joe Bill made their way up a circular boardwalk where a half dozen smaller, more secluded tubs sat in the shadow of towering spruce and hemlock trees. Two barrel-saunas, large enough to accommodate half a dozen people if they were on friendly terms, sat spaced along the same walkway.

A small chalkboard beside a tub to their left read 102 DEGREES.

"This one," Lola said, breathless, hesitant to sacrifice any more words to the cold air. She grudgingly shrugged off the heavy robe and hung it on one of the provided pegs. She took a scant moment to adjust the bum of her cobalt-blue one-piece swimsuit before putting a bare foot on the wooden steps leading up to the tub.

Behind her, Joe Bill gave a low whistle.

"I can help you with that—"

"Nope," she said, hauling herself up the steps and into the hot water.

Her eyes fluttered at half-mast, happy to be bathing in warmth after the ordeal of just getting here. She squatted low, her nose barely above the surface. The air was still well below freezing just a few inches above. Joe Bill spiked his hair to resemble a dark flame. Lola's tresses floated lazily around her broad shoulders, but the top of her head felt like she was wearing a frozen helmet.

She leaned back, looking skyward and warming her noggin. Gunmetal clouds were just becoming visible in the gathering light of morning. A red-breasted nuthatch wheezed and hammered at some seed it had lodged in the bark of a nearby spruce. Lola took a deep breath, chasing away the shadows. Her dad watched birds. Early Polynesians had used them to navigate.

She sank to her ears listening to the whoosh of her own blood. Joe Bill was right. She needed this.

"What's that one?" Joe Bill asked, nodding to a flock of small ash-colored birds pecking at the frozen ground beneath the nearest spruce.

Lola rose out of the cozy warmth enough to peer over the edge of the tub.

"A dark-eyed junco—" She rolled her eyes and sank back into the water when she saw Joe Bill looking at her.

"Did you seriously just ask me what kind of bird that was so you could ogle my boobs?"

"Maybe," Joe Bill said. "We've got about two hours until Regina Orr starts her shift. How about you run down your plan?"

"My plan is to park myself right here forever."

"We could do that," Joe Bill said. "Or we could try that barrel sauna for a while, maybe one of the cold pools. You're supposed to go back and forth—"

"Oh, hell no," Lola said. "I've had enough cold plunges to last a lifetime. I'm a child of the South Pacific, mate."

"It's supposed to be good for you," Joe Bill said. "They've got three pools—sixty-five, a sixty, and a fifty-five degree."

Lola looked like she'd just eaten something awful. "Fifty-five-degree water sounds like the Ninth Circle of Hell. Anyway, I'll bet those pools are even colder in this weather. I'm getting an ice cream headache from the air. Next time, I'm wearing a hat."

"The lady by the towel stand said they heat the cold pools," Joe Bill said. "Keeps them in the fifties."

"Do you even hear yourself?" Lola said. "I'm not setting foot in any pool they have to heat just to keep it cold!"

Joe Bill gazed upward, waving his arms like wings just under the surface. "Thanks for coming out here early with me," he said. "I know what happened at the lake was really bad."

"I'm fine."

Joe Bill heaved a long sigh, deep enough his chest rippled the water's surface.

"I don't think you are. I wouldn't be if the same thing happened to me. I'm not sure anyone would come out of that without bad dreams. It wouldn't hurt you to talk to somebody. Even if that somebody is just me . . . or even Cutter."

Lola leaned forward, eyes narrowed. "You mention a word about this to Cutter and I will cut you deep, wide, and continuous."

"Lola," Joe Bill said. "Arliss Cutter is the most observant dude I've ever even heard of. Pretty sure he already knows."

"I just need some time," she said. "That's all. I'm good."

She leaned forward and kissed him on the cheek. "Like you said, we have two hours before Orr gets to work. Would you please relax and enjoy this time with your half-naked girlfriend."

Joe Bill gave a I-gave-it-shot shrug and then let his gaze fall on her again. "It's just that—"

Lola raised her hands as if in surrender. "Tell you what. You wanted to go to the sauna. Let's go to the sauna. Maybe I can hide from your pitiful stare behind a cloud of steam."

"I just—"

Lola hauled herself up the steps, alternately gripping and then releasing the handrails to be certain her fingers didn't freeze to the bare metal. "I love you, Joe Bill, but you have got to let this drop."

"I apologize," he said. "Please don't be pissed at me—"

She paused, bumping him playfully in the forehead with her butt as he started to climb up the steps behind her. "How could I be pissed at you? As long as you don't make me jump into one of those ice-baths with you, we're right-as."

The boardwalk made a large loop through the forest before meeting back up with itself between two wood *banyas*. Lola and Joe Bill were approaching the main walk when the sauna door on the right opened, belching a cloud of steam. A tall blond woman emerged and grabbed her robe off a peg. Twenty feet out, Joe Bill listed sideways as if to give Lola a kiss. He touched his forehead to hers.

"That's her!" he whispered. "I think she might have recognized me."

Lola stutter stepped, forcing herself to look away from the woman who'd come out of the *banya*.

"You've met Regina Orr before?" she hissed through clenched teeth. "That would have been helpful to know, my dear."

"Almost a year ago," Joe Bill whispered against her neck. "My training officer arrested her pimp but we cut her loose. She had red hair at the time. Didn't look anything like her driver's license photo."

Orr froze mid-step. Her glacier-blue eyes fixed on Joe Bill for a fraction of a second too long. The cowl-like hood of her robe gave her the appearance of a medieval monk. She snugged the belt tight around her waist and then gave what looked like a resigned sigh before turning to walk away. She cut right, instead of continuing toward the main spa, between the larger steam sauna building and the crescent-shaped hot pools.

Lola's brain went into high gear. She pictured a map of the place, avenues of escape, fight scenarios, and possible friends Orr could have in the area. It was far too cold to stand around and wait for something to happen. For all she knew, Pritchard's girlfriend, Tina, planned to meet Orr here. Coworkers were always an unknown. Friends might give up and roll over immediately or they could fight. Lola's gun was in her locker, as was Joe Bill's.

"Looks like she came in early to grab a steam before work," Joe Bill whispered, adding a chuckle so he appeared to be talking about something else.

Orr disappeared around the corner of the barrel sauna.

"Split up," Lola said. "I'll stay on her, you go straight, toward the firepits. Cut her off if she runs."

Joe Bill picked up his pace, splitting off without another word.

Lola rounded the corner to find Orr continuing toward one of the large sauna buildings, cutting between a half a dozen bathers lounging in a steamy hot pool and the vacant cold pool with a stubby wooden tower and waterfall. A young woman in the hot pool waved at Orr and called her by name. Probably a coworker. Orr ignored her. Lola thought about calling out, but Orr surely knew she had warrants. That would cause her to hoof it for sure. It was a complicated dance, following, gaining ground, all without triggering a chase.

Lola made another corner just as Orr passed the glass door leading into the steam room ten feet ahead. Their eyes met in the reflection.

Half a very cold breath later, Orr dropped her towel—and ran.

"Get away from me!" she yelled over her shoulder. "Help!"

Lola bowed her head and dug in, struggling to keep up in the pathetic plastic slippers. The walkways were generally free of ice, but there were spots where the heating elements just couldn't keep up with the rock-bottom temperatures. Lola's feet shot out from under her as she attempted to cut right. She went down hard, sending an excruciating pain through her elbow. She scrambled to her feet, but Orr gained precious ground.

She was getting away.

Stunned spa patrons looked on. A muscular guy in a wool hat grabbed the ladder and started to climb out of the pool nearest the firepit. He yelled something unintelligible, obviously thinking Orr was under attack.

Lola shouted, attempting to identify herself as a marshal, but the words froze hard in her throat. They came out as a strained hiss, like she'd been kicked in the gut.

Joe Bill chuffed up from the other direction. "Police!" he barked. The big guy shrank back into the heated pool, a relieved look on his face.

Shoeless now, Joe Bill made up enough time to get ahead of Orr, rounding the crescent pool in time to block her way to the main building.

Running was one thing, but running in subzero weather while wearing a swimsuit, robe, and the damned plastic slides was nearly impossible. This had to stop. Now.

Lola kicked out of her slippers mid-stride, gaining two precious yards on her quarry.

Less than ten yards ahead now, Orr shot a quick look over her shoulder and tripped on the dragging sash of her robe in the process. She stumbled, bloodying a knee on the frozen concrete before jumping to her feet.

Lola felt a surge of adrenaline as she closed the distance, almost within arm's reach. She tried to call out. Again, frigid air rammed the words back down her throat. It hardly mattered. The splashing waterfall in the cold pool would have drowned her out.

Joe Bill stood directly in Regina Orr's path.

Cursing, she spun, planting her feet to face Lola. She raised her hands as if she were giving up—but the scowl on her face said otherwise. Long fingers balled into fists. Hate blazed in her eyes. She planned to fight.

Orr lowered her shoulders and sprang forward, seemingly intent on bowling Lola over. She was the larger woman, with several inches and at least a twenty-pound advantage. Unlike Lola, Regina Orr had never played rugby with very large Polynesian brothers.

Onlookers might have thought the two women were about to collide like battling bighorn rams. And they would have, had Orr gotten her way. Instead, Lola sidestepped at the last moment, adjusting her attack just enough to catch Orr at an angle, arms around the other woman's hips below her bum in a quartering rugby tackle. Cheek to cheek they called it. Orr folded immediately, caught off guard and off balance. A curdled scream escaped her lips as she flew backwards into the cold pool with a hundred and fifty pounds of angry deputy marshal wrapped tight around her waist.

The fifty-degree water slammed into Lola like a fistful of quarters. It wasn't deep, three feet at most—bright and clear as a swimming pool—but darkness closed in around her. A massive weight gripped her chest. Bolts of liquid fire shocked her skull. This wasn't . . . She couldn't . . .

Then Orr's fist brushed her jaw. Fingers clawed at her face. The attack was frantic and unaimed, but it was enough to remind Lola that there was no time to panic.

The women slammed into the concrete bottom a scant moment

after they hit the surface. Countless bubbles, garbled screams—everything flowed in slow motion. Instead of attempting to surface, Lola kicked downward, driving the point of her shoulder through Orr's midsection. The weight of the waterlogged robes helped hold them under. A cloud of silver bubbles erupted from Orr's mouth. A good sign. That meant less air to fight with. Lola squinted, continuing to kick downward, smiling maniacally at the terrified woman. All the while she imagined it was Butch Pritchard she had pinned to the bottom of the crystalline pool. The entire episode lasted less than ten seconds.

Orr went limp, still conscious but docile as a lamb. Lola gave her another five-count to ensure compliance before dragging her spitting and sputtering to the surface. Joe Bill hauled her out by the shoulders. She slumped to her knees. Her wet robe instantly froze to the ground.

A crowd of some two-dozen people gathered around the pool.

Still in the water, Lola blinked, breathless, dizzy. She wiped a lock of hair out of her face with the back of a cold-pinked forearm and reached for Joe Bill's hand. "You gonna help me out or what?"

He scrambled to pull her up. "I just thought you didn't want—"

She grinned. "Learn to read the room, buddy."

A woman about Lola's age snugged up the collar of her robe and peered down her nose. "Who are you people?"

Lola spat a mouthful of blood. The blow to her face had done more damage than she'd thought.

"US Marshals."

Orr's head snapped around to stare down at her.

"Marshals?" she said. "As in federal cops?"

"Y...yep..."

Joe Bill tried to give her his robe, but she nodded at Orr. "Give it to her."

Orr broke into tears. "I thought... I thought you were..."

"Thought we were who?" Lola said.

Orr closed her eyes tight, struggling to control her runaway breath. "Never mind."

# CHAPTER 16

*I*T WASN'T EVERY DAY UNITED STATES MARSHALS TACKLED SOMEONE into an Alyeska Nordic Spa plunge pool. The two guys from resort security bent over backwards to accommodate once they got a look at Lola's silver star and credentials.

Regina Orr slouched dejectedly against the wall in the spa manager's office, now dressed in dry clothes. Joe Bill went to get the car, leaving one of the security guys at the door. Lola stood, leaning against the edge of the cluttered desk, finally beginning to warm up. She rubbed her aching jaw with one hand while she thumb-typed Cutter's number into her phone with the other.

Orr stared down at her feet. "I thought Anchorage was more interested in payers than players. Why are the feds messing with a solicitation charge?"

The security guy raised a brow at that.

Lola shot him a smile, called him by the name on his vest, like they were on the same team. "Hey, Steve, you mind giving us a minute?"

His shoulders fell, disappointed not to hear the rest of the scoop, but he nodded and slinked out the door.

"Your warrants are for theft," Lola said when they were alone. "Not prostitution."

"Question remains the same," Orr said. "I'm guessing you want something. The Marshals gotta have bigger fish to fry." She tried to talk with her hands out of habit, but the cuffs stopped her, jingling each time she pulled against them. "I mean, look at me, lady. I'm trying to do legitimate work here. Certified masseuse and everything."

"I respect that." Lola moved her jaw back and forth. "You pack a wicked punch."

She paused. If she'd learned anything from Cutter, it was that silence made people uncomfortable. Hell, it made her uncomfortable, but she bit her lip and stood there, bum against the desk.

Orr stared into the distance, not defiant, just somewhere else.

In Lola's experience, hookers, when they weren't strung out on drugs, had the toughest emotional walls of anyone on the planet. They had plenty of practice shutting off unpleasant surroundings.

"And just what is it you want from me?" Orr finally asked.

"What do you think? If you had to guess."

"Just cut the bullshit, will ya? People been wanting things from me since I was a little kid. And if you've read my rap sheet then you know I'm happy to sell what I got."

"You know a woman named Tina Massey."

Orr gave a curt shrug.

"That wasn't a question," Lola said.

"Yeah, I know her," Orr said. "Haven't seen her in . . . I don't know, a couple of months at least."

"Knock it off, Regina." Lola heaved a long sigh. "You just said you want to cut to the chase. Just tell me where Tina spends her days. She still keeping company with Butch?"

"I don't answer questions . . ."

Lola gave a tired chuckle. "You hear that on the internet?"

"I don't answer questions."

"Cool," Lola said. "Cool, cool, cool. Just listen then. I don't care about your piddling little warrants. And I could give two shits about any warrants for Tina. I'm after Butch Pritchard. Everything I read and everyone I talk to tells me you and Tina are besties. Hell, Regina, the two of you have been arrested together, what? . . . five times."

Orr's gaze returned to Lola for a split second, then dissolved into the distance again.

"I'll tell you what I think," Lola said, taking a gamble. "The longer your friend hangs out with that asshole Butch Pritchard, the more danger she's in."

Orr frowned, giving a disgusted shake of her head. "Tina told me one of that idiot's traps nearly drowned your skinny ass."

Lola fought the memory, trying to keep it from flooding in and overwhelming her. She clenched her jaw. "True," she managed to say.

A light flicked on in Orr's blue eyes, giving Lola something to hang on to.

"Listen to me, Regina," she said. "You and I both know Butch is a killer. And here's the thing about people like that—they look after themselves. We're gonna find Butch eventually and when we do, he's very likely to fight. Do you really want your friend to be caught in the crossfire?"

That perked her up.

"So y'all are just going to gun him down."

"Of course not," Lola said. "But let's be honest. Missouri's a death penalty state. Butch Pritchard doesn't have much to lose."

"I wish you would," Orr said. "Gun him down, I mean."

"The outcome is up to him," Lola said.

"He beat the shit outta her, ya know," Orr said. "Cracked her over the head with a beer bottle and then choked her until she blacked out. One of her eyes is still wonky. I'm absolutely positive he thought he killed her. Didn't care either, just left her lying there in her own puke."

"Would she know where he is?"

Orr scoffed. "She'll know how to get in touch with him. I doubt he even went to the trouble of dumping his prepaid. Dumb son of a bitch thinks she's not a problem anymore. I'd love to see the look on his face when he hears her voice again and she's not dead."

Lola was already texting Cutter.

"Listen to me," Regina said. "Tina Massey's dumb as a sack of hammers, but she's not a criminal."

Lola gave an I-don't-know-about-that shrug. "She is running with a hired killer."

"And you never got yourself mixed up in a bad relationship?"

"Fair point," Lola said.

"Are you gonna arrest her?"

"Not unless she does something stupid, like making me tackle her into a freezing cold pool. You help me find Butch Pritchard and I'll see to it he never bothers your friend again."

Orr snorted. "You know, it woulda saved me and you a whole boatload of trouble if you'd led with that. Get these damned handcuffs off me and I'll take you to her right now."

"Where?"

"Across the parking lot," Orr said. "She should be in a hospital but she's cleaning rooms at the hotel. You'll need to hurry, though. News travels fast at this place. She'll haul ass for sure if she hears I've been arrested." She held up her wrists. "I need to go in the room first."

"Not a chance," Lola said.

"I'm serious," Orr said. "You're liable to give her a literal heart attack."

"Who the hell is everyone so scared of?"

Orr held up the handcuffs and shook them again. "You want to get Butch, we'll help you get Butch. That's as far as it goes."


Lola found Tina Massey in a vacant room on the fourth floor of the Alyeska Hotel. Her housekeeping cart was in the hallway but the door was shut and locked instead of propped open as per protocol. The resort security officer swiped his passkey and stepped aside. Lola went in first, hand on the butt of her Glock. Massey was slumped over the desk with her head down and resting on her arms. Her back was to the door, leaving both hands visible. The bed had been stripped and a stack of folded sheets sat on the bare mattress. She'd been in the middle of cleaning.

Lola cleared her throat. "Tina."

Massey sat bolt upright and screamed. The chair fell over with her in it. She continued to scream, holding up an arm as if to ward off a blow.

"Police, Tina!" Lola said. "We're not going to hurt you."

Massey cowered against the heater pipes on the wall, her arm still raised, chest heaving. Her top lip was badly swollen. The zipped collar of her fleece sweater did little to cover the purple bruises that ringed her neck. The hair on the side of her head was crusted with blood.

Hand to her chest, her breathing began to slow. "Police!" she said. "I thought you were . . ."

"US Marshals," Lola said. "I'm Deputy Teariki."

Half an hour later, Lola called Cutter from the back of the ambulance as they sped up the Seward Highway toward Anchorage. Joe Bill knew and vouched for both the EMTs, allowing her to talk with relative freedom about the case.

"It's a go for Pritchard," she said. "We're taking Tina to the hospital now, but she's agreed to help set him up after we get her checked out."

The nearest EMT shook her head. "I'd be surprised if they let her out of the hospital today."

Lola patted the back of Tina's hand while she relayed the new information over the phone. "He beat the crap out of her, Cutter. She's keen to help, but it may not be for a day or two."

"We'll do it tomorrow," Tina whispered. "I been through worse. I'll be fine."

"We'll see," Lola said, patting her hand again.

"Am I on speaker?" Cutter asked.

"No."

"Is Massey in custody?"

"No," Lola said, her voice—and she hoped her face—passive.

"What's to keep her from hoofin' it?"

Lola took a deep breath and looked the bruised and battered woman in the eye. "No worries, boss. She wants to help."

Lola promised to keep him posted and ended the call.

Tina Massey squinted up at her from the cot, eyes heavy from the first warmth and safety she'd probably felt in a good while.

"Your boss, he thinks I might run, doesn't he?"

"Crossed his mind," Lola said. "I have to admit, I'm a little worried about it, too."

"Promise me Butch is going to jail."

"Prison," Lola said.

"I'm not going anywhere." Tina tried to shake her head, but winced at the pain the movement brought her neck. "That asshole tried to kill me."

"You and me both," Lola said. "Listen . . . Tina . . . You mind telling me what has everyone so terrified?"

A flash of fear crossed Massey's face. Her lips began to tremble and she closed her eyes.

"Tina," Lola prodded.

The heart monitor began to chirp faster, climbing to one-twenty then one-thirty-five in a matter of seconds.

The EMT shook her head. "Not now."

Lola leaned back against the ambulance wall and looked out the back window at Joe Bill, following dutifully in his truck.

She took out her phone and typed a text to Cutter.

**Lola: She's scared to death of someone, and it's not Pritchard.**

**Cutter: Same as Butterbean?**

**Lola: Yep. Orr, too. What's going on!!?**

**Cutter: Focus on Pritchard for now.**

She started to give him a thumbs-up, but stopped, deciding on exclamation points and a poop emoji.

This was definitely not a thumbs-up situation.

# CHAPTER 17

*Texas*

*I*T WASN'T MADS NASH'S FAULT SHE HAD TO STAB THE MAN AT 2307 Magnolia Place in the neck with an apple corer. She would have stabbed him one way or another. It just would have been with something more robust, an eighteen-inch L-shaped Japanese fishing gaff. Merciful killing had little to do with her reasoning, but death inflicted by the stainless steel *tegaki* would have been lightning fast and much more humane.

The apple corer appeared to be working. Her target was bleeding out PDQ on the immaculate bamboo floor. He coughed and sputtered, clicking blood-stained teeth, then looked up at Mads, wide-eyed, accusing, like Banquo's ghost from *Macbeth*.

Mads loved *Macbeth*. It was the only Shakespeare she'd ever read, the only play, really.

Banquo of 2307 Magnolia hadn't had time to say a word when he saw her. He hadn't confronted her or cried out. Even now he just made a sort of mewling gurgle. Mads had spoken, though, calming him in her smooth Australian accent. Everyone trusted Aussies, even when they showed up in the kitchen uninvited wearing white Tyvek coveralls.

He'd taken a step toward her as if to get a closer look or even shake her hand. What Mads did next wasn't panic, it was tactical. She'd been doing this long enough to never let anyone get inside her personal space unless it was on her terms. The apple corer had been handy, a fraction of a second faster to grab than the stainless-steel gaff. To the man's astonishment, she'd snatched it off the counter and used it to great effect.

The dude had every right to be pissed. He'd moseyed in from his bedroom, probably hunting a piece of the pie that sat under one of those fancy restaurant glass pie covers. Instead of coconut cream, he'd come face-to-face with Mads. The look on his face wasn't angry or defiant, more like he was disappointed in Mads as a human being.

Her sister, Browny, had surprised the girlfriend. Dressed in the same Tyvek coveralls, Browny now stood at the threshold of the hallway door beside a woman she'd tied to a wooden chair. An old T-shirt gag pulled the poor woman's cheeks into a grotesque lipstick-smudged grin. Tears and mascara had transformed her into a raccoon with dangly emerald earrings. Her chest heaved and shuddered with sobs. Each time she tried to turn away, Browny cuffed her on the back of the head, forcing her to watch Banquo bleed out on the bamboo floor.

Mads gave a soft sigh. Her sister was a piece of work. In another life Browny might have been a guard at an East German women's prison. Now she was a serial killer who got paid to pursue her passions.

Mads stepped over the crimson pool blossoming in fits and starts in time with the man's choking gurgles. Not all the blood was on the floor. A sizable sploosh painted the belly of her coveralls. A couple of drops had hit her in the goggles. Always wear goggles. Mads learned that little rule the hard way. It wouldn't do to get pulled over by the cops with a tear of some dude's blood on your face.

Dying Banquo raised a hand heavenward, pointing a trembling finger, clicking his teeth. He was as good as gone. The ragged wound in his neck virtually assured it. But in Mads's line of work, "as good as" and "virtually" didn't cut the mustard. The people who paid the bills wanted the man at Magnolia Place all-the-way, no-coming-back DRT—dead right there.

Mads watched for a few seconds, then stooped down on her

haunches, avoiding the blood with her Tyvek slippers. There was no point in giving the cops bloody tracks to judge her shoe size. The man's pajamas had hiked up around his shoulders during the struggle. Mads turned up a button nose. For some reason, the sight of the hairy belly, pale and soap-like, struck her as more obscene than his blood-stained teeth or the pulsing kitchen utensil in his neck. What kind of grown man changed into pj's this early in the afternoon—or ever for that matter? Mads pulled the man's near arm out straight and then grabbed his far arm and knee, pulling him toward her so he lay on his left side. She'd learned the maneuver during first-aid training as a teenager. It was called the recovery position. That made her smile. Recovery wasn't in the cards for this guy. Once he was on his side, she stood over him and, pulling the stainless-steel gaff from her back pocket, drove the spike deep into the base of the man's skull. He was already dead, but a mysterious hole in the back of someone's brain stem was just the sort of message her employer wanted her to send.

In the chair across the room, the sobbing woman screamed against her gag. Browny wore a mask but Mads could see the look of amusement in her eyes.

The show over, Browny grabbed the back of the wooden chair and tipped it back on two legs, dragging the sobbing woman around the corner into the bedroom.

Mads twisted at the waist to pop her back as she stood and looked at the door to the hallway. She had to admit it, her sister was better at this than she was.

The girls had grown up on opposite sides of Australia—Mads out west in Perth, Browny in Nerang, a rural bedroom community of Gold Coast, Queensland. Now twenty-nine, they were only five months apart in age. Browny was older. They hadn't met until they were seventeen—at their father's funeral.

Morris Nash had traveled extensively as an executive with Citibank Australia, allowing him to hop back and forth between two families, each unaware of the other. He alternated Christmases but spent nearly every Easter with Mads as her mother was the more religious of his wives. He kept two phones, one for personal use, the other password protected for "sensitive banking matters." Each device swapped roles depending on which family he happened to be with at the time. Browny's mother hadn't pressed for a marriage ceremony, which allowed him to skirt Australia's bigamy laws. Browny had still adopted his last name. His double life came to an abrupt end when a bullet took off the back of his head during a robbery gone bad—while he was enjoying the services of a prostitute in Darwin.

Both Mads and Browny had liked their father well enough— but, unlike their respective mothers, neither was particularly surprised at the circumstances surrounding his death. The girls were excellent spies and while neither suspected Morris Nash had another family on the opposite coast, they'd overheard enough phone calls to suss out the fact that he was a man of enormous appetites.

Mads's mother was a voluptuous woman with mouse-brown hair and lantern-like green eyes. She whispered virtually every word she spoke, even during the rare moments when she was angry. Browny's mother was tall and blond and a natural athlete. Both women got on well with virtually everyone they met including each other after Morris's funeral. They even took to traveling together and set up a charity for battered women with their windfall of insurance money. They were, in short, good souls. Whatever bad blood ran in Mads and Browny Nash's veins, the girls inherited it from their father.

They hadn't discovered each other's natural tendency toward violence until almost five years later. Mads would never forget the electricity in her sister's eyes when Browny ventured behind the bar in Colón, Panama, to find Mads holding a bloody knife and standing over a dead man. For a moment, Mads thought Browny might scream, call the cops, or, at the very least, slink back the way she'd come. Instead, Browny's eyes had locked on the dead man. Nodding at the blade glistening in the streetlight, she'd whispered, "Can I do that part next time?"

The target in Panama was Mads's first job and would have been her last had Browny not stumbled into that alley. A one off, it happened at the beginning of what she called her quarter-life crisis. Show the guy a little leg, lure him into the alley, and cut his throat.

Easy enough work to zero her twenty-grand in gambling debts. Not that Mads wasn't good at killing. She was. Very. But Browny turned out to be a natural.

It was she who'd introduced Mads to the idea of using the *tegaki*. She'd taught English in Japan for two years where she'd dated a man who worked at Tsukiji fish market. She'd become entranced with *ikejime*, the process where a *tegaki* was used to instantly kill the fish and then a long metal wire was inserted into the hole and run quickly back and forth to destroy the nerves in the spinal cord. Browny had even tried the wire technique on a few of their jobs, but it turned out to be overkill. Literally.

Similar wounds on multiple victims tended to lead authorities to the conclusion that they were dealing with the same killer. Browny didn't care. To her, it was all part of the game—and she enjoyed the game so much she took to leaving yet another kind of calling card.

Mads pushed up the sleeve of her Tyvek suit to check her watch, revealing the beginnings of a full sleeve tattoo. Celtic knots, the *wyrd* sisters from *Macbeth* around their cauldron, snakes, a skull with *Macbeth*'s dagger through it, even an unfortunate *My Little Pony* unicorn she'd gotten one drunken night in Bangkok. You had to get close to see that one, and Mads never let anyone get that close.

A low moan carried in from the bedroom. Browny must have removed the gag to get a clear shot with the *tegaki*. Sad deal that the girlfriend had shown up. The target was the board member of a pharmaceutical company who was withholding his vote on a pending merger. The senior executive who'd hired the sisters wanted to send a message to any others on the board who might be entertaining such thoughts.

They almost hadn't taken the job. It came to them from a friend of an acquaintance through their contact point on the Dark Web. Referrals were all well and good. They needed business, but they were also a good way to get tripped up by some FBI sting. Mads had a hard and fast rule—*friends of friends may not refer friends.* "I know a guy" was fine. "I know a guy who knows a guy," could land you in the joint—or get you killed.

Eventually, though, you had to trust somebody enough to take their money. Killing was a decent living if you didn't get caught. The money wasn't like the movies, but it wasn't bad either. Million-dollar paydays stashed away in Cayman Islands accounts was the stuff of spy novels. Nowadays, everything was Bitcoin and the Dark Web. Five-figure jobs were standard, a living wage—but expenses added up fast. Travel, surveillance equipment, none of that came cheap. Just getting the right VPNs and web security burned through money.

Browny stepped around the corner, hand on her hip. She was taller than Mads, broader, built like a rugby player—like their dad.

Mads nodded at the doorway behind her sister. "How'd you go?"

"I'm hungry," Browny said, smearing blood around the front of her Tyvek suit as she rubbed her belly. "You hungry? Let's stop at that catfish place we passed coming across the lake."

Mads took one last look at the man on the floor to be certain he was DRT and then nodded to her sister.

"I could do catfish. We need to call Valeria back on the way, find out about this job that's got her knickers in a twist."

Browny came closer, opening her gloved hand slowly like she was revealing a treasure. Inside was a beautiful emerald and white gold earring—attached to a dainty pink ear.

Mads sighed. That Browny. What a piece of work.

Back in the Land Cruiser, the sisters waited until they were half an hour from Magnolia Place before removing their phones from the Faraday bag.

Browny drove. Mads held up her phone, which was connected to the Dark Web through a virtual private network and anonymizer. It was easy to see they were sisters once they'd ditched the Tyvek suits—same smallish nose, same full lips, pronounced cheekbones, and dark hair. Browny kept hers short where Mads was longer with a shock of silver that ran down one side that she'd had since she was a child. She probably should have dyed it to make her less noticeable, but in the end decided that if a bit of white hair got her caught then she probably deserved to be in jail.

"Five messages from New York," she muttered, nodding at the screen.

"I'm sure it's something of the direst of consequence and importance." Browny affected what she called her snooty voice. "That woman's hair's always ablaze."

"You are right about that," Mads said.

She punched Valeria Kot's private number into her VoIP or Voice over Internet Protocol app and put the smartphone on speaker.

Valeria answered on the first ring, her words buzzing like a chainsaw with an open throttle as soon as they came out of her mouth.

"I've been trying to reach you for the past—"

Browny cut her off. "We're working," she said from behind the wheel.

A muffled grunt filled the line, as if Valeria choked back the remainder of what she'd wanted to say.

Then, "I have a job for you."

Browny took a frontage road off the highway and turned into the restaurant parking lot. She looked at Mads, brow raised, and shrugged.

"We can get to it next week," Mads said.

It was another one of their rules—at least seven days between jobs. They needed the mental rest, but Mads had another, perhaps more important reason to bake in a mandatory waiting period between jobs. Browny needed to stay hungry. Her sister was a handful already. Boredom turned her into a ticking time bomb.

"Next week won't work," Valeria said.

"I'm afraid it has to," Mads said before Browny could say otherwise.

"Five hundred thousand," Valeria snapped.

That was getting close to Hollywood money. Browny gave an emphatic nod. "Where?"

"You'll take the job?"

Mads's hackles went up. For the amount of subterfuge she used in her daily life, she hated when others beat about the bush. The VoIP line was spoofed, anonymized, and bounced all over the world. All these theatrics were pointless.

She was about to say *it depends* when Browny answered for them.

"Five hundred thousand . . . plus expenses. You know where to send the details."

Valeria didn't hesitate.

"On their way to you now. It's a mother and son."

"Where?" Browny asked again.

"Alaska," Valeria said. "My men will explain everything when you get there."

Mads's brow shot up. "You already have men on the ground there?"

"Relax," Valeria said. "You'll get to earn your money. I've told my guys to wait for you—but I needed an insurance policy. This might be my only chance to get this little bastard."

"Alaska's a big place," Mads said. "Care to narrow it down?"

"Fairbanks," Valeria said.

Mads thumb-typed *Fairbanks weather* into her phone, then shook her head when she saw the results.

She gave a low whistle. "Thirty below zero—minus 34 Celsius. That's damn near the surface temperature of Mars."

Browny shrugged, like it might be a fun trip. "We can handle the cold," she said. "But equipment and transportation costs money. And it will take time. I doubt we can get a direct flight."

"Then charter," Valeria said, winding herself up like she might stroke out. "I don't give a shit what it costs. I need you there now!"

Browny looked to Mads. "We'll have to buy cold weather gear—"

"What part of *I don't give a shit what it costs* do you not understand, *słoneczko?*"

*Słoneczko* meant "sunshine." From anyone else, it would be a term of endearment. Valeria spat it like a curse.

Browny licked her lips and grinned. It wasn't in her nature to get offended. She was above that, like some alien predator who laughed at the emotion of these pitiful earthlings.

Mads's phone chimed with the arrival of a photo. She studied it for a moment.

"He's kinda hot." She turned the screen toward Browny. "This the guy who screwed you over?"

A muscular Native man stood with his arm around Valeria.

"It is," Valeria said. "Sam Lujan. The second pic is his mother, Josie."

Mads swiped to the next photo. "Mommy's not hard on the eyes either. Doesn't look much older than Junior."

"She goes first," Valeria said. "I want Sam to know what it feels like to lose someone he loves."

Browny gave an understanding nod. "Feeling bloody."

"Feeling betrayed," Valeria said. "One leads to the other."

"The kid will have time to feel it before we flip his switch," Mads said.

"Yeah, well," Valeria said. "Flip it slowly. This bastard needs to hurt."

"Hell, yeah." Browny gave a smug smirk, as if there were any other way.

# MONDAY

# CHAPTER 18

*16° below*

THE MRI AT ALASKA REGIONAL HOSPITAL REVEALED NO MAJOR damage to Tina Massey's brain. Even so, the severe head wound along with a sprained wrist and three cracked ribs made the doctors decide to keep her in the hospital overnight for observation. Along with the injuries, the admitting nurse had made note of numerous tattoos, including a jagged brand about the size of a silver dollar on the base of Massey's neck: the head of a wolf or maybe a bear and what looked like a small evergreen tree. Lola was with her at the time, providing moral support. Otherwise, she wouldn't have seen it, since Massey wasn't in custody.

A bucketload of pain meds and seventeen stitches in the back of her head saw Massey resting with an ice pack on the black leather couch in the USMS Fugitive Task Force offices in the James M. Fitzgerald United States Courthouse and Federal Building the next day. She didn't know—or at least wasn't telling—why Butch Pritchard had tried to murder her. She was, however, sure he thought he'd succeeded.

Lola rolled her desk chair alongside the couch, providing moral support—and attempting to build rapport. Cutter sat at the small conference table in the middle of the task force common area, carving on a piece of yellow cedar he'd found on his last trip to Juneau. Deputy Hart stuck her head out of an office she temporarily shared with Blodgett. "We're getting nothing on Pritch-ard's cell. Looks like he probably dumped it."

Masscy pipcd up, one hand holding the ice pack to her wounded scalp. "He goes through at least one a week." She looked at the knife in Cutter's hand, then at Lola.

"The pocketknife comes out when he's thinking," Lola said. "You get used to it. So, you have no way to contact Pritchard now?"

"I didn't say that. I can get in touch with him through email." Massey paused. She had to catch her breath from the mere effort of talking. "He bounces the account all over hell and gone though. You probably won't be able to track him . . . or, I don't know, maybe you can. What I do know is that he'll be surprised as hell to hear from me because he thinks he killed me."

"We can use that," Cutter said. "If you're willing to help us."

"Help you grab the guy who tried to cave in my head?" Massey said. "If someone can get me a laptop or phone, I'll send that ass-hole a message right now and tell him I want to see him."

Lola shook her head, smirking in disbelief. "What makes you think he'll meet if he already thinks he killed you?"

Massey gave a long sigh. "Butch looks pretty good on paper. He's not ugly, always has money, never been arrested as far as I know . . . but this isn't the first time he's hurt me. I know it makes me sound stupid—and I guess I am, but he apologizes every sin-gle time. He bawled like a baby the last time . . . the time before this I mean. And I always end up taking him back."

Cutter folded the pocketknife and set it on the table with the piece of cedar. He studied the woman for a long moment, then said, "But this time is different somehow?"

"Hell yeah," she said. "This time he really meant to kill me. But if I play it off like I'm not the wiser and it's just like any of the other times, he'll come pick me up."

Cutter shot a glance a Lola, who shrugged.

"Worth a try."

"I'll have to be there though," Massey said.

"Not a chance," Cutter said.

Lola spun back and forth in her office chair, bleeding off nervous energy. "He's right. You're a loose end. Could be he'd only agree to meet you to finish the job he botched the last time."

"But y'all won't let that happen," Massey said. "Right? I mean it. He has to see me, or he'll just drive on by."

Cutter's cell began to buzz, dancing across the conference table. It was Jill Phillips.

"Excuse me a second," he said. Then, "Hey, Chief."

"You still have Tina Massey in your office?"

"We're talking to her now," Cutter said.

"She know anything about Royce Decker?"

Cutter shot a glance at Massey, catching her eye. "I'm just about to ask her."

"Am I on speaker?"

"No, ma'am."

"Look, Arliss," the chief said. "I know you want to get Pritchard for what he did to Lola. I do too. It sickens me to say it, but headquarters wants us to look at this through a political lens. Missouri wants their bent cop in a bad way."

"Copy that," Cutter said.

Massey started talking as soon as he ended the call. "Listen, I get that you want to find Royce. I'll tell you whatever you want to know. But you gotta swear you won't hurt Suzi."

"I'll do everything I can not to harm your sister," he said. "But the way this goes down . . . I gotta tell you, that depends on how she and Decker respond."

"I get that." Massey closed her eyes in resignation. "I haven't talked to her for over a week. Royce keeps her on a tight leash, never lets her tell me where she's at. To be honest, I was worried they'd already left."

Cutter leaned back, not wanting to appear too interested in this particular information. "Explain what you mean by *left?*"

"Nothing," Massey said. "You know, moved to another place."

"Another place from where?" Lola said.

"Where they are now," Massey said.

"Which is?"

"I told you I don't know!"

"Tina," Cutter said. "You told us you were afraid your sister had left. As in left for a particular destination."

She whimpered. "I really—"

"Tina!" Lola said. "Tell us what you're scared of so we can help you."

Massey slumped, dropping the ice pack in her lap.

"Left the country," she said. "That was what Butch got so pissed about. Decker has a contact in Russia who's gonna help him out. At some point we're all supposed to meet in Nome or Kotzebue or somewhere. They're still working out the details. Butch was with them. The only reason he came down here was to get me. I told him I hadn't done anything, I didn't want to go back."

"Back?"

Massey looked at the floor. "I don't . . . I mean I told him I don't want to go to Russia."

"That's as good a reason as any to try to kill you," Lola said.

"When's all this supposed to happen?" Cutter asked.

"I don't think Butch even knows. The Russian will let Decker know the details. They were afraid new faces would stick out in small places like Nome or Kotzebue."

"Smart," Lola said.

People on the run from the lower forty-eight often seemed to think they could run to Alaska and hide out at the edge of civilization. The problem with that was that there just weren't enough people in those areas to get lost in a crowd.

"You said Butch came *down* to get you," Cutter said. "What do you mean by that?"

"I don't know exactly." Massey pursed her lips and shook her head. "I did hear her talk about seeing the pipeline when they were driving around. She didn't say specifically, but I'm sure they're somewhere around Fairbanks."

"The pipeline goes from Valdez all the way to the Arctic." Cutter nodded. "What makes you so sure? Did Butch tell you?"

"Oh, hell no," Massey said. "I think he woulda made me wear a blindfold or something if I'd agreed to go up. No, our parents were from Fairbanks. They had some land out on Chena Pump Road. It's all been turned into houses by now."

"They still in Fairbanks?" Cutter asked.

"Died in a car wreck when I was twelve. But Suzi would still know people."

"What people?" Lola asked.

"Suzi's six years older than me. That was before my time." Massey looked at the floor and shook her head slowly, as if remembering something. "I hate it there. I hate it here, too, just not as much."

Cutter decided to take a different tack. "Tell us about Butch and Royce Decker. What's their deal?"

"What do you mean?"

"How do they know one another?"

"Through Suzi," Massey said. "Butch's mother is at an assisted living place in Cape Girardeau. We flew out to visit her a couple of years ago . . . in between bruises on my face. Suzi was already seeing Royce so when we got together, we introduced the guys. Butch wasn't too psyched about hanging out with a cop at first, but once he found out Royce wasn't your regular tight-ass, they hit it off. Fact is, as bad as Butch is, I'd say Royce is even worse."

"Why's that?" Lola asked.

"Cause Royce is smart," Massey said. "You get the idea he's always planning, thinking of ways you can best serve him. Royce Decker doesn't have friends. He's got minions. Some of 'em just don't realize it. Anyway, Butch flew down to see his mom again about a month ago. I guess that's when he and Royce . . . did that thing."

"How'd you meet Butch?" Cutter asked.

Massey flattened against the couch like she'd been caught in a spotlight. "I . . . we . . ." She glanced toward the door like she was about to run. "At a bar," she blurted.

Yep. She was definitely hiding something. Rather than quiz her further, he simply waited.

She composed herself and changed the subject. "This could be something. Suzi's got this damned mutt that's mortified of loud noises,"

Cutter tapped his pen on the notebook. "A small dog?"

Massey shook her head. "Oh, no, no. It's a big-ass dog. A malamute I think. Looks like a cross with a wolf or something. That thing'll tear your face off for sure, but fireworks and loud noises make it shit the bed. Suzi told me she's pissed because Royce had set them up someplace with loud jets flying over. You know, sonic boons."

Cutter didn't correct her. Boon, boom, it didn't matter to him what she called it. He finally had information he could work with. They had three possible addresses outside Salcha—all of them rural, any of which could be on the Eielson Air Force Base flight path. He gave a nod to Nancy Alvarez, who stood in the doorway to her office listening to the conversation. She'd already done a workup on the Salcha properties—deeded owners, utilities, previous contacts with law enforcement, Google Earth and any other aerial photos that might exist—anything to pin down the one where Decker was laying his head at night.

"Okay . . ." Cutter mused. "I imagine your sister gave you an email address to contact her? Like the one you're going to use for Butch?"

"Sorry," she said. "I'd be outta luck unless she calls me." Massey darkened, as if she'd just thought of something awful. "You guys do know Royce figures you're trackin' his phones and stuff. He's using prepaids. I didn't recognize the number Suzi called from last time. I'm sure he made her dump it after that call, but the number's on my phone if you think it'll do you any good."

Cutter waited a beat for her to say more. When she didn't, he said, "Give Deputy Hart the number you have, old or not."

Massey looked up with tears in her eyes. "That psycho piece of shit. I'm terrified he's gonna get my moron sister killed."

"We'll do what we can," Cutter said. "I promise you that." He tapped his pocketknife on the table, switching gears. Massey was so weak he wondered if she would even be able to keep her feet long enough for Pritchard to see her. "Does Butch carry a gun?"

"That's funny! Does he have a gun?" Massey looked at Cutter like he'd lost his mind. "Sometimes he has two. Glocks, I think. I don't know guns very well. I just know what they look like when he shoves one of 'em in my face."

* * *

Pritchard's reply to Tina Massey's email pinged on her phone less than two minutes after she sent it. He had to be getting the messages on his own device. Sean Blodgett went to work immediately attempting to backtrack the IP address and get them a location. No luck.

As Massey expected, Pritchard wanted to see her—for some reason, explicable only by his sheer hubris, he didn't think the woman he'd just attempted to murder would ever think to betray him unless she was under duress from the cops.

Cutter allowed Massey free rein in setting up the meet. If he gave her too much direction, the message would sound like the trap that it was.

She told Pritchard that Regina had taken her to the hospital, where they'd had a big fight and now she was in Anchorage with no ride and nowhere to go. As par for their relationship, she intimated that she wanted him to pick her up at the hospital—knowing full well that he'd choose a different location. He told her he'd meet her at Moose's Tooth, a popular pizzeria off the Old Seward Highway in Midtown Anchorage. She reminded him again that she didn't have a car. Rather than offer to come get her where she was, he set the meet for two hours later and signed off his message with: I know things got a little rough earlier. Sorry. Won't happen again.

Massey had nearly thrown her phone across the room.

Lola already had a map of the area around Moose's Tooth pulled up on her computer.

"Are you sure you're up for this?"

"The God's honest truth?" Massey said. "Hell no, I'm not up for this. My head feels like it's gonna fall off my neck, but I am telling you, he has to see my face, or he'll run." She clutched the back of Lola's chair for support and leaned closer, pointing at the screen. "I'm sure he'll pick me up here."

Lola glanced up and shook her head. "That's the alley."

"I know," Massey said. "Butch didn't spell it out in his message, but I guarantee you he'll want to change things up at the last minute. I'll get a text about the time we're supposed to meet telling me to walk out the back door and go into that alley. He's done it before. *Walk through the kitchen like you own the place,* he'll say. He's always pulling shit like that. The idiot thinks he's Jason Bourne." She looked up suddenly, catching Cutter's eye. "Butch isn't a brain surgeon or anything, but he's not stupid. He knows he's looking at the death penalty if you guys grab him. I'm here to tell you, if he sees any weak spot in the way y'all approach, he'll go to guns in a heartbeat." She shrugged. "I don't know. Maybe he will anyway. I mean, what's he got to lose?"

# CHAPTER 19

*19° below*

$C$UTTER HAD NANCY ALVAREZ COORDINATE THE TAKEDOWN WITH her contacts at APD's Investigative Support Unit. ISU was a plainclothes team comprised entirely of SWAT officers who focused on tracking down and arresting the most dangerous elements on the streets of Anchorage. Many on the unit had been sworn in as special deputy US marshals, giving them federal jurisdiction when working alongside the task force—a routine occurrence considering their charter.

ISU had several undercover rigs—older model cars and SUVs that hadn't started off life as a patrol or detective vehicle so were more difficult to ID as belonging to the po-po. Cutter asked them to post across Thirty-Fourth Avenue by the Extended Stay and in the strip mall parking lot on the west side of Moose's Tooth. Marshals Service vehicles weren't marked, but every outlaw on the street suspected dark colored SUVs with tinted windows were chock-full of jack-booted government agents. Many were, but the Alaska Fugitive Task Force had a secret weapon—an all-wheel drive Toyota minivan similar to Mim's.

Just over an hour after Tina Massey's last exchange with Pritchard everything was set. As SWAT operators, ISU routinely practiced integrated arrests including pinning target vehicles with theirs. Men and women who chose law enforcement careers tended to be type A personalities. Those who specialized in fugitive hunting needed a strong predator drive to excel. Without careful coordination, arrest operations involving multiple agencies could easily devolve into dances where everyone tried to lead. It was Cutter's policy that if he asked SWAT or ISU to play, he and the fugitive task force would step back and allow the operators to move in and make the arrest. Deputy US marshals loved to be the ones to slap the cuffs on their fugitive—but the main goal was the arrest, not who got the credit. Historically, the Marshals Service didn't go around bigfooting local cases or thumping its own chest—a sentiment not shared by every federal law enforcement agency.

Per the last-minute ops plan, one of the ISU officers went into the Moose's Tooth with Nancy Alvarez. They ordered a pizza and scanned the occupants to be certain Pritchard hadn't arrived early and set up inside.

Nancy's voice crackled over the radio. "No sign of him in here."

Lola drove the soccer-mom van. Cutter sat in back with his M4 rifle, complete with the USMS-issue HUXWRKS suppressor. ISU would make contact. The task force would provide lethal cover.

"We'll be right outside," Cutter said to Massey before they dropped her off. He'd purposely kept her out of the loop as to exactly where members of the arrest team were posted. Better for her to think they were everywhere. "Call or text Lola as soon as Butch makes contact."

"I'll try," Massey said. "But he'll keep me on the phone as soon as he gets ahold of me. He'll want me to keep moving. Like I said, Jason Bourne."

Cutter chewed on that for a second. "Text her if you can. It'll be helpful if we get a heads-up about what he's driving and which way he's coming from."

Lola dropped Massey off in front of the restaurant and then drove five blocks to the west, waiting a full five minutes before returning, in case Pritchard had arrived early to scope out the area. She parked the minivan in the Kinley's restaurant lot across Thirty-Third, giving them a view of the approaches to Moose's Tooth as well as the alley entrance. Cutter stayed in the back of the van, ready to jump out the side door if the need arose. Lola left the engine running, the defrost roaring against encroaching ice. Everyone else on the arrest team wore micro spikes over their boots in the event their target bailed and tried to run on foot.

Lola slumped in the driver's seat, all but receding into her parka.

"That girl's hiding something."

"Yep," Cutter said.

Lola caught his eye in the rearview mirror. "You ever get the feeling things are about to go terribly wrong?"

Cutter didn't answer right away. He lived with that feeling pretty much every day.

True to form, Lola kept talking. "I mean, I'm sure Heather Decker went to bed the night Pritchard killed her dreaming about what color to paint her nursery or what to give her asshole husband for his birthday. I came to work the other day thinking everything was hunky-dory. And then came a whisker away from getting my head chopped off by a sheet of ice." She looked over her shoulder. "Who's to say today won't be *that* day?"

Cutter waited to see if the question was rhetorical. It must not have been because Lola kept her head craned around as if she expected an answer.

"I wish I had something wise to tell you," Cutter said. "About all we can do is train and plan—and then leave the rest to God or fate or karma or whatever you believe in."

"You think God protected me the other morning?" Lola asked. "Because I'd like to believe He did. But if that's the case, why didn't He protect Royce Decker's pregnant wife? What makes me so special? Or maybe I'm not. Maybe today's the day . . ."

"Lola—"

She cleared her throat, using the wheel to straighten herself up in the seat. "I know. Get my head in the game. Sorry about that, boss. I'm good. Really."

"We'll talk about this some more," Cutter said, though he had no idea what else he could say. The fact was, he'd pondered the same questions a thousand times himself.

"Right-o," Lola said. "But for now, we gotta—what's that you say? Keep our eyes on the prize."

They didn't have long to wait.

Sean Blodgett, who was posted in the hotel parking lot to the south, broke squelch first.

"Red Silverado half-ton just turned north onto Fairbanks Street off Thirty-Fourth. It's the second time he's passed us. Lone male as far as I can tell. Big. Looks white but he's got a ball cap pulled low so I can't make out his face."

"Got him," ISU Sergeant Tom Smith said from the job center parking lot. "Running the plate now."

The Silverado turned right on Thirty-Third Avenue, passing within a hundred feet of the minivan. Lola kept the radio low in her lap. "He's heading east toward the Old Seward. Looks like he's scanning the area, but I can't tell if it's our guy. Repeat, no positive ID. Nothing from Tina Massey."

Operators continued to call out the red pickup's location as it made the block again.

Sergeant Smith spoke again. "The plate on that truck comes back to a black Ford Econoline van."

"Silverados are in high demand with car thieves," Nancy said. "He likely stole this one or bought it for pennies from someone who did."

"If it is Pritchard," Lola said.

An ISU operator named Pendergrass called out next. "He's heading west on Thirty-Fourth, almost to Eagle. We'll lose the eye if he keeps going and makes it to Denali. Want us to stop him?"

Sergeant Smith came back immediately. "Stand by." Then, "Your call, Marshal."

Cutter didn't relish the idea of letting the Silverado out of his sight. Rushing in would blow everything if this was just some random guy waiting on a friend—or a decoy sent in by Pritchard. Cutter lifted his radio to speak but paused when he caught movement in the alley behind Moose's Tooth.

Officer Pendergrass spoke up, sounding relieved. "Silverado turned north on Eagle."

"Massey just exited the back door of Moose's Tooth," Lola said. "She's walking north."

Cutter and Lola watched as Tina Massey limped up the alley toward them, heavy parka pulled tight around her face.

Lola gripped the wheel with both hands, squirming in the driver's seat.

"*Popongi!*" she said.

*Good morning* in Maori, Lola often used the word when she spotted someone they were hunting.

"I'm not sure." Cutter watched the red Silverado grow larger in his binoculars as it came east on Thirty-Third Avenue. "Either way, we're not letting her get in that truck." He picked up the radio and keyed the mic. "Looks like he plans to grab her on Thirty-Third. North end of the alley behind Moose's Tooth. *Initiate! Initiate! Initiate!*"

# CHAPTER 20

*A* WELL-EXECUTED VEHICLE PIN WAS A THING OF BEAUTY—AND THE operators with Anchorage Police ISU were experts.

Still in the alley, Tina Massey stopped in her tracks and clutched her parka around her neck, fifteen feet from Thirty-Third Avenue.

Five unmarked vehicles squealed up on the scene, surrounding the red Silverado as if materializing out of thin air. Officer Pendergrass met the vehicle head-on in an older model Dodge Durango, knocking bumpers and blocking his way forward. Sergeant Smith swooped in from the rear, shoving the Silverado's back bumper and pushing the truck into Officer Pendergrass's Dodge. Two more ISU officers came in from the opposite sides, their vehicles kissing the pickup's doors and pinning the driver inside. A fifth APD unit came in behind Smith, bolstering his vehicle to keep the Silverado from shoving its way out in reverse—a generally lower gear. Two officers riding shotgun—literally— bailed out of the side vehicles, drawing beads on the Silverado's driver, angled to avoid crossfire with their brother officers.

Pinned in his vehicle with nowhere to go, Butch Pritchard raised his hands above his head.

Lola, who'd pulled forward as soon as the dance started, threw the minivan in park and gave a reverent gasp.

"Car-fu," she said.

Cutter looked sideways at her.

"What?"

"Like kung fu," she said. "But with cars."

She and Cutter made it out of the minivan at the same time the ISU contact officers extracted an extremely shaken Butch Pritchard from the stolen pickup truck.

Tina Massey stood outside the ring of unmarked vehicles. Great clouds of vapor billowing out from under her parka hood.

Pritchard's face screwed into a snarling frown when he saw her. "You bitch!" he said, half whispering, as if he'd just taken a boot to the groin. "I can't believe this—"

"You tried to kill me," she said.

He glared at her. "I told you I was sorry!"

The ISU officers passed their catch over to Blodgett and went to work on another target. Cutter assigned Paige Hart to sit with Tina Massey in the minivan out of the cold. Lola stood beside the open rear door to Blodgett's SUV when Cutter approached.

Hands cuffed behind his back, Butch Pritchard leaned sideways, still shaking from adrenaline. "That bitch is going to get us both killed."

Lola leaned in. "What's that now?"

He raised his voice to speak over the roaring heater vents. "I said, how about loosening these cuffs?"

"I checked 'em already," Lola said, as much to Cutter as to Pritchard.

Cutter stomped his way to the open door. His Zamberlan boots were better than average for kicking around the city during the winter, but the temperature had dropped dramatically in the last hour.

Pritchard leaned sideways again, peering over his shoulder at the minivan.

"How much did she tell you?"

"Nice try," Cutter said.

Pritchard threw his head back and groaned. "She's going to get us all killed—me, you, my family, your family."

Lola and Cutter exchanged glances.

"Second time I've heard that," Cutter said.

Pritchard continued to bang his head against the back of his seat. "I can't believe her. She knows what will happen. And she still—"

Lola pounded on the side of the car with her fist. "Focus, Butch."

Pritchard stopped and studied both deputies for a solid minute, then sighed. "She didn't tell you shit, did she?" He shrugged. "About that stuff with the ice . . . I didn't mean anything personal."

"Yeah, nah," Lola said, her Kiwi accent coming on strong. "I get it. Just business. You're morally obliged to murder anyone who happens to get in your way . . ."

He slumped forward, staring at his feet. "Okay then. How about we skip the games. I'm ready to deal."

Lola raised a dark brow. "Deal?"

"Come on, Marshal," Pritchard said. "I'm smart enough to know you weren't lookin' for me."

"That is high-larious, Butch," Lola said. "Going after shitheads who murder pregnant women is damn near the tippy top of our list."

"Easy there, Moana." Pritchard wasn't accustomed to women who stood up to him, let alone gave him up to the cops. Adrenaline from the ambush was wearing off. The outlaw obviously thought he had an ace up his sleeve, giving him a wily glint in his eye.

Lola's lips pulled back in a tight snarl, like she might dive in the back seat. It was exactly what Pritchard wanted. A broken jaw or bruised face would muddy the water around his arrest. Cutter gave Lola the slightest shake of his head.

She stood completely still, her nostrils flared. "Don't worry," she said at length. "He's not worth it."

"You don't like me. I get that." Pritchard's flippant tone said he obviously thought he was the one holding all the cards. "You were just business. Heather was business. It's all just business. Nothing more. I am a dude tryin' to pay my bills like everyone else. The real bad guy here is her husband, the one who hired me. Am I right? I swear to you, Royce never once told me she was gonna have a kid."

"That where you draw the line?" Lola scoffed. "Innocent women are fair game? Kids are off limits? What's your age cutoff? I'm curious. Twelve? Four? Or do you just charge more as the age goes down?"

"Look," Pritchard said. "I am willing to give you what you're looking for. I just need some assurances from your side."

"Assurances?" Cutter stepped in closer. "What exactly are you thinking?"

The outlaw gave a wry chuckle. "I'm thinking I'll give you enough information to put your warheads on Royce Decker's forehead. I'll give you this much for free. You better get him quick, or he'll be out of your reach."

Lola frowned. "Is that so?"

"It is indeed," Pritchard said. "But I need you to take the death penalty off the table. Do that and I'll even give you Royce's Russian connection."

"Fyodor Pugo," Cutter said. "We have that already."

Panic flashed across Pritchard's face. "Listen, if you know about the Russian then you know you're on the clock here. Get me my agreement and I'll draw you a map before he flies the coop."

Cutter gave a slow nod. In truth he was thinking about the conversation with his nephew. If anybody in this world needed hurting, it was Butch Pritchard. With any luck, the state of Missouri would handle that.

"I've thought about it." Cutter looked the outlaw up and down. "And you know what? I think we're good with what we've got." He gave Pritchard a wink to show him exactly who held the cards, and then slammed the door.

Pritchard's face fell as he no doubt tried to process what had just happened. It was unthinkable that cops wouldn't want to deal. His terrified voice went up an octave, muffled behind the frosted window of Blodgett's Tahoe. He threw himself sideways, frantically banging his head against the glass—a drowning man pleading for a lifeline.

"Decker's got traps and trail cams! I can tell you where they are!"

The Tahoe's reverse lights came on as Blodgett prepared to back up a few feet, straightening out his wheels to get around a remaining marked APD patrol car.

Pritchard kept up his tirade, pounding, screaming, finally breaking into tears of desperation. Missouri had him on video. If he didn't make a deal now his life would end on a cold cot with a hot needle in his vein.

"Somebody's gonna get hurt," he screamed. "That blood is on your hands, Marshal!"

Cutter turned to Lola. "What do you think?"

"I think he's a murdering bastard." She turned up her nose. "But he's right. I don't want you or anyone else to get hurt just so Pritchard gets what he deserves."

Cutter raised a gloved hand to wave Blodgett back. The Tahoe's reverse lights lit up immediately, stopped, and he returned to his previous parking spot on the icy lot. Cutter stood stone still and glared at Pritchard through the frosted window. Virtually every big case had some stench of politics, this one more than most. Deals with killers made him sick.

Dying a little inside, Cutter dabbed the moisture off the end of his nose with the back of his glove then took a deep breath, burning his lungs with metallic cold. Penance for what he was about to do.

# CHAPTER 21

"WE CAN HANDLE DECKER," CUTTER SAID AFTER THEY'D DROPPED Tina Massey off with Regina Orr and were on their way back to the federal building to deal with Pritchard.

Lola was behind the wheel.

"What do you mean?"

"I mean I think you should sit this one out," he said. "We'll take care of the stuff in Fairbanks."

He may as well have slapped her.

"Cutter! Have you lost your mind? You say stuff in Fairbanks like you're going up to clean the office instead of arresting one of the sleaziest assholes to ever show his face in Alaska."

"You've been through it these last few days," Cutter said. "It's gonna be cold as hell up there. Better you stay home and recuperate. You can spend some time with Brackett."

"I'm fine," Lola said.

"Just trying to look out for you."

"Well, stop." Lola turned on the wipers to help squeegee away the exterior frost that was forming as she drove.

"Alright," Cutter said. "I thought you might want to stay home and get warm for a change."

"Do you?" she scoffed. "Because Sean and I can handle stuff if—"

"Touché," Cutter said. "Jill's on the horn with the US attorney's office and the DA from St. Louis as we speak. If his information pans out, we'll head up early in the morning." He shucked off a wool glove liner and thumb typed on his cell.

Lola nodded across the console at his phone. "You calling the girl with three first names?"

"I'm calling Micki," Cutter said. "If that's who you mean."

"That's what I said. Micki. Lee. Frank. Three first names."

Formerly a V-22 Osprey pilot for the United States Marine Corps, Deputy US Marshal Micki Frank was the primary pilot for the District of Alaska, flying their Cessna Caravan and a smaller Cessna 185 that prior to seizure by the US government in Operation Just Cause, had belonged to Manuel Noriega.

Chief Jill Phillips had no small amount of political capital in the Marshals Service, but it had still taken her the better part of two years to convince the big brains at headquarters that a state as vast and roadless as Alaska needed aircraft. First, she had to teach them that unlike the maps on their office walls in Arlington, Virginia, Alaska wasn't a little bitty island beside Hawaii, inset below Baja, California. Cutter wasn't privy to whatever backroom deals were made. All he knew or cared to know was that the chief had gotten Alaska a couple of planes, and that made life so much easier for the Fugitive Task Force.

Deputy Frank had, in fact, come with the Cessna Caravan, transferring in from Oklahoma City with all her luggage when she and another pilot for the Marshals Service air wing personally delivered the aircraft to Alaska.

Frank answered on the second ring. Like Jill Phillips, her voice held a soft, almost pensive Kentucky drawl—until something got her blood up.

Cutter put the phone on speaker.

"This is Micki," she said. "What can I do for you, my dear?" Deputy Frank called most everyone "my dear," sometimes even prisoners. It was her way of separating civilian life from her time in the Marine Corps. Sometimes "my dear" could be taken literally, sometimes it meant "hey, you there, asshole." Deputy pilot Micki Frank was a master of inflection and nuance.

Cutter gave her a quick rundown of the situation with their fugitive and the urgent need to fly north.

Computer keys clicked in the background. Micki sucked air in through her teeth. "Fairbanks airport shows clear skies and minus twenty-four." More clicking keys. "Hmmm. That's actually a little warmer than we are in Anchor-town."

"Twenty-four below." Lola gave a thumbs-up. "That's not so bad. Downright toasty . . ."

"Weather guessers say it's supposed to drop like a lead balloon tomorrow though," Micki said.

Lola slumped in her seat, thumb down.

"So," Cutter said. "What do you think?"

"No go for the Caravan is minus fifty-four."

"That's good," Lola said, thumb up again.

"It's not that simple, my dear. We'll lose about three and a half degrees per thousand feet of climb. Say we fly at ten thousand feet. That's a loss of thirty-five degrees—which at this moment would put us at fifty-eight below, four degrees colder than the Caravan's minimum operating temp."

Cutter let the pilot talk without interruption. The last thing he wanted to do was push her into a situation she didn't believe was safe. On the back side of forty, Micki Frank was on the road to being an "old" pilot, and you didn't get that way by being an overly "bold" pilot—her combat flights in the Marine Corps notwithstanding.

The line went quiet for a time while she checked weather en route and did a few calculations.

"We'll need to leave early," she said at length. "Tell your guys to meet me at the hangar at zero four thirty. I'll have everything ready for a zero five hundred departure. How many of you are we talking about?"

"Besides you, five souls plus weapons and winter gear," Cutter said.

"Roger that," Micki said. "Afraid this'll have to be a turn and burn, though. I'll plan on dropping you off and then hauling ass back to Anchorage."

"Be good if you could stay long enough to do a flyover of the target property," Lola said.

"I might be able to make that work. But listen, y'all, this whole deal is contingent on the weather. We all know how fickle that is. Those systems north of the Alaska Range are awfully shallow, notoriously prone to sudden disruptions—which mean they can turn on a dime. Things might go bum overnight and I'd have to call off the whole show. I'd suggest you make plans to fly commercial. You can always cancel in the morning if we're able to go wheels-up."

"Sounds good," Cutter said. "We're on our way to the office as we speak to debrief an informant. I'll be bringing the chief up to speed as soon as we're done with him." He checked his watch. "Maybe two hours if you want to sit in on that."

"I'll be there, my dear," Micki said. "Wish I was kickin' doors with you instead of just driving the bus."

"Me too," Cutter said. "But I get it. Stay if the weather allows. Scoot if you have to."

Cutter ended the call.

"Got any ideas about how we should handle this?" Lola asked. "Decker was SWAT for something like fourteen years, a sniper no less. He's gonna know exactly how we do things, which means he'll be set up and waiting for us when we move in to arrest him."

"That's the one and only reason I'm willing to listen to Pritchard."

"Still . . ." She went quiet for a time, then without warning, careened off on an entirely new subject. "So, how are things going with your mum?"

Already pondering on tactical plans in the warmth of his parka cocoon, Cutter looked up with a sudden start.

"What about her?"

"Are you gonna try and get her daughter back?"

Cutter groaned. He didn't go around blabbing about his prodigal mother, but it was clear Lola and Mim talked far more than he would have preferred.

The truth was, Ursula occupied much more real estate in Cutter's brain than she should have. He'd thought about her a lot as he was growing up, but over time she'd faded out of his mind. A big blank spot, a loss. Not anything important like a limb—more of a dream that slowly disappeared. He'd learned to forget her over the years, and her sudden presence wore on him like an ill-fitting boot. He hated to admit it, but the blisters would only get worse if he didn't do something about them. Mim had plenty of ideas about how he should handle the situation, and she wasn't shy about giving her opinion. After all, Ursula was her children's grandmother, and this estranged daughter was their aunt.

Thinking about this teenage sister was like an icepick to Cutter's forehead.

"I'd rather talk about Mim and me," he said.

Lola perked up, eyes wide. "Really?"

"Not in a million years," Cutter said. "You and I have plenty to think about besides my homelife. Focus on Royce Decker."

"Okay . . ." Lola sighed, obviously feeling cheated out of a juicy conversation.

Relieved to occupy his mind with work, Cutter scrolled through his recent calls but didn't find what he was looking for. "Do you have the contact info for Joe Ikeda? We must have called on your phone."

"The SWAT guy from St. Louis?" Lola said. "Sure." She gave a sideways nod toward the powder-blue warrant folder beside her seat. "His number should be near the back of the file. We've talked to him at least five times. Sounds to me like they were very close. What are you thinking now?"

"I'm thinking we need to fly him up ASAP in the event we need his help to lure Decker out."

Lola grimaced. "Lure his friend out so the state of Missouri can kill him . . ."

Cutter gave a slow nod.

"Yep."

# CHAPTER 22

*Fairbanks*
*26° below*

TWO ROWS AHEAD OF BOBBY GANT, JOSIE LUJAN STOOD FROM HER seat at the sound of the chime. Pushy passengers crowded into the aisle immediately, nearly trampling her as she attempted to reach her duffel in the overhead compartment. She wasn't a tall woman—barely over five feet—and had to tiptoe.

Gant fought the urge to jump up and help her. At least he wouldn't have to be the one to kill her. Mads and Browny would handle that. Valeria wanted to make a statement. Statements were the Aussies' specialty.

Oh, he could have killed her no problem in the beginning, in the days and months after her kid ratted to the feds. Gant had put a lot of bullets in a lot of heads before and since. Killing wasn't the problem. But tailing someone day after day for weeks on end—reading her mail, watching the way she shopped or volunteered at the library or took food to her sick neighbors—that was sure to develop a certain level of intimacy.

Booking at the last minute meant Gant and the others were scattered throughout the plane. He'd hoped Josie's seat might be behind his, meaning she would pass by him as she made her way down the aisle. He would have been able to actually touch her, to inadvertently brush her arm as she walked by in the cramped space, possibly catch a whiff of her perfume.

Gant watched with his peripheral vision as she dragged her bag and heavy red parka out of the overhead. He had to force himself not to stare. Up to now, all his watching had been from a distance. Being this close to her made his stomach hurt.

She was apparently old-school enough to dress nicely when she traveled, heavy leather boots, jeans that hugged her hips, and the fashionable wool sweater. Short black hair peeked from beneath a matching wool tam. The bright lights of the aircraft cabin glinted off hoop earrings Gant had watched her buy at the Fireworks jewelry store during the layover at the Seattle airport.

Gant resolved to take them when the time came and keep them as something to remember her by.

He wished for the ten-thousandth time that they'd met under different circumstances. In a matter of hours—after she led them to her son—Josie Lujan would be dead. Valeria wanted the job done in a certain order—and she was the boss. Kill Josie in front of her kid, let him see it, feel it, then kill him. Gant had been around enough killing to know it was all about to end in a flurry of snot and tears. He rubbed a rough hand across the stubble on his chin. Josie Lujan didn't deserve that . . . or maybe she did for helping her sorry excuse for a son. It wasn't for Gant to decide.

He leaned forward, peering past the passengers on his left to catch a glimpse out the window. Ground personnel waddled back and forth in heavy yellow coats, surrounded by swirling vapor in thick blue-black darkness. An involuntary shiver ran up his spine. This was going to suck, no matter how long they were here.

Gant grabbed his duffel and fell in with the exiting passengers. The rest of his crew had seats behind him. Mads and Browny would come in later.

He knew his Costco winter coat was a terrible mistake the moment he stepped off the plane. Crystals of frost ringed the mouth of the jet bridge like so many fangs. Air so cold it burned, lurked in the scant inches between plane and bridge.

Two of Valeria's crew from New York had joined Gant and

Dusty in Seattle. John Blackwell was lanky and balding, though he didn't like to admit to the latter. He started sporting a hell of a combover until Valeria had threatened to shave his head with a belt sander. He and Gant had been with Mr. Kot since they were both in their teens. Gant wasn't the type to really trust anyone, but he mistrusted Blackwell the least of this crew. Nils Halverson, a monstrous, platinum-haired Swede who everyone called Pee-wee, made Dusty look small.

Apart from Gant, none of the crew had much practice tailing anyone without being noticed. Their duties in New York leaned toward intimidation—and jobs where it was good to cut a wide swath. It was only by sheer luck that Josie hadn't caught on to them during her layover in Seattle. Peewee Halverson, who stood out like a blond mountain to begin with, stomped everywhere he went with such an intensity that people scattered out of his path like he might grind their bones to bake his bread. A toddler leashed to her mother in Seattle had taken one look at the giant and burst into tears.

Like Gant, Blackwell was pushing fifty. Time and experience got rid of a lot of piss and vinegar. Dusty and the Swede were great at thuggish force, but they could be unguided missiles. Some jobs called for a little more finesse.

Gant and Blackwell kept an eye on Josie while the monsters took care of the rental cars. They'd reserved two. That would help shake up the tail with different vehicles now and then.

Gant caught himself staring when Josie grabbed a backpack off the luggage carousel.

Blackwell leaned in. "That woman has got a case of USDA Prime ass," he whispered. "A crying shame we have to whack her."

Even Gant was surprised at the sudden white-hot fury that welled up from his gut. His hands balled into fists; his jaw tensed. He swallowed the feeling, but not before Blackwell clocked the fire in his eyes.

"You good, brother?"

"Just tired," Gant said. "Ready for this to be done."

Blackwell gave a slow nod, eyeing Gant like he didn't quite believe him. "You tell the boss and I'll deny it, but waiting on those crazy Aussie bitches is about the dumbest thing I ever even heard of."

"Valeria wants what Valeria wants." Gant was tired of the New York crew already. He preferred to focus what would be his last few hours with Josie.

Normally one to chat with store clerks and virtually everyone on the street, the professor now kept to herself, looking around the terminal as if scanning for faces. Gant couldn't tell if she was searching for the kid, or checking to see if she was being followed. Probably both. She retrieved a heavy roller bag and backpack from the luggage carousel and dragged them to the rental car counter.

"I guess Junior isn't picking her up," Blackwell said. "Pretty shitty behavior for a son who hasn't seen his mom in four years."

"His car's in the shop," Gant said. "He told her about it on the last phone—"

Peewee Halverson tromped up and handed Gant the keys to a Jeep Compass.

"Still no sign of shitbird?"

Gant shook his head. "She must be going to meet him. Is Dusty out with the other rental?"

"He is." Halverson stuck his hands in his coat pockets and hunched up, still cold from the few seconds he'd spent outside. "I do not know how people live in this place."

"Go on out there with Dusty and be ready when she comes out. John and I will grab the bags and guns and be right behind you."

Halverson took his hands out of his pockets. "You're suddenly the one giving orders now?"

"Look at it this way," Gant said. "Things go sideways, there'll be no one to blame but me."

The big Swede stared at him for a long moment, and then wheeled to stomp his way to the doors.

Blackwell gave a nod toward the rental car counter, speaking under his breath.

"Don't look now," he said, "but the professor Josie's about to crawl across the counter and kick the shit outta the clerk."

"Maybe they don't have her car ready."

"I wish," Blackwell said. "Then she can take an Uber. They're easier to follow."

Whatever the issue with the rental car was, Josie must have gotten it worked out. She got the keys about the same time the two Pelican gun cases tumbled onto the carousel. Wanting to stay nimble, Gant and the others brought only one bag apiece. The gun cases—which were not at all out of place in Alaska—held all six of their handguns, a Remington 870 short shotgun and two H&K MP5 submachine guns with suppressors.

Josie wheeled her luggage toward the exit, stopping to step to the side before she reached the double doors. Gant watched with his peripheral vision as she took a moment to situate a wool scarf over her face and exchange her stylish wool tam for a fur-trapper hat that covered her ears. She took a step toward the doors, then stopped like she'd forgotten something and pulled a pair of heavy fur mittens from the pockets of her parka. The mittens had been there all along, affixed to a red and black cord that ran through the parka's sleeves so she wouldn't lose them if they fell out of the pockets. Bundled like the Michelin Man with only her eyes showing, Josie hoisted the backpack onto her shoulders and dragged the roller bag out the door into the night like she knew exactly what she was getting into.

Gant zipped up his flimsy parka and motioned for Blackwell to pick up the pace. Dusty and Halverson, the two meatheads, were already in the parking lot, but he didn't trust them not to lose her.

Blackwell fell in beside him with the luggage cart, snugging a wool hat over his balding head and ears before they stepped outside. "What if you dragged our asses to this deep freeze and she doesn't lead us to the kid?"

"I'm not wrong."

"You think Mads and Browny will forgive you if you are?"

Gant started to answer at the same time the doors yawned open. Icy air hit him like a wall, freezing his face and shoving the words back down his throat.

# CHAPTER 23

*Wasilla, Alaska*
*21° below*

MIM WATCHED THE TEMPERATURE TICK DOWNWARD ON THE DASH-board as she drove northeast out of Eagle River. It bottomed out at twenty-one below zero as they thumped across the Knik River. Her kids called it the "Star Wars" Bridge because of the yellow lights along the edges to keep drivers from plunging into the river during a blizzard. Mim counted seven moose huddled among the willows on the Palmer Hay Flats, their backs blanketed with frost.

Other than periodic observations about how Alaska didn't meet with her approval, Ursula had barely said a word since leaving Anchorage. She piped up out of the blue from her pile of scarves and blankets about the time they reached the interchange where the George Parks and Glenn Highways split generally northwest and northeast.

Mim kept left, getting on the Parks.

Ursula rubbed frost off her window with the heel of her mitten. "That's gotta be wrong."

Mim groaned. A complaining mother-in-law seemed like an insignificant problem compared to everything else in her life. She painted on a smile.

"What's that?"

"That sign said two-hundred and thirty-two moose have been killed since July. A lot of moose for one highway?"

"That sounds about right," Mim said. "Ethan told me once that there were something like two hundred thousand moose in Alaska."

"Hmph," Ursula said. "Sounds like a factoid he'd remember."

Mim fought the urge to say, *how would you know?* "He was pretty hung up on moving north even back when we were in college."

"Alaska . . ." Ursula said, as if the word tasted bad.

They drove on in silence, heading west through the growing city of Wasilla. Mim's friends in the lower forty-eight tended to picture all Alaskans living in log cabins or igloos and running traplines or mushing dog teams to deliver diphtheria vaccines. Mim thought about how they pitied her for living in a place so devoid of modern conveniences. Sure, the produce she got in Alaska was expensive, but she rarely had trouble finding what she was after. Even off the road system—the Bush, Alaskans called it— milk might cost fourteen bucks a gallon and peanut butter twenty dollars a jar, but it was there. Mim had once found three little kiwi fruit in the tiny store in Emmonak when she was gaining hours toward her nurse practitioner license. They were slightly shriveled, next to a twenty-dollar tub of sour cream in the cooler, but they were available in a Yupik village of eight hundred on the Yukon River. Apart from the thick layers of rime ice that made the Walmart, Lowes, and Red Robin look like they were located on some ice planet, Wasilla, Alaska, could have been every Anytown, USA.

Ursula spoke again as Mim turned left onto the Knik Goose Bay Road—KGB to the locals.

"I do appreciate you helping me with Opal."

The minivan's tires thumped as they rolled over the Alaska Railroad tracks.

"We're family," Mim said. "That's what families do."

"I realize this is hard on Arliss," Ursula said. "I just . . ."

Mim took her eyes off the icy road long enough to turn and meet her mother-in-law's eyes. "I'm not gonna lie," she said. "It's extremely hard. But here's the deal, Ursula. You made your choices, but none of us were in your shoes. We can't know what your life was like."

"I'm not sure I know that myself," Ursula whispered, still gazing out the side window. When she turned, her face was different, harder, more in control.

"How about you, Miriam," she said. "Are you okay?"

Mim settled deeper into the driver's seat, as if bracing herself for an attack. No one but her own mother called her Miriam.

"I'm fine," she said.

"You don't seem fine," Ursula said.

"Well, I am." Mim hoped the look in her eye left the *mind your own business* implied.

"Are you telling me you're not a teensy bit worried about this thing you have with Arliss?"

"That came out of nowhere," Mim said. "This *thing*?"

"You know exactly what I mean," Ursula said. "I've seen photos of Arliss's ex-wives. Any one of them could be your sister. It's obvious he's had feelings for you since . . . forever."

"So what?"

"Did you know?" Ursula asked. "How sweet he was on you back then, I mean."

Mim ignored the question and said, "We're getting close to Opal's."

"Just because I left doesn't mean I stopped loving my boys, you know," Ursula said. "Not a day went by that I didn't think about them."

"Good to know," Mim said. She didn't care if it sounded sarcastic.

Ursula looked Mim up and down. "There's something going on with you," she said. "I can't put my finger on it, but I'll tell you this much. I don't want Arliss to get hurt. This thing you have with him is—"

"Stop calling it a thing!" Mim snapped. Then, more evenly, "Ursula, that little five-year-old boy you left is now truly happy for the first time in years. You want that for him. Right?"

"Of course I do," Ursula said. "But—"

"Nope!" Mim said. "But nothing. You either want him to be happy or you don't. Listen, you don't know me and from the way you act, I'm not sure you even like me. I have no idea what kind of crap you were dealing with back in the day or what you had to put up with during the years since, but if you have to set limits on your son's happiness—"

"Like you said"—Ursula sighed—"life is messy."

"No doubt," Mim said, tight jawed, growing angrier by the moment. "It's messy as hell. I'm just trying to decide how much of your bullshit I'm going to allow into my family." She glanced at the GPS then up at her mother-in-law, breathing hard. "Is this the turn?"

Ursula gave a shaky nod. "Yes. Thank the Lord."

Cold began to creep into the minivan the moment Mim killed the engine. She heaved a heavy sigh and unbuckled her seat belt, turning to look at her mother-in law, happy to be able to focus on anything besides her and Arliss.

"Sorry to snap at you."

Ursula raised a trembling hand. "It's fine."

"I meant what I said, though." She turned toward the fourplex nestled among the birch trees before Ursula could respond. "So this is where you've been coming to every day?"

"I know, right," Ursula said. "I'm an abandoner and a stalker."

"I get it," Mim lied. There was little if anything she understood about Ursula's actions. "How long has it been since you saw her?"

"August," Ursula said. "Just before her dad moved up to take a job in Seattle. She was going to do a couple of weeks with him while I went on a cruise, and then be back before school started. An opportunity came up for me to hike around France for another month, so she ended up starting school with him. She dominated cross country, so I let her stay for that. By the time the season was over, she didn't want to come home. Then he got transferred to Alaska and she moved with him. I missed everything with my boys." Ursula choked back a sob. "I swear on all that is holy, I will not make the same mistake with Opal." She took a deep shuddering breath, composing herself, and then pointed at the four-plex with a manicured hand. "That's it all the way down on the right. Unit D."

Mim nodded at the red Toyota Tacoma backed in the driveway. "Is that Geoff's pickup?"

Ursula looked at the truck as if seeing it for the first time. She shook her head. "Geoff drives a Ford. He should be at work for another hour. I have no earthly idea who that one belongs to."

Mim zipped her parka up to her chin, snugged down her wool hat, and pulled the feather qiviut smoke ring up so it covered her neck and ears. She checked the small can of pepper spray in her pocket—glad to have it with the unknown truck parked out front. Hand on the door, she took one last look at Ursula.

"Ready?"

"No."

Mim chuckled, sounding far braver than she felt. "Too bad. The best way to stop worrying about a thing you have to do—is to do that thing."

"What number Grumpy Rule is that?"

"Funny," Mim said. "Grumpy assigned numbers to his Man-Rules as he went along. There're half a dozen Rule Number Twos depending on what he thought was important on any given day . . ."

"So that was a Number Two?"

"Nope," Mim said. "That one's all me."

Ursula pushed open her door with her shoulder, grunting a little to break the frozen rubber gasket.

Crunching across the frozen gravel with each step, Mim paused at the red truck and slipped her hand out of her mitten long enough to touch the hood and feel that it was still warm. Whoever it belonged to, they'd not been here long. Arliss would have been proud of her for noticing. She patted her pocket with the pepper spray. He'd be proud of her for bringing that, too.

"This was a mistake," Ursula grumbled, ten feet from the door.

"We're here to talk, that's all," Mim said, though she couldn't shake the feeling that this all probably *was* a mistake. Curiosity drove her forward. After all, Opal Rogers was her sister-in-law.

They'd not even reached the front door to unit D before it opened a crack, just wide enough for a bearded young man to poke out his face without letting too much freezing air inside the house. Mim only got a peek, but from what she could see, he was well muscled and compactly built, probably an athlete of some kind. Scruffy with dark curly hair, he looked to be in his early twenties—much too old to be in the apartment alone with fifteen-year-old Opal.

Mim's mama bear instincts kicked in the moment she saw him. Her hand dropped to the pepper spray in her pocket at the same time she put her boot against the door, wedging it open.

The kid frowned.

"I don't know who you are, but you'll want to move that foot before you lose it."

Mim had been through far too much in the past few months to be intimidated by a man-child who happened to be able to grow a good beard. She left her boot planted where it was.

"Is Opal around?" she asked.

A female voice carried into the cold from somewhere inside the apartment.

"Who is it?"

"Some pushy bitch." The kid eyed Mim. "She's asking for you."

The door opened wider, revealing a stocky blonde wearing a white T-shirt and black leggings. Mim recognized Ethan's green eyes and Arliss's blond coloring at once—the blond version of Constance.

Opal.

The girl gasped.

"Mom? What are you doing here?"

"Wait." The boy nodded at Mim. "This pushy bitch is your mom?"

"Not that one," Opal said. "The other one."

Ursula ignored the kid, focusing instead on her daughter. "Where's your dad?"

"He's at work." Opal's hand shot to the top of her head. "I . . . I can't believe you. If you came all the way from Savannah to drag me home . . . I swear, you are wasting your time."

"Your dad's at work and you're here all alone with this guy."

The bearded man-child turned out to be a Mat-Su College nursing student named Brad. He stayed glued to the girl's side.

"Daddy says there's no custody agreement," Opal said. "You're not divorced."

Ursula's lips began to quiver. "Pack your things."

Brad put his arm around the girl's shoulders. "She's not going anywhere—"

Mim cleared her throat. "How old are you?"

"Old enough to know this isn't your house," he said.

"I'm guessing twenty-one," Mim said. "Maybe twenty-two."

Ursula looked from Brad to her daughter. She yanked her phone out of her coat pocket and started punching in numbers. "Does your daddy let you have boys over like this when he's not around?"

"Of course not," Opal said. "Brad loves me, Mama. Nothing's happened—"

"You don't have to talk to them," Brad said. "Just tell them to leave and I'll take care of it—"

Opal squirmed like she was uncomfortable with the embrace.

Mim's fingers thumbed the safety cap off the pepper spray in her pocket.

"That girl's fifteen years old," Mim said. "You need to get your hands off her."

Brad squeezed Opal's shoulders, drawing her closer. "I don't know who you think you are, but she wants you to go. Now!"

Mim gave a deranged chuckle. She'd had it with this kid. "I'll tell you who I am. I'm the one saving your life by not calling Opal's brother. You need to take your shit and go. Now."

"Nice try—"

Opal pulled away, staring wide-eyed at Mim. "Are you serious?" The girl wheeled toward Ursula. "Mama, is that true? I have a brother?"

In the middle of giving her husband an earful over the phone, Ursula looked up and gave an embarrassed nod.

"Yes," Mim said. "You have a brother—and I swear to you, if he were here right now, he would put a boot through Boo-radly's ass—and there's not a thing any of us could do to stop him." She pasted on a smile. "He knows we're here and is expecting a call from me anytime. Shall we take care of that now?"

Ursula ended her call and shoved the phone back in her pocket. "Your daddy's on his way home right now."

"We don't have to sit here and listen to this." Brad tried to put an arm around Opal again, but she shrugged him off, focused on Mim like he wasn't even there.

"A brother?" the girl whispered again. "What's his name?"

Brad put a hand on Opal's arm. "Come on, sweetie," he said. "You don't have to listen to them."

Again, she shrugged him off.

Mim took the girl by the hand and pulled her closer.

"His name is Arliss." She turned to meet Brad's eye. "You should beat feet unless you want to register as a sex offender for the rest of your life."

Brad came up on his toes like he might throw a punch. "Come on, Opal." He actually snapped his fingers, summoning her like a dog. "We're leaving." He took her by the elbow.

Mim pulled the pepper spray out of her pocket.

"Give me that," Ursula said, snatching the canister from Mim's hand and emptying it into young Brad's face. "She is fifteen years old, asshole! I'm an old woman and the worst mother on the planet but the last thing you need to worry about right now is the cops."

Brad fled out the door choking, trailing tears and snot. He never looked back.

Ursula pulled her daughter into a bear hug, both of them crying and coughing from the cloud of pepper spray that filled the room. "Grab your coat," she sputtered. "We'll wait for your daddy in the van."

Mim fought the urge to rub her eyes as she peeked out the miniblinds to make sure Brad was gone and hadn't done something stupid like gone to his truck for a gun.

"Damn . . . Ursula . . ." she said through spasms of coughing as she turned around, desperately trying to blink away the sting in her eyes. "Arliss . . . inherited more . . . from you than . . . I realized."

Ursula herded her daughter out the door.

"Poor thing," she said.

# CHAPTER 24

*Anchorage*
*22° below*

$A$RLISS CUTTER DREW A RED CIRCLE AROUND THE DIAGRAM OF THE cabin where Royce Decker and Suzi Massey were supposed to be staying and then capped the dry-erase marker, stepping away from the board.

Butch Pritchard had sung like the proverbial canary in order to keep lethal injection off the table. Not only did he confirm Cutter's suspicions about Decker's location, but he gave up the design and whereabouts of the improvised explosives, fishhooks, and trail cameras the former SWAT officer had set around the perimeter. The former cop had chosen a spot where virtually every possible approach could be turned into a kill box.

The District of Alaska Marshals Service conference room was relatively small as government conference rooms went, with just enough space for a long oval table, twelve Herman Miller chairs, and a couple of boxy sofas manufactured by prison industries. A two-foot silver star hung in the center of the long wall opposite the door, flanked with a large grizzly bear rug on the left and a black bear rug on the right, both on loan from US Fish and Wildlife Service—"Fish and Feathers" to the deputies. A scrimshawed walrus tusks stood guard on the far wall as soon as you came in the door, along with the requisite John Wayne and Tommy Lee Jones *U.S. Marshals* movie posters.

Cutter had spent the last hour lining out the details of his loose tactical plan for everyone who would be involved in the operation. To his right, at the head of the table, Chief Deputy Jill Phillips leaned back in her chair and tapped a pencil on her leather folio in thought. DUSM pilot Micki Frank sat to Cutter's immediate left listening, nodding when she agreed, raising a brow when she did not.

The decorated V-22 Osprey pilot had spent more than a few hours downrange dropping other Marines into hot zones. Nearly fifty, she was just a couple of years from the KMA Club when federal law enforcement could take early retirement. She could likely have had Cutter's job had she wanted it but had zero desire to promote if it took her out of the cockpit. Like any good pilot, she saw things as they were, not as she wished them to be. Had she not been so busy hauling deputies around Alaska in the district Cessna Caravan or the 185 on floats, Cutter would have lobbied hard to get her assigned to the fugitive-hunting side of the house.

Lola slumped down in her chair at the other end of the table alongside deputies Blodgett and Hart and Task Force Officer Nancy Alvarez. Fairbanks deputies and their Alaska State Trooper detachment counterparts participated through secure video conference.

Chief Phillips was tall and fit with mouse-brown hair that she kept cut short and no-nonsense. The mother of a toddler, not to mention fifteen deputy United States marshals—who were also prone to whine—left her with a tired, bedraggled look. Like the rest of the deputies in the conference room, she wore khaki 5.11 slacks and a blue three-button polo with a silver star embroidered over the left breast. Her badge was clipped to her belt forward of her Marshals-issue Glock 23.

"Let me make sure I understand," the chief said, in a slightly exhausted drawl. "This is your plan in a nutshell. Be where you're not expected to be and do what you're not expected to do—thereby surprising the hell out of this guy?"

"Yes, ma'am," Cutter said.

She glanced at her notes, running her pencil down the margin as if looking for a particular point she wanted to make. "When does this Officer Joe Ikeda arrive? Are you picking him up?"

"He's flying directly to Fairbanks later tonight," Cutter said. "Paul and Ryan are picking him up."

"Are the Fairbanks deputies going to babysit him?" Alvarez asked. "He was Decker's partner for eight years. Do we trust him?"

"His wife and Heather Decker were best friends," Lola said. "He sounded pretty torn up about the whole thing when I talked to him. I think we're good."

"Man," Blodgett said. "That's messed up having to help trap your partner." He turned toward Alvarez and gave what he surely thought was an endearing grin. "You wouldn't do that to me, would you?"

"Hell, Sean, I'll do it right now." Alvarez took out her phone and glanced at the chief. "What's that number for Internal Affairs?"

Blodgett gave her an air smooch.

Phillips let her head fall sideways against the chair. She looked at DUSM Frank. "What do you think, Micki?" she asked. "Are you going to be able to get them up there in this nonsense?"

A head shorter than Phillips, but with the same accent and features, the former Marine pilot could have been the chief's older sister.

"Fairbanks International Airport is showing thirty-one below zero right now," she said. "Which sucks when you're on the ground but it's imminently flyable." She held up her iPad to display a blue orb superimposed over a map of Alaska. Everyone at the table leaned forward to look. "However, this bad mama jama of an extreme low-pressure system bulging down from the Arctic may give us some cause for concern. When and if it does sink into Fairbanks, we're looking at sixty to seventy degrees below zero, possibly even colder. They're talking record lows."

"Well, ain't that toasty," Blodgett said, smug as ever.

Paige Hart, originally from Texas and relatively new to Alaska and its brutal weather, exhaled slowly. "Colder than seventy below? How often does that even happen?"

"Never, my dear," Micki said. "Or, almost never, at least on this side of the Bering Strait. That kind of winter weather isn't at all uncommon for our Siberian neighbors. And life goes on. What does not go on is air travel in small planes. Commercial airliners fly at altitude in those kinds of temps all the time but reciprocating engines—and even a turbine like the Caravan—don't do well when it's that cold. Alaska State Trooper air wing sets their no-go at fifty below. The airplane specs say minus fifty-two for the Caravan. Jet fuel without any additive starts to freeze around that point."

"Frozen fuel," Lola said. "I reckon that wouldn't be fun."

"Seventy below zero," Hart said again. "I'm just having trouble imagining what that would do to my body."

"You may not have to imagine," the chief said. "Make sure and double-check all your winter gear. If it's a crucial piece like gloves, take two pair."

"There's not enough gear on God's green earth to keep me warm at seventy below zero," Lola said from the end of the conference table.

"These Arctic systems are notoriously fragile," Micki said. "Chances are this low will stall over the Brooks Range. I'll know more in the morning."

"I guess we'll see then," Phillips said.

"Something else," Micki said. "The northern lights could actually become a factor with navigation. Sunspot activity is predicted to be off the charts for the next few days—which could, in theory, wreak havoc on my instruments."

"Well, shit!" Nancy Alvarez spun her ink pen like a top on the conference table. "Who had solar storms and a polar vortex on the How-the-World-Ends office pool?"

"Anyway," Micki said. "It looks flyable for the time being. I'd give us better than ninety percent odds."

Phillips stood, ending the meeting. The Fairbanks deputies and their trooper counterparts logged off the call.

Lola glanced up, shaking her head as if coming out of a stupor. "So, you're saying there's only ten percent chance we'll die in a fiery crash?"

"What? No." Micki chuckled. "Ten percent chance we won't fly at all. I can guaran-damn-tee no fiery crashes on my airplane, my dear."

"Can you though?" Lola whispered, half to herself. "Anyway, I need to go home and pack."

"Lola," Phillips said as the others began to file out of the conference room. "Would you mind waiting outside. It'll be just a minute."

A deer in the headlights, Lola nodded.

"I . . . Yes, of course, Chief."

"Hang back a minute, Big Iron." Phillips never missed the opportunity to needle him about his choice to carry his grandfather's Colt Python revolver as his "secondary" weapon.

She took a seat once everyone had gone, and motioned for Cutter to do the same. He was too tired to even try and hide his groan. This obviously wasn't going to be a short meeting.

"I didn't want to jump down the chain of command without talking to her supervisor first," Phillips said.

"You're the chief," he said.

"I'm concerned that incident on the ice really did a number on her."

"How could it not? But without Lola we wouldn't have found Pritchard, which means we wouldn't be this close to Decker."

Phillips stared down at the table, bouncing her pencil on the notebook again. "I have to be honest with you. I'm not just worried about Teariki."

"Meaning?"

"If you are anything, Arliss Cutter, it's self-aware. You know exactly what I mean. I'm the first one to admit that your personal life is none of my business—until it bleeds into the job. But . . ." Her voice trailed off while she studied the Alaska brown bear rug on the wall. "How many fugitive cases would you say you're working at the moment?"

"Felony warrants on the books?" he said. "Hundreds including state and local. The task force is actively working somewhere around forty-three. I can get the exact numbers."

"Tomorrow that number will be forty-seven because you'll get five warrants for new dipshits to take the place of Decker after you arrest him. It never ends. This last couple of months has to have been hard for you. The injuries from catching your brother's killer, your relationship with Mim, your mother showing up out of the blue. It'd be easy to lose focus."

"All due respect, Chief," Cutter said, jaws tight. "Please point out to me when I've lost focus?"

"That came out wrong," Phillips said. "You haven't, at least not that I've seen. But Royce Decker is probably the most dangerous warrant we've seen in the district for some time. I wouldn't be a very good leader if I didn't check your pulse before you head north."

"I get it," Cutter said.

"You know, Big Iron, your home life is your business. It's got to be hard with your mother here, but you don't seem to be bringing any of that baggage to work. Honestly, I don't worry too much about your mental state when it comes to the work or even sunspots playing thunder with Micki's GPS. It's those little things we don't know about that get us."

"Okay . . ." Cutter said.

"Look," she said. "I'm trying to say, ops plans on top of ops plans won't stop that turtle that crawls out in front of your motorcycle tire at just the wrong time. You and Lola are both perfectionists—in different ways, but nonetheless perfectionists. You take the weight of the world on your shoulders. Stop it! Lola fell through the ice. It wasn't your fault. We can do all the planning in the world and someone on your team may still get one of Royce Decker's hanging fishhooks in their eyeball."

She pushed up from the table, standing again. "And on that cheery note, would you send Lola in."

"Okay," Cutter said. "But someday, you're gonna have to tell me that story about the turtle."

# CHAPTER 25

*Fairbanks*
*31° below*

JOSIE LUJAN SWITCHED OFF EVERY LIGHT IN HER SECOND-FLOOR HOTEL room, even going so far as to wrap the bathroom nightlight in damp toilet paper. She wanted to make doubly sure she wasn't backlit before separating the miniblinds just enough to peer out to the snow-covered parking lot below.

A diehard planner, she'd done gobs of research on Alaska as soon as she learned that was where the government had set up her son with his new life. She knew intellectually that Fairbanks was not far south of the Arctic Circle and got little light during the winter months. The early afternoon darkness was surprising, but the cold—this was ridiculous.

Now she couldn't shake the feeling that someone was following her, and that made her even colder. Maybe it was nerves, her mind playing tricks on her, but there was no doubt that people wanted to murder her son. Something felt off, ever since she'd gotten on the plane in Phoenix.

Her room was warm enough, but the heater could only do so much, and the windows were fringed in frost, forcing her to part the blinds much farther than she'd anticipated in order to get a peek outside. The parking lot looked like something out of a science fiction film. Dozens of vehicles, mostly trucks and SUVs, were plugged into upright posts, meant to keep their engine blocks from freezing. Hotel guests came and went, heavily bundled against the bitter cold. From her angle they looked like eggs with feet, kicking their way through swirls of ground fog in the no-man's-land between hotel and vehicle. Many of the SUVs had been left running, producing great clouds of pooling vapor from the exhaust, obscuring the wheels and giving the vehicles the appearance of floating over the frozen pavement. Darkness combined with the angle made it impossible to tell if any of the cars were occupied—if anyone was watching her.

Josie stood at the window and watched until her nose grew cold—which didn't take long. She turned, careful not to move the blinds in case someone really was out there, and dug the phone out of her bag. She opened the Signal app and stood staring at it for a time. An online search had shown no pay phones in Fairbanks. Calling Sam from the cell was risky, probably even on Signal, but he was waiting for her. She needed to warn him.

She punched in the number—it wasn't in her contacts. In the rare instances she had called him from her phone she'd always cleared her history.

Sam answered immediately. His voice was tight with worry—like she felt.

"Where are you?"

"Listen to me, Piñon," she said. "I think someone is following me."

"Are you sure?"

"No, I'm not sure," Josie said, downplaying her instincts. "But who am I to second-guess a feeling that could protect my son. I think it would be safer if I stay at a hotel tonight. I'll slip out and go for a drive sometime early tomorrow morning. I imagine there won't be many cars on the road, then. Should be easy enough to spot anyone trying to follow me."

"Okay . . ." He sounded unconvinced.

"You should go to a friend's house," she said.

"Now you're really being paranoid," Sam said. "Valeria doesn't know where I live. If she did, she would have killed me already."

"Sam—"

"I'll be fine, Mom," he said.

"Have you got protection?"

"What?"

"A gun, Naiche," she said, using the Apache name she'd given him when he was a small boy. "Do you have a gun?"

"I'm not supposed to."

"That wasn't my question."

"Yes," he said. "I do. Now stop being so crazy."

"I'm your mother," Josie said. "It's my job to be crazy as a rabid fox when it comes to you."

"Just be careful," he said. "If you're right, and someone is following you, you're in as much danger as I am."

"Now who's being crazy," Josie said. "Besides, you're not the only one with a gun."

Gant parked the rented Jeep Compass on the west side of the Sophie Station hotel complex. He'd watched Josie hustle across the parking lot toward registration with her roller bag and backpack.

A backpack. It took a special kind of crazy to go hiking in this miserable weather. It was a moot point. This whole mess would be put to bed long before mother or son had a chance.

The trip almost ended not long after they left the airport. Josie had driven north over icy roads up a treacherous hill to what turned out to be the University of Alaska Fairbanks. At first, Gant thought maybe the kid was a student, and she was going to meet him there. Instead, she'd dropped down off the hillside to head east on the Johansen Expressway, eventually turning south to cross the Chena River. She took an exit into downtown where she worked her way back and forth before getting on the expressway again.

Gant had to hide a smile. This woman was impressive. She was trying to shake a tail—or see if she had one.

*Way to go, Josie!*

Gant and Halverson took turns leapfrogging, taking and giving up the eye on the rented Subaru Outback. It was still early, despite the darkness, just the beginning of rush hour. SUVs and trucks filled the narrow streets and slick highways, producing clouds of vapor as they emerged from the ice fog only to disappear again.

Keeping Josie's vehicle in sight became more of a problem than being seen by her.

She'd eventually driven to the hotel, throwing furtive glances over her shoulders as she crossed the parking lot with her backpack and bag.

Every four parking places in the Sophie's Station hotel lot had an upright post with electrical outlets to plug in as many engine block or oil pan heaters. Half a dozen vehicles or more, mostly diesels, rattled away like so many fog machines in the bitter cold. It helped Gant's idling Jeep to blend in.

"Look," John Blackwell said from the passenger seat. "I'm not saying you're wrong but could be you're not completely right either."

Gant put the binoculars to his eyes and spoke into his hands, glancing quickly sideways, not wanting to miss any movement in the window.

"What exactly are you trying to say, John?"

"Maybe the kid is here," Blackwell continued. "But maybe she's not going to meet—"

Gant lowered the binoculars and turned on the other man. "The phone call," he said, more sharply than he'd intended. "Why does everyone keep forgetting about the call?"

A smug look crept over Blackwell's face. "You ever think there might have been another call? Or two or three on a line you didn't trap?"

"Of course I did," Gant conceded. "But I heard them make a specific plan to meet in Fairbanks. And now here she is in Fairbanks. Any other calls would only have been to work out the details."

"Details we don't—"

Blackwell's phone buzzed on the console between the two men. Gant didn't recognize the number, but Blackwell straightened up in his seat when he answered, like it was someone important. Valeria Kot's mumbling buzz poured out until he pressed the device closer to his ear.

"Yes . . . Yes . . ." Blackwell said. "I'm explaining it to him now . . . Yes . . ." He checked his watch. "They get here a little before seven tomorrow morning . . . Yes. I'll let you know when it's done."

He ended the call and set the phone back on the console.

"That was the boss."

"I heard as much." Gant glared at the other man, imagining a bullet hole between his eyes. "I got us where we are. Why is she calling you?"

Blackwell shrugged. "The boss is the boss," he said. "She calls who she calls."

"Sounds like you're pretty cozy with her."

"Lot of things changed in New York while you've been in the desert."

"Sounds like it," Gant said. "What is it you're supposed to tell me about?"

"The thing is," Blackwell said, "Valeria thinks you might . . . how do I put this . . . that you might be going a little soft on the professor."

"Soft?" Gant wanted to throttle the other man. "I'm the one who told Valeria about her trip to Alaska. Why in the world would she think . . ." Looking at his partner's face, he knew exactly why.

"Come on, Bobby," Blackwell said. "We all see the way you look at her with those puppy-dog eyes. Every time you say her name you sound like a lovesick schoolboy."

The muscles in Gant's neck tensed like cables. "And you told all this to Valeria?"

Another shrug. "I told her what I saw. Don't take it personally. You'd do the same and you know it."

Gant shifted in his seat, feeling the weight of the pistol that he wanted so badly to use at this moment. A bullet in Blackwell's face wouldn't solve a single problem, but it would feel oh so good to put one there. He pushed the urge back where it came from. Impulsiveness pushed you down the ladder, not up it.

"You're wrong." He feigned a smile. "But whatever. I got nothing to prove."

"That's the spirit," Blackwell said. "The kid is probably close by, maybe even in this hotel. If the professor doesn't lead us to him soon, we'll grab her and take her someplace private. It might take a while, but she'll give him up eventually."

"And you came up with this idea?"

"Look," Blackwell said. "We both know Mads and Browny aren't the type to sit around on their thumbs. They're apt to start breaking things the minute they step onto this ice planet if they don't have a job. We need to give them the right shit to break."

Gant raised the binoculars again, seething. "You're not only an asshole," he said, "you're an idiot." He closed his eyes, pretending to look at the hotel. It wouldn't do any good to say what he was actually thinking. "We are on the verge of Josie leading us to the rat we been hunting for four years—and you guys cannot dredge up the patience to wait a couple more hours?"

"Do you even hear yourself?" Blackwell said. "You know you're the only one who calls her Josie?"

"This is bullshit," Gant said.

"Think about it, Bobby," Blackwell said. "Maybe she snapped to us following her. If that's the case, we need to grab her sooner rather than later. She could be calling her kid as we speak and telling him to haul ass outta Dodge."

"And if she hasn't," Gant said, "we tip our hand."

"No." Blackwell threw back his head and groaned, as if trying to explain things to a small child. "I'm telling you, it will not matter in the long run. She leads us to him—we whack them both. We snatch her, introduce her to a few power tools . . . You know the drill." He laughed at his own joke. "She tells us where he is. Either way, they both get whacked. We'll grab her in the morning if she hasn't led us to the kid already. We're supposed to have Mommy tied up and ready for them to do the wet work."

"I'm calling Valeria," Gant said.

"Go for it," Blackwell said. "I already ran everything by her. She says if you can't live with it you need to get your ass back to New York."

Blackwell's right hand had dropped out of sight between the seat and the door—surely gripping the butt of his pistol.

"So you're good with this?"

Gant scoffed. "I always knew how this was going to end," he said. He looked at the other man and smiled. *Just maybe not the way you're thinking.*

# CHAPTER 26

*Anchorage*
*23° below*

$G$EAR FOR THE EXTREME COLD WASN'T ESPECIALLY HEAVY, BUT IT took up heaps of space. Lola had to sit on her overstuffed Cordura duffel in order to zip it shut.

She was at the point in her career when the T-shirts she'd bought at Sally's Cop Shop during her four months of Marshals Basic were beginning to get a little threadbare. Time for her to go to advance training so she could buy some replacements. The gray one she wore now had an understated shield marked 1789 (the year the USMS was founded) over the left breast. A sagging collar and cooking oil spots on the belly were a testament to the fact that it was her favorite shirt.

The heater in her condo barely kept up and it was far too cold outside to sleep in her usual tank top and running shorts. The pink terry cloth sweat bottoms were comfortable enough, but the drawstring was broken and they kept wanting to sag low around her hips. Joe Bill seemed to like them alright—probably for that reason.

Hitching up the sweats, Lola padded barefoot into the hallway and stacked clean wool skivvies, thick socks, and the outer layers of clothing she planned to wear in the morning on a chair outside her bedroom. Her new parka was so big it kept falling off the coatrack, so she just left it in a heap on the floor.

Joe Bill called to her from the bedroom.

"Why are you taking all your clothes out there?"

She leaned her head around the corner. "I have to get dressed at three o'clock in the morning and I don't want to wake up my boyfriend."

"Stuff that," Joe Bill said, using one of Lola's favorite euphemisms. "I'm not letting you out of here tomorrow morning without saying goodbye." He tossed his phone on the nightstand and swung his legs off the bed. His white cotton T-shirt showed off his chest. "What can I do to help?"

Lola raised a wary brow. "You want to help because I need help or help so you can get me into bed quicker?"

Joe Bill checked his watch and then gave an impish grin. "Bit of both, if I'm honest."

"Good answer." She bent to pick up her rifle from a case on the floor beside the bed. "You can put fresh batteries in my lights. There's some 123s and my extra SureFire in the drawer by the bed."

Joe Bill gave her a thumbs-up and pitched in, only broaching the subject of her mental health twice. She deflected both times, which he pointed out was a symptom of a bigger problem—until she threatened to shoot him with her Taser.

An hour later, with all essential gear double-checked and packed, Lola pulled back the duvet and climbed into bed beside Joe Bill. She scootched in close and lay her head on his chest, draping an arm and leg across his body.

He groaned playfully under the weight of her. "Feeling parasitic tonight, are we."

She nestled deeper against his chest, drawing him tighter. "I reckon I am, a little."

"And I'm completely fine with that," he said.

They lay there in silence for a time, her listening to his heartbeat, him toying with her hair.

"You know," she said, "if anything happens to me, you should totally hook up with that redheaded chick on patrol."

Joe Bill pulled away enough to look her in the eye.

"What redheaded chick?"

She gave his ribs a little nudge with the point of a knuckle. "You know exactly who I mean. The one who looks like she wants to eat my liver every time she sees me."

"Ah," Joe Bill said. "That redhead. You mean Sandy Jackson. Yeah, she's not much of a federal fan girl. I always think of her hair as auburn."

Lola put the knuckle to his ribs again, slightly harder this time.

He flinched, laughing. "Hey, I'm not the one who brought her up."

"Anywaaay," Lola said, patting the spot over his ribs. "If anything did ever happen to me, she'd be a good one for you."

"Nothing's going to happen to you."

"That's not the point," Lola said. "You're supposed to say, 'I'd never go with her or any woman. I'd be too busy weeping over you.'" She raised up on one elbow, her face hovering over his. "But seriously, if something happens to me, I wouldn't want you to be alone."

He lay there for a long time, looking up at her, then said, "I wouldn't go with her or any woman. I'd be too busy weeping over you."

Lola patted his chest and fell back into the crook of his arm. "Smart boy."

They lay together for a long time, listening to each other breathe. Lola broke the silence.

"You ever think how when most people say goodbye to their significant other, they really mean 'see you at five o'clock' but when we say it, we might well be saying an honest-to-God goodbye . . . as in lights out, kaput, the big *ka kite.*"

"Falling through the ice like that must have been—"

"I can't lie," she said. "It was horrible. But I reckon I'm more pissed at myself than anything."

"It wasn't your fault—"

She came up on her elbow again and rested her head on her hand, meeting his eye. "Royce Decker would already be in jail if I hadn't let that shitbag slip away."

"I really am worried about you."

"I know." She collapsed against his chest again. "I'm worried about me, too. The chief told me something today after the briefing. I reckon it's true enough. I'm just having a hard time putting it into practice."

"What's that?"

"I should have written it down exactly like she said it, but it was something like, *When we take a test and fail, the thing we think is the test isn't the real test. The actual test is the way we handle the failure.*"

"That Jill Phillips is a wise woman," Joe Bill said.

"She was paraphrasing Einstein or Marcus Aurelius. But still."

"Words to live by," Joe Bill said. "Whoever they come from."

He hugged her tight, kissing the top of her head.

"I fail a lot though."

"Lola!" he chided.

She tapped a finger on the point of his chin then ran it down his chest. "Come on," she said. "I just remembered something I am really good at."

# CHAPTER 27

*P*RIOR TO ANY OUT-OF-TOWN TRIP OR ASSIGNMENT, CUTTER MADE IT a habit to lay out his gear on the bed so he could get a visual. The weather forecast for Fairbanks was beyond brutal and he wanted to make doubly sure the things he needed for his trip ended up in his bags. On the internet they called it *knolling*. Some people built their entire online presence around photos of neatly arranged stuff—tactical and otherwise. Scrolling through such pages was a guilty pleasure Cutter admitted to no one, not even Lola.

Packing was a mundane chore, but doing it correctly was vital. Besides, it was a good way to settle his mind from the tsunami of emotions that had crashed into the house. Ursula was more than pissed at her estranged husband, and Cutter didn't even want to think about the scumbag twenty-year-old kid who was trying to get into his half sister's pants—a sister he didn't know he had, let alone had ever met. He hated the idea of leaving Mim to handle all this by herself.

He'd put in for a couple weeks off after this to make it up to her, maybe take the family someplace warm—and let his mother deal with her own shit. They could invite Opal.

First, he had to arrest Royce Decker—and to do that, he needed to have the right gear to operate in the frozen north.

Cutter had watched Grumpy lay out his equipment time and time again before he headed into the Everglades on assignment or on an overnighter out on Gasparilla Sound. When it came to gear, internet pundits often fixated on the sexy stuff: guns, knives, and an endless list of the latest doodads like tactical crowbars or notepads you could write on when it was pouring rain. Cutter had carried many of these items—on occasion. But his everyday carry—his EDC—consisted of five things—a sidearm, a knife, a light, a handkerchief, and something to make fire. The twins knew it and challenged him to see if he had it all virtually every time they saw him leave the house, going so far as to make him ignite his battered orange Zippo to make sure he'd not forgotten to top off the fluid.

EDC weapons were important, vital in his line of work, but in Alaska the odds of freezing to death were much greater than those of getting shot—most of the time.

Like his grandfather taught him, Cutter started FSO—from the skin out—when planning his gear. He began with a base layer of merino wool, then followed that with as many as four layers of outerwear varying in thickness and material. He could shed or add layers depending on how much he sat static vs how much he had to move. Snowshoeing looked much easier in nature documentaries than it was in real life. It was far too easy to become drenched in sweat. Wool was king in the cold, right down to his socks. Cotton was great in Florida. It was the enemy of cold weather survival.

Extreme cold called for extreme footwear. For this operation he opted for a hiking style boot called a Baffin Borealis. Completely waterproof with a removable insulating liner, they could be combined with NEOS overboots for operations well below minus thirty.

For vitally important items like batteries and ammunition, Cutter erred on the side of caution. His time in the Army had taught him that two was one and one was none. Fairbanks wasn't exactly the end of the earth, but it was the frontier, and Salcha, south of Eielson Air Force Base some thirty miles out of Fairbanks, was little more than a wide spot on a very cold and lonely road. It wasn't the place to try and resupply.

He threw in a half dozen extra 123A batteries for his SureFire and some triple As for his headlamp in a pocket near his body to keep the cold from killing them dead. The window of usable daylight in Fairbanks was nearing its shortest point. It was a safe bet they'd be operating in the dark.

The layered clothing and bulky parkas necessary to survive Arctic conditions made reaching a sidearm problematic. For this operation, Cutter opted for a Diamond D chest rig giving him easier access to his grandfather's Colt Python revolver. The Glock 27 would stay on his hip, keeping him within USMS policy.

Three HKS speed loaders held a total of eighteen .357 Magnum rounds for the Colt—plus the six already in the gun. The Glock 27 carried ten in the magazine plus one in the chamber. Three mags of .40 cal Gold Dot gave him thirty more rounds to feed the baby beast if it came to that. In situations where he expected a gunfight, he relied far more on his rifle than any sidearm. His USMS issue Colt M4 had a 14-inch barrel, holographic sight, and HUXWRKS FLOW suppressor. The glass on the sight was covered with a good helping of Cat Crap, an antifog substance he swore by in Alaska winters. He packed six twenty-round magazines for the M4. Though heavy, he'd never known anyone in the military or the Marshals Service to complain about having too many bullets.

He sorted the rest of his gear—water bladder (with insulated hose and bite valve), an incredibly warm sea otter hat, and large beaver-fur mittens—gifts from Birdie Pingayak, an Alaska Native friend from the Kuskokwim River village of Stone Cross.

Soft footfalls on the wood floor caused him to turn. He smiled when he saw it was Mim and dropped the fur hat on the bed beside the rifle mags. He tended to forget things when he was around her and he wanted to make sure the ammo ended up in his bags.

"This is a nice surprise," he said.

Mim stepped in and kissed him, but moved away before he could take it any further—a real danger of late. She'd kissed him often since their trip to South Dakota. He was careful to let her be the one to initiate, but when she did . . .

He took a deep breath to steady himself and swept his rifle magazines toward the center of the bed, clearing a place for her to sit. "I thought you were busy on the phone with your mom."

"She had to run," Mim said, flushing a little from the kiss. This was all still very new to both of them. "She's making cookies for a church social tomorrow and it's past her bedtime in Florida." Mim picked up the hat and ran her fingers over the soft sea otter fur before putting it on and snugging the flaps down over her ears.

"Suits you," Cutter said. "And Ursula? What's she up to?"

Mim lifted a flap. "What? How do you hear in this thing?"

"I don't really," he said. "It's a trade-off between frozen ears and letting someone sneak up on me."

Mim took off the hat and pitched it back on the bed where she got it. Honey-colored hair was already sweating to her forehead. "That thing is warm."

"Yep," Cutter said.

"Anyway, your mother is on the phone with Geoff again, trying to work things out."

Cutter darkened. "Work things out?"

"You know, who gets custody of Opal if they don't get back together. She's been here six weeks, drives over there to spy on him virtually every day, and he had no idea she was even in Alaska."

"My mother the great communicator," Cutter said.

Mim picked up a black long john top and pressed it against her cheek. "I'm telling you, Arliss, she was fearless today." She brandished the underwear top as if to illustrate her sudden change of direction. "This wool is butter soft."

Cutter nodded. Mim often inserted mundane subjects into the middle of a conversation. "New Zealand wool," he said. "Lola tells me it's just like regular wool, only kinder."

Mim chuckled. "Makes sense." She set the long john top back on the pile and ran a hand over it to smooth the wrinkles. "Opal's about as shell-shocked as you," she said at length. "She desperately wants to meet you."

"I want to meet her, too," Cutter said. "As soon as I get back."

"You know, I always thought you took after Grumpy, but you and that girl really favor one another. And your mother . . . when she thought her kid was threatened . . . You must have gotten something from that woman."

Cutter gave a slow nod. "What about this college guy? Is Geoff making sure he's not coming around anymore?"

Mim ran a hand down his arm, trying to calm him. "He drove off after your mom doused him with pepper spray, but yes, Geoff and Wasilla PD have that covered. I doubt young Brad will be visiting anymore. I'm pretty sure I instilled the fear of God into him when I told him you would put a boot in his ass if you'd been there."

"Good thing I wasn't," Cutter said. "I'd be in jail right now."

"No doubt," Mim said. "But the threat of a badass older brother who happens to be a deputy United States marshal probably helped as much as the pepper spray."

"That kid hasn't ever met me," Cutter said. "Frankly, pepper spray might not even keep him away. Heck of a lot of boys throughout history have nosed around the daughters of some very dangerous men." He gave a resigned sigh. "Not to be indelicate, but there are certain parts of a man's body he will follow into places he wouldn't go with a loaded shotgun."

Mim blushed. "So I hear."

She looked at him for a long time without saying a word. In the end she just tiptoed up to kiss him again, longer this time, grabbing him by the collar with both hands as if to prevent his escape.

"I wish you didn't have to go," she said when she finally stepped away.

"Kiss me like that again and maybe I won't," Cutter said.

"You mean that?" she said. "Because I'll kiss you any way you want if—"

"Careful there, hot lips." Cutter touched her nose with the tip of his finger. "I wish I didn't have to go, too. But this guy is a really bad man—"

Mim shoved the pile of clothing to the side, clearing a space on the bed and then fell back on the mattress. Feet on the floor, she stared up at the ceiling. "I'm perfectly aware that Lola needs you right now," she said. "And I know this Royce Decker guy is an ex-cop who killed his wife. There's no doubt that he's an especially evil dude." Still on her back, she shifted her eyes downward, looking directly at Cutter. "You want to know what else I know?

There's always gonna be some evil dude for you to hunt." She threw her forearm across her face, shielding her eyes from the overhead light—and Cutter. "Arliss, we need to—"

Michael and Matthew burst into the room at that moment. If they noticed their mother was on the bed, it didn't seem to bother them. She came up on one elbow, brushing a hand across her face. Cutter did a double take. Had she wiped away a tear?

He turned his attention to the boys, who were jabbering away from the moment they came in. Their chaotic exuberance chased any other emotion out of the room—or at least kept it at bay.

"Uncle Arliss," Matthew said. "Michael and me had an idea. We were thinking that we could—" The boy hung his head when he saw the clothes and gear stacked on the bed around his mother. "Packing to leave again," he groaned. "Who woulda thought . . ."

Cutter mussed the boy's blond curls, the same way Grumpy used to tousle his before driving away in the Marine Patrol boat on some assignment. It was hard to forget how heavy his grandfather's trips had made him feel.

"I should only be gone a day or two," he said.

Michael nodded toward the rifle in the Pelican case. His eyes brightened. "Can you take us shooting with our new .22s we're getting for Christmas when you get back?"

"Wait," Mim said. "What makes you think you're getting new .22s?"

"Mom," Matthew said. "You want us to learn safety. Right?"

"Of course," she said. "But—"

"Well," Michael said, "we figure that between Uncle Arliss, Santa, and Grandma, somebody's gonna get us what we want."

Matthew flashed his mother a sly side-eye. "Plus," he said. "We saw a brick of five hundred .22 bullets in Uncle Arliss's pack and he doesn't even have a .22."

Cutter shot a sheepish look at Mim, who fell back against the mattress with an exaggerated bounce, the exhausted mother of boys. She covered her eyes with her arm again. The waist of her T-shirt rode up exposing her belly. Cutter doubted she realized it. Or maybe she did. The sight of her there was making it incredibly difficult to even think of going to Fairbanks—or anywhere.

He looked away. "I promise to take you shooting," he said. "You boys need to—"

Ursula suddenly appeared in the doorway. Like the twins, she was already midsentence when she came in, oblivious to any other conversations that might have been going on before her arrival.

". . . I've told Geoff, but he just can't get it through his thick head . . ." She paused, looking at Mim on the bed and then Cutter before shifting her gaze to the boys. She appeared to forget about her own problems. "Well, this is interesting."

The twins breezed out as quickly as they'd arrived. "Bye, Grandma," Matthew said on their way past.

"Uncle Arliss is going to take us shooting," Micheal said. "You should come."

Mim sat up, on both elbows this time. She didn't bother fixing her shirt.

"Did you need something?"

Ursula waited at the door, nodding slowly. Her face held the beginnings of something between mild amusement and uncomfortable gas.

"It's none of my business really, but—"

"That's right," Cutter said. "It is none of your business."

Ursula kept going as if she hadn't heard him. "What's that old phrase, 'I don't give a damn what you do as long as you don't do it in the street and scare the horses.'"

Cutter started to say something, but his mother cut him off.

"I'm surprised you two lovebirds don't think you should be a little more discreet in front of the children." She waved her arm around the room with a little flourish. "I mean, what are they going to think when they figure out what all this is?"

Mim sat up straight, her cheeks crimson.

Constance's voice carried in from down the hall before Mim or Cutter had time to respond. She was matter-of-fact, too bored to come out of her room.

"Relax, Grandma," she said. "We figured that out months ago."

"Hundred percent," Matthew said from the kitchen, sounding much older than his nine years. "We're not dumb, ya know."

Michael echoed the sentiment. "Hundred percent. You woulda seen it too if you woulda been here sooner."

Ursula's face reddened. "I . . ."

Mim gave her a wan smile. "I'm sure he didn't mean it like it sounded."

"It's the truth though," Cutter said. "Was there something else?"

"I . . . no. Nothing at all." Ursula shook her head and then disappeared the way she'd come in.

Mim collapsed against the mattress with a groan. This time, she covered her face with a pillow.

"That was mortifying," she said, her voice muffled.

"She's got thick skin," Cutter said.

"I hope so." She peeked out. "How much do you think the kids really know, Arliss?"

"They're smart," Cutter said. "They want their mama to be happy."

Mim clutched the pillow tight against her face.

"You know," Cutter said, "I'll get the blame if you smother yourself."

"Good," Mim said without lifting the pillow.

It was a beautiful picture, her in the middle of the bed surrounded by winter clothing and tactical gear—her soft belly still visible between her T-shirt and jeans.

Cutter chewed on his bottom lip. "You are happy, aren't you?"

The pillow moved up and down as she nodded a muffled reply. "Yes."

Nothing this perfect could ever last, not for him anyway.

"Me too," he said.

# CHAPTER 28

*Salcha*
*32° below*

*R*OYCE DECKER GRABBED A NEW LOG FOR THE FIRE, VAGUELY AWARE that Suzi was talking behind him. She believed he'd had his wife killed so he could run away and spend the rest of his life with her.

Boy was she wrong.

Decker was almost forty years old, and he'd never lived anywhere with a fireplace, let alone someplace that got all its heat from a woodstove. This one seemed on the big side. It had to be to beat back the bitter cold that crept through even the tiniest cracks between the cabin logs. He'd named it Nebuchadnezzar because it reminded him of the fiery furnace the old Babylonian king used to try and burn up those Shadrach, Meshach, and Abednego boys. That's what his mother had called them, *the Shadrach, Meshach, and Abednego boys* like it was the name of their boyband. A devout Lutheran of the strict Missouri Synod variety, Decker's mother had made damn sure she read the Bible to her three children every night when they were growing up.

Decker's sister grew into a successful accountant but had married, according to their mother, Unitarian trash. Their younger brother was in prison for scamming elderly folks out of their life savings with his roofing business. Royce was easily the favorite, followed by the grifting brother, and then the sister who'd married the Unitarian. His mother would have been proud of him for remembering the fiery furnace story, but if she'd known he hired Butch Pritchard to kill Heather, she'd have stuffed him in that furnace alongside those Israelite boys.

Dressed in jeans and a red and black buffalo plaid shirt, Decker squatted in front of the ticking woodstove and opened the door, closing his eyes against the heat that rolled out and bathed his face. When she wasn't bitching at him over their rustic circumstances, Suzi said he looked like a Cabela's catalog model.

Suzi sat on the big four-poster log bed in the corner of the cabin. Her malamute, Moose, lay on the bed beside her, head resting on her thigh, one paw over her leg, as if to stake his claim. The dog made it crystal clear every day that Suzi was his and he did not intend to give her up.

She wore a headlamp—that she kept shining directly into his eyes—and held a Russian language book in her lap.

"Still nothing from Butch?" she asked.

Decker shook his head. "Every time we communicate adds to the risk of getting intercepted."

"Right." Suzi rubbed her ginormous dog behind the ears, clucking to him softly. She was a statuesque woman with a naturally olive complexion and impossibly long legs that were meant for modeling. Her broad smile could turn into a brooding frown if things didn't go her way.

"Eight million smackaroonies to our name," she said. "You'd think we could find a place with an indoor toilet."

Decker smiled at her, picked up a wrought-iron poker and felt the heft of it in his hand. *Our name?* His look earned him a growl from her idiot dog, so he turned away to tend the fire. "I think your godmother's cabin is quaint. And anyone who can connect the two of you is either dead or in this with us, so it's off the radar. You said Tina doesn't even know about it."

"She doesn't," Suzi said. "It was before her time. Listen to me, Royce, a couple of weeks out here is fine, but I wouldn't mind a place with running water. Besides, it's going to get awfully cramped when Butch gets back with Tina."

The dog licked its lips, gazing at Decker with ghostly blue eyes.

It was only a matter of time before good old Moose tore out his throat. Maybe the fat fur ball wasn't such an idiot after all. Maybe Decker's face gave away his plans. Fyodor Pugo had made it clear that there would be "no filthy dogs allowed" on this trip. Decker hadn't mentioned that to Suzi because it really didn't matter. She wasn't going either. It was laughable how she trailed along, bitching at him one minute, dreaming about how they were going to spend all "their" money the next. The simple fact was that bringing her along was a simpler way to keep her quiet than the alternative. She was decent enough to look at, and certainly kept him warm in bed when the fire burned down at night, but Suzi had to have some serious mental issues if she thought she was such a catch that a man would pay someone to murder his pregnant wife and flee to Russia just to be with her.

A romantic, Royce Decker was not. This plan had been in the works for almost three years, ever since he'd arrested one of Fyodor Pugo's associates. Decker had worked a little magic and made twenty-six kilos of cocaine disappear from the evidence locker. He stood to earn fifty grand for fixing it so the mope walked. It was a tidy sum, but instead of taking money, he asked the Russian for a raincheck.

Losing the coke wasn't Officer Decker's first time to cross the line. He'd started bending ethics rules in the academy and never looked back—planted evidence, shaken down his share of dealers, skimmed a little dope to trade to the girls at the strip clubs across the state line in Washington Park. He knew he would eventually get caught. There was no doubt about that. A couple of the guys from his shift had gone from patrol to Internal Affairs—the Rat Squad. They knew him too well for his own good and were just waiting to jam him up so they could hang another scalp on their belt. He'd have to run eventually and might as well do it on his terms. It was a good thing to have an influential friend who owed him a favor. Even if that friend was in Russia.

Royce Decker had a plan, and it was a damn good one.

A hell of a lot of cash came through the PD evidence locker. It wouldn't be as easy to make disappear as the dope. Evidence techs took special care with money, photographing each bill and logging the serial numbers, but if there was ever a big enough haul to make it worth running, he'd need a place to run where the government couldn't haul his ass back for prosecution. That's where the Russian came in.

Decker had first set his benchmark at six million. He'd seen some cartel bundles come in around that amount. Then Internal Affairs had interviewed a couple of his favorite hookers from East St. Louis. He should have dumped them in the Mississippi river a long time ago. Prostitutes made great informants but, they made poor witnesses. IA didn't have a case against him yet, but it was only a matter of time.

He lowered the "go" number to two million. The investment guys on Instagram said you could draw four percent a year and not touch the principle. Eighty grand a year in Russia would be better than prison. Probably.

He just had to wait for two million to show up in evidence.

And show up it did when a seventy-two-year-old retired high school guidance counselor named Bonita Turpin fled a traffic stop on the Mark Twain Expressway. Nobody could blame her for trying. Her Cadillac Blackwing's 6.2-liter supercharged V8 took her from zero to sixty in 3.4 seconds. The traffic officer's Impala proved no match for the Caddy until Turpin lost control and slammed into a concrete barrier at over a hundred and thirty miles an hour. Firefighters used the Jaws of Life to pry her from the vehicle. She was transported to the hospital in critical condition.

The Blackwing was impounded as evidence and taken to the PD warehouse where Decker happened to be photographing a panel van used in a hostage situation where SWAT had responded. It was busy work, assigned to him because his sergeant didn't want him going on callouts until this thing with IA was cleared up.

Burned and twisted metal was like a magnet to Decker—and most humans for that matter. You never knew what kind of body parts you'd find after the fact. As a rookie he'd found a human toe lodged between the cushions in the rear seats of a Suburban. Alone in that corner of the warehouse, he checked out the wrecked Caddy—and found a duffel full of hundred-dollar bills wedged behind the passenger seat. It was heavy, well over fifty pounds. At first, he thought this might be an Internal Affairs sting operation, but the wreck had happened too fast to get a bag-o-Benjamins lined up just to set a trap.

You make enough drug arrests, and you learn that a million in hundreds weighs about twenty-two pounds. Decker estimated this bag was well over fifty as he'd lugged it to his SUV—at least two million. A quick search of the trunk revealed two more identical bags. Three bags in all, each of which turned out to weigh just over sixty pounds. Over eight million dollars.

He'd end up with seven after Pugo took his cut. Favors only went so far among businessmen. The Russian kept his end of the bargain and got things rolling at once.

Bonnie Turpin was in a medically induced coma and the drug cartel she worked for wasn't about to step forward and claim their eight million. No one would have been the wiser, until Decker's wife went poking around in the shed looking for her hot-glue gun.

Heather watched the news. An accident involving a seventy-two-year-old grandma with a record for running drugs and cash was enough to tell her where the money came from. She cried and screamed and invoked their baby's good name for two solid hours. Eventually, she'd calmed enough to draw her line in the sand. He had to put the money back or she'd tell his partner.

Decker had thought about bringing Joe Ikeda in on the deal, but convinced himself that would never work. Joe was an elder in his church, far too straight in the laces to take so much as a department ink pen without paying for it. Beyond that, Decker needed all the money to make his run. He wasn't about to start paying people off to keep them quiet.

Instead, he called Butch Pritchard and invited him out for a beer. Pritchard was a longtime acquaintance if not actual friend. Suzi had introduced them when Pritchard moved to St. Louis with her mousy sister, both of them running away from something. They'd never said what.

Pritchard still knew nothing about the millions and agreed to do what needed to be done for twelve thousand dollars. That night. It would be simple. An in and out job.

Heather had cried herself to sleep on the couch. Decker left with the money and in his haste, had forgotten to tell Pritchard about the cameras. After that, he had no choice but to take Pritchard with them to Alaska.

As luck would have it, Heather's killing had been relatively pointless. It all came out before he even got out of Missouri. Bonnie Turpin, driver of the Cadillac Blackwing, woke from her coma begging the authorities to put it on the news that they'd confiscated the eight million dollars that she'd been transporting. The cartel would cut her head off with a chainsaw if they believed she'd stolen it. The authorities knew nothing about the money until that moment, but it didn't take them long to put two and two together. The timing of Decker's disappearance made him a prime suspect for both the theft and his wife's murder.

Decker shrugged it off. Sure, he hadn't needed to kill Heather to hide the fact that he had the money, but he'd never wanted a kid anyway, so it all turned out for the best.

It cost an extra twenty grand, but Pugo arranged to get all three of them out of St. Louis to a dry cabin in Alaska belonging to Suzi's godmother. They were to wait there for the Russian's instructions. Two days after their arrival, Pritchard had gone to Anchorage. Suzi believed it was to pick up her sister—but that was not the plan at all. Tina didn't know much, but she was far too flighty to trust with what information she did have. Pritchard would put an end to that problem and then come north, expecting to leave with Decker and Suzi and enjoy his share of the money in Russia . . .

Decker stabbed at the burning logs with the fire poker and glanced across the cabin at Suzi and her mutt. Pritchard would arrive any time. Decker needed to take care of her before then. He'd do it after their bath.

Fyodor Pugo had been clear from the beginning. Transport to Russia was only for one.

# TUESDAY

# CHAPTER 29

*Anchorage*
*26° below*

CUTTER ARRIVED AT THE FAA HANGAR AT 4:20 A.M. LOLA HAD rolled in just ahead of him and he had followed her taillights through the parking lot to the east side of the building. Both of the USMS District of Alaska aircraft were parked in the massive beige hangar south of Ted Stevens Anchorage International Airport's east/west runways. Lola had apparently called ahead because the gargantuan door slid open as they pulled up. Blindingly bright gymnasium lights spilled out into the ice-covered parking lot, gleaming off the waxed white floor of the hangar. The head mechanic, a jovial, Santa Claus of a man wearing insulated Carhartt coveralls and two wool hats waved them inside. Pete was good that way. If the hangar was too full to allow them to park inside, he at least let them drive inside to unload. At the moment along with the relatively diminutive Marshals Service Caravan and 185 on wheel skis, they housed an FAA Bombardier Challenger, a NOAA Lockheed Orion "Hurricane Hunter," and an FBI Gulfstream, leaving only enough room for Micki's green Hemi Dodge Durango to stay inside.

Tires squeaked over the highly polished floor as they drove through the door. Alvarez and Hart stood by the Caravan chatting with Micki. They'd already unloaded their gear and moved their vehicles outside. Each was dressed in snow bibs and heavy boots but had taken their parkas off in the warmth of the hangar. Belt badges riding by sidearms or hanging on neck chains glinted like jewelry under the bright lights.

Cutter dragged his two duffels and Pelican case out of his Ford and met Lola as she lugged her gear toward the airplane. He waved at Pete, who was busy checking out some piece of electronics.

"We'll take the vehicle back out to the parking lot when Sean pulls in." Then to Lola, "You good?"

"Right as," she said, almost like she meant it.

"You know the chief wants you to talk to someone."

Lola stopped in her tracks. "All the shit you went through, and she wants me to see a therapist?"

Cutter lowered his voice. "A counselor," he said. "For what it's worth, she did send me."

Lola picked up her bags and started walking toward the plane again. "Whatever she wants. I don't care."

Micki saved them from further conversation.

"Hey, my dears," she said. "You want the okay news or the semi-bad news?"

"Those sound kinda like the same thing," Lola said.

Micki shot Cutter a *what's with her?* look. "Depends on your point of view," she said. "Anyway, I'll just tell you. Weather's holding so we're a go for flying toward Fairbanks."

"Good to hear," Cutter said.

"Now tell us the okay news," Lola said over her shoulder as she heaved a duffel through the Caravan's rear cargo door.

"That *was* the okay news," Micki said. "It's only okay because we may have to do a one eighty if the sky turns to shit when we approach the pass."

Cutter dragged his bag to the rear of the plane and waited for Lola to finish loading. His instincts told him to help with her bags, but experience told him she might bite his head off if he tried.

"What about the semi-bad news?"

"It's going to be booger of a cold trip, my dear," Micki said. "I'll crank up the heat but, as you may have noticed driving in, it's not pretty out there." She gave a Cheshire Cat grin. "And it won't be any better at altitude."

"Hooah," Cutter said, embracing the suck of it all.

"Oo—rah!" the former Marine Corps pilot corrected him. "Don't give me any of that Army horseshit this early in the morning."

Twenty minutes later, Sean Blodgett arrived bearing Krispy Kreme donuts to apologize for his tardiness. The Caravan was loaded, with the rear stanchion removed, ready to be pulled outside. Paige Hart sat up front, in part because she normally worked prisoner operations and didn't get to fly nearly as much as full-time members of the task force. The main reason, though, was because the more senior deputies wanted to curl up in their seats and sleep— hard to do when you had to worry about getting your feet tangled up with the right-seat control pedals.

The USMS Caravan customarily had room for ten, including the pilots, with a row of single seats running down each side of the airplane. Micki had removed the two aft seats in order to accommodate more of their bulky winter gear. Alvarez and Blodgett sat in the two forward seats, directly behind the cockpit. Lola and Cutter sat across from each other in the rear. Backpacks went in the two empty seats between the four deputies.

Pete hit the button to open the rolling hangar doors and took a seat on the boxy aircraft tug, snugging the wool hats down over silver hair. Cutter leaned his head against the side window. The guy really did look like Santa about to drag his sleigh out into the dark night of swirling ground fog and blowing snow.

Micki turned from the left seat to look behind her and make certain everyone had on their earphones.

Pete put the tug in gear and started pulling them outside. The engine off, cold crept into the plane immediately. The thin metal skin of the fuselage began to pop and crack at the sudden change in temperature. Across the aisle, Lola flinched at the noise, shooting a wary glance at Cutter.

Micki turned to look at Paige Hart, tapping her own gray Light-speed headset. Hart reached up and turned hers on.

"How about now?" Micki spoke to Hart, but it was over the intercom, so everyone was able to hear.

Hart gave her a thumbs-up. "Loud and clear."

"Good," Micki said. "Tell me what you have in your pockets."

"What do you mean?"

Micki pulled out a Payday candy bar. "You know, stuff that'll keep you alive if we go down."

"I just assumed we'd all die if we went down," Hart said.

"Fair point," Micki said. "But assuming we don't, you should consider the fact that you may have to survive until rescue with nothing but whatever you happen to have in your pockets." She shot another glance over her shoulder. "Right, Cutter?"

"Yep," Cutter said.

"Just something to think about," Micki said. "Flying in Alaska can turn dicey in the best of times. Forty below, well, when it gets that cold, shit just starts to break."

Cutter could only see Hart from behind, but he felt sure she grew visibly smaller before his eyes.

"Not the plane? Right? That's not going to break?"

"Probably not," Micki said. "But if it does . . ." She drew the Payday again like a gun. "Just remember to have the stuff you need to survive on your person . . . if we survive the landing."

Lola leaned sideways into the aisle toward Cutter, lifting the headset off her ear with one hand and covering the mic with the other. "And the chief thinks *I* need a therapist . . ."

Clearance for takeoff was easy to come by at that time of the morning. Bundled in his parka, Cutter leaned his head against the window and watched the runway lights slip by in the darkness. The Caravan shuddered and then leapt into the darkness, more quickly than usual in the dense winter air.

Anchorage Air Traffic Control vectored Micki west toward Point MacKenzie for other traffic, and then banked her back to the north, taking them across the Knik Arm of the Cook Inlet directly over Willow where she'd intercept the Parks Highway toward Denali. Cruising at just under a hundred and seventy miles an hour, they emerged from the Alaska Range through Broad Pass an hour after wheels up.

Cutter checked his watch. A quarter to five. Daylight was still over four hours away.

Layered clothing and the warm air blowing from the heater combined with the constant drone of the engine lulled Cutter into a wakeful dream, eyes open, staring out the window at the blackness. Micki's voice came over the intercom, filling his head-set and jerking him out of his trance. It was the first time she or anyone had spoken in over half an hour. He was suddenly aware of the odor of the Caravan's interior—new car and, oddly, toasted marshmallows. Probably had something to do with the heater—or maybe he was having a stroke . . . He shook off the early morn-ing stupor and rubbed his eyes with a thumb and forefinger. Nope, a stroke was the smell of burnt toast.

"Ladies and gentlemen," she said. "And I use that term loosely. If you care to look out your windows you will be fortunate to . . . well, see for yourselves."

Cutter opened his eyes to find the sky awash with flowing waves of green and red and purple, dancing, flowing like glowing col-ored sand among the stars.

Lola gasped. Paige Hart whistled low under her breath, and everyone looked on in awe.

"How's this affecting your instruments?" Cutter asked after what he hoped was a proper amount of reverence for the incredi-ble light show.

"All good so far," Micki said. "And I have good news. The wea-ther on this side of the mountains isn't as shabby as I expected. Eielson's reporting a balmy thirty-one below zero. For now. The forecast still calls for the bottom to fall out by this evening."

Arliss sat up a little straighter in his seat. "Does that mean you have time to do a flyover of Decker's?"

"I shore do," the pilot said, exaggerating her accent. "We're heading that way as we speak."

Paige Hart spoke next. "Don't we need to worry about him hearing us if we're low enough to see anything of value? Even with the FLIR."

FLIR was forward-looking infrared—a thermal imaging camera mounted on the belly of the airplane.

"Not likely," Lola said. "He's staying at a cabin on the edge of
an active flyway. Froggy as Decker is, he'd probably start to worry
if he stopped hearing airplanes."

"Agreed," Micki said. "There's a no-fly zone around the base
for civilians—unless you have permission . . ." She turned to grin
over her shoulder at her passengers. "Which I have. We're a government aircraft so there weren't too many hoops to jump
through in order to land and buy some fuel. I've requested an approach that will take us pretty much right over the target house.
It'll still be dark, but we should still be able to get some good images with the FLIR.

"If it was me," Micki continued, "I'd amend my ops plan and
have the Fairbanks DUSMs and Troopers link up with me at Eielson with your rental vehicles. It'd save you some time, and if the
weather turns bum quicker than we expect, I can turn and burn
for home right from there. After we've had a look with the FLIR,
I mean."

"Perfect," Cutter said. He took out the satellite phone and
opened the antenna, holding it against the window.

Nancy Alvarez piped up while he was waiting for a signal.

"Who's stationed at Eielson?" she asked.

"The 354th Fighter Wing," Micki said. "Used to be A-10s. Now
it's F-16s and F-35s."

Across the aisle from Alvarez, Sean Blodgett pumped his fist.
"An A-10 Warthog would have been sweet!" he said. "Still, we
should just get one of those F-35s to do a low flyover. That would
scare the shit outta our guy and we'll swoop in and grab him."

"Not a horrible idea," Lola said.

"Yeah," Cutter said. "Except for that whole posse comitatus
thing. The military doesn't conduct law enforcement ops on US
soil."

"Pesky details," Alvarez said.

"That," Micki said, "and it costs forty grand an hour to operate
said F-35. Would be cool though."

Cutter checked the satellite phone, wanting to get in touch

with Fairbanks deputies with the change of plans regarding a meet at the air force base.

He got nothing but pulsing dots.

Gasps from Hart and Blodgett carried over the intercom. Cutter looked up from the sat phone in time to see Lola press her face to the window.

"And that, my dears," Micki said, "is why I never get tired of flying."

The sky outside the right side of the airplane was on fire with more dancing currents of green and purple light, washing and pulsing against the black even brighter than before.

Micki gave a low whistle, impressed. "They weren't kidding when they said solar activity was through the roof."

"Incredible," Cutter heard himself say. Not easily impressed, this show was easily the brightest he'd ever seen in the aurora. "No wonder I'm not getting a signal."

"GPS is still working," Micki said.

"For now," Lola said. Her face still pressed to the window.

Ten minutes later, with the sky still ablaze, Micki signaled their imminent arrival over the target.

"I'll record as we pass," Micki said. "But if you come forward, you'll be able to watch it in real time." She tapped a glass screen on her console to the right of the GPS map. "Here."

Cutter unbuckled his seat belt and moved up the aisle, crouching so he didn't bang his head.

Micki flipped the switch to activate the FLIR. It took a few seconds, but the screen went from black to an undulating sea of purple, some spots slightly lighter than others.

Micki reached forward and tapped the screen again, animated. "See that red blob," she said.

Cutter leaned in between the cockpit seats for a closer look. "A moose."

"Yep," Micki said. "A moose. The hide's something like an inch thick. Great insulator, otherwise we'd get a better heat signature, and it would show up yellow. See, if you look closely, you can see a hint of yellow every time it breathes. The cold air turns it red then purple in a split second."

Cutter watched the moose disappear from view and the screen turned purple again. Warm red blobs, their borders tinged in warmer orange and even specks of yellow began to dot the purple cold of the landscape. Houses. A neighborhood.

"See that long one with all the red pouring out of it?" Paige Hart said.

"Mobile home," Micki said. "Their heating bill must be atrocious." She turned to Cutter, then back to her GPS, tapping a spot on the screen just ahead of the moving arrow that signified their position. "That's the address you have for Royce Decker."

"Can you slow us down a hair?" Cutter asked.

"Just a hair," Micki said. "I need to keep our speed well above minimums in this weather."

"Safely as you can," Cutter said.

"Roger that." Micki pulled back slightly on the throttle, slowing the aircraft. "We're still gonna zip by at a hundred and forty speed over the ground," she said. "But I'll put the video on a thumb drive for you to study after we land."

"That's it there," Cutter said, as another red blob hove into view. Decker had chosen his location well. There were no other houses within a half mile. The driveway was long and open, a single point of entry by vehicle. It was difficult to tell on the FLIR, but the property was on a slight bench at the base of a slightly higher hill covered by a stretch of woods that ran between the base perimeter fence and what looked to be the main house.

"Another moose," Hart said, pointing at a red spot ghosting through the woods.

"Good eye," Micki said.

Cutter leaned forward, grabbing the back of Hart's seat to keep from falling. "Hey, Micki," he said. "Is that what I think it is?"

Behind the main house, maroon against a deep purple background, was a red oval with a swirl of yellow orange bleeding into it, from a brighter yellow dot.

Micki pulled back on the throttle just a dab more. "If you're thinking hot tub, then that would be correct."

"What's the outside temp?"

"Holding at minus three-three," Micki said.

Cutter nodded. "It would take something hot to keep a spot bright yellow like that."

"It would," Micki said. "Like a fire."

"A wood-fired hot tub," Cutter said. "So that maroon-red water is . . ."

"Warmer than the air," Micki said. "But not particularly hot yet. It's probably one of those snorkel stoves that's mostly underwater. See that orange swirl? That's hot water mixing in."

Lola called out from the back. "Don't forget to fly the airplane, Micki!"

"On it, my dear," Micki said.

"A lot of work to heat the water with a wood-fired stove," Cutter mused. "As soon as he let the fire go out, the water would start to freeze in just a few minutes."

Micki gave a slow nod. "So, if he's going to the trouble of heating the tub at thirty below zero . . ."

Hart turned to look at Cutter, grinning, eyes wide with excitement. "Then we know exactly where he'll be when the water gets hot."

Cutter was thrown slightly backward as Micki bumped the throttle forward and the Caravan picked up speed. She shot a quick glance over her shoulder.

"I assume you'd like me to get this airplane on the ground ASAP."

Cutter looked at the screen, already forming a new plan of approach.

"I would indeed, my dear," he said.

# CHAPTER 30

*Fairbanks*
*33° below*

GANT LEFT JOHN BLACKWELL AND PEEWEE HALVERSON WATCHING Josie's hotel while he and Dusty made the drive to the airport. The Aussie sisters were flying in on a private jet and would arrive at a small aviation services company on the northwest side of Fairbanks International. Gant couldn't decide which was worse, sitting in an idling car watching Josie's hotel without actually getting to see her, or putting up with Dusty's serenade of farts during the drive.

"I can tell you've never met these two," Gant said as he pulled off Airport Way onto the frontage road where the fixed base aviation operation was located north of the main terminal.

Dusty popped the top on the stainless-steel bottle he carried everywhere and took a long—and loud—slug of protein drink.

"What do you mean by that?"

"How do I put this . . ." Gant said. "The Aussies, they're the best at what they do, and what they do is murder people."

"Ha." Dusty wiped errant protein drink off his lip with a fore-arm. "That's not exactly outside our wheelhouse."

"Right," Gant said. "But do you know how they kill people?"

"I heard it was some kinda spike," Dusty said. "There's this chick in the Bible who kills a dude with a stake through the head. Did you know that?"

"I did not," Gant said. "I also did not picture you for a Bible reader."

"Just the good parts." Dusty grinned. "You know, spikes through the head, swords to the gut, shit like that."

"Anyway," Gant said. "The Aussies use something like a meat hook or a gaff." He snapped his fingers. "A single blow at the base of the skull. Wham! Destroys the brainstem—the celery stalk with all the nerves that tells your heart to beat and your lungs to breathe. What does that say to you?"

"It tells me I don't want to get whacked in the brainstem."

"It's a hell of a lot easier to whack someone if you just pop them in the back of the head with a .22 pistol," Gant said. "No muss, no fuss. This spike thing, it takes patience and precision. You hit exactly the right spot at the base of the skull, you get medulla oblongata. Sever that and boom!" Gant clapped his hands. "Poor son of a bitch goes stiff like he's grabbed a live wire. Instant death. But you miss by as little as an inch and you got yourself a very angry dude with a hook in his neck."

"Okay . . ."

"What I'm telling you is that these two are perfectionists. Extremely talented, and with that talent comes certain . . . expectations."

"So?"

"So," Gant said, his voice rising in pitch and volume. "They'll expect us not to pick them up in a vehicle that smells like a dog died in it."

"It's not that—"

Gant cut him off, railing now. "Pull your head outta your ass, kid! You smell like your guts are rotting inside of you."

Dusty blinked like a chastised child. "You don't gotta be—"

"Toss that protein shit out the window," Gant snapped. "And leave it rolled down while you're at it. Geeze, kid, how do you sleep at night? My eyes are burning."

"It's not that bad."

"We'll know when they sit down in the car," Gant said. "Or maybe not. I guess we won't even see the spikes coming."

The Gulfstream commuter jet nosed onto the apron outside the private aircraft operations office and stopped, engines spooling down amid a cloud of ice fog. The only ground crew, a silver-haired woman who before the plane arrived had been filling the popcorn machine in the office lobby, hustled outside to help with luggage and get the fuel truck. The G-5 pilot evidently didn't want to spend the night and was obviously scooting south for warmer climes. Gant couldn't blame him.

The Nash sisters came down the boarding stairs wearing heavy parkas and winter boots—all of which looked to be brand-new. Gant thought they must not have expected to be here very long because they didn't have much in the way of luggage—just a large duffel and a day pack apiece—and, of course, what they had in their pockets. They'd flown private so that could have been anything.

Gant had met the sisters once, three years earlier. He'd seen them work. Browny, the taller one, had a reputation for being the most dangerous, but as far as Gant could tell that was a toss-up. The one called Mads had a white streak in her hair, now barely visible under the edge of a black wool hat pulled down over her ears. She did most of the talking. Browny stood back and glared, eyeing the men like they were roadkill she was just waiting to rot and become tender. It was uncomfortable for Gant, but Dusty looked as if he might pee himself.

The sisters each grabbed a bag of popcorn before they left the office and carried it with them to the car—leaving Gant and Dusty to get their bags.

Mads took the front passenger seat while Browny sat in the back. Gant caught a glimpse of Dusty in the rearview mirror. If he hadn't been such an asshole, Gant might have felt sorry for him.

Browny settled herself in and pulled the seat belt across her chest. "Holy shit!" she said. "Someone opened their lunch in here."

In the rearview, Dusty the musclebound goon, looked like he was shrinking.

"Sorry about that," he said.

Everyone in the Jeep, including Mads, sat completely still, waiting to see what happened next.

Browny elbowed the terrified man in the arm. "That's alright, mate." She chuckled. "Everybody farts!"

"The professor is still in her hotel room?" Mads peeled off her mittens and held her hands in front of the heater vent.

"She is." Gant turned right out of the parking lot onto Old Airport Road, and then onto Airport Way, where he turned right again.

"And no contact with her son?"

"That's right," Gant said.

"And your men are watching her?"

"They are."

Mads slapped her thighs. "Right-o then," she said. "That airplane had a piss-poor excuse for a galley. Nothing but booze and Skittles. I reckon we have time for a proper brekky."

"Yeah, sure." Gant looked at his watch. "Six thirty."

In the back seat, Dusty went to work on his phone.

A half hour later, Gant wound his way through a car dealership on the north side of town to a place called The Cookie Jar. Judging from the crowd waiting to get in, they were either very good, or the only place in town open at this hour.

It turned out to be both. Aptly named, the inside of the place smelled like dessert. To reach the tables, patrons had to walk by a gauntlet of hand-dipped chocolates, monstrous cinnamon rolls, and all manner of cookies.

The waitress brought coffee and Mads ordered before they had a chance to look at the menu.

"Sourdough pancakes," she said, like it was a royal proclamation.

Pen and notepad in hand, the waitress looked at Browny next. "And what'll you have?"

"Sourdough pancakes."

The waitress turned to Dusty for his order. Mads saved him the trouble.

"Sourdough pancakes for everyone at the table."

"Sounds good," Dusty said, as did Gant.

"It just makes sense," Mads said when the waitress had gone. "I reckon sourdough just screams Alaska. You can get bacon and eggs for brekky most anywhere. We're in Alaska, we should do Alaska things."

Gant had planned to order sourdough anyway but kicked himself for not being brave enough to order some bacon on the side.

The sisters—mostly Mads—talked about all things Alaska in between bites, like they'd studied travel books on the plane. Their charm and pleasant chuckles gave Gant the creeps. He knew why they were here. No amount of friendly chatting could make him forget that one of these women would eventually drive a meat hook into the back of Josie's head.

Seemingly oblivious, Dusty wolfed down his breakfast, hunched over, arm wrapped around his plate like he was worried someone might try and steal his pancakes. Prison could do that to a person. Gant was surprised the kid didn't pick up his plate and lick off the syrup. He'd evidently taken Mads's banter as a sign that he could relax—a very dangerous notion.

Still butt-hurt from their conversation in the car, the kid decided to have a little fun at Gant's expense, no doubt hoping to make him look bad in front of the Aussie sisters.

"Good thing you made it when you did," Dusty said, gesturing at Gant with his syrupy fork. "Turns out our man, Mr. Bobby G, is sweet on the professor lady. I thought we might have to whack her and her kid before you even got here just to keep him from going all soft on us."

Browny cut a bite of pancake, then toyed with it against her plate, soaking up a pool of butter. "Is that right?" she said without looking up. "You would have started without us?"

Either Dusty didn't realize the danger he was putting himself in or he was too dumb to think that anything on Gant would blow back on him as well.

Mads met Gant's eye. "Is your mate telling the truth?" She smoothed the white shock of hair back behind her ear. A sad smile crossed her lips, almost like she was jealous. "You got a little thing for Ms. Josie . . . Bobby G?"

"I do not," Gant said, ashamed that these women frightened him as much as they did. He'd ended more than a few people himself. It would have been easy to stand up and shoot them both in the face. And yet—

Browny spoke next, startling him out of his treason.

"I reckon you're the smart one," she said to Dusty. "It takes a keen eye to notice that sort of thing. Ready to take matters into your own hands, are you? Don't want the prof nor her son to get away." She gestured at him with the pancake laden fork, moving it around like a wand. "Valeria needs to keep an eye on you."

Dusty shot Gant a *what was all the fuss* look, wagging his head before turning back to Browny. "Thanks, mate," he said, mimicking her Aussie accent. He scooted away from the table and gave Mads a wink. "You ladies will have to excuse me. I'm not used to so much coffee. I need to hit the head like a big dog."

*And do a line of cocaine,* Gant thought.

The sisters gave polite nods, otherwise ignoring Dusty as he got up and made his way through the other tables toward the restroom.

"What's that mean?" Mads said after Dusty was out of earshot. "Like a big dog? I'm not getting the visual."

"No idea," Gant said.

Browny stood, again startling Gant. "I should go to the loo myself before we leave."

"You know," Mads said when she and Gant were alone at the table, "I'd understand if you developed some feelings for Professor Josie. Valeria sent us photos. She's quite a looker."

"That's not an issue—"

Mads raised a hand to stop him. "How long have you been assigned to follow her?"

"Not quite four years," Gant said. "Off and on."

"Well then," Mads said. "I reckon that makes perfect sense. You watch someone from afar for that length of time, it's only natural to imagine things. You might wonder what life would be like if you were *in* their life instead of merely observing it. I find myself doing that all the time when I observe people." She shrugged.

"Sometimes this job calls on us to do hard things. You know what I mean?"

"I do," Gant said.

"Ace!" Mads said. "You'll be alright."

Her smile looked genuine enough, but Gant was under no illusion that this woman was his friend.

Browny returned a few minutes later and took her seat. The waitress poured her a warmup for her coffee, which she drained like she was dying of thirst.

Gant checked his watch again. Seven thirty.

"I need to call the men at the hotel." He glanced up at the doorway that led to the restrooms. "Dusty's taking his own sweet time. I should go check on him."

Browny shook her head. "The loo's a one holer," she said. "And the door is bolted."

"I'll knock," Gant said, pushing his chair back from the table.

Browny shook her head again, this time pulling a wadded paper napkin from a jacket pocket and sliding it across the table. The napkin fell open to reveal a severed cauliflower ear.

"He won't be able to hear you," she said.

The waitress came back with the check, which she gave to Gant. Instead of shoving the bloody ear back in her pocket, Browny merely covered it with her hand.

Gant paid cash at the register, buying a couple of chocolate clusters that Mads and Browny pointed out in the glass case. He jumped when his phone began to vibrate in his pocket.

The sisters looked on and chuckled. He wondered if they'd just killed Dusty to keep him in line. No. The kid deserved what he got.

Gant answered the call.

It was Blackwell.

"Her car is gone."

Gant felt like he might throw up. "What do you mean, gone?"

Outside the restaurant now, the Aussie sisters stopped in their tracks, blowing clouds of vapor in the predawn darkness.

"I'm saying the bitch slipped away from us," Blackwell said. "I told you one vehicle was not enough to surveil a place like this."

Gant suppressed the urge to fling his phone into the parking lot. "You didn't tell me—Never mind. I'm not doing this. We're on our way."

"You want me to check her room?"

"I don't want you to do anything until I get there."

Gant ended the call and turned to the Aussie sisters, who from the look on their faces had heard everything. Their eyes demanding answers—or, at the very least, accountability. He licked his lips and without thinking, reached up and touched his ear.

Browny saw it—and smiled.

# CHAPTER 31

*Anchorage*
*26° below*

M IM WOKE FROM A FITFUL SLEEP TO THE SOUND OF A SLAMMING car door. She'd spent the first hour after Arliss left intermittently doom-scrolling and dozing before finally drifting off. An engine revved outside, with the whine of half-frozen belts that had yet to fully warm up, lugging as it backed down the driveway. That would be Jessica from down the street, picking up Constance in her dad's stick-shift Jeep for their zero-hour biology class.

The house was eerily quiet. Mim checked her phone. Ten minutes after six. The boys wouldn't drag their butts out of bed until she rousted them at seven, but Ursula was usually up by now, puttering around and hogging the bathroom to put on what the boys called her "Southern Lady" makeup. Odd that she'd still be sleeping. The business yesterday with Opal must have really kept her up late.

Mim resisted the urge to start scrolling on her phone again. She had things to do. Still, she *was* forty-four years old. A couple more minutes in bed couldn't hurt her aching bones one bit.

She'd gotten up at three thirty to make Arliss sourdough toast and creamy scrambled eggs, one of Grumpy's signature dishes. Far from naturally blabby in the best of times, Arliss was even qui-

eter before a big warrant operation—which meant he was quiet a
lot. Mim's mother once told her that the true measure of a good
relationship was how much time you spent enjoying each other's
company in silence. Mim liked the quiet times, especially in the
early mornings when she could sip her coffee wearing her battered Florida State bathrobe and listen to the tick-tick-tick of the
baseboard heaters while Arliss sketched raid plans on his Battle
Board notebook. It was surreal to think that she'd gone from a
house where firearms were generally out of sight in the safe unless
Ethan was going hunting, to this guy who wore two guns virtually
everywhere he went and planned his law enforcement exploits at
her kitchen table. She never mentioned it, just sipped her coffee
and watched, but it made her smile inside.

This morning was different. This morning, Mim wanted desperately to talk, but Arliss was leaving. Horrible timing for a deep
conversation. It was important that he devote his full attention
into not getting shot. So, she'd sat there in her robe, listened to
the baseboard heaters, and kept her thoughts bottled up inside.

She rolled onto her side to take some pressure off her aching
back. The only cure for that was to get out of bed. She needed to
get the boys up anyway.

Surely Ursula was up by now. There was a lot they needed to
talk about today. Mim swung her legs off the bed and sat completely still, holding her breath to concentrate on the sounds of
the house. There were a lot—the boiler in the garage (that fed
the ticking baseboards), her grandmother's clock on the living
room mantel, and the groans and creaks of a fifty-year-old house
whose bones were feeling the effects of below zero temps. But no
creaking floors or running taps. No sign of Ursula.

Mim bribed the boys out of bed with fresh bacon, then helped
Michael with a short math assignment he'd put off while she
talked Matthew off an emotional ledge about a perceived injus-
tice toward him by a lunchroom aide. A typical morning with the
Cutter twins.

She got them out the door trailing crumpled homework papers and winter scarves, seconds before the bus pulled up.

Still in her robe and already exhausted by 8:45 a.m., Mim sat at the table nursing her coffee, happy to have the day off and the house to herself.

Except she didn't have the house to herself. Any minute now, Ursula would make her grand entrance and give some flip comment about how much of the day was already gone, noting that Mim wasn't yet dressed, and her hair looked like some kind of drunken bird's nest.

The boiler kicked on in the garage, startling Mim out of her thoughts and reminding her how cold it was. She checked her phone. Twenty-six below zero. A good day to stay inside. Poor Arliss and Lola up in Fairbanks. She hoped Ursula had the sense not to go out today . . .

It wasn't any of Mim's business how long Ursula stayed in bed. But there was a chance something had happened to her. She wasn't old, but she wasn't young either. She'd been relatively open about the "bohemian" lifestyle she'd led after she left her boys with Grumpy. A heart attack or stroke wasn't out of the realm of possibility.

Mim began to picture the worst.

Knocking on her door wouldn't hurt anything—though her mother-in-law was a lot like a crying babe—much more pleasant when she was asleep.

"Ursula?"

Silence.

"Ursula? Are you up?"

Silence.

"I'm coming in."

The house had settled quite a bit from the last little series of earthquakes. She had to push the door open with her shoulder.

Mim was astonished to see the bed empty and neatly made. Ursula's two suitcases sat in the corner. Her hairbrushes and make-up box were laid out neatly on the nightstand—like Arliss laid out his guns. But no Ursula.

Either she'd slipped away before three a.m. or . . . she'd not come home last night.

Mim left the bedroom to kneel on the couch and look out the

front window. Ursula's rental car was gone, the spot in the drive-way where she usually parked covered in hoarfrost. She'd been gone all night.

Mim called Opal, who answered right away.

"I'm looking for your mother," Mim said.

"No idea where she is," the girl said. "She was supposed to come over this morning, but we haven't seen her."

"We?"

"My dad's here," Opal said. "You want to talk to him?"

Geoff didn't know where she was either.

"I don't mean to scare you," Mim said. "But she left last night and hasn't come home. I tried her cell a couple of times."

"Yeah." He sounded as exhausted as Mim felt. "Ursula's not big on answering. Maybe she moved on?"

"All her stuff is still here," Mim said.

"Look," Geoff said. "I have to be honest with you. Nothing that woman does would surprise me."

"Dad," Opal chided in the background.

"You're right," he said for his daughter's benefit. "Ursula can be a wonderful person, obviously. The thing is, disappearing like this is her superpower."

"It's just really cold out there," Mim said. "I'm a little worried."

Geoff sighed.

"I'll have Opal give her a call," he said. "Maybe she'll answer." He was silent for a time, long enough Mim thought maybe she'd dropped the call.

"Hello?"

"Yeah," he said. "I'm still here. Look, if you've been around Ursula for more than a minute or two you probably already sensed this, but she's hiding something. So, I guess she's got two super-powers. I didn't know about her boys until four or five years ago—and I doubt you knew about us."

"True enough."

"That woman's got secrets for days. I haven't figured them out yet, and to tell you the truth, I'm not sure I really want to."

Mim promised to reach out if she heard anything and ended the call.

"Secrets for days," she said, tapping the phone against her open hand in thought. "I guess Arliss was right."

That had to be it. Ursula was at a secret place neither Mim nor Geoff knew about. Maybe she hadn't even been going to Wasilla every day like she'd said.

Mim looked out the window at the gray morning. A flock of redpolls and juncos flitted on the frozen ground beneath the gnarled birch tree. A small sedan—Mim wasn't great at identifying cars—slid down the road in front of the house, barely maintaining control on the icy pavement. It occurred to her that Ursula didn't have much experience at winter driving. What if something had happened? The roads were dicey at best. Mim had heard of people sliding into the trees and not being found for days. She checked the temps on her phone again. Twenty-seven below. It had dropped a degree.

She stood at the door of the guest room, holding each side of the frame. "Secrets for days," she whispered again. "Ursula, what are you hiding?"

Mim wasn't naturally a snoop, but she truly was worried. She stood there for another five minutes imagining the line she was about to cross. She'd heard Grumpy and Arliss tell dozens of stories about searching houses, looking not only for the outlaw, but for any clue that might lead to that outlaw's whereabouts. Something as small as a receipt or bill might give them away. Mim wasn't trying to catch her mother-in-law in a lie, just rescue her if she was in trouble. Right? It was still an invasion of privacy, like reading Constance's diary to save her from herself. Mim had yet to stoop to that, though she'd been tempted a thousand times.

She decided on a light peek, no rummaging, just looking at stuff that was out in the open. Plain View, Arliss called it. That wouldn't be so bad, would it?

Ursula's suitcases felt empty. Mim shook them, listening for the shuffle of hidden papers. Luckily, she heard none. The closet was a bust. Nothing but clothes. Mostly blacks and greens, Ursula's favorite colors.

There was a copy of *A Gentleman in Moscow* on the nightstand.

Nice to know her mother-in-law had good taste. Mim thumbed through it, breaking her no-rummaging rule. It didn't matter. She found nothing other than a ribbon Ursula used as a bookmark. Garnet and gold for the Florida State Seminoles, just like Mim's robe. Both Mim and Ethan had degrees from FSU. Arliss had attended classes there for a short time before he left for the Army. The ribbon was an interesting detail, but it provided no clues as to Ursula's whereabouts.

Mim replaced the book, slightly embarrassed that she was sneaky enough to leave it at exactly the same position she'd found it. It was like one of those old John D. MacDonald books. *That's me,* she thought. *The Spy in the Ratty Red Robe.*

That left the chest of drawers, a tall Amish piece with a hidden compartment behind the molding that she doubted Ursula even knew existed. An underwear drawer would be the perfect place to hide something—but Ursula needed to be MIA a little longer before Mim braved a pile of granny panties.

Mim stored her wrapping paper in this extra room under the bed—and Christmas *was* right around the corner. She had every right to be here . . . Didn't she?

She knelt and lifted the bed skirt—and there it was, an old-school cardboard valise with riveted leather corners. About the size of a modern-day carryon suitcase, it was painted garnet and gold. Mim lay down on her side, peering under the bed. This would be impossible to explain if Ursula came in now, but she wanted a better look before she moved anything. All she saw were dust bunnies, her wrapping paper, and the valise.

She slid it out from under the bed, gingerly, as if it might be booby-trapped.

The sound of a slamming car door sent her popping to her feet. She kicked the valise back where it came from and smoothed the bed skirt as neatly as she could and bounded into the living room, kneeling on the couch to peer out the window. It was just Katie from next door, walking from her car to the mailbox.

At once disappointed and relieved, Mim all but sprinted back to the guest room. She dropped to the floor and took out the valise again. A couple rolls of gift-wrapping paper on the carpet beside her would help keep up appearances if her mother-in-law suddenly darkened the door.

She sat for a long time just staring at the mysterious case. There looked to be some markings on the sides and a label between the clasps, but they'd been painted over and were impossible to make out. Mim pulled on the handle. The case was heavy, maybe thirty or forty pounds. Not gold bullion or anything, but it was still a heck of a lot for Ursula to lift. Mim hadn't seen her bring it inside. Whatever it contained had to be important. A person didn't drag around an old carboard suitcase with mundane receipts and old airline tickets.

The boys would have guessed it was a human head. If it was, there were a lot of them.

Mim thumbed open both latches and then stopped. She'd told herself she wanted to help find Ursula. And that was true. But she also wanted desperately to see what was in the box.

She lifted the lid—and began to sob.

# CHAPTER 32

*Eielson Air Force Base*
*Salcha, Alaska*
*33° below*

$A$T 07:40, Eielson Air Force Base security police ushered Cutter and the rest of his team from the Cessna's stairs past several trucks and SUVs, two of them pulling trailers with snow machines. Bright yellow lighting pushed back the blue-black darkness. Lola, shuffled along hunched up in her parka, dragging her heavy gear bag and muttering out loud about the "stupid cold."

Cutter walked in the door and stomped the snow and gravel off his boots to be greeted by an Air Force major who wasn't much older than Lola. He noted her nametag: Kalogeropoulos.

She smiled. "Most people just call me 'The Greek.'"

Cutter peeled off his glove liner and shook her hand. "I'll stick with Major. Thanks for having us."

Entering the decades-old military building was like going back in time for Cutter—the smell of stale coffee and whatever glue the government used to hold down the industrial carpet squares. Of course, this was Air Force, so aftershave replaced the men-who'd-just-spent-two-weeks-in-the-field stench that Cutter remembered from the Army. A hint of wintergreen hung in the air with the odor of cleaning supplies—a telltale sign of smokeless to-bacco, the ubiquitous use of which crossed service lines. There was something Spartan about the place, which he preferred over the fancy art and wood-veneer furniture of the civilian side of government. His office desk in the task force was called "The Senator" model, for crying out loud. In the military, his writing platform had been, at best, a BattleBoard, or in a pinch, the inside of his own wrist.

Cutter had to admit, he lived for times like this despite the miserable cold—or maybe because of it. Hardship was his friend. For a time, the best friend he'd had.

The two deputy US marshals assigned to the Fairbanks sub-office had already put a five-foot map of the target house and surrounding terrain on the wall. As far as warrant services in Alaska went, this was a big deal with, as Lola would say, heaps of moving parts. St. Louis Metro officer Joe Ikeda sat with them. The poor guy looked as if he was going to be sick to his stomach at any moment. Cutter couldn't blame him. Partners, especially those in special units like a SWAT sniper cadre, shared an incredibly tight bond. They trusted one another with their lives every day. Cutter could only imagine what a gut punch it must be to know your partner was not only a thief, but a sociopath who'd paid for the murder of his own wife.

Four Alaska state troopers stood along the far wall dressed in insulated snow-machine pants with custom belt loops allowing their gun belts to fit outside of their insulated ski pants, covered only by their heavy parkas. Cutter and his team were in and out of the office, spending the vast majority of their time in vehicles. Rural troopers were in the thick of it, exposed to the elements every day. Blue "Smokey the Bear" Stetsons gave way to fur-trapper hats both issue and "Village Made" like the seal and sea otter Cutter wore. These folks were experts, paramilitary stiffness notwithstanding, and Cutter urged his team to look to them as examples for cold-weather tactics. M4 carbines slung center chest, Styrofoam cups of coffee in hand, each of the four were members of SERT—AST Special Emergency Response Team. In this case, they were acting as individual troopers. If they'd come out as a team, their brass would have demanded they have tactical command—

and Cutter wouldn't have blamed them. They had the training and skills, and Cutter was glad to have them. In the corner near the wall map, two Trooper R44 chopper pilots, one male, one female, pored over an iPad, no doubt getting the latest scoop on the weather while they studied possible routes. Their cranials— white aviation helmets—sat on the end of the conference table next to their mittens. Blue insulated coveralls were rolled down around their waists to bleed off excess heat in the stuffy conference room.

Cutter and the others greeted the rest of the group as they dragged their bulky gear bags into the conference room. Blodgett passed around two boxes of Krispy Kreme donuts he'd brought from Anchorage, making fast friends. They were all focused on arresting Decker, but the deputies took advantage of the impromptu reunion. Everyone in the District of Alaska got along well, but get-togethers were few and far between. Suboffice deputies across the entire Marshals Service did everything within their power not to darken the door of their district headquarters.

Deputies Paul Gutierrez and Ryan Madsen were anything but lazy. They did, however, want to handle life on their terms—the suboffice way. Cutter traveled up with the task force on occasion for big cases like Royce Decker, but by and large Paul and Ryan handled every writ, summons, and warrant on their own.

Gutierrez sported a walking cast from an accident on his personal snow machine. The lines in his forehead said he was none too happy to be on the injured list.

Both he and Ryan Madsen were big men with scruffy beards and the slightly unkempt demeanor of deputies who were lucky enough to work four hundred miles away from their bosses. Chief Phillips had assigned them the two Polaris Voyageur 146 sport utility snow machines that were parked on the trailer outside.

Fairbanks weather was almost always more extreme than in Anchorage, and even when the DUSMs had prisoners in court, their everyday winter attire might be heavy wool sweaters, fleece-lined khakis, and Steger moosehide mukluks laced up to their knees. This was the frontier. Ryan once told Cutter he'd served a civil summons on a man who was in the middle of skinning a wolf carcass hanging from his living room ceiling fan. The poor guy couldn't figure out why he was unable to find a wife.

Being so far from the flagpole—and USMS backup—meant they had to form solid relationships with the state and locals. Madsen had coordinated with an AST lieutenant to have a few troopers help out with the hit. Under normal circumstances, two parttime task force officers from Fairbanks PD would have joined the party, but according to Gutierrez, the entire department was tied up with a murder investigation.

"It is literally happening as we speak," Gutierrez said. "Our guys were nearly here and got turned around. Sounds like a waitress at The Cookie Jar restaurant found a severed ear wadded up in a napkin on the floor beside the register. Turns out the guy belonging to the ear was in the bathroom with a perfect little hole in the back of his neck."

"Shot . . ." Lola mused.

"Could be," Gutierrez said. "But no exit, no powder burns, no singed hair. My buddy says at first glance it looks like a single stab wound. Like someone drove a big nail into the base of his skull and then pulled it out again."

"That's stuffed," Lola said. "Killed like that in the loo?"

"No kidding," Gutierrez said. "The point is, our FPD task force guys have their hands full at the moment."

Cutter made a note of the information and asked Gutierrez to keep them in the loop. It was highly unlikely Royce Decker had anything to do with the murder. He wanted to lay low, but a bloody homicide where the killer cut off ears on the same morning the Marshals showed up was too big to ignore. There were no coincidences.

"Let's get this show on the road," Cutter said. "What are we looking at for daylight?"

"Sunrise at 1044," Micki Frank said. "Little less than three hours from now. Nautical twilight at 0811. Civil Twilight at 0922."

"Got it," Cutter said.

Nautical twilight was the time when mariners could make out

the horizon, but most stars and planets remained visible for navigation—a good time to move quietly into position. Civil twilight was generally bright enough to see without artificial light. Cutter wanted to be well in place before then.

"Decker had a fire going in the hot tub when we flew over the target," he said. "Judging from the FLIR, it looked like it had a ways to go before the water was hot enough to sit out in this weather."

"We want to challenge him when he comes out the door," Lola said.

"Exactly."

"Target is a three-minute flight from here in the chopper once we're airborne," the female Trooper pilot said. Her name was Burns. She traced her finger along the map. "For orientation purposes, this is the Trans-Alaska Pipeline, and this is Pump Station 8."

"Workers there?" Blodgett asked.

"Shouldn't be," Trooper Burns said. "Pump Station 8 was shut down sometime in the mid-nineties." She moved her finger along a darker line north on the map. "Your target residence is here, in this next valley. There's an unmaintained gravel road leading up from the Richardson Highway. Looks like your guy parks his truck down here not far from the pump station and then gets in and out on snow machines."

"That tracks with the information we got from Pritchard," Lola said. "Decker's supposed to have trail cameras set up down there by his truck and a buttload of nasty booby traps the farther up the road you get."

"No doubt," Trooper Burns said, referring to the map again. "We can fly you north up this adjacent valley. We'll stay low to cover our noise. Each bird can carry three pax at a time depending on how much gear you bring."

"You guys got way more snow than we do down south," Blodgett said. "Drifts gotta be hellacious in these mountains. I'm thinking it'll take us hours to hump over that ridge."

"Happy to put you *on* the ridge, or in the same valley as the target if you want," Trooper Haslet, the male pilot said. "The mountains would channel the noise though. Your guy's sure to hear us even from a couple miles away. The R-44 isn't exactly a stealth aircraft."

"Here's another reality," Trooper Burns said. "Y'all brought snowshoes, I assume."

They all nodded.

"Up to you how you do it," she said. "But you'll need a plan to get them on when we set down. I'll keep up the collective so the bird doesn't sink, but, like Deputy Blodgett said, we may get into some deep drifts. I've dropped off troopers who sank up to their armpits."

"Got it," Cutter said. "Everyone pre-stage the bindings on your snowshoes so we can get them on as we leave the aircraft."

Cutter had deployed out of numerous helicopters during his time in the Army and executed more fugitive arrests as a deputy US marshal, but this was the first time he would have hopped out of a chopper into deep snow. There was always something new to learn.

"Is flying in this weather giving you any heartburn?" he asked the chopper pilots on his way for a closer look at the map.

"Not yet," Trooper Haslet said. "Helicopters perform well when it's cold—up to a point. Now if you decide to camp up there until it drops to seventy below like it's supposed to later tonight, we won't be able to fly in and get you out."

"Seventy below . . ." Deputy Hart muttered.

"If we get stuck in the mountains all day," Blodgett said, "just come chip our bodies out in the spring."

Cutter stood in front of the map. He'd studied a smaller version in great detail, but that was before he had the information about the wood-fired hot tub.

"Take time to climb," Cutter said under his breath.

"What do you mean by that?" Lola asked.

"It's something they drum into you in the military," he said. "Take time to climb. We definitely need the high ground with this guy." Cutter's index finger hovered over a spot on the map to the west of Decker's Alamo, on the lee side of the ridge. He stepped back so the chopper pilots could see. "What about this bench here?

Noise will be blocked by the ridge, and it's exposed to wind so the snow may not be as deep."

Lola looked from the map to her watch, a Garmin Fēnix Joe Bill had given her as an early Christmas present. Cutter wasn't necessarily a watch guy, but the topo map and GPS features looked like they might come in handy.

Trooper Burns studied the map a moment. "That's doable," she said. "We could fly nap-of-the-earth up the valley floor to drop you without getting above ridgeline—which should mask our approach."

Nap-of-the-earth, or NOE, was essentially when an aircraft followed the rise and fall of the terrain, staying just above the treetops, mountaintops, and valley floor. Depending on the pilot, it could be a gut-churning experience—better than any roller coaster.

Cutter tapped the map again, thinking through the logistics. "It would be maybe a fifty-yard climb up and over, but that would put us looking down on the target."

"Fifty yards is a hell of a long way in the snow," Blodgett said. "Even with snowshoes." He wasn't so much whining as he was pointing out the reality of the situation. Post-holing through knee-deep snow for fifty feet, let alone fifty yards, could make a healthy person think they were having a heart attack. In some places, the snowdrifts could be waist deep or better.¯¯

"We'll spread out," Cutter continued, "putting Sean and Alvarez to the north, Lola and I here in the center, with Ryan and Hart to the south." He gave the troopers a nod. "If y'all wouldn't mind standing by on snow machines where Decker leaves his truck. You have sketches showing where we believe booby traps to be located. That puts you on the outer ring. The cavalry so to speak. You good with that?"

"Working outer perimeter will bring joy to our brass," a senior trooper said. His name was Ayers, and he had an impeccably trimmed salt-and-pepper mustache. "They would prefer we waited."

"Wait until what?" Lola asked, a skeptical brow disappearing into her wool hat.

Ayers gave a wry grin. "Until something happens, and they don't have to screw with the problem."

"Time would usually be on our side now that we know where he is," Cutter said. "But our bad guy's been in contact with a Russian oligarch who will likely try to chopper him out to the coast. We're looking at a ticking clock."

"Got it," Trooper Ayers said. "If I'm honest, I think it's just that the brass don't want to see us in some mountain standoff alongside the US Marshals."

"Can't blame them," Cutter said. "My brass would prefer that didn't happen as well."

He went over the initial plan one more time, the difference being they now planned to challenge Decker when he came out and got into his hot tub rather than creeping up and attempting to lure him out of the house.

Lola picked up one of the three gray plastic off-the-shelf drones from the table.

"What about these little Chinese-made gizmos?"

Trooper Ayers raised a hand. "Trooper Van Horn and I brought them in case. We're certified operators if you need us."

Cutter thought how his nine-year-old nephews should have been certified drone operators if you counted the hours they flew the little DJI he'd given them last Christmas.

"It may come to that," he said. "Decker's SWAT so he'll expect us to use Throwbots, drones, et cetera. In the event we're wrong and he doesn't come out to the hot tub, we'll have Gutierrez and Ryan try and lure him out while the four of us on the ridge hold our positions. The drones will come in handy then."

"Batteries don't last for shit in this," Trooper Van Horn said.

"We'll take what we can get," Cutter said.

"Where do you want me?" Joe Ikeda said.

Cutter glanced at the Security Forces major. "Is it alright if Officer Ikeda stays here? We may need him if this turns into a negotiation." He turned back to Ikeda. "You armed?"

"No."

"Fair enough," Cutter said. "I know this has to be a kick in the teeth, what we're asking you to do."

"How ever you need me," Ikeda said. "I gotta be honest though.

Do you really think a guy who would kill his pregnant wife is going to listen to his old cop partner?"

"He may not," Cutter said. "What about Suzi? You know her at all?"

"Heather and my wife were best friends," Ikeda said. "Royce and I hung out, but he was smart enough not to mention any of his side . . . other girls."

Lola spoke up. "Her sister, Tina, thinks she'll come out peacefully once she knows it's over."

"If he doesn't use her as a hostage," Alvarez said.

"Never can tell," Lola said. "But according to Tina, Suzi's never even held a gun. Afraid it'll chip her nail polish."

"We'll know soon enough if she's a combatant or a hostage," Cutter said.

"Or doomed bystander," Trooper Van Horn said. "Someone who's just standing around when the bullets start flying. Especially if this asshole's fond of IEDs."

"Alright," Blodgett said when Cutter had finished. "So the plan is we sweat our asses off snowshoeing over the ridge and then hole up and turn into icicles while we wait for this jack wagon to come out and take a bath."

"Yep," Cutter said. He waved his finger in a circle over his head. "Three minutes to offload urine and upload coffee, then let's gear up."

Gearing up essentially meant press-checking weapons and putting on mittens while the rest of the task force did the same, soaking up the last few moments of relative warmth.

"¿Listo?" he said to Lola.

She pulled a white balaclava over her head, leaving only her eyes exposed, then lifted the thumb of an oversized mitten that was tethered to her parka in case she had to shuck it off quickly.

"Ready as, boss," she said, perky as ever. "To quote Bluey—'let's do this!'"

Cutter raised a brow, lost under his own white balaclava. "Bluey?"

"Never mind," Lola said. "But you'd love it."

Alvarez stopped at the door. "Speaking of Bluey, what are we going to do about the dog? I know it's supposed to be aggressive, but I'd sure be happy if we didn't have to shoot it." Her boyfriend was one of APD's K9 officers. Including his working canine, the two of them shared four dogs. She made it her business to watch over any pup during a warrant service.

"I'd like that too," Cutter said. "But I'd also like to not get bit."

"Big-ass malamute," Blodgett said. "According to Tina it'll rip your face off."

Micki Frank raised a hand. "I'll give the wing commander a call," she said. "I think we can take care of that."

# CHAPTER 33

*Fairbanks*
*34° below*

$B$OBBY GANT AND THE NASH SISTERS MET BLACKWELL AND PEEWEE Halverson outside Sophie's Station. Daylight was still hours away. For some reason, the yellow lights in the otherwise blue-black parking lot made it seem even colder than it was. It wasn't likely, but there was an outside chance that Josie would come back. If she did, they planned to grab her there and, as Blackwell had said, hurt her until she told them where her son was. Gant knew her better than that. Josie was a tough lady. She'd die before she ratted on her rat son. Such a shame.

Gant pulled up alongside the other Jeep Cherokee, driver's door to driver's door, and rolled down his window. Mads sat in the front passenger seat. Browny perched in the middle of the back seat, looming forward when she wanted to say something. Gant couldn't help but expect a sharp steel hook to impact his neck at any given moment. At least he wouldn't feel anything.

Blackwell sat behind the wheel of the other vehicle, head tucked turtle-like into the neck of his parka, dark wool hat low over his eyebrows. Peewee Halverson slouched in the passenger seat, no doubt trying to look small.

Mads began to snarl the moment the window came down. She made a sweeping gesture with her hand and gave a toss of her head. "I do not see how two grown men could manage to be so dense. There is hardly any traffic at this time of morning."

"Losers!" Browny muttered.

"Hey," Blackwell said. "We're not—"

"Did you lose her or didn't you?" Mads snapped.

Blackwell looked genuinely hurt. "That's not—"

"You lost our only connection to the target." Browny made a harsh buzzing noise. "Losers!"

Blackwell stared directly at Gant. "She had to have known we were out here," he said. "It wouldn't surprise me if someone called to warn her."

Bile rose in Gant's throat. His hand dropped from the steering wheel to the pistol on his belt.

"You know that's a lie—"

Mads put a hand on his arm but spoke over him to Blackwell. "My experience, the one who makes the most excuses is the one who needs a closer look. Stop with the blaming. You lost her. Own it!"

"I—"

"Own it!" Mads said again. "And then think of a way to fix your screwup."

Peewee Halverson leaned forward in his seat to speak across Blackwell, looking hopeful. Vapor blossomed around his face. "Sam was working at a hotel when the boss hired him. Maybe he's doing the same kind of work. We could start checking the other hotels."

Mads rolled her eyes. "You reckon there's heaps of valet parking going on in this town? What else you got?"

Gant cleared his throat, drawing a surprised look from Mads, as if she'd not expected him to talk.

"She had a disagreement at the rental car counter," he said. "Something about an extra fee."

Blackwell nodded quickly, happy for the lifeline. He pounded the window frame with his fist.

"That's right!"

"What kind of disagreement?" Mads asked.

"We weren't close enough to hear," Gant said. "I thought about stopping to talk to the clerk but decided it was better to stick with . . . the professor." He caught himself before he called her Josie. "We should go talk to her now."

Mads nodded, then shot a glance over her shoulder at Browny, probably deciding who they wanted to hit in the head with their spikes.

"We'll meet you there," Blackwell said.

"Not you," Browny said.

"Peewee will ride with us," Mads said. "You and Browny can start checking all the hotels, on the off chance that Sam's working reception or something."

"You said it wasn't likely," Blackwell said.

"It's not," Mads said. "But it gives you something to do. Browny will go with you."

Peewee Halverson came around, his hulking weight causing the cold car to squeak and groan as he got inside. Hands stuffed deep in her parka pockets, Browny walked to the passenger side of the other vehicle but instead of taking Peewee's spot, she climbed in the back seat and scooted across to the driver's side. Blackwell glanced sideways at Gant, his face suddenly pale, looking like a scared little boy who'd just been sent to sleep in a dark and unfamiliar basement.

Mads pounded on the dash with her mittened hand. "Let's get moving!"

Gant put the Jeep in gear and wondered if this would be the last time he saw John Blackwell alive.

# CHAPTER 34

*Eielson Air Force Base*
*36° below*

MILITARY AND LAW ENFORCEMENT MADE FOR A VERY SMALL WORLD. It turned out that Deputy Micki Frank knew the Eielson Air Force Base wing commander's brother from her time in the Marine Corps. His aggressor squadron of F-16s needed to stay sharp and ready at any and all temperatures. Who knew if the Russian Bear might attack when it was forty below. They were already planning to have birds in the air for training runs this week. He was happy to help by tweaking the schedule.

Two flights of F-16 Fighting Falcons left the runway in pairs two minutes after the AST helicopters lifted off into the blue darkness.

Royce Decker might get hinky at the sound of an approaching chopper, but out here, fighter jets were just par for the course.

Cutter rode in the front left seat of Trooper Burns's helicopter. Rotary wing pilots customarily flew from the right as opposed to the left for fixed-wing aircraft. Burns and Haslet set their respective birds down on the protected bench moments before two pair of fighter jets roared past less than a thousand feet above the ridgeline.

On the ground and squinting in the bitter cold downwash, Cutter rallied Lola and Sean on the rocky ledge. Driven snow whipped and seared his face. He could feel the skin tighten—beginning to freeze, even behind the wool face mask he and the others on the team wore. His blinking became more rapid in a vain effort to keep his eyes warm. Bowing his head, he made certain everyone had all their gear before squinting back at Burns to give her a thumbs-up. Backlit by the faint glow of her instrument panel, she returned the gesture and added collective, taking the bird into the air. With nowhere to go on the small bench, Cutter and his team each took a knee, protecting their gear. The second flight of Flying Falcons roared overhead, covering the two choppers' egress as they thumped down the valley the same way they'd come in.

Some might have said the military was helping with civilian law enforcement. It was a gray area Cutter was happy to exploit.

There are few silences more intense than the moments after an aircraft insertion when the noise of jet engines and rotors fade and the quiet alone settles in.

Alvarez linked up with Blodgett, and the task force began to move up toward the ridgeline. It was steeper than Cutter anticipated, which helped with the snow depth, but required frequent side-hilling to get enough traction without sliding back down to the landing zone. All were in decent shape—and a decade younger than Cutter. It wasn't long before they achieved an efficient, if not graceful, rhythm. Lift, push, lift, push, careful not to overexert and start to sweat. It took almost half an hour to cover the fifty yards. It was like the worst calisthenics he'd ever experienced—in the military or the Marshals Service—all done in a deep freeze.

"'Take time to climb' my ass," Lola whispered.

Cutter darkened.

"What?"

"It sounded better in my head." She turned toward him, speaking in low hushed tones, barely above a whisper. Anything else would have seemed sacrilegious in this cathedral-like mountainside.

She held up her watch and then pointed to the line of black rock above them. Clouds of vapor enveloped their faces. A smile of frost from Lola's breath covered the front of Lola's balaclava. Complaints notwithstanding, she was nearly giddy from the impromptu quad workout.

She touched the face of her watch with the tip of her gloved finger. "We should be looking down on him as soon as we get over that lip."

Cutter blinked, squinting in the pre-dawn darkness. He hated to admit it, but he'd need reading glasses if he wanted to read a map that small.

"Good deal," he said and started upward again, taking Lola's word for it. He smelled woodsmoke a few feet from the top. A dog barked somewhere in the distance. Stopping, Cutter checked his own watch, a Seiko Turtle that was much easier to read. "Anytime now," he said.

Ninety seconds later, two F-16s thundered over again, rumbling the mountain and sending skitters of snow toward the valley floor.

"That should take care of our killer dog for a few minutes," Lola said.

Cutter had hoped to find some cover on the other side of the ridge. Instead, he found a snowy face and a large pocket of spruce between them and the cabin. The sun still wasn't up but in the gray light of dawn he was just able to make out bits and pieces of Decker's cabin through the trees some two hundred feet below, built on the same sort of bench where they'd landed the helicopters. It gave a commanding view of anyone who approached from the valley below.

"I reckon Decker wanted the higher ground as well," Lola whispered, her lashes fringed with crystalline ice. Clouds of vapor enveloped her face with each breathless word in the super-chilled air. The freezer in Mim's garage was twenty degrees warmer than this.

Cutter whispered into his mic, "One and Two are moving down the east side of the mountain to get a better view."

"Leave our snowshoes here?" Lola whispered. "These metal tubes will make a shit ton of noise."

Cutter scanned the rocks and trees below. "I think so. Looks pretty windswept for the most part. Sure to be some drifts but we should be good when we get down to the trees. We just need to be there before it gets light."

Darkness, even darkness combined with bitter cold, was a man-hunter's friend.

Fifteen agonizing minutes later, they'd worked and wallowed their way down through knee-deep drifts and tangled deadfall to reach a vantage point less than a hundred feet from the sixteen-by-twenty A-frame cabin of plywood, tin, and tar paper. The hill-side flattened when they came out of the thickest portion of the forest, leaving Cutter and Lola at roughly the same level as the cabin. Smoke poured from a metal stovepipe, flattening into a grimy gray layer when it hit the sub-zero air. Decker had to be up and stoking the fire.

Cutter slung his rifle and moved forward with his binoculars, nestling belly-down in a trough of deep snow. Lola took up a similar position at the base of a fat spruce ten yards to his right. The tree's feathered boughs had protected the ground below from most of the falling snow, leaving a well some four feet deep that served as a passable hide. The black of her hair spilling from beneath her white wool blended perfectly with the shadows beneath the spruce.

Cutter cupped his hand around his radio mic. "One and Two in place. Eyes on." He described their position as best he could relative to the cabin and the ridgeline.

Blodgett and Hart both checked in for their respective teams.

Cutter keyed the mic twice to show he'd received the message.

Belly down, Cutter continued to scan with his binoculars. As he suspected, he found a second plume of smoke curling from a metal chimney that jutted from what looked like the bottom half of a very large wooden barrel. He caught another smell, realizing what it was at the same moment he saw movement in the scant light near the hot tub. A cigar. Cutter blinked, clearing his eyes. From his vantage point, Cutter could just make out the top of a man's head—already soaking in the tub.

He clicked his tongue softly to get Lola's attention, then mouthed the word "Decker," nodding at the outdoor tub. She settled in behind her rifle, giving him a thumbs-up with her gun hand. Cutter depressed the push-to-talk switch in his mitten. "Male subject already in the tub, fifty feet northeast of the rear door. Can't see anything but the top of his head but he's got curly brown hair."

"Gotta be Decker," Alvarez said.

"Copy," Paige Hart said. "You want us to work around so we have a better angle?"

"Hold," Cutter said. "We don't have eyes on Suzi Massey yet."

All but invisible in the depression of snow, Lola peered down the barrel of her rifle. "Who goes for a soak in this weather. I'm freezing my ass off and he's lounging around in the nip."

Cutter slowed down his scan, moving his head from left to right. Scanning by moving just the eyes forced the brain to fill in the gaps, leaving out critical information.

The two-person soaking tub was a simple affair—hooped cedar slats six feet tall, coopered to become water tight. This one listed sullenly to one side, bleached and scarred from many years of use. Wooden steps, surely lumpy with packed snow and ice, led up to a platform of rough-hewn timber that kept the tub off the ground. A portion of the interior was devoted to a water-tight Snorkel Stove, all but the top of which was hidden from Cutter's view by his angle and the tall slats.

Though he couldn't see it, he knew the stove's firebox was sunk below the surface and partitioned off from bathers by a wood-slat divider wall. The stove was vented and fed through openings on the top to keep the firebox dry. A series of looped pipes through the wooden partition circulated heated water through the rest of the tub. Temperature was controlled by adding more wood or adjusting the damper—and stirring the water with a small canoe paddle that rested across the rim of the tub—now gray-white from hoarfrost created by billowing steam when it hit the near forty-below air.

Hart spoke again. "We're looking at an outhouse set back in the trees a hundred feet or so off the southwest corner—Stand by . . . Door's opening. White female coming out. That's positive ID on Suzi Massey."

"We're still too far away to move in and grab her," Nancy Alvarez said. "At least not without alerting Decker."

Sean Blodgett's voice crackled in Cutter's ear. "You want us to come on down, boss?"

"Stay put for now," Cutter whispered. "We'll just watch. I want to be reasonably sure we know what we're getting into. Decker's not above setting traps. No telling what surprises he's got lined up for us."

"I'll vouch for that," Lola said.

"Copy," Alvarez said.

Two minutes later, Suzi Massey emerged from the cabin wearing nothing but a red and black buffalo-plaid robe and matching slippers.

Massey hustled quickly against the cold, stepping out of the robe and draping it on a two-by-four rail. Doing so nudged Decker's robe to the side, just enough Cutter could see the black pistol grip of a firearm. An MP5 submachine gun or some variant, from the look of it.

Cutter called out the gun over the radio, letting the others know what he'd seen as well as the fact that it was within lunging distance of Decker. Suzi was unarmed. There was no doubt of that once she shed the robe. She stepped straight out of her slippers over the rim of the tub, grimacing when her leg came in contact with the frosty edge, frowning and looking at the sky like she'd rather be anywhere else as she lowered herself into the water. The hot water sent a flush of blood to her face. Decker grabbed her and yanked her toward him, causing her to cry out. Cutter tensed, suspecting Decker had spotted one of the team. He rested the front sight of his rifle over a spot over the outlaw's left ear.

Decker laughed, splashing Massey with water. He was just playing.

Just the tops of their heads were visible over the fortress-like lip of the cedar slats, but it was easy to tell when Decker pulled Massey close. She disappeared from sight for an instant, then shot upward, throwing her head so her long red hair flew into the super-cooled air. It froze solid immediately, sticking skyward like a giant flame. Decker roared with laughter. Massey sank back into the hot water, melting her hair at once. Decker leaned against the wooden rim and barked at her to do it again.

"Time to let them know we're here," Cutter said over the radio. "Troopers, you can start this way on the snow machines." Then, settling himself behind the gun, barked across the frozen landscape, "US Marshals! Royce Decker! Do not move!"

# CHAPTER 35

*R*OYCE AND SUZI TURNED IN UNISON TOWARD THE SOUND OF CUT-ter's voice.

"Hands!" Cutter yelled. "Let us see those hands! Both of you!"

Massey raised her hands and stood, rising half out of the water. Even from a distance it was easy to see she shook with cold and terror. Decker jerked her sideways placing her body between him and the direction of Cutter's voice. Her hair froze again, helmet-like. She tried to pull away, but the confines of the tub gave her no place to go.

"Aren't you a tough guy," Cutter yelled. "Using her as a human shield. How about you get into some warm clothes, and we handle this like adults—"

"Nice try, Marshal," Decker yelled. "It'd be better for all involved if you back off before she gets hurt."

"You can show me your hands and put a peaceful end to this." Cutter's voice grew darker. "Or, I wait until she kicks you in the balls and then I shoot off the top of your skull when you go for your gun."

"Bullshit!" Decker said. He talked a big game but his voice thrummed, tight with tension. "You're not gonna shoot a couple of naked lovebirds on the side of a mountain. Half the country already thinks you feds are jackbooted thugs. I can imagine the avalanche of civil suits that would rain down on you."

"You're smarter than that, Royce," Cutter yelled. "Let the woman go and we'll handle this like men."

"What happened to knocking on the door when we're fully dressed?" Decker said.

Decker glanced toward the cabin. "Thermometer says minus thirty-eight. You perverts have to be freezing your asses off sitting out there in the snow."

"Get out of the tub, Royce!" Cutter barked.

"I don't think I will," Decker said. "Not just yet. Now look, you go ahead and shoot us if you feel like you have to—"

Suzi's head snapped around at that. Decker yanked her to him to keep her in line.

"Thirty-eight below zero," Cutter shouted, as if driving home a point. He whispered over the radio, "Everyone hold what you got. I'm going to put a round through the stove."

Cutter was vaguely aware of Lola taking her eyes off her gun long enough to turn and look his way.

"You're what?" she whispered.

Cutter answered by pulling the trigger.

The .223 round from his M4 was miniscule—less than a quarter inch in diameter, but it had no trouble punching a hole in the tub's cedar slats and continuing through the aluminum wall of the submerged woodstove.

Cutter keyed the radio without getting off his gun. "Everyone move on up," he said. "Lola and I have him if he goes for the gun."

Suzi shrank away from the thwack of metal, pressing herself against the opposite end of the tub. Visible now, she was submerged to her nose. Decker's head snapped around toward the sound of the report. His right hand reached for his rifle. Cutter had a clean shot, but the idiot had a point. An avalanche of paperwork would follow if he killed a naked guy out for a soak, even if said naked guy was reaching for a gun. Cutter sent two quick follow-up shots, all in the same spot on the tub.

Decker froze at the report, hands in the air.

Steam bubbled and hissed to the surface, billowing out the stovepipe as water poured into the firebox and hit the flame.

Decker yanked Massey close again and hunkered behind her, squatting lower in the water, almost completely out of sight.

"What the hell, man?" he crowed. "You're gonna hit her."

"Do the math, Royce," Cutter said. "Your fire's gone out. And you said it yourself, we're looking at nearly forty below zero up here on this lonely old mountain. That water's what? A hundred, hundred-and-two tops. I doubt it'll take ten minutes to drop to sixty degrees. That's hypothermia time, my friend. You'll be looking at near freezing in half an hour. Much longer than that and I expect we'll have to chip your body out of there . . ."

In a burst of herculean strength, Suzi jerked loose from Decker's grasp and threw herself over the side of the tub, floundering like a pale and hairless seal on the ice. She pushed up like a sprinter and started for the cabin, high kneeing it to keep her wet feet from freezing to the wooden deck.

"Suzi! Stay away from that door!" Lola barked.

Cutter nodded at Lola's order. Massey was still an unknown. No way they were letting her get to any guns she might have stashed inside.

Lola continued to shout. "Go around front! Troopers will meet you there."

Suzi complied, tiptoeing quickly as if she were stepping over hot lava. In truth, the feeling was probably similar. Cold was already seeping through Cutter's snow pants and into his bones. Suzi was naked as the day she'd been born.

Royce Decker lasted another eight minutes before his hands rose shakily above the rim of the tub.

"Okay, okay!"

"Keep away from that gun," Cutter barked.

"Okay, okay." Decker's teeth clicked and chattered so hard it sounded like they might break. "Coming up."

# CHAPTER 36

*T*HE FAIRBANKS INTERNATIONAL AIRPORT TERMINAL WAS A LARGE boxy affair tucked in a forest of leafless white birch and the occasional snow-flocked spruce. The front of the building was almost entirely glass, good for letting in the scant sunlight during the short days of their Arctic winters.

Any airport was bound to be bristling with security cameras, collecting data that investigators would, no doubt, scour at some point in the near future in hopes of finding who had slipped in to whack a federal witness. Gant and Peewee Halverson traded wool hats for ball caps. Brims low, they would avoid looking up. Mads tucked her hair—including the silver streak—into a thick wool beanie with a decorative fur ball on top. Someone was bound to remember her Australian accent, but she'd come in on a private jet so her name would not appear on any commercial manifest.

Gant and Mads entered through the ticketing lobby while Peewee went in separately three doors to their right at baggage claim and the rental car counters. Inside, partially hidden from view by the stuffed polar bear, Gant and Mads waited under the bush plane suspended from the ceiling and watched Peewee approach the rental car counters like they'd planned on the way over. Gant breathed a sigh of relief when he saw the same doe-eyed clerk from the day before working at the rental car counter. They were in between flights and, apart from a man riding a large vacuum cleaner and a couple of blue-shirted TSA officers debating politics in the corner, the terminal was deserted.

There was no one else in line, leaving the clerk time to lean against the wall and pop her gum while she surfed her phone. Peewee banged on the counter with a huge fist and demanded she check into a reservation that didn't exist. He understood the assignment and did everything in the book to make an ass out of himself. After a full three-minute rant, he stomped off. The clerk, whose nametag said she was Cheryl, shot him the bird as soon as he turned his back.

She was exactly where they wanted her when they approached.

Mads did most of the talking, putting on her smooth Aussie voice that everyone seemed to trust—far more than they should have.

"What in the world had his knickers in such a twist?" she said.

Cheryl gave a little harrumph, watching Peewee as he stomped out the door. "Asshole," she said under her breath before turning to Gant and Mads. "Big guys like that never get their ass kicked enough to learn some manners . . . Anyway, how can I help you?"

"I have to say you handled that brilliantly," Mads said. "Does that happen to you a lot? Customers being such dicks?"

Cheryl snorted. "Too often for what they pay me. That's for sure."

Gant gave her an understanding nod. "I was picking up a friend yesterday afternoon and there was this Native lady giving the clerk all kinds of grief."

"That was me," Cheryl said. "Yeah. That lady wasn't so bad though. She was just pissed about an extra fee she had to pay."

"A fee?"

"Yeah." Instead of elaborating, Cheryl decided to get down to business. "So, what can I do for you?"

"We're hoping you rent four-wheel-drive pickups," Mads said.

"Only kind we rent." Cheryl tapped a few keys on her computer. "We still have one available," she said.

"About this extra fee?" Mads asked.

The clerk's fingers hovered over her keyboard. "What extra fee?"

Mads turned up her smile. "The one that Native lady got so upset about yesterday."

"Depends on where you plan to drive."

"Just around town I reckon," Mads said.

"Then you don't have to worry about it. The fee is if you planned to go up the Haul Road. It's some real *Ice Road Trucker* shit going on right now. Most companies won't even allow you to take their rentals up there. Stupid, especially in this weather. Fifty, sixty below is a battery killer. Shit tends to break when you just look at it. And there aren't many people to stop and help you when your car conks out."

"Why would anyone want to drive up the Haul Road?" Gant asked. "Seems like they'd be playing chicken with a bunch of eighteen-wheelers. What's the draw?"

"The cabins," Cheryl said. "That's what that Native lady was doing. Sounds like she plans to go out to one of the BLM cabins out toward Wickersham Dome. Guess she didn't read the fine print when she rented online and got pissed about the fee we charge for wear and tear. I mean, if she plans to go to one of the cabins that means she's leaving the car in the parking—"

Gant felt his gut tighten. "You said it would be stupid to go up there in this weather."

"It is," Cheryl said. "But totally worth it. I don't know if you saw, but the auroras were on fire last night. Those BLM cabins are a great place to see them. My boyfriend and I skied out to one last year. Pretty damned incredible."

Mads gave a low whistle. "Must really be out in the *woop-woop* if you made that woman pay extra."

"It's not the distance," Cheryl said. "It's the location." She pulled a tearaway map of the area off a large pad and spun it so it was oriented toward Mads and Gant, following the highway with her index finger. "The Steese Highway goes north out of Fairbanks . . . here up to Fox."

She looked up, finger holding her place on the map. "Y'all ever been to the Turtle Club?"

Gant shook his head.

"It's in Fox," she said. "Best prime rib in Alaska . . . Anyway, the

Steese turns into the Elliott here. The Wickersham Trailhead is something like fifty miles out, an hour and a half or so in this weather—if your car doesn't break down." She slid the paper map across the counter to Mads. "You can keep this. I'll need a driver's license and credit card to get going on the pickup truck."

Mads took Gant by the hand, gently, like they were actually friends. Gant was accustomed to hanging out with killers, but something about this woman curdled his blood. She smiled benignly. "What do you think, love?" she said. "Should we wait a couple of days?"

"Good idea," Gant managed to say.

Cheryl shrugged. "Suit yourself. I'm guessing it'll still be here. Gobs of people canceling their reservations when it's gonna drop to seventy below. Nobody wants to freeze their nose off just walking out to the car. Excuse my French, but everyone dreams of being an Arctic explorer until it's time to start doing Arctic explorer shit."

Mads put her phone on speaker and called the Bureau of Land Management main office as soon as they made it back out to the Jeep. Huddled in her parka, she put a finger to her lips warning Gant to be quiet and then laid on the charm with her sweet Crocodile Dundee voice. The young woman on the other end of the line hadn't likely been called "love" this many times during one conversation in her entire life.

"I'll cut right to it, love," Mads said. "This is so, so embarrassing, but my sister and I met this legend named Sam when we were skiing down in Anchorage. A real ripper if you know what I mean. Anyhoo, he invited us to come meet him at one of your cabins. I know it's somewhere around Fairbanks, but for the life of me, can't remember which. White Mountains, maybe . . ."

Two minutes of friendly chat later, the BLM clerk confided that there was no one named Sam on her books, but could his name have been Luke? They had a Luke Trejo registered in Lee's Cabin for the next two nights. Two different couples were staying at the Moose Creek and Eleazer's cabins, but she had no way of knowing if any of them had actually shown up on account of the horrible weather. A family of five were staying at Crowberry, the third cabin on the Trail Creek trail, nearly thirty miles in. They'd already been there two days and had either hunkered down for the weather or were on their way out a day early.

"They're calling for it to get really bad tonight," the BLM clerk said. "Lee's Cabin is about seven miles in. You'll need to get out there early if you want to meet your friend. I've fat-tire biked and skijored to it a bunch of times, but I'd definitely recommend snow machines in this weath—"

"Ta!" Mads said. "Brilliant. We'll be alright then. Thanks so much!"

She ended the call just as Peewee Halverson lumbered up and climbed in the back seat. She raised a brow at Gant. "I don't suppose you know where we can get some snowmobiles?"

"I'm sure we can find a place, but that would be more face-to-face interaction, paperwork—"

"No time for that," Mads said. "It's only seven miles and we may find them on the trail."

"Wait," Halverson said, unaware of the previous conversation. "Seven miles to what?"

"To Lee's Cabin where your government snitch is hiding out with his dear mum." She turned to Gant again. "We need to find a store with some of those fat tire bikes."

Peewee laughed out loud. "Sure. Bicycle seven miles in this? I haven't been on a bicycle in twenty years. It's thirty below out there. We'll freeze our asses off."

"Suit yourself," Mads said, deadpan. "You can ski."

# CHAPTER 37

*Girdwood*
*32° below*

TEN THIRTY IN THE MORNING WAS WAY TOO EARLY FOR TINA MASSEY to get out of bed, especially with the puke-inducing headache she'd been carrying around since Butch tried to murder her. But, the smell of frying bacon and woodsmoke curled up to the loft of her tiny ski-bum condo and pulled her out of the covers. She dabbed at her head, then checked the pillow. Dammit. Still bleeding. The first night she'd seen a piece of red fuzz on her sheet and thought it was a hunk of her brain. It wouldn't have surprised her. The pain was bad enough.

A feeble beam of light worked its way around the edges of the miniblinds. The sun was up, but cloud cover and the surrounding mountains put the little ski town in near perpetual shadow during winter.

Tina summoned enough strength to swing her legs over the edge of the bed. The wood planking creaked under the weight of her feet as she stood, holding on to the headboard to stop the room from spinning.

"She's awake!" Regina called from the combination kitchen, living room, and guest quarters below. "Hang on and I'll come up and get you."

In retrospect, it was stupid for Tina to have climbed the stairs in her condition, but her bed was way more comfortable than the couch. Regina had insisted on helping her up. Tina had gotten three anonymous calls after the Marshals picked up Butch. All three came from different numbers. She wouldn't have answered but she thought it might be Suzi. If it was, she didn't say anything. She'd made enough calls on smuggled cell phones from jail that she thought it might have been Butch, but the grouchy-faced marshal had said they'd keep him in lockdown so he wouldn't be able to call Royce. Whoever it was, they hadn't said a word, just sat there and breathed until she hung up. A threat would have been less unnerving. Tina had been threatened hundreds of times. The silence let her imagination run. Not good. Not good at all.

"You're a better than average friend," Tina said when Regina covered her with a quilt on the sagging sleeper sofa downstairs and handed her a giant cup of coffee to chase down two Tylenol and three Advil. It didn't touch the headache but took the edge off the pain in her neck and ribs—as long as she didn't move.

A fire cracked and popped in the woodstove.

Regina took a tray of bacon out of the oven and bumped the door shut with her hip. "How'd you sleep?"

"Crappy," Tina said. "I couldn't stop thinking about the phantom caller."

Regina gave a full body shiver. "I know what you mean. I got no proof, but I can't shake the feeling that someone is following me." Her face darkened. "Butch did make a deal to help the Marshals get Royce. Maybe they let him have a phone."

Tina took a sip of coffee. "No way," she said. "They got no love for Butch."

"What if he escaped?"

"You've been in the Anchorage jail," Tina said. "You ever see a way to escape unless you were a trustee? No way they're gonna let Butch Pritchard the baby killer be a trustee."

"You're right." Regina sighed. "Want some eggs?"

"You know what I'd really like? Some of that bacon between two slices of French bread with a lot of mayo and a slice of tomato."

Bacon, fresh bread, and fresh tomatoes were not normally things Tina had on hand, but the big marshal had given her fifty bucks out of his own pocket and told her to get something to eat. She'd blown it all at Crow Creek Mercantile in Girdwood—where the clerk was surprised to see her buy something besides her usual fried beef and bean chimichanga.

"Glad you're getting an appetite again," Regina said, going to work immediately. She prepped the bread and mayo and had just sliced the tomato when she looked up, knife in hand. "If it's not Butch . . . you think it might be—"

"Don't even say it out loud!"

"You still have dreams?" Regina said. "Because I do, almost every night. I'd see a therapist if I had the money."

"You can't see a therapist," Tina said. "You know what they say—they'll kill you, they'll kill me—"

"They'll kill my family," Regina said. "They'll kill your family . . ." She closed her eyes. "Better to just put it behind—"

A car door slammed at the end of the street.

Tina set her coffee mug down on the side table and pushed away the blanket. Like an idiot, she'd left her revolver upstairs. Regina started to say something, but Tina raised her hand, shushing her. She canted an ear toward the door, straining to hear.

No footfalls. Boots on snow would have squeaked like an ill-fitting Styrofoam cooler in this bitter cold. The silence should have comforted her, but like the calls, it left her thinking the worst. Her neighbor, Mr. McFadden, was still in Hawaii. The only other reason for anyone to park in front of his house was to hike the trail into the woods—and it was way too cold for a stroll.

A soft knock sent Tina retreating deeper into her quilts. Regina turned to face the door, the tomato knife clutched in her fist. Neither woman spoke. Both had worked the hotel circuit to know. Cops banged on the door. Friends just knocked. Soft knocks were always from the worst people . . .

# CHAPTER 38

*Salcha*
*38° below*

GETTING DECKER AND MASSEY DOWN THE MOUNTAIN ON THE Troopers' snow machines proved to be an exercise in creativity. For all his planning, Cutter had neglected to think about extra clothing for naked prisoners. Given the intelligence that Decker had set booby traps all around the property, there was a better than average chance he'd rigged some kind of surprises in the house as well. The guy was looking at the death penalty with nothing left to lose. Nancy Alvarez was able to coax the big malamute out with a little patience and some bacon treats she had in her pocket. It would follow the snow machines down when the time came. Cutter wasn't about to allow any of the arrest team to go in and get a fresh set of clothes. But he couldn't let them freeze either.

He considered giving Decker and Massey two of their parkas and sending them down the mountain in the sleds behind the Trooper snow machines. The parkas were warm enough for their upper bodies, but at forty below, the prisoners would quite literally freeze their asses to the sleds. Trees and scrub surrounded the cabin, preventing the AST choppers from landing anywhere but two hundred meters up the ridge, much of that through knee-deep snow. Negotiable for Cutter and his team when they were coming down, but a hell of a trip if you were naked and handcuffed.

In the end, Cutter asked Trooper Burns to fly over and drop a couple of insulated jump suits. It took ten minutes to get everything squared away. Until then, Cutter had the prisoners stand on folded bathrobes. He and Blodgett gave them their outer parkas. From the outside looking in, it seemed a chivalrous act, but the last thing Cutter wanted was for this bastard to have any complaints about ill treatment that might give him grounds for appeal. Giving him a coat just helped grease the wheels of justice—which, if the State of Missouri had its way, would eventually send Decker to the death chamber.

Trooper Burns proved to be a good shot as well as an outstanding pilot, dropping the bundle of two insulated snow-machine suits and two pairs of white military bunny boots less than ten yards from the hot-tub deck where Cutter and his team were gathered.

Cutter had to remove the handcuffs in order to get Decker into his one-piece suit. Without being told, Lola took a step back. She shucked off her beaver fur mittens and let them dangle by her side, leaving her with only merino wool glove liners as she drew her Glock and held it muzzle down toward the snow.

Handcuff key in one hand, Cutter gripped Decker's wrist with the other. "You were on the job a good while."

Decker cleared his throat to hide a sob. The cold as well as the reality of his situation were getting to him. "Long enough to know you're the contact officer, she's your lethal cover."

"Absolutely right," Cutter said. "What you may not know is I'm too tired and cold to fight with you. If you move . . . Well, tell him what will happen, Deputy Teariki."

"If you do anything other than what you're directed, Deputy Cutter will push away, and I will shoot you in the head."

Another sob. "I'm naked!" he bleated like a wounded fawn. "Not even the US Marshals would just gun down an unarmed man with no clothes."

"You're not unarmed," Cutter said. "We have it on good authority you have this entire place rigged to explode. One step the wrong way could put my team in jeopardy. And we can't have that." He glanced at Lola. "¿*Listo?*"

"*Listo.*"

Shivering badly, Decker did exactly as he was told.

Two troopers pulled around in their snow machines, pulling large black plastic sleds with room enough for two. Deputies Madsen and Hart volunteered to ride out, essentially holding the prisoners on their laps on the way down the mountain. The trooper pulling Madsen and Decker took the lead so the second trooper could keep them in view during the trip. No one wanted Decker to escape.

Butch Pritchard had provided a fairly extensive list of improvised explosives and dangerous devices in and around Decker's cabin. Alaska State Troopers EOD team anticipated it would take them the better part of the day to deem the area safe.

Adrenaline waning post arrest, Cutter and the others made the cold trudge back up the ridge to the waiting choppers for egress.

Less than an hour after Cutter had slapped the cuffs on Decker, the Alaska Fugitive Task Force was back in the warmth of the Eielson Security Forces office with their prisoners. The temperature had fallen by seven degrees from the time they'd initiated the hit. Micki Frank, still at the ad hoc command post, had arranged for a tray of sandwiches. Exposure to this kind of bitter cold burned a massive number of calories and everyone wolfed down the sandwiches like hungry huskies just off the trail.

Getting a murderer off the street should have been cause for celebration, but the look on Officer Joe Ikeda's face when he saw his old partner marched through the door was worse than a drop kick to the groin.

"Heather was my friend, you son of a bitch," Ikeda said under his breath.

Decker looked away.

The Security Police sergeant let Cutter put the prisoners in his holding cells, as long as someone other than Air Force personnel stood by and guarded them. "Posse comitatus and all."

Blodgett and Hart volunteered to take their sandwiches to the cellblock and babysit. The prisoners got sandwiches too.

"Outstanding job, my dear," Micki Frank said to Cutter. "I can run you back if y'all tend to all your business in the next hour. As suspected, this weather's goin' titties up, as they say, awfully fast."

"Hooah," Cutter said. Getting back home to Mim was just what his cold bones needed. "Let me call the chief so she can let Missouri know the good news. Thanks for the sandwiches by the way . . ."

Jill Phillips answered on the first ring as Cutter knew she would. The best chief he'd ever even heard of, she was either ready with the phone when her people were in the field or out there with them. Like a good boss, she let him speak before butting in to ask for details.

"No injuries and we're off the mountain with Decker and Suzi Massey in custody."

"Good to hear," Phillips said.

"Micki's still here. We'll jump in with her and be back in a couple of hours. Maybe early enough for Decker to see a judge. He knows the drill. He'll probably ask for an identity hearing just to drag things out."

"Sounds about right," Phillips said. "Listen, Arliss, a couple of things."

Cutter didn't like the sound of her voice. She rarely called him Arliss unless she was going to talk about something personal, or heavy. Often it turned out to be both.

"Everything okay?"

Phillips ignored the question and plowed ahead.

"Am I on speaker?"

"You are not, Chief."

"Good. I got a call from an inspector in the lower forty-eight today who seems to have lost contact with his protected witness, a kid named Luke Trejo."

"His real name?"

"No idea," Phillips said. "Inspector Smith didn't tell me much. He asked if we could swing by this guy's apartment and tell him to call in."

"Does this inspector suspect something's happened?"

"Nothing like that," Phillips said. "He's just been trying to get in touch with what's-his-name for two days now."

"Hmm." Cutter told her about the murder in Fairbanks, and the severed ear.

"Pretty damned coincidental," she said. "They have an ID on the victim?"

"Not that I've heard," Cutter said. "I'll keep an ear to the ground . . . Sorry. Tired. This Trejo kid have a history of not checking in?"

"Like I said, Inspector Smith wasn't very forthcoming. I hesitate to bring the Fairbanks deputies in on this unless you find a reason to believe the ear guy is connected to this somehow. Do me a favor, get with Paul or Ryan and borrow one of the Fairbanks G-rides. You and Lola run and give this Luke kid one of those patented looks from your Arliss Cutter mean mug. Any of the others want to know what you're doing, tell them you're on a special assignment from me. Don't mention that I want you to go scare the pee-water out of a protected witness."

"Roger that, Chief," Cutter said. "You had something else?"

"Afraid I do," Phillips said. "Girdwood EMS found Tina Massey and Regina Orr dead in their apartment about fifteen minutes ago."

"What?" Cutter said, loud enough to draw looks from everyone else in the room. He turned away and lowered his voice. "How?"

"There was some product at the scene that tested positive for fentanyl," Phillips said. "They're calling both deaths overdoses."

"Nope," Cutter said, loud again. "That doesn't track. Could be Pritchard made some calls. He did just try to kill her."

"That was my first thought, too," Phillips said. "Anchorage jail assures me he's been in solitary since you booked him. No contact with anyone. Even the jail staff is limited."

"She was terrified of someone," Cutter mused. "And it wasn't necessarily Butch. That someone is who killed her."

"Agreed," Phillips said. "But investigations into possible homicides are so far outside of our swim lanes . . . Anyway, I just wanted you to know it happened."

Murder, suicide, overdose—Cutter and his team dealt with one kind of death or another a couple of times a month. Their clients—

the folks they hunted—rarely lived the healthiest lives. But Tina Massey and her friend both overdosing on the same night in the middle of all this, that rubbed against the grain of reason.

"You okay?" Phillips asked.

"I'm fine," Cutter said. "Lola and I will go light a fire under Luke Trejo and then fly back commercial."

"Good deal," Phillips said. "With any luck you'll be home before dinner."

# CHAPTER 39

*40° below*

O<small>N LIGHT DUTY DUE TO HIS BROKEN FOOT, P</small>AUL G<small>UTIERREZ GAVE</small> up his G-ride. He removed his gear bag and a padded Cordura hunting rifle case from the back of his government issue forest-green Chevy Tahoe. Cutter gave a nod to the case.

"Whatcha packing, Paul?" The gun was surely out of policy, but in a place as remote as the Arctic, Cutter wasn't going to second-guess the guys on the ground. He was genuinely interested in what kind of rifle a frontier deputy would opt to carry.

"Winchester Safari Express," Gutierrez said. The deputy braced himself for a correction.

Cutter gave a nod of approval. "Looks like a .375 H&H."

"It's a .416 Remington Magnum." The deputy rubbed his shoulder. "A brute for sure, but it'll knock down anything on the planet."

"A projectile the size of your index finger," Cutter said. "I imagine it would come in handy in a pinch."

"I know it's outside policy," Gutierrez said. "I just—"

"What's outside policy?"

"The .416."

Cutter peeked in the back of the Tahoe. "I don't see a .416."

"You're a hell of a boss," Lola said ten minutes later when they were in the Tahoe and braving the icy noontime twilight on the

Richardson Highway through North Pole. The little suburb of Fairbanks lived up to its name, with candy cane streetlights and a Santa Claus House store that stayed open year around.

Cutter shrugged off the compliment. "Don't know what you're talking about." He glanced across the center console. "Lola, I've been pretty hard on you these last couple of days."

She managed a pretty good imitation of his Florida drawl and stone face. "Don't know what you're talking about." Her Kiwi accent came crashing back a half second later. "What do you reckon really happened with Tina Massey? Poor thing. Regina too. I'm not buying the overdose theory."

"Neither am I," Cutter said. "The chief was crystal clear though. Homicide investigations are outside our—"

"I know," Lola said, exasperated. "Outside our swim lanes. Bosses and headquarters people say that all the time. We're deputy United States marshals, for pity's sake and, last I checked, peace officers in the state of Alaska. We swim in the whole frickin' pool!"

Cutter didn't respond, but he couldn't disagree with the sentiment.

"Butterbean was scared of something, too," Lola said.

"Yes, he was." Cutter turned left off the Steese onto College Road, which would take him to Luke Trejo's address of record.

Lola twisted slightly in her seat, arm on the console, and studied Cutter's face. "We're going to talk to Butterbean when we get back, aren't we?"

Cutter parked the Tahoe in front of Trejo's building. Surely built in the 1970s, the apartments were boxy prefab affairs with flat roofs and weathered cedar shake fascia and dismal-looking brown balconies covered in frost. Alaska Pipeline chic.

"Aren't we?" Lola prodded.

Cutter put a hand on the door handle. "Yep."

Lola smacked a fist into her opposing hand. "You're a hell of a good boss," she said.

Trejo's apartment was on the second floor halfway down the hall. Cutter had half expected to find yellow shag carpet and dark wood paneling in the hallway but instead found shining waxed tile and Alaska-themed prints. He stood to the side of the door out of habit, giving it four solid raps with the meat of his closed fist. Three knuckle knocks might be a salesman or some kind of missionary. Four good smacks hefty enough to bring a shower of dust raining down from the ceiling inside said *I'm not going away.*

Nothing.

He tried again, this time jiggling the knob.

Lola groaned. "What now? Did this blabby inspector give us anything else to go on?"

"Not a—"

The door across the hall opened and a young Native woman backed out, AirPods in her ears, housekey in hand to secure the door as she pulled it closed. She gave a little yelp when she turned around and realized she wasn't alone in the hallway. On the smallish side, Cutter guessed her to be in her mid-twenties. Her traditional caribou fur parka was trimmed in startlingly white Arctic fox and sported a thick wolverine fur ruff the color of spun molasses—the kind of coat you spent thousands of dollars on at a fur shop in the city—or got for free when your aunty sewed it for you in a bush village.

Cutter suspected this was the latter.

Rather than rouse suspicion by identifying themselves as deputies, he gave the young woman a wave.

Lola stuck out her hand. "My name's Lola," she said. "We're friends of Luke's."

The young woman took the offered hand. "Carina."

"Seen him around today?" Lola asked.

"He left early this morning," she said. "Not like he gives me the time of day. You know, when he first moved in, I thought, *Fantastic. A cute Native guy living right across the hall from me.* But, no, that Indian keeps to himself."

"He's always been kind of a loner," Lola said.

Carina looked at Lola and cringed. "I'm sorry," she said. "I wasn't thinking. You're probably . . . I mean, here I am telling you how I wanted to hook up with Luke and you're probably his girlfriend."

"Nothing like that," Lola said. She nodded at Cutter. "Just friends. My uncle and I have done a couple of business deals with him. You know, online investments and stuff. He happen to say where he was going? We're in town for a couple of days and thought we'd stop by and say hello."

Cutter was happy to let her do the talking. She was good at this.

"He had a map of the White Mountains under his arm a couple of weeks ago," Carina said. "His truck's still in the parking lot, bad starter from the sound of it, but he never asked me. Anyway, I saw him hooking up his snow machine trailer to a little Subaru early this morning. Hell of a job in this cold, I'll tell you that."

Cutter raised a brow. "The White Mountains?"

"Up toward Wickersham Dome," Carina said. "On the Haul Road. It's way too cold to go snow-machining for fun. I figure him and his new girlfriend are planning to hole up at one of the Bureau of Land Management cabins. He had a couple of those plastic totes with him. Probably full of grub and such. If he'd asked I woulda told him he should take like a Yeti or something heavier duty. Those thin plastic ones from the hardware store will shatter like glass if you so much as bump them at fifty below—and we'll be wishing for fifty below by sunset."

"New girlfriend?" Lola asked.

"The one in the Subaru," Carina said. "I only saw her through my window, but she looked a little too old for him if you ask me."

"Holding at forty below." Lola nodded at the thermometer when they were back in the Tahoe. "The place where Fahrenheit and Celsius meet up . . ."

Rather than leaving with them, Carina had gone back inside her apartment, and now peered out her window at them through a pair of binoculars.

"Weirdo," Lola said. "No wonder she was able to tell Luke's new girlfriend looked older than him through her second-floor window in the dark. It occurs to me Carina could be making up this shit about the White Mountains BLM cabins and she's really got our guy tied up in her bed like that *Misery* movie."

Cutter checked his watch. Twenty minutes after noon. He started the Tahoe and pulled around the corner, out from under Carina's prying gaze.

"Give the BLM offices a call," he said. "You have to give a name to reserve a public use cabin. See if they have a Luke Trejo on their list."

"Lee's Cabin," Lola said after she hung up. "The clerk was cagey, like she was holding something back."

"Like what?" He'd learned to trust Lola's intuition. Mostly.

"Probably nothing," Lola said.

Cutter fished the phone out of his parka. "I'll let the chief know what we've got."

Again, Jill Phillips answered like she was already holding the phone to her ear. Cutter briefed her quickly and then ended the call so she could pass the information to the inspector.

In the meantime, Lola called FPD for an update on the homicide at The Cookie Jar. The victim still hadn't been identified, but he wasn't a Native American. Finished with the call, Lola reclined her seat and stared up at the headliner. "The chief's gonna make us stay up here forever . . ."

Cutter's phone rang as if on cue. The caller ID said CDUSM.

"We're about to find out." He answered. "Hey, Jill. You're on speaker with Teariki."

"Hey, Lola," Phillips said. "So listen, our friendly neighborhood inspector about shit a brick when I mentioned the homicide at The Cookie Jar. The severed ear is especially bothersome. Seems like the kind of message you'd send to intimidate a government witness."

"Hard to argue with that," Cutter said.

"The inspector wants you to, and I quote, *run out to the cabin and check in with Luke,*" Phillips said.

Lola laughed out loud. "That is so stuffed. There's no running out to check the cabin. We'd be talking a winter expedition to a remote cabin seven miles from the trailhead. It's forty-three below and falling. AST's no-fly temp is minus fifty—which we'll pass in another hour. They couldn't even drop us if they wanted to."

"She's right, Chief," Cutter said. "We're talking Arctic expedition here."

"You still have your winter gear from this morning or did you send it back with Micki?"

"We have it with us," Cutter said.

"Let's split the difference then," Phillips said. "Get with Gutierrez and Madsen and tell them you need to borrow their snow machines. You and Lola drive out to the trailhead and take a look. If you think it's too dangerous, then turn around and come home. You're boots on the ground so I'll leave the final decision up to you."

"What should we tell the Fairbanks guys?" Lola asked.

"Just tell him I'm sending you on an errand," Phillips said. "At forty below, Madsen will be happy he doesn't have to go with you."

# CHAPTER 40

*Anchorage*
*34° below*

MIM SAT ON THE FLOOR WITH HER BACK AGAINST THE WALL AND legs akimbo, combing piece by piece through the contents of her mother-in-law's secret suitcase. Tears streamed down her cheeks. Benson Boone songs played on her phone in an endless loop.

Ursula had run away when Ethan was seven and Arliss was five, but over the ensuing years, she'd collected a copy of virtually every certificate, award, and diploma from her boys' lives. Ethan's sixth grade report card, with a note recommending him for high school algebra in the seventh grade. A note to D. Wayne Cutter from Arliss's elementary school nurse, lamenting the fact that the boy was forever getting in fights defending other kids, often getting himself beaten up in the process. "Our boy is fearless," the note said. The nurse didn't seem to mind that Arliss was getting a few licks in on the bullies. She just didn't like to see him hurt.

There were copies of Ethan's diplomas, their wedding photos, school pictures of Constance and the boys. She found a photo of Arliss's baby face and buzzed blond hair the day he graduated from Army boot camp. Then another, where he looked even more gaunt shortly after he'd finished Selection and joined the 75th Ranger Regiment. Ursula had photos from when Arliss graduated boot camp and copies of his military citations. At the bottom of the case was a pair of blue hand crocheted baby booties.

Until she'd opened the valise, Mim had no idea Arliss had anything beyond a rudimentary ability to draw. Somehow, Ursula had gotten her hands on two original pencil sketches, each signed Arliss C. One was of a motorcycle cop in jodhpurs standing beside his bike. The other was the profile of a young woman standing in the surf, half turned toward the sea. The hair, the cheekbones, it was obviously Mim. It was dated 1994, the year after they'd first met in that little bait shop where she worked. She was dating Ethan by then.

"Oh, Arliss," she sobbed, whispering to herself. "What we must have done to you . . ."

"I think I have you beat on that account, hon." Ursula's voice cut through Mim's tears, causing her to sit bolt upright and clutch her robe tight across her chest.

"I wondered when you might do a little investigating," Ursula said. "Took you a hell of a lot longer than it would've taken me."

"I'm sorry," Mim said. "You didn't come back last night and I—"

"Relax," Ursula said. "I'm smart enough to know. You leave something a mystery for too long and people are gonna try to find an answer, with or without you."

Ursula tossed her purse on the bed and lowered herself down beside Mim, arching her back with a little grimace from the effort. She picked up the military citation that went along with Arliss's Bronze Star with a V device for valor.

"My sons," she said. "The finest men I never knew . . ." She choked up, hand to her chest, tears coursing lines through her powdery makeup.

"Arliss has absolutely got to see this," Mim said. "He needs to know that you never stopped loving him."

Ursula picked up the blue baby booties. "Nana Cutter made these for Arliss . . ." She sniffed back a tear. "I was such a hot mess back then. You have to believe me. Wayne . . . Grumpy was so . . . he was just so solid. Exactly what the boys needed." She reached across the open case and touched Mim's arm, is if to make sure she had her full attention. "I was dating a string of very questionable men, which made me drink, which made me date more questionable men, which made me drink even more. Grumpy helped me get into the Betty Ford clinic in Naples . . . twice." She rubbed her eyes with a thumb and forefinger, taking care not to smudge her liner.

"Did he help you get all this stuff?"

She nodded, nearly breaking down again. "We talked. A lot. He kept me up to speed on what was going on with their lives. I kept all his letters, too, in another box, all written in pencil."

"Treasures," Mim said. "I'm sure Arliss would love to see them as well."

"I wish Ethan could have seen them," Ursula said.

"Me too."

"You know, I always intended to come back and get them. First, I thought, I just need to be two years sober. But two years turned into five and then six, and by then, I'd stayed away too long. They had such a good life with Grumpy." Ursula looked up, suddenly brighter. She patted Mim's arm again. "And if they'd been with me, who knows if they would have gone in that bait shop on Manasota Key. If they hadn't met you, neither of my boys would ever have been truly happy."

# CHAPTER 41

*Wickersham Dome Trailhead*
*48° below*

JUST AS HEAT BECAME FIRE, COLD MORPHED INTO SOMETHING TANGI-
ble when temperatures dropped far enough, a physical thing. Ice
was too benign a word. Bouncing along on the back of the screaming snow machine, bitter wind invading every seam and zipper of
her insulated clothing, Josie Lujan imagined something worse
than fire. Something that burned cold.

Whatever it was, she'd dressed for it. Or thought she had. Steger moosehide Arctic mukluks and thick alpaca socks, wool long
johns, insulated ski bibs and a goose down parka with a wolf-fur
ruff, wool glove liners, heavy over-mitts, face mask and goggles.
No part of her was left exposed—and still the wind cut through.

If there was a post card image for bitter cold, the Twenty-Three
mile trail was it. A pitifully weak sun threw a crystalline glare off
endless moguls of white, blinding, deafening, breathtaking,
rolling into snow-covered mountains or falling away to drifted val-
leys. The endless landscape was broken only by patchy forests of
spruce. Not the towering evergreens of the Arizona mountains or
even downtown Fairbanks. These dark and gnarled little trees
might have given the land a mangy look, but now, flocked with
frost and bowed under whipped-cream dollops of heavy snow

they resembled something out of the Dr. Seuss books Josie had read to Sam when he was a boy.

Josie sat behind her son, helmet against his back, mittened hands gripping the side passenger handles. She'd started the seven-mile journey to their rented cabin with her arms wrapped around Sam's waist—partly to hold on, mostly because she was ecstatic to see her boy in person after four long years apart. He would never know the pain he'd caused her, but she consoled herself that he was here with her now.

He was a good boy at heart, her son, strong and kind, albeit with a mushy moral compass. He was learning though. She hoped.

He must have bought the machine to impress her. It was a brand-new Skandic, octane blue with the sticker from the Ski-Doo dealership in Fairbanks still on the windscreen. It had taken less than a mile for Josie to realize he wasn't a very good rider. She didn't have much experience either—a few tours into the Yellowstone or with friends outside of Jackson Hole—enough to know he should have been using his own body more to steer, even on these groomed trails.

Ten minutes into the ride, her helmet visor was so fogged with ice she couldn't see anything. Blind now, she ducked her head between his shoulder blades and imagined sitting in front of a warm wood fire. A few bitter minutes later, he suddenly cut left as if he'd almost missed a turn. Thrown to the right, she gripped the rail.

Sam slowed the machine, grunting something Josie couldn't make out over the engine. She turned her head to peer sideways out of the only clear spot in her visor.

Two snow machines sat parked in a snowy clearing in front of a ten-by-fourteen cabin of blond logs.

Sam flipped up his visor, blowing steam with each word. "I know this is the right place," he said. "It says Lee's Cabin right above the door."

"Checkout's at eleven," Josie said, doubting herself even as she said the words. "Maybe they're just a little late—"

A shadowed face filled the tiny window on the door, peering out. Josie waved. "Hello the cabin!"

The door creaked open a crack, releasing a puff of white smoke into the cold. Josie could make out a strip of youngish face, a few years older than Sam, one deep-set eye and a long aquiline nose. Though inside the cabin, the man still wore a wool hat, his parka and leather gloves.

"Help you?" He coughed, then rubbed his eye with the knuckle of his glove. More smoke rolled out.

Sam held up his phone. "We've got reservations starting at noon today."

"Are you . . ." The man coughed again. "Are you sure? Must have been some mix-up. We have it reserved."

Josie's teeth were beginning to chatter. "Mind if we come inside and get warm while we get this sorted?"

The man turned to look behind him, consulting with someone. He opened the door and then turned, leaving it ajar as he went back inside.

"Come on then," he said over his shoulder.

Josie noted the thermometer outside the door on the simple wooden plank porch.

Minus 52°—a drop of eight degrees since they'd left the parking lot. It wasn't much warmer inside the cabin.

A set of bunk benches ran the length of the left wall, giving access to a loft along the back third of the little cabin. On the right was a woodstove and a small plywood table. Josie was surprised to see the stove piled with wood but unlit. A tall woman wearing a bright purple snow-machine suit hunched at the table warming her hands over a gas lantern turned to the highest setting. The cabin windows and the lantern light cast odd shadows over the smokey room.

"Something's wrong with the stove," the woman said. She wore a startling amount of makeup to be in the wilderness. Blond braids trailed from either side of her wool Sherpa-style hat. Her voice was husky, sultry, like Kathleen Turner, but far less pleasant. It wasn't hard to imagine her in a horned helmet and breastplate belting out a Wagnerian opera.

"I'm Josie and this is my son—"

Sam stuck out his hand. "Luke," he said. "Luke Trejo."

"Evan," the slender man said grudgingly. "My wife, Adrianne."

Sam held up his phone to prove his point about the reservation, but Josie interrupted. They needed to get warm.

"What's this about the stove?" she asked.

"I told you," Adrianne grumbled. "It's broken." This winter camping stuff was definitely not her jam.

Josie directed her questions to Evan. "Broken how?"

"I'm thinking the damper," Evan said. "I get the fire going but I can't get it to pull smoke."

Still in her parka, gloves, and hat, Josie got down on her knees and peered into the metal box. The damper appeared to be open.

"Can I get a wad of paper or curl of birch bark?"

Evan handed her a stack of white paper plates. Burned remnants in the stove said he'd been using the same thing to try and start his fire.

Instead of putting the crumpled paper under the kindling where conventional fire-building wisdom said it should go, Josie wadded two of the plates and pushed them up past the damper into the chimney before lighting them. Once they were burning, she lit another wad of paper under the kindling. Flames were soon licking the logs. The chimney puffed away, drawing all the smoke up and out.

"What did you do?" Evan asked, genuinely interested.

Josie squatted in front of the door, warming her bare hands on the flame. "My grannie used to have a cabin in the mountains outside Flagstaff. Never got this cold but we had some pretty brutal winters. Sometimes you get a column of cold air hanging out in the chimney. The initial flame can't warm it enough to lift it out, so it never draws, and your fire never gets going. I just stuffed a little paper in there and heated it up to push out the stagnant air and start her going."

"Smart," Evan said.

Adrianne rolled her eyes, but she moved from the lantern to the stove to warm her hands as well.

Josie turned to her son. "I was reading on the plane," she said. "We need to cut some spruce boughs and stuff them under the skis and tracks of the snow machine, so it doesn't freeze to the ground in this weather."

Adrianne looked up. "So you're leaving?"

"Tomorrow," Josie said, matter-of-fact. "Our reservations are through tonight until eleven tomorrow."

Sam held up his phone. "I can send a message to BLM via my inReach and we'll sort this out if they double-booked us. Mind if I take a look at your reservation?"

Evan got his phone from a duffel on the bunk. Instead of showing it to Sam, he held it by his side, sighing. He was nearly as tall as Sam but ten years older and doughy around the middle. "Truth is," he said, "we booked the Moose Creek Cabin."

"I hear that's a good one," Sam said.

"You're welcome to get warmed up here before you push on," Josie said.

"We're already unpacked," Adrianne said. "If you think it's such a good place, how about you trade with us."

Josie shot a glance at Sam.

"We'll stick with this one," he said. "It's what we reserved. Like my mother said, you're welcome to stay here and warm up a bit before you push on."

"It's fifty below," Adrianne groused. She was close enough that for the first time, Josie smelled alcohol on her breath. Much larger than Josie, she loomed over her, crowding her away from the stove. "We were here first."

Josie stood, unzipping her parka. "That's not how reservations work."

"I'll give you five hundred dollars," Evan said.

"No!" Sam said. "I reserved this place weeks ago and we're staying here."

"Then we'll all stay," Adrianne said. "Because I am not going out there again. You guys can have the loft and we'll take the—"

Josie took several deep breaths, keeping her voice calm. "That is not an option," she said.

"Oh"—Adrianne gave a low chuckle as she waved a hand around the cabin interior—"it's this simple. Our shit's already unpacked. Yours is still on your machine. You can warm up by the fire a few minutes and push on to our cabin at Moose Creek, or you can stay upstairs in the loft." She glowered, orange flames reflecting off her heavy makeup. "Unless you feel like you can physically throw me out."

Josie just looked at the woman and smiled, thinking how simple it would be to cut the woman's heart out and toss it into the snow. Her great-grandmother probably would have. Josie had heard stories.

# CHAPTER 42

*48° below*

MADS HAD BLACKWELL WRITE DOWN EVERYONE'S SIZES AND GO with her and Browny to buy better winter clothing at the Sportsman's Warehouse and a place called Big Ray's. Gant's Jeep had a top rack so she sent him and Peewee to pick up fat-tire bikes at a shop north of Ester, about five miles out of town.

Peewee began to make excuses from the moment they were alone in the car.

"It's not that I couldn't ride a bike," he said. "I just never had cause to learn. You know what I mean, Bobby. When are guys like us gonna ride a bicycle?"

"You learned how to ski but never learned how to ride a bike when you were a kid?"

"What can I say? My mother used to send me to her sister's place in Schenectady for a couple of weeks every winter. Not much call for bicycling upstate that time of year, but a shitload of opportunity to ski. I got pretty good."

"But no bike," Gant said.

"I'd fall on my ass."

Gant pulled into the Goldstream Sports parking lot. "This place has skis," he said. "The cabin is only seven miles from the trail. We should be in and out in a couple of hours."

"As long as Mads gets us warm enough gear and we don't freeze to death," Peewee said.

"There is that." Gant bailed out of the Jeep and made a beeline for the store. The cold hit him like an axe handle to the face, tightening the skin so it felt like plastic.

Forty-five minutes later, he'd paid cash for four fat-tire bicycles—with insulated handlebar covers called pogies—and a pair of cross-country skis with backcountry bindings that were surely ten times better than anything Peewee Halverson had ever skied in at his aunt's house in upstate New York. Before he left the store, Gant picked up a pair of Outdoor Research down mittens, and boots called Baffin Snow Monsters. Big and clunky as its name implied, the boot didn't look like it would be especially easy to pedal a bicycle in—but at least he'd have feet when he got to where he was going. Looking at Halverson's miniscule ski boots—Gant couldn't say the same for him. Served him right. He should have learned how to ride a bike.

The clerk, an overly energetic young man who had to be drinking far too many Red Bulls, helped them bungee all the bikes to the top rack. Finished, the young man banged a gloved hand on the back fender and gave a sort of sloppy salute.

"Thanks for shopping with us," he said. "Hope it warms up enough for you to ride soon . . ."

Gant didn't know whether to laugh or cry. He couldn't shake the feeling that they were all doomed.

Belying their terrifying demeanor, Mads and Browny bought four large pizzas for the group to share on the hour-and-a-half drive out to Wickersham Dome Trailhead. They picked up a couple of boxes of granola bars, too, along with water bottles for everyone. They didn't plan to be gone long, but they were riding into the wilderness in subzero temperatures. Granola bars, water bottles, and a couple of butane lighters—a pretty legit survival kit.

They found Josie's rented Outback in the parking lot—with a snowmobile trailer attached. Must have belonged to the kid.

The Jeep's thermometer bottomed out at minus 40° where Fahrenheit and Celsius met, but it had been minus 48° when they left Fairbanks. If the speed with which Gant's legs went numb was any indication, it was a hell of a lot colder here.

Moving quickly, the team stuffed uneaten pizza and water bottles into their day packs, pulled balaclavas over faces and wool hats over balaclavas. Mads had bought everyone Sorrel PAC boots, which seemed like they would be warm enough. Gant opted for his new Snow Monsters.

Peewee slung a CZ Scorpion sub-gun on under his parka and then clipped into his skis.

Gant couldn't remember anything quite so torturous as adjusting the height of a bicycle seat at fifty below. Mittens made the task impossible, bare skin would freeze to the metal in seconds. Glove liners were clumsy but workable—eventually.

Pistols and smaller rifles went under coats. Gant had the short shotgun. Blackwell carried another Scorpion that would kill Sam Lujan and his mother just as dead as one of the nasty little metal spikes Mads and Browny were so fond of.

Peewee strode across the flat parking lot, skis hissing and squeaking over the snow. He stopped long enough to study the map on the trail board.

"There's a warning about a sow grizzly and two cubs!" he shouted.

"That's gotta be old," Gant said, astonished at how the cold seemed to shove the air back down his throat. His lungs convulsed with each word even with the face covering, turning "bears would be sleeping by now" into "bears . . . guh . . . sleep . . . guh."

Straddling the bike, Gant tugged back his parka sleeve long enough to check his watch. One forty-five. An hour and a half until sunset. No way they were getting in and out before that. Josie and her rat kid would make good time on a snowmobile, but that didn't matter. They were just seven miles in at the Lee's Cabin, the first in a long line of cabins and a million acres of frozen wilderness.

Mads led the way on her bike. Day pack cinched down snugly over the puffy Arctic parka, she was wobbly at first. Blackwell went next, then Gant. Browny brought up the rear like the sisters were afraid one of them might try to turn back. Extreme cold turned the fat rubber tires into stone wheels, which made the bike feel like riding on a two-by-four on the frozen trail.

One by one the riders passed Peewee Halverson. He'd made it maybe two hundred yards up the trail, grunting with each kick of his skis, sliding backward almost as much as forward. The clerk at Goldstream Sports had stressed the fact that he'd need to match the ski wax to the temperature. He'd also said they didn't have wax for temperatures this low.

"You okay, Peewee?" Gant managed to get out on a series of gasps as he pedaled by.

"Walk . . . in . . . the park . . ."

Gant dug in, doing the best he could to keep up without freezing his lungs.

The muscular Swede fell farther and farther behind.

# CHAPTER 43

*61° below*

CUTTER TOLD THE FAIRBANKS DEPUTIES WHERE HE AND LOLA WERE going, but not why. Deputy Paul Gutierrez was naturally curious as to what Cutter and Lola were up to in his stomping grounds, but he and his partner were both smart enough to assume they weren't working a warrant. If that were the case, they would have asked for help. It had something to do with a protected witness—generally the most sensitive operations USMS personnel ever had to deal with. They were so sensitive in fact that rank-and-file deputies rarely knew when a protectee had been relocated to their area—until something went wrong.

Ryan Madsen gave Cutter and Lola a quick briefing on the snow machines—brand-new Polaris 146s—bright red over gray. Each sled had its own bag of survival gear—bivvy sack, matches, hand warmers, and high-calorie rations that tasted like a mixture of coconut and sawdust.

Enough gear packed to survive on the ice planet Hoth, Cutter pulled out of the Fairbanks federal building garage with the snow machine trailer in tow. The Tahoe's defrost roaring on high to keep the windshield and side windows relatively clear.

The sky was a brutal cobalt blue when they set out. An hour later, when they'd arrived at the Wickersham Dome parking lot, a low sun set the horizon on fire, bathing the White Mountains in alpenglow.

The aftermarket thermometer in the Tahoe read minus 63°.

Lola peered out the window as Cutter pulled up to the line of five other vehicles parked near the trailhead. Two of them pulled empty trailers.

Stalactites of dirty ice hung from the bumpers and wheel wells like so many fangs. Heavy frost webbed the inside of the windows.

Lola held up her phone. "I've got service," she said. "At least they'll know where to find our frozen carcasses."

She called Ryan Madsen, who was still at the office, to run the license plates. He told her he'd call her right back.

Ending the call, she opened the door as if to get out but quickly slammed it against the cold.

"You know I'm game for just about any adventure," she gasped. "But going out in this shit seems like a good way to freeze off body parts we might need later on. Our guy has the cabin rented until tomorrow. If our only aim is to get him in trouble, we can be here waiting on him when he comes out. Hard to believe this inspector wants us to risk life and limb just to catch up with him and slap his peepee."

"Agreed," Cutter said. "He is awfully insistent that we put eyes on Mr. Trejo ASAP. I'm thinking there are details about this case he's not sharing with the chief."

Lola's phone chirped in her hand. She put it on speaker.

Ryan Madsen read back the plate numbers.

"The green 4Runner comes back to Evan and Adrianne Barton of Anchorage. Red Tacoma to Sandy Liu of Wasilla. The two Jeeps and the Subaru are airport rentals. Paul's on the line now with the car company to see who signed the paperwork."

"Thanks, Ryan," Cutter said.

"You guys really going out in this crud?" Madsen said. "You could die, ya know. I'm serious."

"It's looking less and less likely," Cutter said.

"Glad to hear—"

Paul Gutierrez interrupted his partner. "I hate to say it, but you may change your mind after this," he said. "The Subaru was rented

by a Josie Lujan with an Arizona DL. But the name on the contracts
for both Jeep Cherokees is Dusty Baldwin out of New Jersey."

"And . . ." Lola prodded.

"Rental company emailed me copies of their DL photos. Dusty
Baldwin looks an awful lot like our earless dead guy from this
morning at The Cookie Jar."

"Well shit!" Lola hissed. "Looks like we're going for a snow machine ride."

"Lola's right," Cutter said. He made the command decision to
let the Fairbanks deputies know they were dealing with a protected witness, giving them what little information he had.

"Figured as much," Gutierrez said. "I googled Josie Lujan while
we were talking. Turns out her son, Sam, testified against a Polish
mob boss in New York four years ago."

"Sam Lujan," Lola said. "Luke Trejo. Makes sense."

Cutter looked at the thermometer again. "It's minus sixty-four
at the trailhead," he said. "I know AST air support is out of the
question, but I wouldn't mind a dozen more guys with snow machines and guns, as soon as possible."

"I'll get on the horn with the Troopers," Gutierrez said. "Get
some backup headed your way. The BLM ranger who handles
that area lives in Fox so he may reach you first—if he answers his
phone."

"Hold what you got," Madsen said. "I'll head that way with my
personal sled."

"Appreciate it," Cutter said. "But we'll go ahead and hit the trail.
Whatever it is that's happening here, I have a feeling it's going
down as we speak. I've got the sat phone and the inReach. We'll
check in when we know more."

"Keep them next to your skin," Gutierrez said. "Otherwise, the
batteries will freeze."

"Got it," Cutter said.

"Holy crap," Gutierrez said under his breath. "I'm looking at
my windchill calculator. At minus sixty-two if you ride at twenty
miles an hour, you're looking at a windchill of, get this, one hundred and three below zero! You aren't careful and our vic at The
Cookie Jar won't be the only one to lose an ear."

"Got it," Cutter said again. "Go ahead and make your calls. We need to let the chief know what's going on."

"Call Jill and bring her up to speed," Cutter said after Lola ended the call with Gutierrez. "I'm going to have a look inside those Jeeps while we still have a little light. I'll just be a minute. Keep her on the line until I get back."

"Don't die," Lola said. It didn't look like she was joking.

He left the motor running and shut the door behind him as quickly as possible to leave more heat for Lola.

There were plenty of things in Alaska that could kill you. Bears, moose, volcanoes, mudflats, plane crashes, runaway trains . . . thin ice. But those were all sometimes threats. The cold was always there, creeping around in the wings, no matter the season. Cutter thought he would have been used to it by now.

Where minus forty bludgeoned you senseless, fifty below was a vise that pressed energy and good sense out of body and soul.

At first, sixty below feels little different than fifty. The proof is in what it does.

At sixty below zero, plastic shatters at a nudge, metal parts snap off at the most inopportune times, trees explode as if hit with unseen artillery. Aviation fuel thickens like hair gel. Simply picking up a set of dropped keys with bare fingers can bring frostbite and blisters. Everything hurts. Even breathing brings pain. Overexertion—or exertion period, freezes and destroys delicate lung tissue. Even schools in Siberia—where people were accustomed to bitter cold—closed when temperatures dropped below minus fifty. Physical processes that you normally didn't have to think about turn into burdensome chores. The brain becomes preoccupied with sending blood to the body's core rather than wasting precious heat on pesky trivialities like fingers and toes.

Every inch of skin needed to be covered.

Cutter's boots squeaked across the parking lot as he walked around the two rented Cherokees. He didn't risk taking off his mittens to touch the hoods. He could tell from the lack of rime ice on the glass and metal that these vehicles hadn't been there for more than an hour. Josie Lujan's Subaru, on the other hand, was covered in frost. Several sets of boot prints walked circles around it, different from the boots that exited in the first place and unloaded a single snow machine from the aluminum trailer.

He made another round, taking mental notes before climbing back in the Tahoe. He took off his fur hat and mittens immediately, absorbing the precious warmth from the heater.

"Here he is now, Chief," Lola said.

Cutter brought them both up to speed. "Looks like they're on fat-tire bikes," he said. "Four or five of them. Lots of clothing and gear tags in the vehicles."

"Meaning?" Phillips asked.

Lola gave a slow nod. "This is an unforgiving place, Chief," she said. "I'm thinking anyone who's brave or dumb enough to strike out from here in this weather owns their own gear."

"Lola's correct," Cutter said. "For whoever is on the fat bikes, this is a last-minute trip."

"Like they've just found Sam Lujan."

"Exactly," Cutter said. "This is a hit. Lola and I will both turn on an inReach. You can follow our breadcrumb trails."

"Be safe," Phillips said.

"Safe is to stay in the Tahoe," Lola said.

"Safe as you can," Phillips said.

"Yep," Cutter said, ending the call. He pulled the balaclava and goggles over his face and then put the fur hat and mittens back on. He'd exchange the fur hat for a helmet once they got the sleds unloaded. He then turned to Lola. "Ready?"

"Nope," she said.

Hand on the door, Cutter took one last breath of warm air.

"Me neither."

"I want to punch that inspector in the face," Lola said.

Cutter opened the door.

"Yep."

# CHAPTER 44

*F*OUR MILES UP THE TRAIL PEEWEE HALVERSON KICKED OUT OF HIS skis. He'd discovered too late that it was far too cold for skis to function correctly. Cross-country skis worked by friction when the slightly arched center of the ski directly under the boot was pressed down against the snow by the weight of the skier. Friction between the snow and, in the case of Peewee's skis, small unidirectional protrusions that looked like fish scales, kept the ski from sliding backwards with each push. Under normal, more temperate circumstances this combination of weight and friction melted the snow just enough to make a thin layer of water, allowing the ski to slide forward and then catch the snow when the skier bore down, providing enough traction to stay in place while the opposite ski glided forward, repeating the process back and forth.

Snow turned the consistency of powdered sugar at sixty below. Nothing worked.

The trail was well enough groomed that he didn't need the skis to move forward. If he'd had the keys to the vehicles he would have turned back. Skiing, and now walking, was too much work, and it made him hot. And he couldn't remember a time when he was so tired. One of his ski poles was broken. He couldn't remember how it had happened. He flung the useless thing into the woods, drawing a curse from his mother, who, for some reason, followed him along the trail but wouldn't come out of the trees. He knew better than to break his equipment. She'd paid good money for those skis!

What was she doing out here? She hated skiing.

Halverson unzipped his parka, opening and closing it like a fan in an attempt to cool off before he got heat stroke. He was surprised to find a gun hanging there on a sling around his neck. That's right. They were here to kill the rat. He couldn't remember the rat's name but was sure he'd know him when he saw him. You could tell a rat by his eyes . . .

Halverson's mother called to him again, kinder now, humming softly, telling him it was alright to have a little rest.

He took off his coat, drawing another curse from his mother when he dropped it on the side of the trail. He stumbled forward, debating on whether he should take off his boots. His feet were burning up.

The goggles went next, then his hat.

Frost coated the face of his balaclava, threatening to suffocate him. He peeled it off, aware enough to feel a sharp pain in his cheeks like he'd cut himself with a razor. He looked down dully to find pieces of dead frostbitten flesh had frozen to the balaclava and peeled away from his face with the wool. He shrugged. Couldn't be helped. He tossed the bloody mess away and plodded on, peeling off clothing as he went.

His mother continued to call out from somewhere in the trees, first humming, then sighing, then cursing him for not taking her advice. Her curses turned to screams and the screams turned into the growl of a snow machine engine.

He tensed at the sound, raising the rifle. Maybe it was the rat.

Overhead, the northern lights danced and flowed in curtains of green and purple, bright enough to cast eerie shadows on the snow. Halverson didn't notice.

Naked from the waist up, blood crusted to what was left of his frostbitten face, the muscular Swede began to fire blindly into the snowy woods.

# CHAPTER 45

*Five minutes earlier*

*L*OLA TEARIKI SCREAMED UP THE GROOMED TRAIL, UNABLE TO GET Paul Gutierrez's windchill calculation out of her head. *One hundred and three below zero.* That was insane!

She kept her eyes up, following the pool of her headlight as best she could. Both her goggles and helmet visor were mottled with fog even with a heated shield. She imagined that was how her grandfather saw the world everyday through his cataracts. Mittened hands clutching heated grips, she hunched as low as she could behind the windscreen in a useless attempt to avoid the wind that cut like a razor through her parka anytime she leaned out of the protective bubble provided by the snow machine's cowling.

She'd never been this cold.

Twilight was short-lived this far north. She was vaguely aware that the aurora had come out to play, but there was no time to enjoy it. Instead, she kept her focus ahead, where every gnarled tree or drift cast wild, sinister shadows as she maneuvered her sled in a series of S curves to play the headlamp back and forth, searching for any threat in the snow.

Cutter rode behind her, surely eating the spray of snow her machine threw into the air.

Lola eased off the throttle, slowing when she saw the black

lump in the middle of the trail. At first, she thought it was a body. An abandoned parka. Cutter pulled up alongside her, his machine at idle.

She shucked off her right mitten and wearing only a light wool glove, lifted her rifle to cover the trail ahead while Cutter dismounted and checked out the parka, retrieving a phone from the breast pocket.

He tucked the device deep inside his own coat and stomped his feet, the warming dance familiar to anyone who lived and worked in this frozen North.

"Look at this," he said. He'd raised his visor, but his voice was muffled, his face hidden beneath the thick balaclava. "Someone took a leak right here in the middle of the trail. Dark amber."

"Dehydrated," Lola said. She doubted Cutter heard her behind her helmet and the rattling engines.

Cutter took a few steps up the trail then stooped to pick up what looked like a dead animal. It was a facemask, crusted with blood and bits of blackened flesh—including a marble-like glob that turned out to be the tip of a nose.

"He's crashing," Cutter said as he heaved a leg over his machine—made more difficult by the heavy snow bibs. "Bad hypothermia. Starting to shuck off clothes. I'll be surprised if we don't find his body in the next quarter mile."

Riding on, they passed a wool hat, and then a flannel shirt. A divot in the snow said the man had likely fallen but floundered to his feet and continued to stagger up the trail. Lola found it impossible to believe a human being was capable of walking ten steps without a shirt in this miserable weather, let alone several hundred yards without turning into an ice statue.

The first volley of shots cracked the darkness at the same time she rounded the corner doing a solid twenty miles an hour. Still behind her, Cutter had moved his machine forward, close enough to see if she turned her head slightly and glanced to the left.

A hundred feet ahead, standing dead center in the trail, a bare-chested man fired at them with a short-barreled rifle. What was left of his face was a mass of swollen crimson flesh.

Three seconds to impact, Lola poured on the throttle. Ignoring the immediate bitter increase in windchill, she aimed to clip the man as she sped past—before he shot Cutter.

Hyper focused on the grotesque image, she didn't see the spruce sapling that bent like an arc under the cold and snow until it was too late. The front pan of her machine took the tree dead center between the skis at thirty miles an hour, causing her to run up on it at an angle as surely as if she'd hit a ramp. Airborne, her left ski slammed into the faceless man's shoulder, spinning him and ripping the gun out of his hands, sling and all. Lola hit the ground hard, barely keeping her snow machine upright. She threw her body to the left, trying to bring the screaming Polaris back around to face the shooter. Instead, everything came to an almost immediate stop as if she'd hit an invisible wall. Lola flew forward, shearing off the windscreen with her hip. The ski had shattered, leaving nothing but a naked shock absorber that dug into the snow, arresting the snow machine's forward momentum and stopping it cold. She'd clipped the automatic kill switch with her parka, so the motor died as soon as she flew off.

Cutter had stopped and was standing on the ground, mittens dangling, rifle raised by the time she clambered to her feet. Lola arched her back and swung her arms. She was sure to hurt in the morning, but at the moment, everything bent the way God intended it to.

"I'm good," she said to Cutter. Flushed with adrenaline, she was momentarily numb to the worst of the cold—dangerous since even a short exposure would still do tremendous damage.

Bulky clothing and the glaring headlight of his snow machine made Cutter loom twice as large as usual as he stooped over the shirtless man. He found a handgun and passed it to Lola, who kept her eyes on the trail ahead just in case there were more faceless dudes with guns.

The wounded man stirred, blinking up at Cutter. He whispered something unintelligible. It sounded like he was being strangled.

"Nils Halverson," Cutter said after he'd thumbed through the man's wallet and ID. "How many more of you are there?" Puffs of vapor hung around his face at every word.

"My mother," the man said. "Did you see her back there?"

Cold beyond shaking, the man's movements were absurdly smooth, like he was moving in slow motion. He shuddered, spat a clot of blood that instantly froze to his chest. Lola thought he was gone, but he asked for his mother again.

Cutter dug the phone out of his parka and held it up, obviously trying to use the man's face to unlock the screen. It didn't work. There just wasn't enough of his face left.

Cutter squatted down beside him. "Let's give your mother a call," he said. "How about that?" He put the phone to Halverson's thumb to unlock it. Cutter took the phone back immediately, scrolling through the text messages.

"Anything?" Lola asked.

"Not much," Cutter said. "The cold killed the battery before I could get anything useful. There's a text thread with 'Dusty the Regulator,' who I assume is the dead guy from The Cookie Jar, along with two others. Somebody named John and another named Bobby G. I didn't have time to read the contents."

Lola stomped her feet. A numbing cold seeped up through the soles of her boots and into her bones if she stood in one place for more than a few seconds.

"Likely thugs working for the guy our kid testified against," she said. "Dusty's out of the picture, but it's safe to assume we're dealing with these other two."

"Four sets of fat tires at the trailhead," Cutter said, breathless now. He bent down, gloved hand to Halverson's bare chest, then stood with a groan. He shook his head.

"Gone."

Lola nodded to her snow machine, the movement surely lost between her helmet and the fur ruff of her parka. Breathing deeply enough to speak was becoming painful. She chose her words carefully.

She lifted a fur mitten toward Cutter's machine. "Two up?"

He gave a curt nod and threw his leg over the seat. "Jump on behind me and hang on," he said. "Still about five miles from the cabin. Those fat bikes are probably already there."

Cutter scooted forward, giving Lola just enough room to sit

half on the luggage rack, half on the smallish seat that was never meant for two-up riding. Fortunately, the duffel of survival gear provided some cushion. She pushed her slung rifle to one side, and wrapped her arms around Cutter's waist, fighting back tears at the sudden closeness and human touch. She couldn't shake the image of a shirtless Nils Halverson, skin red and dying and swollen, his face destroyed by the cold. It had to be seventy below by now. Dressed in virtually every piece of cold weather gear she owned, she still couldn't feel her hands. Maybe her own face was even now freezing to the inside of her balaclava under the snow machine helmet. No way they could walk five miles in the grip of this unspeakable cold. If they shattered another ski or simply broke down, they would die. That was all there was to it.

She held on tight, face against the small of Arliss Cutter's back. Six hours ago, they were celebrating the arrest of the killer they'd been hunting for weeks. Now, they were steadily freezing to death.

# CHAPTER 46

*68° below*

GANT ROLLED TO A STOP IN FRONT OF THE LONELY LOG CABIN perched on the edge of a snow hill that fell away behind it. His bicycle tires squealed and crunched on the snow. Mads and Browny already flanked the door. Blackwell pushed his bike around to the left of the cabin toward the little privy, out of sight.

Gant didn't realize his legs had stopped working until he tried getting off the bike. Oh, he could pedal enough to stay upright, but standing was an entirely different story. He fell to his knees, dropping the bike in the process. Mads turned to glare at him. It was impossible to tell in the dark with only her eyes visible in the frost-covered balaclava, but he thought she might have shown a flash of concern. Browny snarled something he couldn't quite make out but that sounded like a threat.

Gant noted two snow machines parked out front. Odd. He could have sworn there had been only one set of tracks coming off Josie's trailer. Even more curious were the fresh spruce boughs stuffed under the skis of each machine, like someone had made them a nest.

Light spilled out of a small window in the door and another that took up much of the right wall.

Browny waved, pointing with a ludicrously large wool mitten. "Watch the back," she whispered.

There was only one door. Gant supposed they could try to escape through the window. He'd followed Josie long enough to know her propensity for changing into plush house slippers the moment she got home. She wouldn't make it fifty feet without her boots.

Mads pounded on the door while Blackwell and Gant stayed out of sight. Everyone trusted an Aussie, especially one who was half frozen.

The door opened just enough for a doughy man to stick his long face out the opening.

"Can I help you with something?"

It wasn't Sam or Josie.

"Sorry to b . . . bother, mate," Mads said. Her stammer wasn't an act. "My s . . . sister and me got a late s . . . start. Was w . . . wondering if we might c . . . come in and g . . . get warm."

A woman's voice carried out through the crack. It was too snide to be Josie.

"Tell them there's another cabin up the trail," she said.

"S . . . seriously, mate?" Mads said. "We are literally f . . . freezing to d . . . death out here, and you'd s . . . send us up the trail? P-p-please. J . . . just let us warm up by your f . . . fire a minute and we'll g . . . go."

Gant could see Browny had her stainless-steel gaff behind her back. It would have been smarter to use a gun until they figured out who all was inside, but he wasn't about to suggest this crazy woman give up her favorite toy.

The man looked Mads up and down, nose scrunched as he made his decision.

"Okay."

"What the hell, Evan?" the woman groused from somewhere inside the cabin.

He opened the door. "You can come in and get warm then—"

"Cheers!" Mads said, pushing her way inside. Browny followed, nearly running over the startled man. Blackwell came next. Gant followed tight on his heels.

A big-boned woman in red flannel underwear swung long legs off the side bunk at the far end of the little cabin and stood to face the intruders. Browny brought the gaff around hard, hitting the woman with the blunt side and knocking her jaw out of place.

Mads advanced on Evan, who retreated backwards until he tripped over the wooden table under the loft. There was nowhere else to go.

"Where's Sam?" she demanded.

"Get out now!" the man snarled. "I don't give a shit how cold you—"

Blackwell moved past Mads, slamming a wicked right into the man's temple. He should have fallen. Instead, he rallied, arms up, tucking his chin. It was as if he'd suddenly realized he was in the middle of a fight.

"The kid and his mother," Mads asked again. "Where are they?"

"Gone!" Evan spat.

Browny shot a glance at her sister, giving the big woman the opening she'd been looking for. She sprang forward, screaming like a banshee, her jaw jutting grotesquely to one side. Throwing one of the heavy wooden chairs at Blackwell, she grabbed a stick of spruce the size of her wrist and swung it like a bat, connecting with a loud crack to the side of Browny's head. Blackwell staggered backward. He caught himself on the woodstove and screamed as he seared both hands.

Browny fell, blood pouring out a gaping wound above her ear.

Blackwell turned to face the crazed woman and her stick, but Evan intercepted him, straight-arming the wooden table so it slid across the floor. It smashed against Blackwell's knees, knocking him to the ground beside a moaning Browny.

The fight would have ended much sooner if there had been more room. The cramped confines of the little ten-by-fourteen cabin made it impossible to mount a coordinated attack.

Gant sprang sideways to avoid the oncoming table, putting him directly in front of the door, which was still open and filling the cabin with bone-chilling cold.

Browny tried to push herself up with her knees. The gaff clattered to the wooden floor and she fell again, clutching the bleeding wound above her ear.

Infuriated, Mads swung her own gaff as the big woman charged at Blackwell, catching her in the back of the head, a perfect shot to the base of the skull. The woman froze mid-stride. Her entire body went rigid, arms shoved down at her sides, fingers splayed, wrists drawn unnaturally inward as if she'd stepped on a live wire. She fell forward like a toppled tree.

Evan roared at the sight, grabbing up one of the chairs and lifting it above Mads. Gant shot him twice in the throat. He landed on top of his wife.

Mads put a foot on the side of the dead woman's face and pushed as she yanked the gaff out of her skull. She dropped to her knees with her arm around Browny's shoulders.

"You flaming *galah!*" she said over her shoulder.

Gant stepped inside and shut the door, moving toward the stove now that the immediate threat was over. He'd just saved Mads's life. Surely, she wasn't talking to him.

She was.

"What?"

"Nah, mate, I reckon it never occurred to you that Sam and his dear old mum might hear a gunshot?"

"I . . . he was . . ."

"I . . . I . . . I," she mocked, then turned her attention to Browny. "Let's have a look at that, sis."

Blackwell took a roll of gauze out of his pocket and passed it to Mads—the suck-up. He shrugged. "A couple of gunshots might just be enough to warn Gant's girlfriend that we're coming—"

Gant rushed in, hitting him just above the hips, intent on shattering his ribs. They fell backward, clawing and gouging until Mads stood and began kicking them both with her heavy winter boot.

"I will personally gut you both," she said, "if you do not stop this now!" She seemed oblivious to the fact that both men had guns.

Mads helped Browny to the wooden side bunk where Evan and the tall woman had rolled out their sleeping bags. Even from a distance it was clear from Browny's mismatched eyes that she had a concussion.

Gant shook his head. "She shouldn't go to sleep—"

"Shut it!" Mads snapped. "You two take a couple of minutes to get warm and then go find Sam Lujan and his mother. Kill her if she gives you any trouble, but bring him back to me. I'm staying with my sister."

Gant felt the air leave his lungs.

Blackwell stared at the darkness beyond the picture window. "It's fourteen miles to the next cabin."

"Take their snowmobiles, you flamin' *galah*."

Gant didn't know what *galah* meant but it was safe to assume it wasn't good.

Gant and Blackwell took off their parkas and stood over the stove, warming their torsos until their clothing steamed. They were able to turn "a couple" of minutes into five before Mads ran them out the door. Gant was quick enough he grabbed the larger of the two snow machine helmets.

The machines were identical, both beefy Polaris Titans. Working sleds, they would have been comfortable in normal winter conditions. Seventy below was far from normal.

"Who told that looney bitch she was in charge?" Blackwell said as they worked in the bitter cold, with only headlamps and the northern lights overhead, to pull spruce boughs out from under the snow machines and wipe frost off the seats.

Gant swung a leg over the snow machine and scanned the controls, figuring it all out on the fly.

"She is in charge," he said. "I know that because we're outside freezing our asses off doing what she tells us while she's inside with the fire."

Blackwell got on his machine and started it, lowering his visor and pulling away into the night without another word. The snow machines would be far better than the fat bikes, but Gant could tell the wind was going to be a killer at these temperatures. He'd already forgotten what it was like to feel his feet and he hadn't even started the fourteen-mile trip.

Gant got his machine started about the time Blackwell's turned the corner heading northeast, flickering through the trees on the main trail toward the next cabin on the line—Moose Creek. Gant gave a low groan, not so much from the assaulting cold—though that was bad enough, but from the realization that he was less than an hour away from having to watch Josie die. There was no way around it—as long as John Blackwell was alive.

# CHAPTER 47

*Anchorage*
*38° below*

$M$IM WOKE TO THE SNAP OF BURNING SPRUCE IN THE FIREPLACE. Blinking, she patted the chest of her cashmere sweater, feeling around for the phone she knew was there. She'd nodded off again. Ethan's old Eames chair cradled her like a well-worn catcher's mitt but that didn't stop the pangs of guilt she felt for being so warm and comfortable while Arliss was out risking his life in the cold. She reached for the pair of reading glasses she'd left on the side table, putting them on to check the weather app for Livengood (pronounced to rhyme with "alive and good" by Alaskans). It was the closest reporting spot to the Wickersham Dome trailhead. Seventy-two below. Even with the heat from her fireplace she shivered just thinking about it, unable to even imagine.

She took off the glasses and set them on her chest.

Opal's father had dropped her off an hour earlier. That was interesting, watching her and Constance get to know each other while trying to remain cool in the process. Arliss would have called it the "butt sniffing" stage—young dogs meeting on the trail, figuring each other out. The boys had it easier. The fact that their new aunt was the same age as their sister was slightly amusing, but other than that they didn't give a rip. Relatives had to like you. It was a rule as far as they were concerned. Fortunately, Constance was actually a year and a half older than her aunt. But they felt more like cousins than aunt and niece, which made it slightly less awkward. They appeared to have the same taste in music. It was headbanging stuff that Mim didn't understand, but she was grateful it gave them something to talk about in Constance's room.

Ursula was fairly glowing that her daughter had now met her daughter-in-law and grandchildren. Mim couldn't help but believe she and her mother-in-law had made some real headway looking through her box of memorabilia. It certainly made it easier for Mim to give Ursula a touch of grace for what she'd done to Ethan and Arliss.

She scrolled to Arliss's inReach page, checking his breadcrumbs to see where he was. He was moving. That was good. All he'd told her was that he and Lola had to go check something at a wilderness cabin in the White Mountains—by snow machine. He'd not told her why it was so important that the chief would send them out into this terrible weather. This was one of those times when she knew not to ask for details.

Shortly after he arrived in Alaska—she couldn't believe it had been almost three years—Arliss had told her he'd rather not make up a story when he had to do something secret. He'd rather just tell her he couldn't tell her. It made sense. She would have known if he was lying . . .

Ursula came in with two mugs of coffee and set one on the side table next to the Eames chair.

"The girls are getting along great," she said. "Like sisters."

"That's good to hear," Mim said.

Ursula sat on the couch, leaning closer to the fire.

"It's a little late in the day for coffee," she said. "But I assumed you wouldn't be sleeping until he's safely off that trail."

Mim scooted back in the chair to sit more upright and to take a sip from the mug. "This is perfect," she said. "Thank you, Ursula." She took another sip. "And you're right. I'm not going to bed until I hear from Arliss again. Maybe not even then. It's bad up there. I'm really worried about him."

"I should think so," Ursula said, "considering . . ."

Mim couldn't put a finger on her mother-in-law's inflection, but she was definitely insinuating something—which in and of itself was odd. In the short few weeks Mim had known her, Ursula had been one to come out and say what she meant, even if it was hurtful or rude.

"There's something I can't figure out," Ursula said.

Mim braced herself. Here it came. "What's that?"

"Well," Ursula said, "it seems to me that a girl who's been through what you have would want a relationship with someone a touch more . . . how do I put this . . . plain vanilla than my son. You know, someone with a safer career path."

Mim scoffed. "You mean safer like a petroleum engineer? I thought *that* was the safe job."

"Touché," Ursula said. She took a sip of coffee and nodded like she was considering the logic.

"You know," Mim said, "up until fairly recently I thought I was pretty damned immortal. I mean, we had money and clothes, food on the table when I was growing up. My parents didn't beat me—"

Ursula gave an impish nod. "Or run off and leave you."

Mim chuckled. "This is about me," she said. "But you're right. They were always there for me. They paid for volleyball, soccer, a school trip to Europe, and whatever else my teenage brain decided I should do. I didn't have to study too hard to pass nursing school . . . And you know what? Your sons—two of the best men I've ever even heard of—both loved me unconditionally right from the get-go. I chose the safe, 'plain vanilla' brother and he gave me three wonderful children. Life was near perfect. Nothing bad ever happened to me . . . until it did."

She took another drink of coffee, letting that sink in before continuing.

"Then those guys murdered Ethan, and my little family nearly fell apart with grief . . ."

"I'm sorry I wasn't there for—"

Mim raised a hand. "I'm done judging you, Ursula. I'm not telling you this to make you feel guilty. My point is that when I lost one of your sons, the other one came and saved me. I knew Arliss was in love with me shortly after he and I met. It's not like he's ever been good at hiding it. I also knew he was a dangerous man. I could sense it even back then. You know what I mean."

Ursula nodded. "I do."

"It was incredibly cruel of me to let him move to Alaska and live in the same house and help me with my children when I had no intention of loving him as anything more than a brother-in-law and friend. But I let him come up here anyway. Hell, I even encouraged it. And you know what I learned? He really is a dangerous man. Extremely dangerous. But a dangerous man is what I needed. In the nearly three years Arliss has been here, people have tried to run me down with a truck, feed me to polar bears, and murder my children. But not one of those things was his fault. It all had to do with Ethan. Is being a deputy US marshal risky as all get-out? Sure, it is. I'm not stupid. I'm worried sick about him when he's in the bush like this—but I trust him to know what he's doing. It's a calling for him and he's good at it."

"I hear what you're saying," Ursula said. "But I have to admit, it's been extremely hard for me, always worrying about him. I can't help but wish he'd chosen a safer life."

"There's no such thing as a safe life, Ursula," Mim said. "There's only life. At some point, that life's gonna hurt. Bad. And when it does, a dangerous man is pretty handy to have around."

# CHAPTER 48

*White Mountains*
*72° below*

TWO MILES AWAY FROM LEE'S CABIN THE TRAIL BEGAN TO CURVE from east to north. Josie Lujan gave her son's waist a squeeze. Curtains of dancing aurora shimmered and danced across a star-filled sky—and she was missing it beneath her stupid foggy helmet.

Sam slowed the snow machine to a crawl and craned his neck around so he could see what she wanted.

"Are you okay, Mom?"

"I came to see lights," she said. "Let's stop and look at lights."

"Stop?" he said, muffled under his face mask. "Let's wait and stop at the cabin."

"It's another half an hour to the cabin," she said. "We'll be half frozen when we get there."

"I'm half frozen now."

"I'm saying the lure of the cabin will draw us in," Josie said. "We'll want to rush to get a fire going. Who knows if the lights will be as brilliant by then."

"A fire sounds like a smart idea," Sam said.

She knew he was upset with her for deciding to move on instead of making Evan and Adrianne leave. Any other time she would have. Adrianne looked as though she might actually get physical. Josie had been in more than a few fights in her life and wasn't too worried about winning, but causing a scene when your son was a federally protected witness seemed like a poor choice. It was better to move on than risk pushing until someone did something they would all regret later.

"I came to see northern lights," Josie said again. "We are dressed as we should be. Your snow machine is in good working order but we are speeding through life without taking the time to notice anything. I'm only asking that we stop on the side of this beautiful mountain and take a few minutes to be quiet and look up."

"What if the snow machine won't start?"

"It will start," she said.

"The battery could freeze."

"What will you do if it freezes overnight at the cabin?"

"First off," he said, "we'd be at the cabin, with a fire in the stove. But if that happens, I have a small rope I can use to pull-start it."

"Four minutes," Josie said. "The battery should be fine for that long."

Sam switched off the motor, throwing the mountain into immediate silence. Josie closed her eyes, feeling the cold creep through all her layers of clothing, sinking into her bones.

"Is this what you imagined?" Sam asked.

Josie chuckled. "I didn't imagine my face would hurt like this," she said. She leaned sideways, against her son's arm.

"I'm glad you came," he said. "It's been a long time."

"We can't do this anymore," Josie said. "I'm pretty sure I was followed from the airport, but even if I wasn't, I'm not sure my nerves can take the stress."

Sam nodded slowly. "This is all my fault . . ."

Shimmering veils of iridescent green morphed into red and pulsed purple before flashing green again. The sky didn't just seem alive. It was.

"Many Plains tribes believed the aurora were made up of the campfires of the northern peoples roasting the flesh of their enemies."

Sam scoffed, pointing his chin at the sky. "They look at this and get flesh-eating?" Still looking upward, he blew a cloud of vapor like a freight train. "Ten points for imagination."

"I read that the Inupiaq believe the lights are the torches of walrus spirits—"

Two distinct cracks carried over the mountains, pulling both Sam and Josie's attention back the way they'd come.

"Gunfire?" Sam said.

Josie shivered. Snow and bitter cold dampened sound, making it difficult to be sure where the shots originated.

"Hunters?" Sam said. "Wolves, snowshoe hares . . . ?"

"No, son," Josie said. "Whoever that is, they're hunting you."

# CHAPTER 49

*72° below*

*T*HE WOODSTOVE WORKED SO WELL MADS HAD TO STRIP DOWN TO her long john bottoms and a T-shirt to keep from sweating to death. As far as she'd seen, that was the thing about Alaska. She was either too hot or too cold. There was no in-between. Mads fed the fire anyway, choosing too hot over the freezing nonsense on the other side of the walls. She put on a pot of water to boil and rummaged through a nylon stuff sack on the wooden table— Evan and Adrianne Barton's food cache.

"What do you say, sis?" Mads asked. "Looks like they brought along some pretty good tucker." She held up a packet of freeze-dried biscuits and gravy. Peak. The good stuff. "This looks delicious."

Browny hung her head, squinting, dabbing at the oozing wound with a bandana. "I'm not hungry."

"You gotta eat," Mads said. "It'll help you heal, not to mention keep you warm when the fire dies down at night."

Gant and Blackwell had dragged Adrianne and Evan outside and stashed them in the trees behind the cabin. The woman hadn't bled much. They rarely did when the spike came into play. Evan Barton was a different story. Mads busied herself scrubbing up the blood while she waited for the water to boil. "*Out, out, damned spot,*" she said under her breath.

"You should have had Bobby Gant do that before he left," Browny said.

"We needed him to finish the job," Mads said. "Or we wouldn't get paid."

Browny leaned back against the log wall. Eyes closed.

"Don't go to sleep!" Mads snapped.

Browny's eyes flicked open. "I don't really feel bad," she said. "Just this headache." She looked up again. "I don't know if you've noticed or not, but Bobby Gant has a thing for you."

Mads scrubbed at a particularly stubborn spot of blood on the plywood floor. "You think?"

"I know," Browny said. "Anyone can see it."

"He's cute," she said. "He's the only one of that crew with any sense, and that includes Valeria. Bobby Gant has the balls to step up and do something. You notice Blackwell didn't shoot when that guy was going to cream the shit out of us with a twenty-pound wooden chair. Gant stepped up when he needed to. I think that's a good thing."

"His beard looks like a skunk's ass."

Mads laughed, happy her sister felt good enough to joke. She reached up with the hand that held the bloody towel and touched her white streak. "I think his beard matches my hair."

The rattling whine of snow machine engines vibrated the windows.

Mads got to her feet. "Dammit! What are they doing back? No way they made it to the Moose Creek." She dug through her bag and brought out a small revolver. "I'm going to blow their brains out."

Browny scooted to the edge of the bed. "You said he was cute."

"He's not that cute." Mads marched to the door where she stood with the gun behind her thigh.

Browny stood, wobbly at first, but she was soon standing steadily enough. "If you're going to do this," she said, "at least let me help." She searched the crumpled sleeping bags until she found her stainless steel gaff, still red from Adrianne Barton's blood.

Cutter and Lola stopped their snow machines as soon as the light spilling from Lee's Cabin came into view. Smoke poured out of the metal stove pipe, flattening as if it had run into an invisible ceiling when it hit the cold air, to settle into a blue gray cloud around the cabin. They approached the last fifty yards slowly on foot, side by side, rifles at the ready. Both of them still wore their mittens. Their fingers had to stay functional if the need suddenly arose.

The cabin was set in the middle of a clearing with zero cover. Twenty yards out, Cutter stopped and scanned the area. Fortunately, the aurora was doing the tango overhead, providing enough ambient light to get a lay of the land.

"I have never been this cold in my life," Lola said. "It's like this shit is cumulative. I finally get warm, then end up even colder the next time I'm out."

"I know what you mean," Cutter said, deadpan. "My toes have stopped hurting. Pretty sure that's not a good sign." He nodded toward the front of the cabin. "I count four fat bikes, but I don't see a snow machine."

"Weird," Lola said. "We know Josie and Sam came in with one on the trailer." She looked over her shoulder at the trail. "I wonder where Ryan is with that backup?"

Cutter didn't have to check his watch. His internal clock had been counting down since he'd first spoken with Madsen. Even if he'd been able to get everyone on the road a half hour after he'd hung up, it would still take them over an hour to reach the trailhead from Fairbanks, then another half hour to unload and make it to the cabin. Cutter had sent a quick inReach text message warning them about Nils Halverson's frozen half naked body, but any responding LEOs would certainly stop and check it out, if only to be sure it was the same shirtless dead man Cutter had told them about.

"Backup?" Cutter said. "I suppose we could wait here until they arrive . . . in around ninety minutes if we're lucky."

"Wait here?" Lola said. "You mean wait in this blistering, no good, very bad cold?"

"Yep."

"So, what you're saying is that there is no backup."

"Nope."

"What are you saying then?"

"I'm saying I'm your backup."

"Sweet!" Lola said. "I'm going to remind you of this cavalier shit next time you yell at me for . . . doing cavalier shit."

"Thought you might," Cutter said.

"I'll circle around back," Lola said. "Right to left. Meet you by the door."

"Remember," he whispered. "Online photos show a big window on the side and a small one in the back."

"I'll stay low," Lola said. "Ready?"

"I'll wait to knock until you get there."

Cutter had just shucked off his mittens and pulled the balaclava up to his forehead when a brunette with a shock of silver in her greasy hair flung open the door. He didn't have a chance to knock or announce. Lola was still working her way around the cabin. The brunette's eyes flew wide when she saw him standing there, as if she'd expected someone else. Surprised as he was, it wasn't lost on Cutter that her right hand was hidden behind her thigh.

He stepped to the side, rifle at low ready, prepared to use the heavy door frame as cover if it came to that. He kept his voice low and calm.

"US Marshals," he said. "Do me a favor and let me see both of your hands."

The woman ignored his command but let go of the door and took a step back inside the cabin. He scanned the area behind her—small, cluttered, drying clothes and gear around the stove and piled on a heavy wood table.

He couldn't see all the way into the loft at the back but at first glance, the woman appeared to be alone.

"US Marshals?" she said. "What in the world would bring you all the way out here in this weather?"

"Hands!" Cutter said again. He noted her Australian accent.

The woman gave a mock pout and raised her left hand. "You're scaring me, Marshal," she said. "All the way out here by myself. Of course I have a gun. I'll put it on the bunk if you promise not to shoot me."

"Slowly," he said.

Now the woman complied, gingerly setting a blue steel revolver on the wooden bunk to her right.

"Now move away," Cutter said. *Where is Lola?*

The woman took another step back, both hands up now. The hot metal stove ticked against the bitter cold that flooded through the open door.

"You never answered my question," the woman said. "What's a US marshal doing out here in this weather?"

Cutter needed to deal with this woman so he could check on Lola.

"Turn around," he said. "Put your hands behind your back."

Mads gave a purring growl. "Owww," she said. "A kinky marshal . . ."

Cutter took a half step in when the back window of the cabin blew out with three explosive cracks, the last two much louder than the first.

Lola!

The brunette lunged for the bunk.

Cutter shot her twice as her hand curled around the butt of the revolver. Still at the back window, Lola shot her as well. Four .223 rounds ended the threat.

Cutter was vaguely aware of the sound of clanging metal behind him. Rifle in his right hand, he scooped up the revolver from the bunk and turned to see a second woman, this one with three bullet wounds, two to her upper torso and another that had taken off the left side of her face, including her ear. A sharpened steel hook lay on the wooden floor beside her in a rapidly growing pool of blood.

"Did you see her?" Lola coughed from the cold, catching her breath as she padded around from the back of the cabin. "She was waiting to clobber you with that metal hook thingy."

Cutter took a deep breath, slowing his heart rate. "Thanks for that."

"Two dead stiffs in the snow out back," Lola said in between coughs. "Not our witnesses. I bet it's that Barton couple from Anchorage." She shivered. "Creepy as hell when you sneak up on them in the dark. You're lucky I didn't scream. Looks like Jack Nicholson at the end of *The Shining*." She let loose with another coughing fit.

Cutter made his rifle safe and put a hand on her back. "You okay?"

She nodded, tight lipped, stifling another chest spasm. "Ran too fast getting around front," she said. "I'll be fine."

"Don't run," Cutter said. "No matter what. Running is suicide."

Lola looked at the carnage at her feet, taking a moment to squat down and study the steel hook without touching it. They'd need to leave it in place for the post-shooting investigation.

"This accounts for two of the killers who came in on fat bikes," Lola said. "That leaves two more."

"They took the Bartons' snow machines," Cutter said.

"We need . . . to . . . g . . . go." Her cough grew worse, doubling her over. She dabbed at her lip when she stood up. "Well, shit," she said, her face falling when she saw the frothy pink blood on her hand.

"That's it," Cutter said. "You're staying put here."

"I'm not going to argue with you," Lola said in between coughs.

Cutter threw a parka over each of the dead women. Not out of any sense of propriety but for Lola's benefit.

"I need to go," he said. "Send a text on your inReach. Let Jill know what's happened. Tell her you're going to need medical attention."

"Copy."

"I'm serious, Lola," Cutter said.

"Wait two minutes," she said, rummaging through a pile of food on the table. She poured hot water from the stove into a cardboard cup of instant mashed potatoes into which she stuffed an entire stick of butter she found in a soft-sided cooler on the floor. She mashed up the whole mess with a plastic spork and shoved it at Cutter. "Eat this. It's about a thousand calories."

The butter was still in chunks, but he wolfed it down anyway. She was right. He needed the energy.

"You should have enough wood in here to keep you until help arrives," he said. "I'll send you a message when I find our witness. Until then, stay in the cabin. Do not come looking for me. You understand?"

"Got it." She stared down at the bodies. "You know what else I'm going to do?"

"What's that?"

"I'm going to go see one of those damned shrinks."

Four minutes later, Cutter was bundled up again and speeding at forty miles an hour toward the Moose Creek cabin with the rifle across his lap. He was far too cold and preoccupied to do the math to calculate the cold's effect at that speed. Had he been able to do so, he would have learned that the air outside the protected bubble of the snow machine's cowling had a windchill of one hundred and thirty-three degrees below zero.

# CHAPTER 50

$S$AM PULLED UP BESIDE THE MOOSE CREEK CABIN AND KILLED THE Skandic's engine. Josie strained her ears in the silence, unsure of what she was hearing. She shook her head. It was the growl of another machine in the distance.

She felt Sam tense in front of her. He'd heard it too.

"It's getting closer," he said.

"We'll be sitting ducks once we're inside," she said. "No way out."

"At least we'll have the log walls," Sam said. He waved his arm overhead. "The lights are beautiful but they're going to make it impossible to hide. We'll be sitting ducks on this snow machine, too. Especially if they have a rifle."

Sam got off the machine and gave her his hand, helping her stand in her bulky gear. He was a good boy. Short-sighted, but good. She couldn't let anything happen to him.

"You go on in and get a fire going." She nodded toward the lonely little outhouse. "I need to take care of something."

"Suit yourself," Sam said. "But hurry up. And sit on your mittens so your . . . so you don't freeze to the seat."

"I've done this before," Josie said. "Now hurry and get a fire going. If this is going to be our stand, I want it to be warm."

Cutter figured he was less than a mile from the cabin when the idling snow machine appeared in his headlights on the side of the trail. The machine had nosed into a drift. Some twenty feet behind it, a bundled form, presumably its rider, lay face down in the snow. Cutter had a fleeting notion that the prone figure might be bait for an ambush, but anyone foolish enough to lie face down in these temperatures risked losing body parts. Even so, he approached slowly.

The ground told him what he needed to know.

The man had fallen off the machine while it was underway. Without the kill switch attached, it had continued up the trail until it veered into the drift. A shotgun blast had torn through the back of the man's parka, between the shoulder blades. Most of the blood from the resulting wound had been retained in the layers of bulky clothing, but a quick examination showed the man was clearly dead.

Cutter took his weapons—a short-barrel CZ Scorpion EVO semi-auto with an extendable slider stock, and a nine-millimeter pistol, also a CZ. Cutter cleared both weapons. He shoved the pistol in the pocket of his parka and slung the Scorpion over his shoulder.

"Why?" Cutter whispered to himself. The sign on the ground was clear enough, but it made no sense. Why would one of the bad guys shoot the other? Or did Sam Lujan have a shotgun? Had he done this?

Cutter jumped on his snow machine and rolled on the throttle. Up until now, there had been three sets of tracks. Now there were two. One belonged to Sam Lujan and his mother, the other to a man who wanted to kill them.

Bobby Gant rode his snow machine almost to the front door of the Moose Creek cabin. Delirious from cold and the adrenaline of taking out John Blackwell, he staggered as he made his way to the door. This whole shitshow was finally over. He had to take care of the kid or Valeria and the crazy Aussie sisters would never stop hunting him. But they wouldn't care about Josie. He had some money stashed away. A lot of money really. Enough to go a hell of a long way in Panama or Thailand—or someplace without an extradition treaty with the US. He'd have to check on that.

Smoke chugged from the stovepipe. Good. They were inside.

He stood in front of the rough wooden porch. He clutched the short shotgun in both hands. He'd been shivering so badly he thought he might not be able to hit anything even with the shotgun. But the shaking had stopped. The world seemed to be closing in around him and he was so incredibly hot. He unzipped his parka, trying to get some cool air.

"Josie!" He coughed when he took a breath to shout. "Josie Lujan! Come to the door!"

The sound of a snow machine carried up the trail behind him. He chanced a look over his shoulder, astonished to see the approaching headlight. Blackwell had taken two rounds of double-ought buckshot to the spine.

"Josie!" Gant yelled again. "Come to the door!"

Behind him, the snow machine grew closer. No way it could be Blackwell. Could it? Gant ripped away his balaclava, hunting relief from this sudden oppressive heat.

"Josie! You know me! We can end this now!"

Cutter came through the trees in time to see a lone man standing in front of the cabin brandishing a shotgun. A hundred feet away, he killed the engine and raised his rifle, still straddling the machine. The front door yawned open and lantern light spilled out on the snow, silhouetting a muscular young man—their witness.

Cutter leaned over the windscreen, aiming in when a series of sudden flashes from under the raised porch caught his eye. Gunshots. The man with the shotgun dropped to his knees, teetering there for a long moment before falling on his face.

A parka-clad figure scuttled out from under the porch holding a pistol. She peered across the snow directly at Cutter.

He lowered his rifle.

"United States Marshal!" he yelled through cupped hands, stifling a cough. "My headquarters sent me out here with a message to call Inspector Smith!"

# CHAPTER 51

*The following morning*

THE TEMPERATURE BOTTOMED OUT AT SEVENTY-TWO BELOW, SHATtering the previous official record by six degrees.

Fairbanks Deputy Ryan Madsen led a cavalry of six Alaska State Troopers, FBI Special Agent Stoney Issaac, and two Bureau of Land Management rangers.

There were seven bodies to deal with. The Bartons in Lee's Cabin had been murdered. It would be up to the crime scene techs and ballistics to figure out exactly who did it. Josie admitted to shooting Robert Gant when he raised his shotgun at her son. Lola and Arliss were responsible for two, four if you counted Nils Halverson who froze on the trail—his death likely sped along with a little help from Lola's snow machine ski. Troopers posted at both cabins to guard the scene of the homicides, the officer-involved shootings, and Josie Lujan's self-defense shooting until crime scene folks could make it out. By policy Cutter and Lola would have to be interviewed by USMS Office of Professional Responsibility as well as the Bureau of Land Management special agent and the FBI, since the deaths had taken place on federal land. A satellite phone call to the chief smoothed the way for Cutter and Lola to accompany their protected witness and his mother to the trailhead via snow machine. Deputy Madsen stayed with them as far as Fairbanks, where everyone went to be checked out at the hospital and treated for exposure. It was impossible to spend more than a few moments at seventy below without suffering some kind of injury from exposure. Lola would likely have a chronic cough for the foreseeable future and Cutter was fairly certain he was going to lose the nails on both his big toes. Josie Lujan had frostbite on the backs of both hands as well as the apples of her cheeks from lying in wait under the porch. Her son, the man whose bad decisions had been the catalyst for all this, came away with nothing more than strips of mahogany skin that had been exposed above and below his goggles during the ride.

Medical clearance in hand, Cutter and Lola accompanied their witnesses to the airport and passed through security, handing mother and son over to the inspector as soon as his flight arrived.

Lola did a yeoman's job not clobbering the man when he came off the jetway. The plane was doing a turn and burn back to Seattle, so the gate agent let them right back on while the wings got their mandatory de-icing.

Cutter and Lola all but collapsed in the boarding area while they waited for the aircraft to go "wheels up."

"I used to think WitSec would be sexy," Lola said, covering her cough with a forearm. "Remind me not to ever put in for that job. Give me a good old-fashioned fugitive to chase any day of the week—or even a highfalutin judge to protect."

Cutter slouched in his seat and punched the chief's number into his cell, holding it to his ear. He turned to Lola while it rang. "I hear you," he said. "And I agree."

Phillips picked up.

"Inspector Smith already called me," she said. "Good work. Glad you're safe."

"Thank you, Chief," Cutter said. "I know Lola and I have to give our statements on the shootings, but we're hoping to catch a plane home sometime today."

"Of course," Phillips said. "Unusual circumstances, for sure. I can't give you legal advice, but I imagine you can get your FLEOA attorney to tell them you need a couple of days."

"Honestly, Chief," he said, "I'd rather get it over with."

"Me too," Lola said, her eyes closed in the seat beside him. Understandable. Intense cold had a way of draining energy more completely than running a marathon. It was almost seven a.m. and other than short catnaps on Micki's plane, neither of them had slept since four the previous morning. Cutter had burned through the mashed potatoes and stick of butter and his gut was now an aching pit.

"I'll see if I can get them to expedite," Phillips said. "On our end at least."

"Good deal," Cutter said. "Is there anything else?"

"As a matter of fact, there is," Phillips said. "I thought you'd want to know, your prisoner Merlin Tops, the one you call Butterbean, he and Butch Pritchard were both killed in jail."

"Killed?"

Lola sat up at the word.

"Oh, yeah," Phillips said.

Lola scooted over to the seat next to Cutter and leaned in. He held the phone away from his ear so she could get the gist of the conversation. "Pritchard had two of those little jailhouse soaps shoved down his windpipe and Butterbean had his throat cut in the showers."

"Holy shit," Lola gasped. "Sorry, Chief."

"No," Phillips said. "Holy shit about covers it. DOC is reviewing video footage as we speak but it sounds like the respective cameras were in-op."

"Staff?" Lola said.

"Or a trustee," Phillips said. "I'm afraid there's more. The autopsy reports on Tina Massey and Regina Orr show they both have similar markings on the nape of their necks."

"The tattoo," Lola said. "I saw Tina's when I took her to the hospital. Sort of a wolf head and pine tree looking thing."

"That's right," Phillips said. "But it's not a tattoo. The ME said the marks are brands, like with one of those wood-burning sets."

Cutter frowned. "Burned?"

"Burned," Phillips said. "Slowly, from the looks of it, with a none too steady hand."

"Hey, Chief," Lola said. "I thought you told us investigating the Massey and Orr homicides was outside our swim lanes?"

"It is," Phillips said, "insofar as their killings are concerned, but those girls have ties to Butterbean and Pritchard—two of our prisoners who have also been murdered. We're not going to step on anyone else's toes, but that's enough of a nexus for us to do a little concurrent investigating. I'd like you two to run down what you can on this in your spare time—when OPR clears you for full duty, of course."

"Chief," Lola said. "Have I ever told you I love you?"

# CHAPTER 52

*Anchorage*
*2° above*

CUTTER PULLED INTO MIM'S DRIVEWAY JUST AFTER EIGHT P.M., MORE than a little loopy from cold, lack of sleep, and thirty-six hours of near constant adrenaline. He'd given his statements to the FBI and BLM special agent in person and then spoken with a USMS Office of Professional Responsibility inspector by Zoom. His attorney was on the call. The USMS was a relatively small organization, and he knew the female OPR inspector from a couple of high-threat trial assignments they'd worked together over the years. She and Cutter had never socialized, so her boss deemed there to be no conflict of interest. The inspector took notes, asked some good questions, and then remarked off the record that this event was "about as cut-and-dried as a shooting on the surface of Mars could be."

It sounded like Lola's interview had gone equally well, though neither would be cleared for full duty for several days. That was just fine with Cutter. They both needed the sleep.

Mim met him when he came through the door.

"Hey there." She tiptoed up to give him a kiss. "Ursula took Opal and the rest of the kiddos to see that new Dwayne Johnson movie."

"Nice of her," Cutter said.

"How are you feeling?"

"Right as, as Lola would say."

"I know you probably just want to go to sleep," Mim said. "But do you mind if I show you something first?"

"Of course not," Cutter said. "Watcha got?"

She led him down the hall to her bedroom, where she had an open cardboard suitcase laid out on the bed.

"It's your mother's." Mim took a seat on the mattress, leaning against the headboard, and patted her lap. "Come lie down. I want you to see what she's been saving for the past forty something years . . ."

Twenty minutes later, Cutter held up a photograph of him getting his silver star and credentials on graduation day from the United States Marshals Academy at FLETC. On his back, his head in Mim's lap, he looked up at her and shook his head. "How in the world did she get this picture? I don't even have it."

"Grumpy helped her." Mim stroked his forehead with one hand while she picked up a pencil sketch with the other. Signed *A. Cutter*, it was obviously supposed to be Mim standing in the surf, wearing a sundress and looking out to sea.

"I don't remember you drawing," she said. "You're pretty good . . . Though you endowed me with a more ample bottom than I had at that age."

"I drew it like I saw it."

"You were seventeen," she said. "I suppose that's where you focused."

He picked up a pair of blue baby booties.

"Your grandma made those, before you were born."

"Nana Cutter," he whispered. "Wish I'd known her . . ."

Mim studied another photo from the pile and then showed it to Cutter.

"Don't you think Michael looks like this pic of Ethan?"

"He sure does," Cutter said.

"And Matthew and Constance look like you."

"Their cross to bear," Cutter said.

"Stop it," Mim said. "I think they're fortunate. They could have inherited Aunt Chester Mae's nose."

Mim ran a finger down Cutter's jaw. "I wonder what our kids would have looked like."

"Yeah," Cutter said through a melancholy sigh. "Pretty sure our daughter would be gorgeous, just like her mama."

"Welp," Mim said, popping the P, "what if it's not a she?"

Cutter shifted in place, looking up at her. "What do you mean?"

"If my math is right, less than seven months from now, you and I are gonna find out."

Cutter sat bolt upright. His mouth went dry.

"But we only . . ."

"Guess that's all it took."

"But you're . . ."

"That's right, buster," Mim said. "I'm forty-four years old."

Cutter's hand shot to the top of his head. He'd never felt so dizzy in his life, and he'd been hit in the head a lot.

"W . . . wait," he stammered. "Are you saying you're going to . . . ?"

Mim slid down and buried her head against his chest, holding him so tight her arms began to tremble.

"Yep."

# EPILOGUE

*Kodiak Island*
*Two weeks later*

KODIAK PD OFFICER RODNEY ROBINSON WALKED DOWN THE floating dock in St. Paul Harbor, thinking of how he needed to finish his reports and get off work on time so he could pick up his little girl from play practice after school.

Rolf Svenson, who ran the fishing vessel *Julie Ann*, had contacted dispatch five minutes earlier, freaked out about something. Weird, because Svenson wasn't one to get excited about much of anything.

Robinson called out as he approached. The big Swede jumped off his boat and ran to him, grabbing the officer's hand and tugging him down the pier.

"Settle down, Lassie," Robinson chuckled. "Is little Timmy in trouble?"

Svenson either didn't get the TV reference or ignored it entirely. "She's still fresh," he said. "Been in the water no more'n a few hours, I'd say."

Robinson stopped cold. "Hold on. Who's been in the water?"

Svenson leaned and pointed over the gunwale of his boat at the nude body of a dead woman. She looked to be in her teens or early twenties.

Robinson snatched his handheld radio from his belt and called it in immediately.

"Found her floating on the south side of Near Island. Brought her straight over here and called you. This is just how we found her, poor thing."

Robinson climbed over the rail. "No ID."

"None that I found," Svenson said. "Just that curious little mark on the nape of her neck."

Robinson took out his phone and snapped a photo. "Wolf's head . . . or maybe a bear . . ." He zoomed in on the photograph. "Looks like she was branded."

# ACKNOWLEDGMENTS

By the time this book is published it will have been twenty-seven years since I transferred to Alaska with the United States Marshals Service. Not long after I arrived, my friend and partner, Deputy Ty Cunningham, convinced our chief that the District of Alaska needed a tactical tracking unit—akin to a rural SWAT team. My membership on that team took me to, among other fascinating parts of Alaska, Prince of Wales Island, Pioneer Peak, and the remote cabins in the White Mountains—all of which have made excellent settings for Arliss Cutter novels. Our tracking mission in the White Mountains saw temperatures fall to fifty-eight degrees below zero. For *Dead Line*, I needed colder. Much colder. My friends, Ty Cunningham and Alaska State Trooper Chris Terry, both have plenty of experience with temperatures colder than sixty below. Their firsthand knowledge let me take my own uncomfortable experiences at minus fifty-eight and bring down the chill factor in ways that I hope come across to the reader.

It would be impossible to write about crime fighting in Alaska without including aviation. Marshals Service pilots Rich Cobb, Sonny Caudill, Randy Johnson, and Mick Bunn, and Alaska State Trooper pilot Earl Samuelson have not only flown me all over the Great Land but stand ready to answer my endless what-ifs when it comes to aviating in the extreme cold (and I mean freeze-aircraft-tires-off-the-wheels extreme). I'm grateful for their expertise and friendship.

I've been out of the game for twelve years now. Numerous friends who are former and still active personnel with the US Marshals Service, Anchorage Police Department, Alaska State Troopers, and FBI help me get the details right about criminal justice here in Alaska and elsewhere. I want to thank Anchorage PD Officer Brent Pelkey and Trooper Chris Terry in particular for letting me pick their brains.

I'm fortunate to have worked with the amazing folks at Kensington Publishing for over twenty years now. *Dead Line* marks a change in editors. Gary Goldstein, who shepherded me from my first ghost-written paperbacks, through Mark Henry Westerns, Jericho Quinn Thrillers, and the first six Arliss Cutters, retired before I turned in the manuscript. Gary has become a friend over the years. I was sad to see him go, but happy to see him start this new chapter of his life. My new editor, John Scognamiglio, editor-in-chief at Kensington, has been nothing short of fantastic to work with. I'm looking forward to a long and productive relationship.

Barnes and Noble Anchorage has always treated me well and kept my books on the shelves. I'm extremely indebted to Title Wave in Anchorage, Mosquito Books at the Anchorage Airport, Fireside in Palmer, Hearthside in Juneau, Parnassus in Ketchikan, and Skaguay News Depot and Books in Skagway and all the independent bookstores in Alaska—not only for carrying my books, but for introducing new readers to Arliss, Mim, and Lola!

And of course, I'm grateful for my agent, Robin Rue and her assistant, Beth Miller at Writers House. They streamline the business side of all of this. Beyond that, they are my friends. I am lucky to have them in my corner.

Special thanks to my sister, Julie, the real pair of oven mitts behind Aunt Chester Mae's Chocolate Pie.

None of these books would have happened were it not for my wife, Victoria. She provides encouragement and critique in just the right ratio—plotting, editing—and prodding when I need it. She's an amazing partner. Speaking of my wife, I often say that some aspect of every female character I write, even the villains, is inspired in one way or another by Vic. *Dead Line* is an exception. I've met plenty of very bad people in my life. The Nash sisters, Mads and Browny, lean heavily on those experiences, not anything I've ever observed in my sweet bride. Though, come to think of it, she does like to fish . . . and she is pretty handy with a halibut gaff.

# RECIPE

## Aunt Chester Mae's Rich Chocolate Cream Pie

**Pie Crust:**
1 cup flour
⅓ cup + 1½ Tablespoons Crisco
½ teaspoon salt
~2-½ Tablespoons ice water

Preheat oven to 425°.

In a bowl—combine flour and salt. Using a fork or pastry blender, cut shortening into flour/salt mixture until it forms BB or pea-size pieces. Add water a tablespoon at a time, mixing lightly until dough holds together. Do not overwork dough. Form into a ball, then flatten into a thick disk and wrap in plastic wrap. Chill for 20–30 minutes.

Remove plastic wrap and roll out dough on a floured surface to ~11 inches. Transfer to a 9-inch pie crust. Flute edges as desired. Use fork to pierce the bottom & sides of the crust to avoid puffing up.

Bake for 10–15 minutes, until just golden.

Remove from oven and pour ¼ cup semi-sweet chocolate chips in hot crust. After the chocolate is completely melted, use offset spatula to smooth it across bottom of crust.

Cool completely prior to pouring in filling.

**Filling:**
1 cup sugar
5 Tablespoons cornstarch
¼ teaspoon salt
5 large egg yolks
2 cups milk
1 cup heavy cream

10 oz bag chocolate chips (I use Ghirardelli 72%–purple bag)
4 Tablespoons unsalted butter
2 teaspoons pure vanilla extract

## Topping:
1 pint heavy cream
4 Tablespoons powdered sugar
1 teaspoon vanilla extract
Shaved/grated chocolate

Combine dry ingredients in a medium saucepan: sugar, cornstarch and salt.

Whisk liquid ingredients in a large measuring cup or bowl: milk, cream and yolks.

Pour liquid into saucepan with dry ingredients. Whisk together dry and wet ingredients, heating over medium high heat for 3–5 minutes. Turn stove down to medium low heat, whisking constantly. When mixture begins to thicken and bubble, whisk for an additional 45 seconds. Remove from heat and whisk in butter, chocolate chips and vanilla.

Pour filling into prepared pie crust and cover the filling surface with parchment/plastic wrap so that it does not form a skin.

Cool and then refrigerate for ~6 hours.

Prepare whipped cream. Remove the parchment/plastic from the pie, slice and serve.

Top each slice with whipped cream and garnish with shaved/grated chocolate.

If preferred—cover the entire pie with whipped cream & chocolate shavings and serve.

# BOOK CLUB DISCUSSION QUESTIONS

1. Much of the action in the plot is impacted by the freezing weather. The temperatures are listed at the beginning of many of the chapters and the impacts of the cold on persons and nature are described in detail. Were you able to empathize with these situations? Have you experienced this type of freezing environment?

2. Arliss is Lola's supervisor and mentor, but they are good friends and act as partners. When Lola takes risks while chasing a suspect early in the book, Arliss is upset and disapproving. What are your thoughts on how this affects their relationship? Do you think his reactions are justified, and why? Do you believe that Lola's responses are reasonable, and why?

3. Before reading this book, what was your understanding of the Witness Protection Program as run by the US Marshals Service? Has your understanding of it changed since you read this book? How likely would you be to make the sacrifices required to enter the Witness Protection Program if your life was in danger? Would it be a different choice if it was the life of a family member?

4. A recurring theme in this book is motherhood. There are choices and actions made by three different mothers: Mim, Ursula, and Josie Lujan. What are your thoughts on their differing mothering styles?

5. What is your opinion about the state of Arliss and Mim's relationship? Was your opinion altered by the end of the book?

6. New information about Ursula as a mother is revealed in this book. Do you think she has changed as a mother over the years? How much trust should Arliss allow her?

7. Josie Lujan, Sam/Luke Trejo's mother, takes a risk to contact her son and see him in person. What do you think
   about their relationship, her choices and the way she treats
   him? Would you do the same? Why or why not?

8. There are several villains portrayed in this book, both fugitive criminals and hired assassins. Some seem to be more
   "evil" in nature than others. What is your personal philosophy about the goodness of mankind? What are your thoughts
   on humans' tendency to do evil? Can people change, and
   how do they change?